STRONG
SPIRITS

A Daisy Gumm Majesty Mystery

Book One

Alice Duncan

AWARDS & ACCOLADES

Romantic Times Top Pick
Reviewer's Choice Awards, finalist

"…teems with period detail…[and] characters who make
it so enjoyable, especially effervescent Daisy."
~Booklist

CHAPTER 1

It all started with my aunt Viola's Ouija Board. It was an old one, and sort of shabby. I guess Mrs. Kincaid had been using it ever since she bought it in '03 when they first came out, but she claimed it still worked.

Whether it worked or not, Mrs. Kincaid gave it to Aunt Vi after her own custom-made one with a large emerald in the center arrived from overseas. Mrs. Kincaid declared it had been made by a Gypsy woman in Rumania but I had my doubts then, and I have my doubts now. After all, Mrs. Kincaid was rich, and we all know how gullible some rich people are. I suppose I should amend that to read that I know how gullible *some* rich people are. Lord knows, I've had plenty of experience in gulling them.

On the other hand, my aunt Viola Gumm, like the rest of my Gumm kin, wasn't at all gullible. Or rich. In fact, Aunt Vi worked as a cook at Mrs. Kincaid's mansion on Orange Grove Boulevard in Pasadena, which is how she came to be involved with the Ouija Board to begin with.

Aunt Vi claimed to be a little scared of the thing, but I think she was only teasing. Everybody knew Ouija

Boards were just pieces of wood some smart guy painted and patented to swindle people with money out of it—money, that is to say. You didn't have to look any farther than Mrs. Kincaid if you doubted it.

So that's what started it. What kept it going was Aunt Vi taking the thing out on Christmas Eve to show the relations. Everybody laughed at it, but nobody wanted to touch it. I thought that was strange, since if Ouija Boards weren't truly conduits to a Great Beyond somewhere past death, what harm were they?

I decided to take a crack at it. Why not? I had no morals to speak of, being only ten years old at the time. Back then my main concern was in not making the adults in my life so mad they'd spank me. Since they seemed crazy for this silly board, I decided to have some fun on my own.

You could have heard a pin drop when I sat down across from my cousin Eula and we settled our fingers lightly on a triangular shaped piece of wood Aunt Vi told me was a planchette which, I assumed, was a French word for a triangular piece of wood. Eula, who was sixteen and showing it in every detail, wanted to know if there would be any beaux in her future. I didn't much like Eula, since she wouldn't let me beautify myself with her new eyelash curler, so I made the planchette tell her she'd have three boyfriends, turn Catholic, and enter a nunnery.

Needless to say, my spelling wasn't great, but I invented a spirit control named Rolly, who'd lived in 1055, and who'd never been to school. Therefore, since nobody expected Rolly to spell well, it worked out all right.

I was quite proud of Rolly. I'd listened hard when Aunt Vi explained the Ouija Board to Ma. She'd said that people conjured up some sort of spirit control from the Other Side, whatever that was, with which they communicated through the Ouija Board. That's how I came up with Rolly when I felt a need to explain my rotten spelling. Nobody else in the family could spell worth beans anyhow, so I probably could have dispensed with the control altogether, but Rolly added a touch of panache to an otherwise childish exercise.

To my utter astonishment and her absolute horror, Eula believed me. Everyone joined in communicating with the Ouija Board and Rolly through me after that, except Uncle Ernie, who'd already drunk most of the punch and had taken to snoring in his big easy chair. Uncle Ernie, Aunt Vi's husband and my father's younger brother, snored through most of our family get-togethers.

The thing you've got to understand is that back then, in 1910, Pasadena was a rich man's town. Wealthy folks from back East would build winter homes in Pasadena, or stay at the Green Hotel during the winter months, or even, if they were rich enough, spend the whole year there except when they were jauntering off to Europe or Egypt or somewhere else exotic.

What's more, Pasadena was a sophisticated place. We had 24-hour telephone service before the turn of the century, electrical lighting on our streets shortly thereafter, and several electrical car lines. Daphne, some of our friends, and I would ride the cars from Pasadena to the beach at Santa Monica for picnics sometimes, although most of the time we were too busy trying to make money.

And then there was the Tournament of Roses. There's nothing like a parade, and ours was (and still is) spectacular. People from back East are astonished to see so many flowers abloom in January. Believe me, the city fathers knew it, too, and did everything in their power to promote Pasadena's friendly weather conditions.

Consumptive people, too, came to Pasadena, if they had money enough. There were two or three sanatoria in the area. I suppose that was a good selling point for our fair city, but knowing about those sick people, even if they were rich, struggling for the breath of life itself always made me sad.

And several presidents have made trips here, too. Theodore Roosevelt, my personal favorite, stayed in Pasadena in 1903, so I don't remember his visit. Harrison, Taft, and Wilson also sojourned in the lovely city of roses.

My family would have had no business being in Pasadena at all except that all those rich people needed poor people like us to work for them. Aunt Vi was Mrs. Kincaid's cook, my pa was a chauffeur to several rich millionaires in the moving pictures, Uncle Ernie ran the concession stand at the Annandale Golf Club, my mother was head bookkeeper at the Hotel Marengo, and Eula and my brother Walter worked at the Raymond Hotel.

My sister Daphne and I went to school. Daphne cleaned houses for a couple of rich families in Altadena after school. I helped Daphne with that unpleasant task until Christmas Eve, 1910. After that seemingly trivial but eventually momentous date, I worked the Ouija Board and tried to learn everything I could about other forms of spiritualism.

Even with the success of Christmas Eve, 1910, I guess I would have continued cleaning houses with Daphne and maintained the poor but proud Gumm tradition, except that Aunt Vi told Mrs. Kincaid about my so-called "gift." The "gift," according to her, was my ability to work the Ouija Board through a spiritual control. Mrs. Kincaid asked Aunt Vi to ask me to work at one of her big society parties, entertaining her rich society friends. She even offered to pay me. Sure as shooting, I wasn't going to turn down money for doing something as easy as manipulating the Ouija Board.

The only problem was my name. As well as my appearance, come to think of it. A red-headed, blue-eyed, freckle-faced kid named Daisy Gumm didn't convey, to me, the appropriate image of a Gypsy fortune teller. At the time I thought all fortune tellers were Gypsies. So I had Aunt Vi tell Mrs. Kincaid my real name was Desdemona. When I was ten, I only thought the name sounded mystical and dramatic. I didn't know Desdemona was a world-famous murderee, or I might have adopted someone else's cognomen.

I wowed 'em on the night of the party. I wore Daphne's peasant blouse, the one she'd bought when her church group visited Tijuana, Mexico, in order to buy flowers and spread the Gospel. I did so without her permission and caught holy hell for it from Daphne the next morning, but by that time I was rich and didn't care. Mrs. Kincaid had paid me twenty dollars—*twenty dollars*—for playing with the Ouija Board at her party.

For the record, Mrs. Kincaid really took to Rolly. She spelled his name Raleigh and told me his English spelling was odd because he grew up speaking Gaelic, which is what people spoke in Scotland a long time ago. Back then, I didn't know Scottish people spoke anything other than English. For that matter, I don't know why I'd decided on Scotland as the homeland of my spiritual control. Maybe it was because I'd been reading *Rob Roy* right before the Ouija Board appeared in my life.

Mrs. Kincaid also pronounced the name of Rolly's language "gahlic." I thought she'd said "garlic." Speaking garlic seemed a trifle odd to me, but for twenty bucks Rolly could have spelled his name Raleigh or dozen other ways, and he could have spoken in onions or scallions or even turnips, and I wouldn't have cared.

What really mattered was that I'd found my calling in life. And I was only ten years old. From that day on, I read up on every aspect of mysticism, occultism, and transcendentalism, from turning tables to rapping to reading tea leaves to astrology. Fortunately for me, there was a First Spiritualist Church on Garfield Avenue in Pasadena, and I managed to talk my mother into letting me attend it a couple of times. It was interesting, to say the least.

Along with the genuine beliefs adhered to by people in the transcendentalist movement, I talked to lots of other folks about lots of other things. I've always been friendly and already tended to collect unusual people. My experience with the Ouija Board increased my attentions to such folks.

From some of my buddies, I learned how to read cards (both Tarot and playing), palms, crystal balls, astrological signs (I'm a Sagittarius), and I even studied up on how to summon people from the grave to chat with their living relatives, a notion that sounded appalling to me. I mean, who wants a moldy old corpse yakking in his ear? But people are funny, and a true Gumm never turns down a business opportunity.

I don't mean to sound cynical, because I'm not. Since my tenth year, when I fooled with the Ouija Board as a lark, I've learned that there are, more or less in Shakespeare's words, more things on heaven and earth than are dreamed of in our normal, everyday lives and philosophies. A lot of the learning has been hard, and I long ago ceased disparaging people for believing in or needing my services.

By the time I graduated from Pasadena High School, my classmates thought Daisy was a nickname for Desdemona. Some of them were actually afraid to do me wrong for fear I'd put the evil eye on them. But I'd stopped doing stuff like that when I was eleven, pretended to cast a spell on Billy Majesty, and he fell out of a tree and broke his collarbone. That scared me, and I never pretended to cast a spell again.

It also scared Billy, although not much, as you'll soon see. When I was seventeen and the United States entered the Great War I married him, in fact. He'd forgiven me for his broken collarbone long since. We were in love as only adolescents can be, never having been tested by life. As I soon discovered to my dismay, not even high-school algebra can hold a candle to life when it came to difficulties.

But it was a hellishly romantic time, what with the uniforms, the flag-waving, and the tears and all, and Billy and I both needed the attachment. We, like most of the other people in this great nation, were both proud and scared, and it helped to know Billy and I were united in the eyes of God and man, even though we had to part almost immediately after the marriage ceremony ended.

I can still remember how he looked on that day. He was so handsome in his new uniform, and I'd made a pretty, lacy white dress and carried orange blossoms. Everybody cried, although there really wasn't any reason to at the time. I didn't know that then, although I discovered my mistake not long afterwards.

The truth is that I can still look at the photographs taken at our wedding and get teary-eyed. We were both different people that day.

We were married in April. In June the Kaiser's men gassed Billy out of his trench on the French frontier and shot him when he tried to crawl to safety. He was shipped home in September, more dead than alive, and languished in the army hospital in Los Angeles for months. This broke my heart, needless to say, even though Billy and I didn't really know each other very well for all that we'd grown up together and been man and wife for six months. Because of his terrible injuries that rendered him unable to work, he received a small pension. Unfortunately, it wasn't anywhere near enough by which to support a family.

That being the case, when Billy was finally able to leave the hospital and come home to Pasadena, he was confined to a wheelchair, his lungs were ruined, his legs were bad, and I was one of the legion of women who suddenly had to make a living for their families. Out of that legion, I was one of the few who was more or less prepared to do so.

Fortunately for me, if not for Billy, when the war ended in November of 1918, even though Congress never did ratify the Treaty and eventually came up with separate Resolution officially ending the war with Germany, the spiritualist movement boomed. Lots of mothers wanted to get in touch with their dead fathers, sons, and lovers. Some of them even wanted to make contact with deceased husbands.

At first I felt like a rat for taking advantage of the bereaved. Gradually, however, I realized that people needed to hear that their late loved ones were content on the other side of life, and that they still thought with fondness of the ones they'd left behind. Everybody needs to know their kin want them to be happy. I learned after the War that the desire to communicate with those we love extends beyond life's boundaries.

In the beginning of this rush for my services, it shocked me that people were so eager to pay me for my sort of work, which was basically a sham. Then I began to view what I did as a form of necessary spiritual healing. That probably sounds blasphemous, but it's not meant to. Besides all that, I had a crippled husband and several other family members to help support.

Billy's mother and father had died in the influenza pandemic that had swept the world in 1918 and 1919. His sister had married a nice man who trained horses for Mr. Lucky Baldwin. They were living in a cottage on his ranch in Arcadia, which is a small community about twelve miles across the Arroyo Seco from Pasadena. Therefore, my family became Billy's.

We lived with my parents, and my work helped to put bread on their table, too. By that time Pa had come down with a bum heart and couldn't work as much as he used to. My cousin Paul had died in the war. He's buried in France, and I've told Aunt Vi I'll take her there one day to visit the site of his burial. Uncle Ernie had succumbed to his excesses as well, so Aunt Vi, twice-bereaved and heartsick to her bones, came to live with us.

The plain truth was that Ma needed all the financial help she could get. Since both my brother Walter and my sister Daphne were married and had families of their own to provide for, that left me.

The only problem with working as a spiritualist is that you tend to meet a lot of strange people. Sometimes that can be interesting and even amusing, at least for me, because I like all kinds of people. At other times, it can be merely bizarre, and sometimes it's downright frightening.

For some reason, too, I seem to attract weirdness. I don't understand it. A policeman friend of mine once told me it's because I'm cursed, but I think—I hope—he was only kidding. He won't admit it.

The first real hint of this characteristic of mine happened in 1920, not even two full years after the war ended, and about six months before my own twentieth birthday. Everyone's life had been changed by the World War. Not only had I, a very young female person, become the virtual support of my entire family, including a crippled husband, but everyone was still shaken by the atrocities the world had seen in that most brutal of conflicts.

I still felt a pang of trepidation every day when I picked up the *Star News,* one of Pasadena's two daily newspapers, because it continued to print the casualty lists for nearly a year after the official end of the war. I guess they kept finding bodies, which is a terrible thought. My heart aches to this day when I remember reading, day after day, row upon row of names of the dead and wounded, searching for those of my friends and family.

The nation was having a hard time recovering from the war, too. It wasn't only my family that was suffering. In other words, times were hard.

I've read Mr. F. Scott Fitzgerald's books about all those rich, bored, alienated people back East, who can't find anything worthwhile to see or do in life, and his work only makes me mad. What do those people have to complain about, for Pete's sake? Heck, if I had all that money, I'd *do* something with it; something worthwhile. Not them. They just wallow in their disenchantment and pretend to suffer.

Phooey. They don't know what suffering is. Anyhow, if they hate the good old U.S.A. so much, why don't they move to Europe? I have a sneaking hunch they could be miserable anywhere. Even Paris, France, or Egypt (I've always wanted to see the pyramids).

I don't understand people who claim to have lost hope and have no dreams for the future, either. For so many years after that horrid, awful war, all I lived on was hope. Heck, I dished it out for a living, to people who *needed* it. Besides, the way I see it, it's only the rich in this world who can afford to be disenchanted and blasé. The rest of us are too busy trying to earn a living.

Anyhow, when it comes to reading for entertainment, I'll take a good old murder mystery or a rip-roaring western any day over Fitzgerald's books. I like it when the good guys win in the end. None of your moral ambiguity for me, thank you very much. If I want to be depressed, all I have to do is live. I'd as soon be entertained when I read. Mary Roberts Rinehart and Zane Grey are my heroes.

Maybe I'm just bitter, but I think Mr. Fitzgerald ought to have talked to me about what was going on with *real* people after the war before he wrote his books. Or he might have talked to Billy, who was not only shell-shocked to his soul, but physically ruined into the bargain. Mr. Fitzgerald's so-called "lost generation" might not find life so darned boring if they got jobs of real work and did something useful with their lives. They might even consider helping somebody else for a change instead of sitting around being miserable all the time. Most of us *real* people can't afford to wallow, darn it.

Sorry. Sometimes I get angry about things I can't change. It's a foolish habit, but there you go.

For my part, when the war ended I gave up flamboyant Gypsy attire in favor of more sober clothing. Bright Gypsy stripes didn't fit my mood or the profound melancholy that seemed to have a hold on my family underneath its surface pretense of well-being. I now wore dark colors, either blue or black, for my spiritualist work.

In my heart of hearts, I knew better times were coming, but with my husband a ruin of himself, my cousin and uncle both dead, and so many of my friends and relatives similarly bereaved, I couldn't have made myself wear bright colors even for money, which was a distinct change for a Gumm.

Billy didn't like how I brought home the bacon, but he was unable to work at all. Neither his legs nor his lungs worked any longer. Telling fortunes and conducting séances was the only way I could make a decent living. Sure, I could have worked as a housekeeper at the Huntington or Green Hotels, or cleaned houses as I used to do with Daphne, but spiritualism paid more.

I don't mean to whine or anything, but I really do think my policeman friend might have been a little kinder to a poor young woman who was only trying to make a living when we first met. It wasn't my fault Mrs. Kincaid's daughter liked to think of herself as a member of the "lost" generation. And it certainly wasn't my fault that Mr. Kincaid was a louse. Heck, before my spiritualist business took off, my family was so poor we could scarcely keep food in the cupboard, much less skeletons.

Then again, my policeman friend might possibly have had a valid point when he claimed I'm too darned nosy.

He's wrong to suggest I attract these things, however. I swear to you, none of this was my fault.

At any rate, my life's work has been interesting, even if it's also been a little bumpy in spots.

CHAPTER 2

"Don't go, Daisy." Billy grabbed my hand before I could pick up my hat. "Stay here, with me."

I held on to my patience and Billy's hand because I knew his pain, both physical and psychological, drove him to say these things. He'd once been a happy-go-lucky fellow and one of the human race's cheerier specimens. His experiences in France and the results thereof had changed all that.

"I have to, Billy. You know that." I smiled at him to let him know everything was ginger-peachy, even though we both knew better.

He didn't mean to be fussy. I kept telling myself that in order to keep my temper in check. The truth of the matter was that I got tired of his whining at me all the time about leaving him to go to work. I didn't think he was being fair to me, although I also didn't think I had any right to think so, if that makes any sense. After all, *life* hadn't been fair to poor Billy. Indeed, it had dealt him a wicked blow. And anyhow, he was a wounded war hero. I was only a woman.

But blast it all, *somebody* had to make a living for us,

and I was the only one left. That this was so only because Billy had run off to fight the Huns wasn't either of our faults. We'd both been swept up in the fervor of the moment, and we'd both thought his had been a noble sacrifice for a just cause.

Besides, it made me sad to look at him. He used to be so young and straight and strong. Now he was like the shell of himself. A human ruin. A blasted-out husk of a once-proud young man. When I didn't want to cry about it, I wanted to rush over to Germany and shoot Huns. Never mind that the war was over and that most of those German soldiers had believed their cause to be a just one. The war wasn't over in our house, and what the Kaiser's men had done to my husband was unforgivable in my book.

When he'd left for France, Billy had been nineteen years old. I'd been seventeen. Now he looked a hundred and ten, and I felt at least that old.

Another terrible truth that I didn't often feel like facing was that exhaustion and worry had very nearly depleted my supply of love for poor Billy, although my devotion to him remained unswayed. I couldn't afford to be swayed. I had too darned many people to support.

Which brought me back to leaving our house so that I could toddle over to Mrs. Kincaid's and pretend to raise the spirit of her dead nephew, Bartholomew Septimus Withers Lilley (rich people give their kids far too many names sometimes), from the Great Beyond, wherever that was.

Every time I thought about doing a séance, I had to fight hysteria. For some reason I envisioned those poor dead people rising from their graves, still swaddled in their burial finery, dripping dirt, and looking skeletal, except for who were still in the process of rotting. Especially when it came to the soldiers who'd lost their lives overseas, the visions were hideous and bloody and made me feel sick to my stomach. They were unpleasant mental images, but I couldn't help it that they invaded my mind's eye any more than I could help Billy.

"I don't know why you can't get a normal job." Billy let go of my hand and hunched in his wheelchair. He could walk a few steps at a time, but his lungs were so bad from the mustard gas, and his legs were so badly damaged from grapeshot, that he couldn't walk like he used to walk: forever and ever without even thinking about it. Or run. When we were kids, we used to run everywhere. He'd pretend to find me annoying because I liked to follow him around, but I didn't believe him then. I believed him now. Nevertheless, his tone of voice riled me. Still, I tried to keep my anger from showing.

"A normal job wouldn't pay as well as this one." I'd pointed out this trenchant fact before, but Billy didn't buy it. Or maybe he did and just didn't want to admit it. Sometimes I felt as if I didn't know anything for certain any longer.

"Money's not the only thing that's important in this world, you know," Billy said in the strange, querulous voice that seemed to belong to someone other than the Billy Majesty I'd known all my life.

"Maybe not, but money keeps food on the table and clothes on our backs." Every now and then, when I remembered how his rich laugh and deep baritone voice used to thrill me when I was a starry-eyed bride, I wanted to cry. At the moment, I wanted to shove his wheelchair down the front porch steps and save us both more pain and grief.

"It's sinful, what you do."

"*What*?" It was too much. I snatched up my handbag and whirled around, my fists planted on my hips, and glared down at my poor, destroyed husband. "What I do is *not* sinful, Billy Majesty. What I do is called *work*. I can't help it if you don't like it. It's all I know how to do, and it pays a lot of money." I hated that I had to pass the back of my hand under my eyes to catch tears. "Besides, it helps people, whether you want to believe it or not."

"Hunh. You're only fooling yourself, Daisy. It's wicked."

"It's not wicked! What I do gives comfort to bereaved people." That there wasn't a darned thing I could do to comfort Billy was a fact that seemed to shimmer in the air between us. I wanted to stamp my foot and scream.

His bitter expression didn't alter appreciably, even in the face of my fury and well-reasoned arguments. He ignored my impassioned speech. Sometimes I thought he ignored all of my impassioned speeches because he knew it was the best way to hurt my feelings. I knew I was being unfair to both of us.

"Who's going to be there?"

I turned around, slammed my handbag on the dresser since I hadn't meant to pick it up in the first place—these arguments always rattled me—and picked up my elegant black cloche. I tried to keep my hands from shaking as I settled the hat over my knot-in-a-pouf hair-do. The style was a little old-fashioned, but I was afraid I'd look like Irene Castle if I got my hair bobbed. I'd have liked to get a bob. It would have been so free and easy and simple, especially since my hair was thick would have taken to the "do" with relative simplicity. But then, nothing in my whole life was free and easy any longer.

As you can probably tell, every once in a while I'd get to feeling sorry for myself no matter how much I tried not to.

"How should I know who's going to be there? I'll probably see Edie." Edwina "Edie" Marsh was one of my friends from high school. She worked as a housemaid for the Kincaids, and we always had a good time trading gossip when I conducted séances the mansion. "And I'm sure there will be some of Mrs. Kincaid's rich friends there. Oh, and her sister, Mrs. Lilley, I guess, since it's her son we're trying to reach."

"That's horrible," Billy said in a low voice.

It was, kind of. I'd never say so. "Maybe, but it pays the milk man and the grocer."

Without another word, Billy pushed his chair around and rolled out of the room. I turned and watched him go, my heart aching. Thanks to my work, we'd managed to get him one of those newfangled chairs with wheels big enough so that Billy could maneuver himself around without help. That was some kind of blessing, I guess, because he felt helpless enough without having to have an attendant push him every time he wanted to, say, go to the kitchen or, worse, the bathroom.

Not for the first time, I was glad America had climbed aboard the water wagon. I could envision poor Billy, bitter and incurable, turning to the bottle for escape. Life was hard enough for us already. We didn't need the Demon Rum living with us, too. I worried a little about the morphine the doctor prescribed for him, but without the drug his pain was too great to bear. In other words, there wasn't any happy solution to the Billy problem.

Poor Billy. Great God, but I felt sorry for him. Ruthlessly, I swallowed the tears swelling in my throat. I reminded myself that lots and lots of women were in a state similar to mine, with their husbands dead or crippled. I was fortunate, I told myself, because I had a skill I could use to earn a fair income.

Blast and heck, it was more than a "fair" income! Why, I'd bought a little bungalow on South Marengo Avenue for my family with my earnings. That was more than a lot of *men* could do, working at their so-called "normal" jobs. It hurt like fire that Billy didn't appreciate me and how nobly I was contributing to the family's welfare.

Father Frederick, the Episcopal priest who often visited Mrs. Kincaid and whom I'd met at her house, had told me to go easy on Billy because he felt diminished as a man. I could understand that and agreed with him, but it sure was hard not to be resentful sometimes.

I liked Father Frederick, and not only because he was a genuinely kind man who offered helpful advice, such as the above. He also never looked at me askance because of what I did. Some religious folks were scared of fortune tellers. Even more of them were of Billy's opinion and considered what we did sinful. Although, in fairness, Billy's criticism wasn't based so much on religious belief as on bitterness.

But Father Frederick wasn't like that. His soft brown eyes always appeared a little sad, as if he wished he could cure the world's ills and knew he couldn't. I understood that, all right. Shoot, I couldn't even cure my own husband.

Darn, but life was hard sometimes.

The air outdoors was fresh and balmy, the spring evening cool and slightly breezy, and the San Gabriel Mountains loomed large to the north, evoking a majesty that those of us who bore the name Majesty couldn't come close to projecting. The pure spring weather and the enchantingly sweet aroma of orange blossoms emanating from the tree growing beside the back porch went some way toward soothing my battered spirits.

Sometimes I picked sprigs from the orange tree and put them in a vase in the living room, even though the blossoms never lasted more than a day. The dark glossy leaves and the tiny ivory flowers, not to mention their intoxicating scent, cheered me in a way nothing else could, probably because they reminded me of my wedding and the days of our innocence, before the War had spoiled everything. I didn't even mind dusting up the fallen blossoms every hour or so, although my mother complained about the mess.

I had got into the habit of telling the people who hired me that I fasted and meditated upon spiritual matters before a séance, but that was a lie. Or, rather, it was part of the job. The truth was that I went about doing whatever it was I was doing until it was time to leave for a séance. This day I paused on the back porch steps to inhale several gallons of orange-blossom-scented air and decided life was worth living for a little while longer, Billy or no Billy.

"Gee, Miss Desdemona, you look swell."

This reverent comment was delivered in a tone of absolute adoration by Pudge Wilson, the neighbor's kid. He was skinny as a rail and had more freckles than the Pasadena Fire Department's resident Dalmatian. I don't know why or when anybody'd thought to call him Pudge, but Pudge he'd always been, and Pudge he was. And bless his heart, he appreciated me, even when my own husband didn't.

"Thanks, Pudge." I gave him a gracious smile. I had learned to smile graciously as part of my trade. People seemed to be awed by gracious smiles delivered by ladies who conducted séances; don't ask me why.

"That's a real pretty dress." Pudge had harnessed Brownie, the horse my dad had brought home from work one day several years before, to the pony cart. We had a dumpy little Model T Ford, also delivered by my father. It was one that had been given to him by some now-rich movie star who didn't need it any longer, but I liked to exercise Brownie when I could. He didn't appreciate my consideration, deeming exercise as akin to torture. Pudge, holding Brownie's reins, stared at me as if he intended to fall on his knees and start worshiping at my feet any second.

"Thanks, Pudge." I kept the gracious smile going as I handed him a nickel. Pudge was a nice kid.

He was also correct about my attire. I'd made the dress myself using the new, side-pedal White rotary sewing machine I'd bought for Ma, and it was a stunner—the dress, I mean. The sewing machine was, too, but I wasn't wearing that. The gown was a long black silk number, and it tied at the side hip with glossy black-satin ribbons.

It would have been straight, too, except that I had one or two bulges that marred its sleek lines. On the other hand, I was a woman, for the good Lord's sake, and women were supposed to have those bulges, whether the prevailing fashion called for a "boyish slimness" in American women or not. Naturally, I bound my breasts, but that didn't help a whole lot.

At any rate, where the dress tied at my hip, I'd sewn on a big, scalloped appliqué of shiny black beads and silk embroidery (also created by yours truly) that glimmered in the late evening sunlight. The effect would be truly dazzling by candlelight. Which, actually, was the whole point.

One red lamp with one candle burning inside was the only light I allowed during a séance. I was fortunate that the cranberry glass through which the candlelight glowed brought out the best in me.

My hair had darkened over the years from a bright coppery color to a darker, more sedate reddish chestnut. My skin, thanks to my mother strong-arming me into wearing sunbonnets all the time when I was a little kid, bore a few faded freckles, but no more than that. Those few I managed to hide with pale, pearly rice powder. I wore no lipstick, which gave me an interesting pallor. I'd developed a walk that was kind of like a waft, if you know what I mean, and which made people think of spirits even before the séance began.

Over the years, in fact, I'd polished my act to a high gloss. I was darned good at my job, which made Billy's complaints and harangues that much harder to take.

Pudge removed his hat, as if he'd just remembered his manners. "Are you sure you don't want me to drive you, Miss Desdemona?"

"No, thanks, Pudge. I don't know how long I'll be, and I don't want you to stay up too late. You have to go to school tomorrow."

He made a face, which made me laugh, which made

for a distinct improvement in my mood. "I don't mind,"
he said in a pleading sort of voice.

It was nice to know that at least one male member of
the human race appreciated me, even if he was only
eight years old. "I'm afraid your mama would mind,
though. Not to mention Miss West." Miss West was
Pudge's teacher, and she was a true Tarter. I knew it for a
certified fact, because she'd taught me when I was in the
third grade, and I could still feel that ruler come down on
my knuckles; I flexed my hands in remembrance. I'd
been a lighthearted girl and not the best-disciplined
student in the universe.

"Sorry, Pudge." I chirped to Brownie, who grumbled
once and started walking. I don't know what Brownie
would do if a real emergency occurred, since his pace
was either slow or slower, except when he stopped
walking altogether.

Fortunately, Mrs. Kincaid's house wasn't very far away
from ours, geographically speaking. Socially, the
Kincaids were about as far above my family as the stars
were from the earth. Not to mention money-wise. She
and her husband and daughter lived in the huge mansion
her father had built on Orange Grove Boulevard, the
street where the rich people lived. Lots of rich people
lived in Pasadena, and not all of them lived on Orange
Grove, but nobody who lived on Orange Grove wasn't
rich. They had a son, too, but he didn't live with his
parents.

I loved visiting the Kincaids' mansion, and not only
because one of my best friends worked there. While I
was supposed to be either preparing myself for séances
or taking tea afterwards, I absorbed my surroundings and
pretended the house was mine. Fat chance. I might make
a relatively good living, but I'd need to own a railroad or
a gold mine or a South American country before I could
have an estate like that.

Still, it was nice of Mrs. Kincaid not to treat me like a

servant. After a séance she always asked me to stay and take tea with her friends. She even introduced me to everyone, and they all talked to me as if I were their equal. Which I was in the overall scheme of American life. But we all know that rich people are different from the rest of us, if only because they can buy stuff we can't. The truth was that Mrs. Kincaid seemed a little in awe of me, as Pudge was. It might have been laughable if I didn't appreciate it so much in both of them.

I drove the three-quarters of a mile to the Kincaid mansion, urging Brownie on with promises of sugar cubes and carrots. Brownie pretty much ignored everything but food, including motorcars and me. The first was a blessing since there were so many more of them on the streets by 1920 than there had been only a couple of years earlier, and the second didn't bother me since he did what I wanted him to do anyhow. I haven't met very many horses, but it seemed to me that Brownie was a particularly phlegmatic example of the species. He plodded on, looking like a horse who hated what he was doing but had no choice. Which might have been true, come to think of it.

Brownie perked up when we approached the huge iron gate in the huge iron fence surrounding the Kincaid estate. He'd been there before, and he knew the Kincaids' stable hands liked him and always gave him treats.

Jackson, the guardian of the gate, saw us coming and pressed the button that made the electrically operated gate open. It was an impressive sight, those massive black gates sliding apart—and doing so to admit *me*, of all unworthy objects.

The first time my family had used electricity was when I moved them into the house on Marengo. Until then we, like most people in Pasadena who weren't living in mansions, used gas lighting and wood-burning stoves. Not to mention outhouses. It was still a thrill to sit in a bathtub, turn on the tap and feel that porcelain beauty fill up with warm water.

Back to the Kincaids. I hollered my thanks at Jackson, who nodded and grinned, his teeth gleaming like pearls in his mouth and his onyx face shining.

I liked Jackson. He was a friendly man, and he'd taught me lots of interesting things about spirits that most white people never learn. His family had come from the Caribbean where, I presume, they'd been slaves. He had all sorts of fascinating stories about Caribbean spirits, voodoo, zombies, casting spells and curses, and the like.

Jackson was only one of my sources. I'd garnered spiritual information from all sorts and varieties of people. I used every one of the tidbits people had related to me in my work (although I'd never sacrificed chickens, as Jackson claimed his kin sometimes did) which might be one of the reasons I was so successful. My brand of spirit-raising was unlike anybody else's.

Brownie's pace quickened marginally as he pulled the pony cart down the gigantic, deodar-lined drive to the back of the house and the stables. Most of the Kincaids' horses had been replaced by several automobiles, but Harold, the Kincaids' son, liked to play polo, so the Kincaids still kept a few horses. I fancied the Kincaid horses didn't deign to speak to poor old Brownie, but Brownie was man enough or, more likely, cranky enough, to endure their slights.

Quincy and James, the stable hands, were ready for me. They both grinned, and Quincy tipped his hat while James helped me down from the cart. I'd come to know Quincy pretty well, because he and my friend Edie were in love with each other. That was my conclusion about their relationship, at any rate. Edie blushed every time I asked her about Quincy, and Quincy got tongue-tied every time I asked him about Edie. You figure it out.

The most interesting thing about Quincy, in my opinion, was that he'd been born in Nevada, and had worked as an honest-to-gosh cowboy on a ranch there until he moved to California. He'd come here because he wanted to become a cowboy star in the moving pictures, like William S. Hart. He'd worked in one picture, broken his leg, and that had ended his aspiring career. Boom. Just like that. Sort of like my Billy, although nowhere near as catastrophically. Still, it must have been a disappointment to poor Quincy, although he never let on. After the accident, unable to do the trick riding he'd learned as a boy, Quincy had quit on the pictures and had come to work at the Kincaids'.

I think Quincy and James and I felt somehow akin to each other. We were all three trying to make a living from wealthy people, and both of our professions were dependent upon people who possessed more money than sense. I mean, face it, most people couldn't afford to own a dozen horses in those days any more than they could afford to hire spiritualists.

Be that as it may, I liked Mrs. Kincaid. I know there's a big Red movement in the country, even to this day. In 1920 there were strikes in progress everywhere, and there had been a depression raging since the war ended. Lots of soldiers couldn't find jobs, and the dollar's value had dropped to less than fifty cents of its value in pre-war money, which hurt us more than it did people like the Kincaids. A few people thought they were being funny when they said that a man without a dollar was fifty cents better off than he once was, but it wasn't funny to us. There's always been a huge division between rich folks and the rest of us and there probably always will be.

But as far as I'm concerned, you can keep Communism, Anarchism, Socialism and all the other political "isms." I'd bet money, if I had any to throw around on any pursuit so useless, that nobody in Russia would hire me to communicate with their dead relatives. Only rich people could afford to do that then, and only rich people can afford to do that now.

Not only that, but it was the Kincaids of this world who gave me hope. Or people like that fellow Hearst, who started the Spanish-American War and then bought the newspapers. Shoot, all he'd had were money and words, and look what he's done with them. You couldn't do that in Russia, especially now, with the Czar dead and that crazy man Lenin in charge.

"Thanks, fellas." I saluted Quincy and James and headed for the front door. I wouldn't have minded using the back door, but Mrs. Kincaid had been shocked when I'd asked her if she'd rather I come in that way. That had made me feel quite good, actually, and it was one of the reasons I never refused to work for Mrs. Kincaid, even when her séances were inconvenient.

Sometimes I wondered how much money a family had to have if they wanted to hire a butler. Not that we needed one on Marengo. Heck, there'd be no place to put him if we could afford one. Everyone called the Kincaids' butler Featherstone. Just Featherstone. Not Mr. Featherstone or First Name Featherstone. He was just Featherstone, as if he didn't have a first name or a title.

To judge by Featherstone's accent, he'd come from England. I thought that was elegant. Imagine, importing a man from England just to answer your door and carry things on trays.

On the other hand, sometimes I wondered about old Featherstone. He was so perfect for the job, it was difficult for me to believe he wasn't acting the role of a butler, sort of like I was acting the role of a medium. Then again, maybe because my own line of work was based on misrepresentation and flummery, I was jaded.

Because I couldn't help myself, I grinned at Featherstone when he opened the door. I always grinned at him. He never grinned back. "Hi-ho, Featherstone. Lead me to the ghouls."

Stepping aside, his back as stiff as his countenance and his demeanor much more formal than that of anyone else

I'd ever seen even in Pasadena, Featherstone said somberly, "Mrs. Majesty. Please come this way." Not a smile. Not a wink. Nothing to tell me if he believed in the spiritualist nonsense I perpetrated or not. He was quite a guy, Featherstone.

"Sure thing," I said brightly. I followed him down the hall, contemplating whether or not it would be a good idea to whistle. I decided against it. My own physical demeanor practically radiated mysticism and the occult arts; a whistle would have been out of character, no matter what my innards felt like.

Unfortunately, although they seldom felt jolly in those days, my innards never felt mystical or cryptic, either. Therefore, I composed myself as I followed Featherstone through the massive entrance hall and to the right, where Mrs. Kincaid had everyone gather before one of my séances.

To most of us normal, every-day folks the room would have been called the parlor or the living room. To Mrs. Kincaid, it was the drawing room. That used to puzzle me until somebody, can't remember who, told me "drawing room" was short for "withdrawing room," because it was the room where people retired, or "withdrew," to chat and visit. That kind of made sense to me, but not much.

I had just caught sight of Edie, who was serving canapés and drinks to the guests, and had only had time to nod at her when I heard my name spoken loudly. "Mrs. Majesty!" Mrs. Kincaid had clearly been awaiting my arrival with more anxiety than was usual for her, because she was generally more composed than this.

Maybe she was edgy because of the purpose for this séance. It was one thing to raise a long-dead uncle from the Great Beyond. It must be unnerving to be trying to get in touch with a young man who was only a year or so dead, and who was still deeply mourned. Thinking about it made me want to shudder, so I stopped thinking.

Anyhow, Mrs. Kincaid was rushing over to me, holding both hands out, so I didn't have time to entertain gruesome thoughts or walk across the room and chat with Edie. Besides, we were both working, so I couldn't have done more than say hello.

"Good evening, Mrs. Kincaid." She was a truly nice woman. I appreciated her friendliness to me, a Gumm. We Gumms weren't accustomed to being fawned over by rich people. Not even I, who'd been dealing with them for years, more or less on an equal footing. I was no longer skittish as a cat in huge mansions, but I didn't think I'd ever get really used to them.

"I'm so glad you've come, Mrs. Majesty. Here, let me introduce you to everyone." Still holding on to my hand—I was glad I'd remembered to put on my black gloves—she led me into the thick of things.

There must have been more than twenty people there including Mrs. Kincaid's husband, who didn't join in these social gatherings as a rule. He wasn't a sociable man and he never smiled, maybe because he, like Billy, was confined to a wheelchair.

I don't think he'd ever been cheerful like Billy, though. He looked as if he'd been a grump from birth, and I wondered why Mrs. Kincaid had married him. After all, she was the one with the money. She might have married Mr. Algernon Pinkerton, who was a good friend of hers and was very friendly and merry, or even Father Frederick, who was as nice as they come, and since he was an Episcopalian, even though he was a priest, he was allowed to marry. I think. Then again, maybe he was married already. I never saw him with a wife in tow, but it isn't wise to suppose too much, even though I love to do it.

But she hadn't. She'd married Mr. Eustace Kincaid for some reason beyond my ken. Rumor had it that Mr. Kincaid had been a clerk in her father's stock-brokerage firm in New York when they'd met. Now he sat stoop-

Alice Duncan

shouldered in his wheelchair, his face a mask of glowering disapproval. His eyes, which were black and piggy and small, made him look mean and hateful even before you realized he really *was* mean and hateful.

He nodded to me, giving me a smile that reminded me of lemon juice and unripe persimmons. Wrinkles radiated from his pinched lips, and his eyebrows were gray and bushy and recalled to my mind caterpillars or unshorn sheep. His voice was as thin as his hair, both of which were far thinner than his eyebrows. "Good evening, Mrs. Majesty."

Thank God for my supply of gracious smiles. I tossed one at Mr. Kincaid and said, "How do you do, Mr. Kincaid?" in the deep velvety voice I'd cultivated for my business.

"Not well," he said.

He said no more, which left me sort of dangling there uncertainly. After mulling it over for a second or two, still smiling graciously, I murmured, "I'm so sorry," and moved away from the old goat, wondering if reading the Spanish phrase book I glimpsed when his lap robe stirred would cheer him up. Perusing Spanish phrases didn't sound like my idea of a cheery occupation. I'd rather read a novel, but maybe it was a rich man's thing. Whatever the reason for the phrase book, I don't like cranky people, and I *really* didn't like Mr. Kincaid.

Fortunately, Mrs. Kincaid never paid much attention to her husband. She'd already flitted off to another group of people where she stood, looking at me in anticipation. I wafted after her, leaving old Kincaid to his wheelchair, his Spanish phrase book, and his crotchets, and went up to the group with which Mrs. Kincaid stood.

Mr. Pinkerton was there, smiling at my approach, as was his wont. It felt as if I were leaving winter behind and entering a springtime garden, so different was Mr. Kincaid from Mr. Pinkerton. He'd even asked me to call him Algie, although I never did, mainly because every time I said his name I thought of moss and scum on a pond, and I tended to giggle.

"This is my sister Ruth Lilley, Mrs. Majesty," Mrs. Kincaid said when I joined her group. "Ruth, let me introduce you to Mrs. Desdemona Majesty. We call her Daisy." Mrs. Kincaid smiled as if I were her favorite child or a playful puppy.

"How do you do, Mrs. Majesty." Mrs. Lilley listlessly extended her right hand to me.

I didn't have any trouble knowing what to say to this lady. I recognized the lines of anguish on her face as the same kind I'd seen on lots of faces since the war started, including my own. I took her hand in both of mind and applied gentle pressure. "I'm so sorry for your loss, Mrs. Lilley. I hope I can help you this evening, if only for a little while."

Tears welled in her eyes, and I felt awful for her. "Thank you, Mrs. Majesty." She returned the pressure of my hands. "I must say, I wasn't very enthusiastic when Madeline suggested we hold a séance for Bartholomew, but you seem like a kind woman. I'm sure you mean well."

"Oh, yes," I said, almost bursting into tears myself. "What I do is only meant to ease the hearts of those of us who are left behind on this plane." I'd learned to talk like that, about planes, dimensions, altered states and so forth years before. It was second nature to me now.

"Mrs. Majesty suffered her own tragedy, Ruth," Mrs. Kincaid said in something of a stage whisper. "Her husband of only a few months was grievously wounded in the war and is now confined to a wheelchair." I expected her to add something about her own husband who was similarly confined, but she didn't. I got the feeling she didn't think about Mr. Kincaid any more often than she was forced to, which made sense to me.

"Oh, my dear, I'm so sorry." Mrs. Lilley tightened her grip on my hands and looked even more miserable than she'd looked before.

Darn it. I hated it when people felt sorry for me. "We're coping. Thank you for your sympathy. My loss is nothing compared with yours." This was getting deep and sticky, and I really wanted to change the subject.

Mrs. Lilley left off squeezing my hand and patted it before letting it go, as if it was too heavy for her to hold any longer. "You're a nice girl, Mrs. Majesty."

"Please," I said, "call me Daisy. Everyone does."

"Very well. Daisy." For the first time since I'd entered the room, Mrs. Lilley appeared interested in something. "Is Daisy short for Desdemona?"

At least one person asked me that every time I did one of these things. I gave her my standard answer. "In a manner of speaking." I wasn't going to admit to this poor sad woman that I'd adopted the name when I was ten years old because I thought I was merely playing a silly game.

Algie Pinkerton beamed at me as if I were something wonderful when Mrs. Kincaid dragged me off. I didn't feel wonderful. I felt terrible when I looked back and saw Mrs. Lilley standing there, looking small and lost and alone.

It was hard losing a husband and a cousin to war, as I knew full well; but it must be pure hell to lose a child. I couldn't bear thinking about it. Not that I'd ever have children if things continued the way they were going, since poor Billy was unable to sire kids any longer. That was too unhappy a situation to contemplate at present, so I concentrated on comparing the sisters.

Mrs. Madeline Kincaid was a well-preserved woman of middle age, maybe fifty or thereabouts. She had brown hair that I imagined she dyed, because my ma was fifty, and she had gray hair. Of course, Ma'd had to work for a living all her life, and hard work might have faded the color from her hair follicles. I understand that sometimes happens.

I don't know for a fact that Mrs. Kincaid dyed her hair, but she was a nice-looking woman. Not pretty exactly, but *nice*, as in friendly and kind. Her clothes were something wonderful. I'm sure she didn't make them herself, although they were custom-made, like her Ouija Board had been. Well, I knew for a fact that she had a lady come in to her house and sew for her, because I knew the lady, Mrs. Liljenwall, who was a friend of my mother's.

Mrs. Kincaid always dressed in the latest fashions even though she was a teensy bit plump. She never looked dowdy, though. She was tall enough to wear her clothes well in spite of her heft.

Her sister, Ruth Lilley, was something else again. She looked like she'd been through hell and come back singed. She was very thin. Actually, emaciated is the word that springs to mind when I think about Mrs. Lilley. I don't know if she she'd always been thin, or if she'd lost weight after her son was killed overseas, but she could stand to borrow a few pounds from her sister. She, too, was dressed in the height of fashion, although she looked sort of as though somebody had thrown her dress over her head while she wasn't looking, like a department store mannequin. Her gown was black and had an interesting lacy bodice, her hair was a mousy brown and had recently been marcelled. And she was as pale as a ghost.

Now I cultivate my interesting pallor for my job. People don't expect a medium to be robust and healthy-looking, with rosy cheeks and a bouncy step. I can be bouncy and rosy enough during the day when I'm with my friends and family, but when I'm working I aim for wan and interesting. Mrs. Lilley's face looked as if somebody had deliberately and maliciously drained the color from it.

In short, she looked sick, I felt sorry for her, and I hoped I could help her at the séance. That probably

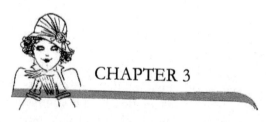

CHAPTER 3

Mrs. Kincaid presented me to the other people who were going to be attending the séance and to a few who weren't, thank God. When I'd first set eyes on that gang, I'd worried that they all aimed to participate. That would have been cumbersome, unwieldy, and difficult to manage, and I didn't want to work with such a huge group.

Mrs. Kincaid reassured me on that point when she whispered in my ear, "I'm only having eight at the séance, Daisy. I'm sure you wouldn't want to contend with much larger a group."

She was right as rain about that. I said, "I'm glad. It's more difficult to summon the spirits when there's a crowd. They can be shy in front of strangers." It was sort of funny—or maybe it wasn't—but I could lay stuff like that on as thick as paste and not even blink by this time.

"I thought sure that was so," she said. Mrs. Kincaid, on the other hand, was absolutely serious about this séance stuff. "You probably know some of my guests already."

She was right about that, too. I'd done séances for a few of the other women there, and I also already knew

Mr. Pinkerton and Father Frederick through other séances held at Mrs. Kincaid's house.

This was, however, the first time I'd seen Mr. and Mrs. Kincaid's son, Harold Larson Kincaid, since I'd grown up. He was one of the few rich men's sons I'd met who had only three names, although two of them were last names. He seemed like a nice fellow, of middle height, sort of soft, with brown hair, hazel eyes that twinkled, and a jovial personality. He sure didn't take after his dad, bless him.

Harold exemplified the modern male. To me, anyhow. Mind you, I didn't really have any idea how the modern male was supposed to look except by reading the movie magazines, but even I could tell that he was dressed in a genuine, albeit casual, Palm Beach suit, complete with belt sewed on across his back and patch pockets. I imagined it was made of mohair or some other expensive fabric and that it must have set his mother back a pretty penny, unless Harold actually held a job, unlike all those lazy fellows in Mr. Fitzgerald's books who only played at working. He was as sharp as a tack, in fact, and the sheen on him had been buffed to perfection.

"Mrs. Majesty!" His voice was high and loud, and his grin was really friendly. "It's so good to meet you at last. Mother talks about you constantly. I seem to recall a little red-headed urchin selling blackberries at the back door a few years ago." He shook my hand heartily.

I didn't mind him bringing up my penniless past. What the heck; it was the truth and anyone who had lived in Pasadena for a while knew all about it. I grinned back at him. "That was me, all right. My sister Daphne and I used to pick berries and wheel them around to all the big houses in our wagon."

He leaned over and whispered conspiratorially, "It's good that you changed professions, Mrs. Majesty. Blackberries are seasonal, but gullibility lasts forever."

He winked at me, and I knew he didn't mean to be unkind. Nevertheless, I felt it would be prudent to take him to task.

"Why, Mr. Kincaid, I don't know what you mean."

He laughed. "Of course not. Here, Mrs. Majesty. Let me introduce you to someone." He grabbed my hand and turned me around, and I darned near collapsed in a heap when, I swear to heaven, I saw Billy standing there. The impression lasted only a second, but it kicked my heart into high speed.

A soldier stood before the unlit fireplace, his back to me. He was talking to Father Frederick, and he was so tall and so slim and so jaunty, and he looked *so* much like Billy when I'd married him, that I felt like bursting into tears again. We Gumms are made of stern stuff, though, and I didn't do anything so stupid.

Besides, when I looked at him harder, I realized the resemblance wasn't as close as my first glimpse had led me to think. This man was a little taller than Billy and had shiny blond hair that curled like a girl's. Billy's hair was dark and straight. Also, this man looked much less rugged than Billy ever had. This guy had class. My Billy had class, too, but it was a different sort. This man would look right at home playing a violin in a symphony orchestra or dancing at a debutante ball. Billy, until the tragedy, would have been more comfortable swinging a baseball bat.

I had my nerves under control by the time we reached the man and Father Frederick. The good Father smiled at me warmly. We Gumms have always attended the First Methodist Episcopal Church on Marengo and Colorado in Pasadena, and I've never set foot in St. Mark's, the Episcopal church on Washington between Los Robles and Garfield, but if all Episcopal priests are as nice as Father Frederick, I wouldn't mind being an Episcopalian. I'd never tell my ma that, though. She thinks Episcopalians, like their Catholic kin, are idol-worshipers.

"Daisy Majesty," Father Frederick said, taking both my hands in his and squeezing them. "You look lovely tonight, my dear. Quite spiritual." He winked.

That's another thing about Father Frederick: He might be a priest, but he isn't judgmental, and he knows how to make a woman feel good about herself. It would be nice if more men, and not all of them priests, did.

Harold tipped Father Frederick a wink in his turn and turned to his friend, who wore the uniform of an Army First Lieutenant. I guess most girls are suckers for a man in uniform, but this fellow looked particularly good in his. Truth to tell, he was about the most gorgeous man I'd ever seen, even including Billy, who was mighty good looking even in his wheelchair.

"Del," said Harold, "look who I have here."

The man named Del smiled at me. His smile was enough to make a good girl think bad thoughts.

"Mrs. Desdemona Majesty, please allow me to present my best friend, former Lieutenant Delroy Crowe Farrington. Del works at my father's bank." Another three-named rich man, only this time all three were last names. "Del, this is Mrs. Desdemona Majesty. She'll be conducting Mother's séance this evening." Harold put his hand up to frame his mouth, as if he were imparting a big secret, and said to me, "Mother asked Del to wear his uniform tonight. She thought poor Bartholomew might be lured from beyond the grave more freely if he sensed another soldier present."

Unable to do anything more cogent at the moment, I blinked and said, "Uh…"

Lieutenant Farrington took my hand and bowed over it. Just like a duke or a prince or something. I swallowed. Never, in my whole life, had I seen anything to rival him in looks or manners. "How do you do?" His voice was smooth and rich. I thought I detected a southern accent, but I'm no expert on such things.

Although I felt unusually tongue-tied I managed to say, "Very well, thank you," as he lifted my hand and brushed it with his lips. Pasadena, California, wasn't overflowing with hand-kissers, and I have to admit that my thundering heart stumbled a tad.

"You have a wonderful name, ma'am."

After gulping—I'm usually pretty self-possessed because it goes with the job, but this guy was something else again—I said, "Thank you." I almost added that I'd chosen the name myself, but decided not to. "How do you do?"

"Very well, thank you."

Lieutenant Farrington couldn't possibly have grown up in Pasadena, or I'd have known about him. Even though the rich kids didn't play with my type, we knew what went on in town, and this fellow was new, or all the girls in Pasadena would have been talking about him long before this.

"Um," I added, interested because of the Billy connection, "were you a soldier in the War?"

He grimaced. "Yes, unfortunately. Thank God, I didn't have to go farther afield than Cleveland, Ohio, during my term of service."

I nodded, agreeing with him that his service had been fortunate, and wishing Billy's could have been thus.

Luckily, Harold took over and guided the conversation away from the recent tragedy. "Daisy is a real master— or is it mistress? Oh, it doesn't matter. Daisy is truly a master of the mystical arts, Del. You'll love getting to know her."

I didn't know what to say. I mean, I didn't even know Harold Kincaid; how the heck was I supposed to get to know Lieutenant Delroy Farrington? I murmured, "Nonsense," because I thought I should.

"Just look at her!" Harold continued, flinging an arm out as if he were presenting me at a bathing-beauty pageant. "Isn't she simply perfect?"

"Harry, you're disconcerting the lady," Mr. Farrington said, laughing.

"Not at all," I said. Rather, I kind of stammered. Okay, it's embarrassing, but the fact is that I wasn't even twenty years old, and I still liked to look at, and be looked at by, handsome men. I know I was a married woman, and I know I shouldn't even have noticed men like Lieutenant Delroy Farrington, but who could help it? Since Lieutenant Farrington still had hold of my hand, I shook his, recalling rather late that I was supposed to be meeting him, not gawking at him.

Harold laughed, too. "I don't mean to embarrass you, Mrs. Majesty. I'm honestly impressed by your demeanor and elegance. If I were to dress a medium for a moving picture, I'd dress her just like you."

"Thank you. I think." In spite of myself, I was beginning to enjoy these attentions, probably because there was nothing malicious in Harold's attitude, and he wasn't being flirty, as some men were even when they knew I was married. Rather, it was as if he were complementing me on how well I'd created my mediumistic persona. I appreciated his appreciation.

Both men laughed again. "Harry's impossible, Mrs. Majesty, but he works in the pictures, so he's constantly thinking of things in terms of costuming and so forth."

"I didn't know that." I looked upon Harold with more interest. "Your work must be fascinating, Mr. Kincaid."

"It is, but I'm sure it's not nearly as fascinating as yours."

"I don't know about that. My husband and I saw *The Cabinet of Dr. Caligari* last month, and it gave both of us the creeps for days afterwards. It was much scarier than anything I do."

"Lord, I hope so." Father Frederick crossed himself, but I think he was making a little joke.

Mrs. Kincaid rapped on a table to get everyone's attention then, so we had to stop conversing. I wanted to find out more about the pictures, since they were about the only refuge I had in those days. Even with Billy accompanying me I could get lost in a good, engrossing moving picture. I saw *Birth of a Nation* six times when it played at the Crown Theater.

I'd have loved to talk to Harold about Charlie Chaplin and Mary Pickford and a lot of other actors and actresses, but I guessed I wouldn't have a chance now. And, since we didn't exactly run in the same circles, my chances of talking to him after tonight were minimal. It looked as though I'd have to keep reading the movie magazines.

Conversation ceased so fast at the sound of Mrs. Kincaid's rap that my ears rang, and everyone in the room turned to look at her. I noticed expressions of mingled interest, fear, and amusement on many faces, which was typical. People pretended not to take my work seriously, but almost all of them weren't quite sure about it.

"Everyone who's attending the séance, let's move to the dining room. It isn't wise for Mrs. Majesty to communicate with the living too much before a séance, she tells me, because she has to maintain the spiritual aura she's fostered during her prior meditations."

"That's rich," murmured Harold at my side. "I'm terribly impressed, Mrs. Majesty."

I decided I'd better not thank him again, because people had turned around and were now staring at me. Instead, I nodded graciously at Mrs. Kincaid and slathered on the mystical aura, knowing my black clothes, pale skin, and dark red hair added to the overall impression of ghostliness.

When Mrs. Kincaid spoke again, I started searching for Mrs. Lilley in the room. She was standing against a far wall and looked as if she wished she could disappear. I felt really bad for her and vowed that I'd help her if I could.

A few people started moving to the drawing room door, so I turned to Harold and Mr. Farrington. "I must leave now. It's been a pleasure meeting both of you."

Mr. Farrington shook my hand like the gentleman he was. Harold pumped it as if he were trying to get water to spout. Father Frederick, who never attended my séances, smiled one of his sweet smiles at me.

Harold said, "I intend to cultivate your acquaintance, Mrs. Majesty. You're too precious to lose."

Whatever that meant. But it gave me something to think about as I wafted to the door and down the hall.

I always entered the séance room before my guests because I needed to make sure everything was set up the way I wanted it. Not that there was much more to set up than the cranberry lamp, but I liked to settle in; get myself in the mood, if you know what I mean. Maybe this quiet time might be considered meditation. I don't know, but I needed it, especially since I hated conducting séances in this room. I preferred to hold them in the drawing room, but that room was full of people tonight.

The dining room bothered me, perhaps because it had a musician's gallery hanging out over the table. I know it sounds silly coming from a medium, but the darned gallery spooked me. I always had the feeling someone was lurking up there, and the feeling gave me shivers. I did think that somebody like Mary Roberts Rinehart might use a gallery like that in one of her books. She could have a body fall out of it during a séance, for instance.

Never mind. My imagination carries me away sometimes.

Be that as it may, I wasn't going to give up a paying job just because the ambience in which I had to do it made my spine tingle. A Gumm knows better. Therefore, after I made sure the lamp was low enough and the chairs were the proper distance apart, I removed my hat and my black gloves—according to my spiel, you need a flesh-on-flesh connection if you expected to communicate with the spirits—and went to the door and opened it. I always ushered folks in to let them know who was in charge. I was, after all, not quite twenty; I needed all the help I could get in the being-in-charge department.

Good old Featherstone stood on the other side of the open door. Now *he* never had any trouble looking as though he were in charge, even when he wasn't. He stood there, as stiff as stone, with his nose and chin in the air as if he didn't care to look at the people he worked for, and ushered all the ladies and gents into the room. He was a master of his art, old Featherstone. I admired him tremendously.

Mrs. Kincaid stood beside her sister, holding Mrs. Lilley by the hand. Poor Mrs. Lilley looked as if she'd have rather been anywhere and doing pretty much anything other than this. I took pity on her.

Smiling courteously, as usual, I extended a hand to her. "Please come in, Mrs. Lilley. I assure you, this won't be difficult."

Reluctantly, the woman entered the room. She didn't return my smile, but I didn't hold that against her. I felt too sorry for her for that.

"Where would you like me to sit?" Her voice was low and it sounded as reluctant as she appeared.

"Beside me, if you please," I answered, sitting at the head of the table and waving at the chair to my left.

She walked slowly to the chair I'd indicated and sank into it with a sigh. Her every movement seemed to be carried out with difficulty, as if it were hard for her to come up with the strength to exist, much less move. I patted her hand and gave her a soothing smile, hoping to impart some of my strength to her.

Mrs. Kincaid sat at my right. The darned gallery

loomed over all of us like the wing of an enormous black bat. I saw Harold and Lieutenant Farrington enter the room. They sat together opposite me. Harold grinned like an imp, although Lieutenant Farrington appeared sober enough. Good thing. It would be terrible if I burst out laughing when I was supposed to be summoning the dead. It was also a good thing that the light was so low I wouldn't have Lieutenant Farrington's gorgeous face to ignore. It was difficult enough to maintain my air of mystery and mastery with Featherstone standing beside the door, looking superior.

After everyone had settled into their chairs, which always took a while, although I don't know why, Featherstone shut the door and I scanned my audience. Mrs. Walsh was there; her husband had made a fortune manufacturing chewing gum. The Walshes lived in an estate an acre or two down the street from the Kincaids and had a huge orange grove behind their house. It smelled really good on Orange Grove Boulevard in the springtime. I'd done two séances for Mrs. Walsh that had gone quite well. There were a couple of new faces, and I hoped they'd be impressed enough to hire me, too. Every time I did a séance, I picked up new customers. It was one of the benefits of my line of work.

When chit-chat ceased, which happened after everyone realized I was being silent and staring at them—it always unsettled them—I spoke in my cultured, low, séance voice. "I'm going to ask Featherstone to turn the electrical lights off now." I nodded at the butler, who only acknowledged my request by carrying it out. He didn't even glance at me. I always got the impression Featherstone didn't admire me as much as I admired him.

The room went black. It was only after folks got used to the decreased level of light that the red lamp made an impression.

"Everyone please take hands," I instructed, keeping my voice soft and as mysterious as possible. "We are going to attempt to communicate with Mrs. Lilley's son this evening." Because I felt so sorry for her, I squeezed her hand lightly. I don't know for sure, but I think she appreciated the gesture, because she returned the pressure.

Somebody sighed and somebody else coughed. Things like that always happened. Stray noises had stopped bothering me about seven years before. I didn't pay any attention to them any longer.

"In order to communicate with the spirits, I will have to go into a trance-like state. If the spirits are happy with us, my control will join us soon. I will need absolute silence in the meantime."

It was stuff and nonsense, of course. They could have chattered away like magpies and it wouldn't have made any difference, because it was all a sham. I'd come to understand that people needed the trappings that went along with the séance, though, so I always strove to give them a good show.

A few shuffles of a few feet constituted silence according to these séance attendees. I could tell the group was receptive and that they were eager for me to commune with their ghosts. Sometimes you could sense a skeptic in the group, but this time everything seemed fine and dandy. The red lamp did its part in mesmerizing people. After a little while of thinking about spirits and staring at the red lamp, almost anyone could conjure up a ghost if he tried hard enough. I moved my act along by slumping slightly in my chair after a few minutes of maintaining relative quiet in the room.

Mrs. Kincaid, who had been through this before and knew what my slump presaged, tightened her hold on my right hand. It hurt a little, but since I was supposed to be falling under the influence of Rolly—Raleigh— whoever he was—I didn't flinch. On my left, Mrs. Lilley's hand fluttered slightly, as if she were unsure what was going on.

Now came the fun part.

In an accent I'd been cultivating since my tenth year, and which I'd modeled on a phonograph record featuring John Barrymore playing Macbeth, I rolled out my Rolly introduction.

"Och, m'love, ye've come nigh to me again." I had to lower my voice an octave, but I just adored doing the Scottish burr. If I didn't value my livelihood so much, I might have used it in the neighborhood, but I couldn't afford to jeopardize my medium business by playing around with an accent. I also made Rolly refer to me as "m'love," since we were supposed to have been soul mates a thousand years or so before. I hate to admit it, but it was nice to think some man had once cherished me madly, even if he was make-believe, not to mention a thousand years' dead.

"Oh, my," whispered my left-hand neighbor, Mrs. Lilley. I hoped she wasn't going to panic, so I hurried on with my mediumistic part in this farce.

"Rolly," said I, in an overjoyed sort of voice. "I'm so glad you could join us."

"M'love," I said. Or he said. Oh, you know what I mean. "I am yours to command."

Would that it were true. I could use some strong male person at my command. "Rolly, another new spirit has crossed over to your plane, alas, another victim of the Great War."

"Och," said Rolly, and I was pleased to hear the sadness in his voice. I was really good at this.

"This young man is the son of Mrs. Lilley, and his name is Bartholomew Lilley, Rolly. He was killed in France." Next to me, I heard Mrs. Lilley give a muffled sob. I felt wretched all of a sudden.

However, I persisted. I had Rolly offer the sympathy I felt. "Och, such a loss, such a loss. 'Tis a crime to send young lads off to perish in wars." I thought about having him say something about the futility of war, but decided that would probably just make Mrs. Lilley feel worse, if such a thing was possible.

"Have you encountered Bartholomew Lilley, Rolly?" I asked, striving for a sweet, consoling tone of voice. I wanted to hug Mrs. Lilley and let her use my shoulder to cry on.

Rolly didn't answer at once. I did this from time to time, especially when I was being asked to communicate with a new spirit. So to speak. Sometimes I get to feeling really ridiculous when I try to describe my work.

When I felt Mrs. Lilley getting tense, I decided I'd waited long enough. Gently prodding, I said, "Rolly?"

"Aye, lass. Aye. Another moment, m'love. I think—yes. Yes, I have summoned Bartholomew Lilley."

Mrs. Lilley cried out this time. Mrs. Kincaid whispered harshly, "Hush, Ruth! This is the important part."

I wished I could run interference between the sisters, but I was supposed to be in a trance. Fortunately, Mrs. Lilley didn't get hysterical or anything. She was tense, though. I could feel the tension coursing from her body to mine.

You know, I guess I truly must be a little sensitive to mystical auras and stuff like that, because I honestly felt some sort of new force in the room. It should have been a prickly sensation but oddly enough, the force made me feel better. It was like a benevolent energy. I can't really explain it, and I don't expect anyone to believe me, but I swear that it might as well have been the spirit of Mrs. Lilley's son arriving in order to console his mother.

That probably sounds creepy, but it wasn't. Anyhow, even if it was creepy, I wouldn't have run away from it. We Gumms are a tough lot, and I had a job to do. Therefore, I stuck. "Rolly," I said, "does Bartholomew have a message for his mother? She misses him terribly and mourns him every minute of every day."

Mrs. Lilley squeezed my hand again, and I felt like a

rat. That had never stopped me before, and it didn't stop me then. "Yes," Rolly said. "Bartholomew wishes his mother to be at ease. He is happy here, with his kin."

"His kin?" Mrs. Lilley whispered desperately. "Does he mean my father and grandfather and grandmother?"

I felt like saying, "Beats me," but didn't. Rather, good medium that I was, I said, "Rolly?"

Rolly said, "He is with his kinfolk who passed before him." I don't know what made me add the next part, but I did. "And your cousin Paul is with him, too, me darlin' Daisy. Guiding him in his new home." It's stupid and I know it, but thinking of Paul and Mrs. Lilley's son as friends made me feel better. Rolly continued. "Aye, and he wishes his mother"—I had him pronounce it something like "mither"—"not to grieve overmuch. He will be here to welcome her when her time comes."

Another sob from Mrs. Lilley. I hastened to have Rolly add, "And not before. Bartholomew begs his mother to remain a true Christian woman. There's much left she needs to do on the earthly plane before she joins Bartholomew in the hereafter."

Before the war, I never once thought about preventing possible suicides among those I served, but since the war I'd been thinking about it a lot. People who are lost in grief are liable to do anything, and I felt a responsibility to let them know their loved ones didn't want them to join them on the Other Side before God called them. If you know what I mean.

All right, I suppose it sounds silly. It didn't seem silly to me at the time. And I expect it didn't seem silly to Mrs. Lilley or Mrs. Kincaid, either.

This time, a sigh emanated from the woman on my left. It was better than a sob.

What happened next wasn't better than anything. Overcome by the mystical drama of the moment (I did mention that I'm good at my job, didn't I?) a young woman named Medora Louise Trunick uttered a heartrending moan, slid out of her chair and landed with a plunk on the dining room floor. The plunk would have been louder if she'd weighed more, but she was as skinny as Pudge Wilson. I'd seen Medora making eyes at Lieutenant Farrington in the drawing room earlier, so I chalked up this theatrical moment to her desire to make an impression.

The interruption startled everyone into jumps and gasps of alarm. Harold leaped up from the table and ran for the light switch. His mother, I presume fearing for my spiritual health, hissed at him not to do it, because the light might do something awful but unspecified to my humble self who was, if you'll recall, supposed to be lost in a trance and communing with a bunch of dead people.

To say that I was vexed would be an understatement. I could have whacked the fallen woman. I wasn't allowed that luxury. Rather, I had to mutter a few disjointed syllables, look dazed, blink several times, and press a hand to my brow, as if I were awakening from a trance—which was the whole point.

CHAPTER 4

Medora's fainting spell ended the séance. Harold, thwarted in his attempt to shed light on the subject, rushed back to Medora and stood looking down at her as if he, too, wished he could smack her. Lieutenant Farrington was already kneeling beside her, chafing her hands and murmuring soft words. It was probably better that he, and not Harold, was tending to the stricken woman, given the latter's facial expression.

I watched these ministrations through slightly slitted eyes, thinking malevolently that I'd like to do more than chafe those delicate, never-worked-a-day-in-their-life hands. Since I was supposed to be recovering from summoning the dead, I didn't say a word, but only continued to murmur a few incoherent phrases here and there as Mrs. Kincaid did her best to revive me.

"We need light," Harold announced peevishly, fists planted firmly on hips. "Can't I turn on the switch yet?"

Since I didn't need anyone, and especially not a Kincaid, getting cranky because of me, I sped up my recovery. It wasn't more than fifteen seconds later that I blinked, smiled wanly, and said, "Why aren't the lights on?" An instant later, they were. I pretended to see Medora on the floor for the first time and murmured, "Oh, my. Whatever happened?"

Harold snarled, "She fainted."

"Oh, dear," I said in a weak voice. "I hope it was nothing I—"

"Nonsense," Mrs. Kincaid said as sternly as she could, which wasn't very. "You were wonderful, Daisy."

"Yes," whispered Mrs. Lilley. I'd almost forgotten about her in the muted uproar then transpiring in the dining room. "Thank you so much."

I turned my head and blinked a couple of times at her, trying to convey my interest and also my state of trance-induced befuddlement. "Oh? What happened?"

"I told you," said Harold. "She fainted."

"She means during the séance, darling," his fond mother said soothingly.

"Ah." Harold grinned at me, which was a definite improvement over the scowl he'd been directing floorwards at Medora. "Yes, indeedy, Mrs. Majesty. You were superb. In fact, you were better than that. You were absolutely magnificent. Called old Bartie right up, you did."

"Harold." This time Mrs. Kincaid sounded as if she were issuing a warning. Since she was a kind, rather ineffectual disciplinarian, I'm sure Harold wasn't frightened in the least, but I appreciated her trying to call a halt to his cynical enjoyment of my efforts at communing with the dear departed.

"She's coming around."

Thank God for Lieutenant Farrington and his interruption, because Harold had opened his mouth, I feared to spout more jolly comments. His friend's words made him transfer his attention back to Medora.

"Good," said he. "Let's heave her up onto her chair, old boy." Intending to suit the action to the words, he reached for one of Medora's more grab-able appendages.

"For heaven's sake, Harold. Don't put her on the chair. She might fall out of it again." Mrs. Kincaid left me in her sister's care and hurried to her son's side. "Please carry her into the back parlor. Thank you, Del." She smiled sweetly at Lieutenant Farrington.

Everyone but Mrs. Lilley and I trooped out of the room. Although I don't generally press the point that talking to dead people is an exhausting business, that's part of the performance, so I didn't dare perk up right away. I was glad Mrs. Lilley seemed satisfied with my work or the evening might have been a complete disaster.

"Are you all right, Mrs. Majesty?" she asked tenderly. Nice woman. I truly hoped my act would help her cope with her devastating loss.

"I'm...fine," I said with just a jot of breathlessness.

"Are you well enough to stand, or would you like me to bring you something first? Tea? Water?"

This was getting ridiculous. I wasn't the one with the problem here; it was Mrs. Lilley. Yet here she was, trying to help me. I decided I'd acted faint for long enough. "I'm fine. Thank you so much for your concern. Sometimes it takes me a little while to recover from a trance, but I'm feeling quite well now." I turned to her and took her hand. "Did your son come through, Mrs. Lilley? I had hoped to be able to find him for you, through Rolly." It was my custom to pretend to recall nothing from one of my séances, once I was under the spell of my control.

Her smile was as radiant as a woman who looked like a wraith could produce. "Yes, dear. My darling Bartholomew came through. He sounded just like himself, too."

Well, that was a wonder. I pressed her hand. "I'm so glad."

"You're really a marvel, Mrs. Majesty. You ought to be so proud of the usefulness of your work."

I wished Billy could have been there to hear her. He probably wouldn't have believed it anyway. But there was no use fretting over what couldn't be. Besides, the party seemed to be getting away from me, so I stood up, making sure I held on to the table for support. Not that I needed any. "Thank you," I said modestly. "I do try to use the gifts God has seen fit to give me to good purpose."

We walked out of the dining room together, Mrs. Lilley holding my arm, supporting me. She had it exactly backwards, but this, too, was part of my job, so I allowed her to help me. Then again, perhaps her believing she was being of use to me was one more step toward her own recovery. People seem to like knowing other people need them. On a personal level, I was kind of tired of helping everybody, especially Billy, but I didn't resent it too much.

Medora Trunick had revived enough to join everyone in the drawing room by the time Mrs. Lilley and I got there. Featherstone was supervising the laying-out of refreshments on a table at one end of the room. I saw Edie Marsh there, looking flushed and nervous.

She also looked as if she'd been crying. It distressed me to see her thus, so I decided to find out what the matter was. I didn't like my friends to be unhappy. Edie slipped out of the room as soon as she'd finished her work, and it took me another fifteen or twenty minutes to make my own escape, since I didn't want to appear to be in a rush.

Harold and Lieutenant Farrington cornered me shortly before I departed. Both men praised me to the skies, which was a relief. I had feared Harold would hold Medora's faint against me, but he didn't.

"You're *fabulous*, my dear!" he exclaimed, sounding an awful lot like one of my girlfriends talking about Douglas Fairbanks. "I've never *seen* such a magnificent performance as the one you just gave us!"

"Thank you."

"It really was a splendid séance, Mrs. Majesty." This, from Delroy Farrington, who was nowhere near as effusive as Harold. I was glad of it, since one person effusing over me was already almost more than I could take. "You do a spectacular job. I honestly think your efforts were of comfort to Mrs. Lilley."

"Oh, my, yes," Harold concurred. "Why, Aunt Ruth looks better than I've seen her look in months, and all it took was a little spirit-dabbling from a true professional." He beamed at me, and I decided he'd meant his comment as a tribute to my skill as a spiritualist.

"That," I said in a voice pitched to convince, "is the whole point of the service I offer. I'm not in this for the fun of it. It's a serious enterprise." I slid a glance at Harold to see if he was buying it. I couldn't tell, although he still smiled. I took that as a good omen.

"Well," continued Lieutenant Farrington, "I think you're wonderful."

I bowed my head, portraying the very image (I hoped) of mediumistic modesty. "Thank you."

"I should say so!" boomed Harold. "Say, Mrs. Majesty, I really want to talk to you about doing a séance of my own."

"You do?"

"Absolutely!" He turned to Lieutenant Farrington. "Wouldn't the boys love it, Del?"

"I'm sure they would." Lieutenant Farrington gazed upon Harold with an expression I'd seen from Billy as he looked at me occasionally. It sort of combined happiness with worship, if you know what I mean. I decided the two men must be *very* close friends.

Turning back to me, Harold said, "Do you have a card, Mrs. Majesty? I'll give you a ring after I look at my appointment book, and maybe we can set up a date and time." He rubbed his hands in what looked like glee to me. "Oh, this will be great!"

"I'll be happy to talk to you about it," said I. Billy would pitch a fit if he found out I was doing a séance with Harold and "the boys," whoever they were. "But I'd better be getting along now. My husband is…He's not been well." I didn't have to pretend distress about poor Billy. I lowered my gaze to the absolutely gorgeous Persian rug upon which my little Gumm feet rested.

Lieutenant Farrington took my hand and gazed at me with an intensity that surprised me. "Mrs. Kincaid told us about your husband's wounds and subsequent distress, Mrs. Majesty. Please allow me to offer you my sympathy and best wishes for his full recovery."

"I fear there's not much chance of that, but I do thank you."

The nice man shook his head sorrowfully. "I heard he took some mustard gas in France."

"Yes."

"The Kaiser ought to be executed for ever even thinking of using that pernicious gas," he said with a good deal more vehemence than I'd heretofore believed his magnificently handsome body contained.

"I agree." I sounded bitter. And why not? I felt bitter.

"Tut, tut," murmured Harold, trying to sound sympathetic, I'm sure, but not quite achieving it. "Let's not get maudlin, kiddies."

"Really, Harry," Lieutenant Farrington said repressively. "Have you no heart?"

"Not much, I fear." Harold cocked his head at me, then grinned. "That's not true. I *am* sorry for your poor husband, Mrs. Majesty. And for you. It must be a trial for one of your tender years to have to support a family. And I know very well that women don't get paid as much as men."

For some reason, Harold's matter-of-fact statement of the facts of my case made tears fill my eyes. I felt stupid. "Thanks," I said, which was about as much as I *could* say at the moment.

He patted me on the back. Lieutenant Farrington offered me a clean white hankie he hastily pulled from his uniform pocket. I shook my head, in control again, more or less. "Thank you. I'm all right." With a ruthlessness I'd been forced to cultivate since the war, I swallowed my tears. "And I do appreciate your— understanding." I'd been going to say "sympathy," but it was the understanding I truly appreciated.

Medora Trunick rushed over to me then, probably because I was with Lieutenant Farrington, and grabbed my hands. "Oh, Mrs. Majesty, I'm *so utterly* embarrassed at having interrupted your séance."

I'll just bet she was. I wasted one of my gracious smiles on her and told her it was nothing, that things like that happened all the time, which was a lie, and that everything was fine. She began simpering for Lieutenant Farrington then, and I almost managed to escape. Unfortunately, at that very moment Miss Anastasia Kincaid, sister to Harold and approximately my age, made her sneering entrance.

Stacy, as she liked to be called, had bobbed hair and wore a high-brimmed hat with about a million dollars worth of beads on it. She was clad in a thin sleeveless dress, likewise heavily beaded and that revealed the whole of her bare arms. It had a skirt I considered scandalously short (and I'm no prude). She'd obviously rolled her stockings below her knees, because her kneecaps showed, carried a lit cigarette in a long, expensive-looking cigarette holder, had dipped heavily into the rouge pot before going out for the evening, had lips the color of red barn paint, and looked as if she were perishing from ennui. Taking in the full glory of her, I thought it was small wonder parents had begun to moan and groan about the immorality of the younger generation.

I'd met Stacy Kincaid once or twice before, and I didn't

like her. At all. She was one of those spoiled rich kids who liked to think of themselves as superior to everyone else in the world and bored by everything in it.

As far as I was concerned, she hadn't lived long enough to be bored. Also, as near as I could figure, she'd never done a single solitary thing either for herself or for anyone else, so her demeanor of condescending superiority fell as flat as a lead pancake with me. She slithered over to her brother, Medora, and Lieutenant Farrington, leaving a trail of cigarette smoke in her wake and ignoring the shocked glances she was generating from the adults in the room.

"Daisy Majesty. So you're at it again, are you?" She smirked as she said it.

I smirked back. "Been reading *This Side of Paradise*, have you, Stacy?"

"Heh," she said, lifting her nose as if something smelled bad. From this, I deduced that she didn't like being reminded that she'd borrowed her going-to-hell-as-fast-as-possible manners from F. Scott Fitzgerald. I felt as if I'd made my point and was rather proud of myself, although I didn't let on.

I wanted to give her a hard whack on the fanny. According to my mother, a sharp smack delivered to the rear portion of the anatomy did wonders to clear up fuzzy thinking in the head portion of the same body. I thought Stacy deserved several years' worth of smacks, and also thought it would be swell if every single one of them were to be imparted at one time.

"I was just leaving," I murmured, smiling graciously. Another smile wasted.

"Ah," said she, exhaling a thin stream of smoke in my direction, probably in the attempt to kill me via suffocation or smoke inhalation. She'd think it was funny.

"Stop being a pig, Stacy, and get rid of that stinking weed." Harold snatched the cigarette, holder and all, from his sister's hand and threw both into the fireplace. I decided I liked him even better than I thought I did.

The gracious smile I bestowed upon him wasn't wasted. As Stacy turned purple and began spitting profanities at her brother, I beat a retreat. Without too many more minutes spent on taking my leave of Mrs. Kincaid and Mrs. Lilley, I managed to get the heck out of there.

The latter seemed to be in a strange mood, caught somewhere between ecstasy and puzzlement. No surprise there. Heck, anybody who believed she'd just received a message from a dead son deserved to be both of those things. She and Mrs. Kincaid showered praise and thanks upon my head, and I effected my escape feeling like the fraud I was, which wasn't awfully comfortable. Ah, well. One does what one must.

I found Edie outside the swinging doors of the kitchen, leaning against the wall and wiping her eyes. Concerned, I rushed over to her before she could flee, which I could tell she wanted to do as soon as she saw me coming.

"Edie!"

She sniffled, although I could tell she didn't want to, and brushed her cheeks with the back of her hand. "Hi, Daisy. How'd the séance go."

"Fine, fine. But what's the matter, Edie? Is something wrong with Eddie?" Eddie was Edie's brother. He'd been hit hard by the influenza when it was going around. It had gone into meningitis, which had done awful things to his spine and affected his brain. I don't think his wits will ever come back entirely.

"Eddie's getting better." She sniffled again. "There's nothing the matter, Daisy. Honest."

"Nuts." I took her by the shoulder and turned her around. We went through the swinging doors leading into the pantry, walked through the pantry, and went into the kitchen.

I was familiar with the Kincaids' kitchen, since my

Aunt Vi had worked there for so many years. Putting a kettle on the fancy Jewel gas range with moderated heat, two ovens, and a built-in soup warmer, I let Edie collect herself as I made tea.

She sniffled a couple more times and sighed. "Thanks, Daisy. You really don't need to make tea for me."

"Nonsense. I don't like to see my friends upset." Carrying the teapot and two cups over to the table, I sat down next to her. "Will Featherstone bother us?"

She shook her head. "He's waiting for the guests to leave. He's got to get their wraps and bags and bow them out the door, you know."

"Shoot, I didn't know being rich was such a formal proposition." That was another lie, and Edie knew it. Rich people were the only ones who could afford to be formal. I'd intended it as a little joke, poor person to poor person, but Edie didn't crack a smile.

Worried in earnest, I took her hand. "Tell me what's the matter, Edie. Is there anything I can do to help? Is anything wrong with Quincy?"

"What?"

Shoot. I'd forgotten I'd never been officially informed that the two of them were an item. Shrugging, I said, "Just wondered. He seemed fine to me." In order to collect myself, I took a sip of tea. "There must be something I can do to help you, Edie. Please let me help."

Shaking her head again, she said, "No," in a sighing sort of voice. "Nobody can do anything."

I set my cup down with a clink. "Jeez Louise, this sounds serious."

Shrugging, she said, "I don't think it's serious. It's only…It's only…Oh, nuts." Another tear or three leaked from her eyes.

"Come on, Edie, spit it out."

She sucked in a huge breath, then blurted, "It's Mr. Kincaid."

I cocked my head, wondering if I'd misunderstood her. Then I thought I understood, and my heart crunched. As much as I didn't like the man, I didn't want anything frightful to befall him. "Is Mr. Kincaid sick?" If he was, his wife was sure putting on a cool front. She hadn't looked at him once when they'd been in the drawing room at the same time. On the other hand, if I were married to him, I wouldn't want to look at him either.

"No. He..." Again she stopped speaking before revealing why Mr. Kincaid was causing her trouble.

Another thought, this one more horrible than the last, occurred to me. Shocked, I whispered, "Good Lord, Edie, don't tell me he's trying to—to—" I, too, stumbled verbally as I tried to think of a polite way to say it. I finally came up with a weak but time-honored euphemism. "Is he trying to take advantage of you?"

Her nod was so tiny I wouldn't have noticed it if I hadn't been watching. I gasped. "Good Lord! That miserable, lousy skunk! What's he done? Oh, Edie, this is ghastly!"

She sighed so hard into her teacup that tea splashed out into the saucer. "He traps me with that wretched wheelchair of his, and—and he touches me."

My mouth pursed up and my nose wrinkled against my will. But...ew. Mr. Kincaid? "My Lord." I couldn't think of anything else to say, I was so dumbstruck.

Now that she'd owned up to the source of her distress, Edie's words practically tripped over themselves as they raced out of her mouth. "And not only that, Daisy, but he pinches me. On my rear end. And he tries to feel my— my—bosom when he wheels past me."

The image of the despicable Mr. Kincaid playing fast and loose with my friend was so grotesque, it cleared up the roadblock in my head. I could think of lots of things to say now, and I wanted to say every single one of them to Mr. Kincaid. "The bounder!" I leaped to my feet and had taken several brisk steps toward the kitchen door before Edie grabbed me. I tried to get away, but she hooked her other arm around a column supporting a cupboard and dug in her heels. I couldn't move.

"No, Daisy, don't!"

"Darn it, Edie, I want to tell that buzzard what I think of him! He has no right to do that to you! I'll bet his wife doesn't know!" I tugged.

Edie tugged harder. "Daisy, will you quit it?"

"No! Somebody needs to tell him what's what, and I'll be more than happy to do it. The skunk! The stinker! The rat!"

"Darn it, I won't let you talk to Mr. Kincaid!"

"Then I'll talk to *Mrs.* Kincaid! She deserves to know what kind of hound dog her husband is!"

"If you tell Mrs. Kincaid, how do you think she'll feel?"

I stopped tugging. I didn't want to, but Edie was right. I liked Mrs. Kincaid and didn't want to hurt her feelings. Still, I fought on weakly, because the notion of Mr. Kincaid pawing Edie made me sick. "If she doesn't know he's a rat by this time, she's stupider than I think she is," I muttered. "She probably hates him already."

"Maybe, but I sure don't want to make her unhappy. I like Mrs. Kincaid. She's a nice woman and treats me well. It's not her fault her husband's a creep."

I gave it up and turned to go back to the kitchen. Edie was visibly relieved. She was also right about Mrs. Kincaid, although I didn't think Mr. Kincaid should be let off the hook so easily. Still and all, it really wasn't my place to butt into Edie's business. Plunking myself back into the chair I'd just vacated, I grumbled, "I still think you ought to do something."

"Yeah? What do you suggest?"

When my jaw started aching, I realized I'd been gritting my teeth. "For one thing, I think you ought to let me talk to Mr. Kincaid." Boy, I'd love to tell that so-and-so what I thought of him.

"If you did that, he'd fire me," Edie pointed out with impeccable logic. "And he'd probably see to it that you never worked another séance in Pasadena, too."

"Blast. You're right." I hated when that happened. "But you could quit, Edie. Why don't you just quit this place and get another job? I know jobs aren't as easy to come by as they were before the war, but still and all, you shouldn't have to put up with that sort of thing."

Edie's fiery blush and obvious embarrassment astonished me. I stared at her hard. "What?" I asked. "What's up, Edie?"

She didn't speak for a couple of seconds. Then she laid a hand over mine. "Promise you won't tell or say a word to anyone, Daisy. I won't tell you unless you promise."

I also hated to make a promise before I knew what I was supposed to keep secret. Then again, I suppose that was the whole point. "I promise."

Her cheeks remained pink, but she looked happier. In fact, she sort of began to glow. The change was amazing. "It's Quincy."

I tried to look surprised. "Quincy Applewood? The stable boy?"

Her mouth twisted, and she gave me a look that told me what she thought about my show of disingenuity. "Come on, Daisy."

I gave a sheepish gesture with my hands. "Okay, so I'd already figured it out."

"And he's a handler, Daisy, not a stable boy." She made the word stable sound like something that smelled bad—which it probably did, come to think of it. The stable, not the word.

"Ah."

"He's brilliant with horses. Why, did you know he was a trick rider in the pictures before his injury?"

I knew he'd been in a movie. Once. Not wanting to burst Edie's bubble, I didn't mention the once part. "Er, yes, I knew that."

"He claims he can't ride like he used to, but I've never seen anyone do the things he can do with a horse. He's no mere stable boy, Daisy. He's working hard to get a job with the races."

"My goodness. I thought horse racing was illegal in California."

"It is, for the time being, but it won't be for long. Believe me. People want the races back." She sounded as if she were quoting somebody else. I suspected Quincy. "And there's always the track in Caliente."

Edie was willing to follow her love to Mexico? I was impressed—and a trifle appalled.

"I see. Er, isn't he a little large to be a jockey? I thought they were supposed to be—"

Edie cut me off scornfully. "Not a jockey. He's a trainer."

"Oh." I didn't know a thing about horses, but I took her word for it that jockeys and trainers were different animals.

"Quincy and I want to keep working for the Kincaids until we've saved up enough money to get married."

"Ah. I see. Of course." My tone was as soft and squishy as a marshmallow. I was still a romantic at heart, in spite of my own unhappiness in marriage. I figured it was the War's fault that Billy and I weren't happy, and Edie and Quincy wouldn't have to face that obstacle to their own marital success.

"These are the best jobs we can expect to get unless one of us moves to Los Angeles or something and works for a studio, and we don't want to be separated."

Aw. How sweet. "I guess I can understand that. Does Quincy know about Mr. Kincaid?"

Her cheeks quit blooming. "No! And don't you dare tell him, either!"

"Why not, for heaven's sake?"

"Because he might do something."

"Isn't that the whole point? Doesn't he deserve to know?" I didn't roll my eyes, which I think showed considerable restraint.

"Darn it, Daisy, I don't want Quincy to lose his job, any more than I want to lose mine! I just told you that! Don't you understand?"

"No." I was beginning to feel as a person might feel if he were watching another person deliberately walk in front of a speeding train. "I don't understand anything about this. Darn it, Edie! You won't let me talk to Mr. or Mrs. Kincaid. You won't tell Quincy. You won't quit. How the heck do you expect to solve this problem if you don't do anything about it?"

"I can take care of it myself."

"Right. That's why you were crying in the hall." My voice held a degree of sourness I hadn't intended.

Edie glared at me. "You promised, Daisy."

"I know, I know. But you're *not* taking care of it."

"I will."

"Oh, brother." I glared back at her for a second or two, then gave up. Edie was a good friend, even if I did think she was being stupid about Mr. Kincaid and Quincy. Still and all, it was her life, and if she didn't want me poking into it, that was her choice. I still had an urge to scream at Mr. Kincaid. Even kick him, although that was a mean thought since he was confined to a wheelchair.

Which he used for immoral purposes. All right; he deserved to be kicked.

Screaming at and kicking Mr. Kincaid weren't within my list of allowable options, however, thanks to that dumb promise I'd made to Edie. Standing and looking down at her, I sighed. "I don't like leaving you here with that awful man, Edie. He can get around faster with his wheels than you can with your feet."

"I know." She sounded as if she'd had vast experience learning the truth of this, actually.

"I still think you ought to tell Quincy, if not Mrs.

Kincaid."

She heaved one more gigantic sigh. "I know you do."

Another second of silence ensued. After I realized I'd said everything I had to say and to repeat any of it might only produce a rip in the fabric of our friendship, I allowed my shoulders to relax. They'd been squared for battle. "I'd better get Brownie home now, Edie. Take care of yourself."

She stood, too. "Thanks, Daisy. I know you're only trying to help."

"Yeah. I am." Too bad she didn't have a dead relative I could talk to for her. I could get Rolly to tell her to quit this stupid job and find another one. Unfortunately, Edie didn't have the money to hire me. Anyhow, I'm sure she was too smart to believe I could really communicate with the dead. I could offer her my assistance if she ever needed it, though, so I did. "If you ever need me, don't hesitate to call, Edie."

Her countenance softened and she gave me a shaky smile. "Thanks, Daisy." She reached out and took my arm to walk me to the back door. "I appreciate your offer, and if I ever do need help, I'll be sure to call."

I gave her a mock-stern scowl. "You'd better. I'll be mighty mad if you don't."

We parted on good terms, thank goodness, although I still thought she was being pretty dumb for a smart girl. I couldn't stand the thought of being touched by the monster Mr. Kincaid. The mere notion gave me the willies.

It was Quincy who brought Brownie out to me. I itched to talk to him about Edie, but I'd promised. Darn it.

"How'd it go?" he asked, handing over the reins.

Now that I knew from the horse's mouth, so to speak, that he and Edie were in love with each other, I understood why he seemed so cheerful all the time. Edie was a good catch, because she was a good person. And a pretty one. I'm sure men cared about that sort of thing, although I gave Quincy credit for being interested in more than beauty in a wife. This might yet prove to be credit not earned, but I liked to give people the benefit of the doubt.

Brownie looked as if he was a good deal put out with me for forcing him to take me home after he'd gone to the effort of bringing me here, but I was used to it. "Great," said I, meaning the séance and being unable to talk about anything else. "Everything went very well."

"Glad to hear it." He took off his cap and scratched his head, as if he'd like to say something else. About Edie? I smiled at him, hoping to encourage confidences.

"Say, Daisy…"

"Yes?" I smiled harder.

"Um, did you see Edie Marsh in there?"

Aha. Triumphant and trying not to let it show, I said gently, "Yes, I did. Edie and I are great friends, you know."

"I know. She's always talking about you."

"Really? You two talk a lot?"

He scuffed a toe in the dirt. "We're aiming to get married as soon as I've saved up enough money to give her a good life."

I gave him a quick peck on the cheek which made him turn pink with embarrassment. "I'm so happy for you both, Quincy."

"Thanks. Er…Did she seem okay to you? She's been sort of nervous lately, unless it's my imagination."

Oh, boy. I wanted so much to break my promise to Edie that my jaw ached from holding the words in. "She seemed fine to me."

"Oh." He nodded. "Good."

I climbed aboard the pony cart and clucked to Brownie, who turned his head and frowned at me before beginning the short walk home. Quincy walked alongside the pony cart down the long driveway, undoubtedly having to slow his pace so as not to reach the gate first. Brownie walked slowly enough for a herd of babies to crawl along with him; in fact, they'd probably beat him home.

"How come you named this horse Brownie?" Quincy asked, grinning, hands shoved into his pockets, looking like a cowboy. He really was a cutie-pie, but I was sure glad he'd dropped the Edie subject.

The question was a valid one, too, since Brownie was sort of a dirty white color. I shrugged. "Not sure. When Pa brought him home, he said his name was Brownie, and that's what we've always called him."

"Hmmm."

Quincy appeared as stumped as the rest of us over why anyone would name a white horse Brownie. It had occurred to me on occasion that Brownie's name might be one of the reasons he was such a grump all the time, but that was certainly mere fancy on my part. I mean, what would a horse know about colors?

Billy was waiting up for me when I got home. Fortunately, he seemed to have overcome his nasty mood, and we laughed a lot about the séance and Stacy Kincaid. I didn't tell him Harold wanted me to do a séance for him.

As the Good Book says, "sufficient unto the day is the evil thereof." I've never been quite sure what that meant, but it seemed to fit this occasion.

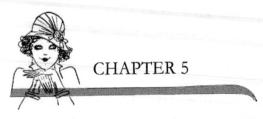

CHAPTER 5

Our house on Marengo Avenue was what they called a "bungalow." Bungalows are popular in Pasadena. A couple of brothers, Greene and Greene, are building them all over the place, and other architects copied them. Ours had three bedrooms downstairs, one of which we used as a back parlor and for sewing, a large kitchen, a dining room, and a living room. There were two rooms upstairs, too, that would have been perfect for a young married couple, provided they could both climb stairs.

Only one of us could do that. Therefore, Billy and I shared a back bedroom, the one off the kitchen. It was large, and had a door to the back yard. God bless Pa, who was a truly wonderful man, he built us a little screened-in sun porch right outside our bedroom door. He and Ma gave us a small but pretty wrought iron table and two chairs for furniture.

Thanks to Pa's thoughtfulness, Billy and I could sit out there and be private sometimes, smelling the orange blossoms and roses and looking at the San Gabriel Mountains. The sun porch wasn't a whole lot of privacy, but it was the best we could do, and we both liked to take advantage of it.

When I woke up the morning after the séance, Billy was already awake and dressed. I saw him sitting on the sun porch, reading the *Pasadena Star News*. Every new day brought with it a certain degree of edginess in my soul until I gauged Billy's mood. Today he seemed perfectly happy, or as happy as a man his age who's in constant pain and confined to a wheelchair can be.

After throwing on a robe, I went out and kissed his glossy black hair. "Morning, Billy."

"Morning, love. Beautiful day."

It was, and my heart leaped in my chest to hear him acknowledge it. Poor Billy no longer had the capacity to enjoy the weather very often. "Be right back." I went back through our bedroom to the kitchen, kissed Ma on the cheek, and poured Billy and me each a cup of coffee. I could tell by Ma's worried eyes that she, too, wondered how Billy felt this morning, so I gave her a thumbs-up sign. The expression of relief on her face made my heart ache. Damn the Kaiser, anyhow.

I tried always to show only a pleasant demeanor to Billy, so I braced myself as I walked back to the sun porch. When I set Billy's coffee cup down in front of him and plopped myself into the wrought-iron chair across from him, I asked, "So what's new in the world?"

Women had finally, after decades and decades of struggle, been given the vote. It burned me up that I wasn't old enough to take advantage of the new law. I liked to keep up with the candidates, though, in spite of the fact that I wouldn't be allowed a voice in choosing one. Not this time. In four years, the whole country'd better watch out. Daisy Majesty would darned well flex her political muscles and exercise her right to vote.

Billy glanced up at me, his old twinkle back. Broke my heart to see it, since it happened so seldom nowadays. "Say, Daisy, you're good with words. Is *normalcy* a word?"

Furrowing my brow in mock concentration, I pondered the question. "I don't think so. What's it mean? The same as *normality*?"

"I don't know, but according to Harding, we all want a return to it."

"Normalcy?"

"Yup."

"Interesting." Sometimes, like this morning, all of the old feelings rushed back and fairly swamped me, and I loved Billy so much I ached with it. "Didn't he want to give somebody a generalcy the other day?"

Billy laughed. "I think so."

I sighed as I took in the full glory of my husband. Only the evening before, I'd decided Lieutenant Delroy Farrington was the most splendid-looking man I'd ever seen. Looking at my husband this morning, I had to alter my opinion. Billy had always been a looker. Nowadays, even though his black hair contained a few premature silver streaks—and why not, given the circumstances?—and even though his legs had lost their muscular tone and he tended to slump, he looked like heaven to me.

He'd dressed in tan slacks, a soft-collared white outing shirt, a blue-striped tie, and a smart and casual smoking jacket, although Billy didn't smoke. Couldn't. Not with his lungs in the shape they were. Except for the lungs part, I was glad he didn't smoke, since I didn't like the smell.

"Who do you favor, Billy? Harding or Cox?"

He shrugged. "Don't know. Harding tends to make up words, and I'm not sure if he has a brain. Then again, maybe a president with a brain is a bad idea. We already had one of those, and look where it got us."

I didn't have to look. I knew. I'd probably feel sorrier for President Wilson, whose health had been permanently ruined by the war and its aftermath, if I weren't married to Billy. I mean, Wilson was an old man and his infirmity hadn't been visited upon him until after he'd fulfilled his life's goals. Most of them, anyhow. Nobody but him seemed enthralled with his League of Nations idea, but at least he'd been president. My Billy'd been a boy and a soldier, and now he was a cripple. Didn't seem fair to me.

"I think I like Harding," I decided, "even if he's a chucklehead and has trouble with his suffixes."

"Yeah," said Billy. "Me, too. At least he looks the part."

"True."

After I'd drunk half my coffee, I went back into the bedroom and pulled on a pretty pink plaid gingham house dress, again made by yours truly's own ten talented fingers, and trimmed with organdy lace. No corset. Thank God corsets were no longer considered a necessity of a lady's toilette, because I hated them.

I wandered back out to the sun porch and sat down across from Billy again. "Have you had breakfast yet, Billy?"

"No, I waited for you."

"Want some eggs and bacon? Pancakes? Waffles?" I'd wound my hair in a bun, stabbed pins into it as I talked to my husband, and recalled with longing Stacy Kincaid's simple bob. Darn, I wished I could get a bob.

He grinned over his newspaper at me. "Feeling domestic this morning, Daisy?"

I grinned back. "You bet."

"Eggs and toast would be nice. Maybe a little ham, if there's any left."

There was always ham. Thanks to Aunt Vi, we ate really well. Outside of Delmonico's in San Francisco, she was possibly the best cook in California. She was assuredly the best cook in Pasadena.

I got up again. Billy grabbed my hand and pulled me into his lap. I loved it when we got along like this. Every time we had a good time together, I hated the Kaiser more, damn his eyes.

We smooched for a while, and I'm sure we both wished Billy was the man he once was. It might be nice to have a real marriage. And kids. I know Billy would have been a good father if he'd had the chance.

The blasted phone rang just when things were getting interesting. I sighed. Billy said, "Damn."

You could never be quite sure in those days if the call was for you, since there were so many other people sharing the line. Even though every family was supposed to have a distinctive number and length of rings, a person wasn't always paying attention. When I hiked over to the phone on the wall in the kitchen and lifted the receiver, I heard a duet of "Hello's" before I added mine and made it a trio.

"Mrs. Majesty, please," came a masculine voice over the wire.

"This is Mrs. Majesty," said I.

I heard one of the party line members hang up her receiver. I knew who was left. "Mrs. Barrow?" I said it sweetly, although there were times I wanted to holler at our snoopy neighbor. She was from New York City, a place called the Bronx, and she talked like nobody I'd ever heard before. "This call is for me. Will you please hang up your wire?"

"Oh," she said, clearly disappointed. "Sure." The receiver on her end landed in the cradle with a sharp smack. I sighed.

"Mrs. Majesty?" the masculine voice said once more.

"Yes, this is she."

"This is Harold Kincaid, Mrs. Majesty, and I wanted to talk to you about what we discussed last night."

Crumb, what had we discussed last night? "Oh! A séance. Of course, I remember."

"Can we talk about it?"

"Um, sure." I glanced out at Billy, who appeared to be absorbed in the newspaper. "Absolutely."

"Would you like me to come to your house so that we

can discuss arrangements?"

Brother, wouldn't Billy just love that? "No, no. I'd probably better meet you at your house, if you don't mind. Or somewhere else."

"If that's what you'd prefer." Harold clearly didn't understand. I'd have told him, but the circumstances didn't lend themselves to explanations. I could just imagine Billy's reaction if I told Harold Kincaid that my husband might be jealous if a strange man came to the house, even to talk about business.

"Yes," I said, "I'd prefer that." For the same reason as the aforementioned, I hoped like heck Harold would suggest a meeting place so I wouldn't have to. Even though Billy seemed to be immersed in the local news, I didn't want to chance ruining his perky mood. Since he'd come home from France, he'd been sensitive to what he perceived as my longing to escape a hopeless marriage. I guess our marriage was pretty hopeless, but I'd never desert Billy.

"Why don't I pick you up," Harold suggested, although not as helpfully as I'd hoped. "I can take you to lunch at the club."

Bad idea, Harold. "Um, I don't think I can do that, but I'll be happy to meet you at Mrs. Kincaid's."

Sure enough, Billy's paper lowered, and he squinted at me. Darn it. I smiled, hoping he'd think it was one of Mrs. Kincaid's friends on the wire.

"Mother's house?" Harold paused. "Um, I don't think that's a good idea. If you don't want me to pick you up, can you get to Kress's on Colorado?"

Kress's was a drug store. It also had a soda fountain, which Billy and I used to visit all the time before the war, when he could still walk. Meeting another man there felt like a betrayal, although I knew that was silly. "Certainly. That would be fine." And even though I didn't like the notion of meeting a man other than Billy there, it was also a relief, since I didn't have to suggest another meeting place with my husband listening.

"Good. Can we meet in an hour? I have to drive to the set in Mojave this afternoon."

Mojave? Good heavens. "An hour would be fine."

"Great. See you then."

"Good. Good-bye."

Harold hung up, and I was rather more pleased than not with the conversation. In all probability it meant another séance, which meant more money, which was a good thing. I went to the ice box and removed the eggs and ham. "I'll have breakfast fixed in a jiff, Billy."

"What was that all about?"

I knew he'd ask, although I wished he hadn't. "I think it's going to be another séance at the Kincaids'." It was only a little fib, and one that was spoken out of kindness. Oh, very well, it was also spoken out of a disinclination to argue.

Billy grunted, not noticeably gratified by the prospect of money. I didn't understand why he was so opposed to my job. It was a good job, as jobs went, and helped the family enormously. He said no more on the subject, though, and went back to his paper, so I breathed more easily.

After breakfast, I told Billy I had to dash out to talk to a Kincaid about séances. This was true. The fact that it was Harold with whom I planned to discuss séances was neither here nor there. At least, that's what I told myself.

"I'd hoped we could take a walk after breakfast," Billy said. "It's a pretty spring day, and we hardly ever get to be together anymore."

He sounded sulky, but I didn't really blame him. "I'd like that, Billy. Can we do it after I get home?"

"I suppose so." He didn't want to do it after I got home; he wanted to do it now.

I didn't blame him for that, either. I'd much rather stay home and be a wife to Billy than have to hoof it all over creation pretending to talk to dead people.

Such was my lot in life, however, so I changed out of my pretty pink house dress and put on a day suit. I hadn't sewn this one by myself, but had bought it at J. C. Penney's Department Store. More and more ready-made goods were being sold since the war, and some of them were even worth buying.

I liked this suit, which was a springy number in a gray-checked cotton-and-wool blend with black trim. The skirt ended a discreet six inches from my ankles, which was considered proper. The Stacy Kincaids of this world might think they were being bold and dashing by raising their skirts almost to knee length, but some of us preferred good old American modesty.

Besides, modesty and mystery were closely linked, and I needed both for my job. This suit filled the bill perfectly. I still felt as if I were exuding spiritualist vibrations, but it wasn't a stuffy outfit, especially when I put on my wide-brimmed black straw hat. It was a simple hat, with only a band of gray encircling the brim. I considered the ensemble rather elegant, actually.

When Pudge Wilson wasn't in school, he generally turned the crank on the Model T for me. That way I didn't have to hurtle from the crank into the car to press the pedals before it could stall out. At present Pudge was under the jurisdiction of Miss West, so I had to set the spark and throttle levers, turn the crank myself, reach inside to pull the spark lever down, then leap inside the too-tall-for-me car, and press the low-speed pedal. I got it right eventually, eased out of the driveway, and started on my way up Marengo to Colorado Boulevard, the main east-west street in Pasadena.

The little old Model T chugged gallantly to Colorado. Like most automobiles of the day, the Model T was open. My hat brim got caught in the wind generated by a speed of almost twenty miles per hour, and I had to pull over and remove the hat, which put me into a peevish mood. I was sure I could never replace it on my head at the same perfect angle at which it had sat originally. I also knew the wind would mess up my hair. I'd wanted to look so professional, too. Stupid car.

If my business remained good, I aimed to by a closed car one of these days. Maybe a Hudson or a Buick. Something not too expensive, but less open to the wind and weather. The Kincaids and people of their ilk drove around in chauffeur-driven Daimlers and Pierce Arrows and so forth, but I'd be happy with a Chevrolet or a Hudson.

As I approached Kress's, I saw a long, low-slung, sleek and sporty, not to mention bright red, Stutz Bearcat residing at the curb. I had a hunch it belonged to Harold. It just looked like the kind of car he'd drive. A spiritualist could never get away with owning a machine like that; nobody'd ever take her seriously. But a man who worked in the pictures…Well, that Bearcat was definitely a picture-person's automobile.

It took me a minute to get my hair under control and to replace my hat, and I wasn't sure I'd done a good job of either. In an attempt to see what I was doing, I squinted at the store window (in those days most cars didn't have rear-view mirrors). But my reflection wasn't clear enough for me to judge very well. Anyhow, I didn't want to look as though I were preening if Harold was watching from inside the store, because I didn't want to give him the wrong idea, if you know what I mean. With a sigh, I decided I'd done the best I could under the circumstances and exited the Model T.

I'd no more than approached Kress's door when it was pushed open, hard, from inside, and I saw Harold standing there, holding the door and smiling at me like an elf out of a fairy tale. There was something so likable about Harold; it was difficult to feature him and Stacy coming from the same parents, although I'm sure stranger things have happened.

He looked as dapper this morning as he had the

evening before. Today he wore a springy seersucker suit and a pink shirt. I didn't think I'd ever seen a man in a pink shirt, but it suited Harold somehow. On my Billy it would have looked ridiculous.

"Good morning, good morning," he cried, evidently enraptured that I should have come all this way (approximately five short blocks) just to see him. Obviously, Harold had never been poor. We poor folk will do just about anything if someone intends to pay us.

"Good morning, Mr. Kincaid." I spoke in a much more formal tone of voice than he had, since I was supposed to be a medium and spiritualism was supposed to be a serious business.

"For God's sake, call me Harold!" he exclaimed, laughing as if I were the most adorable thing he'd seen in a month of Sundays. He led me to a stool at the lunch counter and gestured for me to sit.

I sat. "Thank you. Please call me Daisy." I spoke stiffly. I also didn't mean it. I would have preferred that he call me Mrs. Majesty. I preferred that everyone call me Mrs. Majesty, in point of fact, because the formality put a degree of distance between my clients and me. That distance worked to my advantage because it made my work seem more important, it made me seem older, and it added a soupcon of mystery even to my every-day dealings with people.

And besides all that, I feared that I'd misjudged Harold's motive. I would be very unhappy to discover that his show of friendliness meant that his true purpose wasn't business but hanky-panky.

If that turned out to be the case, I would, naturally, refuse him. Then he'd get mad, he'd probably tell his mother I was a fiend and a fraud, and then I'd never be asked into the Kincaids' house again, and Mrs. Kincaid would tell all her friends I was a miserable seductress who'd tried to ravish her son, and nobody else would ever hire me, and the Kincaids would tell all their rich friends that my family was composed of villains and charlatans, and Ma and Aunt Vi would lose their jobs, and my family would starve to death. Not that I was at all insecure in those days, you understand.

"Let me buy you an ice-cream soda, Daisy," Harold said in his high-pitched, rather piercing voice.

I demurred. "No, thank you, Harold." Darned if I'd call him Harry, as Lieutenant Farrington had.

He eyed me as if he didn't understand my reluctance to be treated to an ice-cream soda. Then, as if the lights had just gone on in his head, he put said head back and laughed. Loudly. I felt my cheeks get hot. Darn, but I hated people laughing at me.

After hauling out a pristine white handkerchief and mopping his streaming eyes, Harold laid a hand on my cotton-and-wool-blend arm. I must have stiffened up like a setter pointing, because he removed it again instantly.

"Oh, my, I'm so sorry, Daisy. I didn't mean to laugh like that."

I smiled but didn't speak, mainly because I couldn't think of anything appropriate to say. The destruction of my career and of my family's happiness loomed large in my mind's eye.

"I wasn't laughing at you, but at myself."

"Oh?" I didn't buy that one for a minute.

"I know what you must be thinking."

"Oh?" I doubted it.

"You're afraid I'm going to try to do something untoward or make unsavory advances to you."

Since he was right but I didn't want to say so, I lifted my eyebrows, striving for an expression of neutral interest, if there is such a thing.

Harold choked on another laugh. "Oh, my dear, Daisy, please forgive me."

Maybe I would. Maybe I wouldn't. It all depended. I kept silent. I'd learned in my pursuit of spiritualism that silence could be a woman's best friend if used wisely. It had been a hard lesson to learn, too, since I love to gab.

"Mind you, I think you're a pippin, and if I were interested in women, I'm sure you'd be my first choice."

What was the man talking about? Since I didn't know, I remained mute. I did, however, lift my brows even higher, attempting to produce a gesture that was quelling when used by several elderly ladies of my acquaintance. I didn't think I could quell anything, ever, even with lifted brows, but it didn't hurt to try.

"Mrs. Majesty," he said, sobering. "I'm sorry. Of course, you have no idea what I'm talking about."

"No," said I icily. "I don't."

"I'm awfully sorry. You see, I'm so accustomed to picture people, I forget that not everyone is as—ah—up to date on the modern world as they are."

"I read the newspapers, Harold, and I keep informed of the news." And here I'd thought I liked this man. Showed how much I knew about anything.

"Yes, yes, yes, I'm sure you do. This is definitely not something you'd read about in the papers, however. Especially," he added, wrinkling his alabaster brow, "not the *Pasadena Star News*."

"Oh?"

Harold sighed. Then he smiled. "I beg your pardon. I don't know how we got onto that subject."

Since I didn't even know what subject we were on, I opted to talk business. "You mentioned you were interested in holding a séance for some of your friends?"

"Yes. Thank you for keeping me on track. I tend to be a trifle scatterbrained sometimes. I think my friends would adore you, Daisy, as I do—in a brotherly way, you understand."

I smiled, not understanding anything.

"But Del and I talked last night, and we both think the boys would find a séance conducted by you something special."

Uh-oh. "The boys? Um, would there be only men there?" Good God, I could envision Billy's reaction when I told him I was going to conduct a séance for a bunch of men.

Harold grinned, again reminding me of an elf. "Only men. Yes, Daisy. Del and I thought we'd invite four other men, which would make a grand total of six. Mother said you don't care to work with large groups and that eight is the maximum you've ever allowed her to invite. Would that be all right with you? Six, I mean?"

Oh, boy. This was dreadful. I took a deep breath, wondering how to explain to this man, whom I'd believed was a nice, friendly sort, that it wasn't proper for a lady to go to a gentleman's house and conduct a séance for a pack of his male friends. Since I couldn't perceive of any way to avoid the truth, I blurted it out in plain English. "I'm sorry, Harold, but I really don't think my husband would approve of my conducting a séance for you and five other gentlemen." I said it with a smile, in hopes that he'd take it in the right way, whatever way that was.

He peered at me as if I'd lost my mind. I resented that. Heck, any right-thinking person, even a man, would understand my point of view on this subject. I was a married woman, for heaven's sake. Not that I'd have done it if I hadn't been married. That would have been even worse, actually.

After staring at me for a moment, Harold gave a start as if understanding had finally hit him between the eyes. He looked as if he wanted to laugh again, didn't, leaned over, put his elbows on the counter, and lowered his voice. Thank God. I really didn't want everyone in Kress's to overhear this conversation.

"Daisy, my dear, I had hoped I wouldn't have to do this, but I feel I really must explain something to you about my friends and me."

"Yes?" My fingers started aching, and I realized I had

a death grip on the handbag in my lap. I endeavored to relax, but it was rough going.

Harold's mouth pursed, and he looked as if he were thinking hard. "I guess the best thing to do is just come out with it."

"Perhaps that might be a good idea."

Harold sucked in about a ton of air, chewed his lip for a couple of seconds, and let his breath out in a whoosh. I tried to keep my expression bland but encouraging.

He lifted his eyebrows then, not as I'd done, in an effort to quell, but in a questioning sort of way, as if to ask if I understood what he meant. "None of the men at the séance at my house would touch you in any way of which you'd disapprove." He smiled, as if he'd just explained the secret of the universe.

I still didn't understand anything. "Um…is that so?"

Harold heaved another sigh. "Oh, dear. How can I explain this?"

Darned if I knew. I tried to look friendly, interested, and puzzled, a not-necessarily-compatible trio of emotions.

He leaned over farther and lowered his voice even more. "Daisy, have you ever heard the term *homosexual*?"

Hmmm. Had I? "Um, I don't think so."

Harold looked disappointed. "Have you ever heard of a writer named Oscar Wilde?"

"Oh, sure. I loved The Picture of Dorian Gray."

"Everyone does."

That was nice to know. I mean, it's good to feel that one fits in every now and then.

"Did you know that Oscar Wilde was imprisoned for several years because of his proclivities?"

His proclivities? If I knew what they were, I might be shocked. "Er, no, I didn't know that. He died before I was born."

Perceiving that I had no idea what he was talking about, Harold got more specific. He lowered his voice and leaned closer. "He was jailed because he was a homosexual, Daisy."

"Oh." That cleared up a whole lot (I'm being sarcastic).

Harold sighed. "You see, Daisy, there are men in the world who aren't interested in women. They prefer to have…ah…love affairs with members of their own sex."

I started on my stool. I'd heard about *that*! Good Lord! Was Harold one of *those*? I'm afraid my face must have revealed my shock, because Harold backed off an inch or so.

"I see you finally take my meaning." He spoke in a dry voice.

I hastened to pour oil on the troubled waters. After all, while I'd not heard much about…well…the kinds of people about which Harold was talking, and what I *had* heard about them was bad, maybe there was another side to the issue. I doubted it, but who knew? "Um, well, actually…" Discovering that my oil supply was seriously low, I allowed my voice to trail off.

Harold seemed to understand, which made one of us. "Daisy, my dear, we're not evil. Honestly, we're not. Not any more evil than any other group of people, that is to say. I'm sure there are some of us who are bad, but I'll wager there are more people who aren't like us who are bad than who are. If you can see what I'm saying."

I swallowed. I have to admit that my first reaction to Harold's revelation was to spring from the stool at Kress's lunch counter and run screaming out of the store and into the Model T. My initial stunned reaction didn't last long, though, and I'm proud of myself for that. I mean, what he'd said was shocking, and most people would consider it objectionable, if not downright wicked. Still and all, Harold was Harold, and Harold seemed to be a nice man. If rather effeminate—and he'd just explained why, I guess. The fact that he was…one of those…didn't negate the fact that he was pleasant and cordial.

And rich. A Gumm couldn't afford to forget the undeniable fact that it was the rich people in the world who had the money. Besides all that, Harold obviously wanted to throw some of his own money my way. And I sure wouldn't have to worry about having my virtue compromised as he did it.

"Um," I said, and I had to swallow again, "I think I understand want you're saying, Harold."

He smiled broadly. "Good! That's good! Then you'll surely see that there would be absolutely no danger of anything disgraceful happening to you. None of my friends would even think of doing anything to you that your husband wouldn't approve of. If you see what I mean."

I smiled back, although it was an effort. "Er, yes, I believe I see what you mean." I wasn't sure Billy would like this situation any better than the other one, but he ought to. I mean, what could happen to me if I held a séance for a half dozen of…of those kinds of men?

"So," said Harold, sitting back and grinning. "Are you willing to conduct a séance for some of my friends and me?"

I made up my mind. I was sure I could ease any worries Billy might have about the job. "I'll be happy to, Harold."

We set a date and parted on the best of terms, and I went home to Billy. I planned to explain this latest job to him as we took a gentle walk on a pleasant spring day.

CHAPTER 6

It didn't work out exactly as I'd planned. Billy was furious. "You're going to hold a séance for a group of *faggots*?"

Since we were strolling down Marengo Avenue, me pushing his wheelchair, magnolia blossoms scenting the warm spring air, and Mrs. Longnecker eavesdropping like mad, I endeavored to ease his worries. Or at least get him to quit yelling.

Mrs. Longnecker, who lived two houses down from us and who was ostensibly weeding her flower garden, frowned at us as we passed. I smiled at her and gave her a little finger wave, but she didn't appear to be mollified, the fussy old cow.

I could feature her running into the house and calling all her friends as soon as we were out of sight, telling them in a loud whisper that for her passed as a secret-conveyor that Billy and I were fighting and wasn't it just as she'd always said it would be? That Daisy Gumm always was a flighty piece of goods, and now that her husband was a cripple, she just *knew* I was up to no good. Mrs. Longnecker was by far the worst gossip in the neighborhood.

"Shhh, Billy. Please."

"Darn it, Daisy, I won't shhh. You have no business working for a lot of men!"

"Billy, they aren't like *you*, for heaven's sake! They don't *like* women." I'd clued him in on the Oscar-Wilde angle, but it hadn't placated him much, if at all.

"And you think that makes it all right?"

Well, yes, actually. I got the feeling Billy didn't share my opinion, so I tried another tack. "Harold's really a nice person, Billy. Even if he liked women, he wouldn't do anything wrong. He's a good, moral man."

"Ha! He's a moral degenerate."

"He isn't, either. Truly, he's not. He's friendly and polite and kindhearted. And he works in the movies. I'm sure you'd like him."

"A faggot? I don't think so."

"How come you call him a faggot?" I'd always thought a faggot was a piece of wood.

He shrugged and hunched in his chair. He always hunched when he was mad at me. He hunched a lot. "That's what we called them in the army."

"But why?"

"How should I know?" Now he sounded irked as well as irate. It was becoming obvious that I couldn't win, which had become a normal state of affairs in our married life, so I used the best reason I could think of to make my husband view the situation my way. Aside from the money reason. Billy had never been able to appreciate the money I made as a spiritualist, although I didn't know why then, and I still don't. "At least you can rest assured that nobody will try to…do anything to me. You know what I mean."

"Small comfort."

By this time I was getting sort of irked, too. I didn't think Billy was being fair to me. "It's a comfort to me," I snapped. "I don't want men making passes at me, and I know these men won't."

This approach didn't work, either, as I might have predicted. There were times when I swear to heaven, *nothing* worked with Billy. I think it was because his physical pain and mental bitterness made him cranky and mulish. Although I honestly tried to be compassionate and understanding, my feelings got mangled more often than not.

"You think that makes it right?" he demanded. "Those men are perverted and depraved, for God's sake!"

"They are not. At least Harold isn't. And Lieutenant Farrington sure didn't act depraved. In fact, he was very nice. So's Harold." It seemed to me I was using the word *nice* too much, but I couldn't think of another one. Darn it, the two men *were* nice.

"Let's go home."

You'd have thought I'd done something so terrible that Billy couldn't stand to be in my company any longer. I felt like crying, although I wouldn't give Mrs. Longnecker the pleasure of seeing me do so. Or Billy, darn him. "You're being unreasonable," I said frigidly.

"Take me home, damn it."

"There's no need to swear."

I took him home. No sooner had I walked through the front door than the telephone rang. I left Billy to take himself wherever he wanted to and dashed into the kitchen to answer it, hoping it was somebody nice. There was that word again.

"Daisy! Oh, Daisy, is that you?"

Several voices had answered the ring, but since I was the only Daisy on the party line, I knew it was my call. I also recognized Mrs. Kincaid's voice, although she sounded almost hysterical.

"Yes, it's Daisy. Mrs. Kincaid? Is that you?"

"Yes. Oh, yes!" She burst into tears.

I took that opportunity to make sure Mrs. Barrow had

hung up on her end. She did after I asked her to. Some people are just too nosy for words.

After I knew we were alone on the wire, I tried to find out what was going on with Mrs. Kincaid. "Is something the matter?" Obviously, something was the matter, but I was straining to be diplomatic. Diplomacy was never easy after a fight with Billy.

After snuffling for a minute or two and blowing her nose, Mrs. Kincaid said in a voice as thick as mud, "It's—it's—" She sobbed. "It's Stacy!"

I'd always figured Stacy for a rotter. I didn't say so. "What's the matter with Stacy?" If she'd managed to get herself killed, I'd be sorry for Mrs. Kincaid's sake. Mr. Kincaid would deserve it. So would Stacy.

A gasp and another several sniffles and a swallow or two. "She's been arrested!"

"Good heavens!" I was truly stunned. And appalled. And even pretty darned horrified. "What in the world did she do?" That didn't sound very tactful. "I mean, what happened?"

"She was picked up in a raid on a speakeasy. Oh, it's just awful!"

"Yes," I said. "It certainly is." The girl deserved to be horsewhipped, in point of fact. "Is there anything I can do for you, Mrs. Kincaid?" That sounded stupid after it popped out of my mouth. I mean, Mrs. Kincaid was as rich as Croesus, and I was only a Gumm. Still and all, the poor woman was in distress and I wanted to help if I could because even though she was rich, she'd always been kind to me.

"Oh, Daisy, I hate to impose, but I'm in such terrible distress."

"I can tell."

"Will you come over to the house? And bring your cards. We can use my Ouija board. I need to get some comfort out of this mess, and if you can only tell me that the future is going to be bright, I'm sure I can bear up under this dreadful crisis."

Shoot. I wasn't sure of anything of the sort. I mean, what if the cards foretold disaster? Not that I'd let on to Mrs. Kincaid if they did. But you never could tell about the cards. Or the Ouija board, either, for that matter, although the board was easier to manipulate than the cards. I was good at maneuvering my fortune-telling accouterments, but even I couldn't predict which way the cards were going to shuffle themselves.

That had never stopped me before, and it didn't stop me now. "Of course, Mrs. Kincaid. I'll be there as soon as I can."

"Thank you." She sobbed a few more times. "Oh, thank you so much, Daisy!"

"Any time." I hung up and saw Billy glowering at me from his wheelchair.

"I thought you just got through meeting with that woman."

Fiddle. I'd sort of fudged on the detail that it had been Harold I'd met at Kress's. When Billy had assumed it was Harold's mother who'd arranged for her son's séance, I hadn't felt the need to correct his false impression. No matter how hard I tried to protect Billy— or myself, if truth be known—I always got caught somehow. "Um, no. Actually, it was Harold I met."

"I see. In other words, you lied to me."

"I didn't lie, Billy. If I'd told you I'd gone to meet Harold, you'd have been even angrier than you were when I told you about the séance he wanted."

His lips curled in a bitter smile. I hated when they did that. "Sins of omission are no less deadly than sins of commission, Daisy."

I heaved a heavy sigh. "It wasn't a sin, Billy. He's a faggot, remember?"

"You didn't know that when you met him."

He had me there. "Maybe, but I knew good and well he wasn't interested in anything but my job."

"Huh."

"Anyhow, that's not the point. The point is that Mrs. Kincaid has asked me to go to her house, because she's in terrible distress and she thinks I can help her."

"You could help me if you'd stick around more."

There was no good answer for that one, I supposed. "Well, I'm sorry you don't think I'm a good wife, Billy, but Stacy Kincaid has just been arrested, and Mrs. Kincaid is in an awful state. She needs me more than you do at the moment." I didn't know that for a fact, but hoped Billy would go for it.

"Arrested? Good God, Daisy, what sort of people do you work for, anyhow?"

Good question. "Mrs. Kincaid is a very generous and considerate lady. Her son is a nice man. Her daughter is a stinker. She got picked up in a raid on a speakeasy."

"Huh. Fine set of people you hang out with." And with that last snipe, he wheeled himself out of the kitchen and into the bedroom. I decided I didn't have to change clothes again, mainly because I didn't fancy changing clothes with my husband glaring at me as if he hated me. Maybe by the time I got home from the Kincaids', Billy would be over his sulk.

It was still too early for Pudge to be out of school, so I had to fight the Model T by myself again. When the weather was warm, as it was on that day, the thing started pretty easily. I drove slowly so as not to disarrange my hair and hat, and by the time I got to the Kincaids' mansion, the gate already stood open. Either Jackson had anticipated my arrival, or the entire household was in too much of an uproar to follow normal rules.

Although this could probably be considered an emergency, I didn't pull up in front of the huge porch, but drove around to the stable area, mainly because I wanted to say hello to Quincy Applewood and Aunt Vi.

Quincy ran to open the door for me, which was polite

of him, although I'd have rather he hadn't. The Model T didn't have a driver's side door, and it was kind of awkward sliding across the seat to get out on the right-hand side of the car when one wore a skirt. When someone stood there holding the door, it could also be downright indelicate. I managed to keep my skirt from bunching up, however. Billy would have been happy with me. Actually, he probably wouldn't have been, because he'd have resented my being there in the first place. Nuts. I couldn't win.

"Did you hear?" Quincy asked as I shook out the wrinkles from my skirt.

"That's why I'm here. Mrs. Kincaid asked me to come and bring my Tarot cards."

He rolled his eyes. I didn't take offense. Quincy and I were in the same boat; we both did what we had to do to get by. I took his expression to mean what I felt: I wish I had enough money to enable me to believe in Tarot cards. When you're struggling to make a living, you tended to focus on tangible things and leave the spirits to take care of themselves.

The back door of the house opened, and Edie Marsh hurried outside. I knew it was Edie even before I turned around to look, because the expression on Quincy's face softened to one of imbecilic adoration. "Hey, Edie!" I said, friendly.

"Oh, Daisy, have you heard?"

It seemed to me that everyone had heard. "Yup. That's why I'm here. Mrs. Kincaid asked me to come."

"Oh, Lord, it's just awful." Edie's eyes sparkled. I got the impression she was about as fond of Stacy Kincaid as I was. "Poor Mrs. Kincaid is so upset."

"I don't blame her." Quincy looked as if he thoroughly disapproved of young ladies getting caught in speakeasy raids.

I did, too, for that matter. "Neither do I."

Edie and Quincy exchanged a speaking look, although

they didn't touch or kiss or even talk to each other. I guess they saved demonstrations of affection until after working hours, which was both prudent and sensible.

"Come on, Daisy. Mrs. Kincaid's in the drawing room, walking in circles and wringing her hands. She asked me to keep an eye out for you." She hooked a hand around my elbow and we walked to the house together.

"How about Mr. Kincaid?" I spoke softly, since I didn't want Quincy to overhear anything either of us had to say about Mr. Kincaid.

Edie's nose wrinkled and her mouth pruned up. "Who knows? He's such a devil. I don't think he cares about anyone in his family, if you want to know the truth."

Made sense to me. "If he did, he wouldn't do the things he does."

"Absolutely."

It came out as sort of a huff, and I wondered if Mr. Kincaid had cornered her again today. I didn't ask, but it occurred to me that I might compare Mr. Kincaid to Harold for Billy's sake. At once, I nixed the idea. If Billy thought Mr. Kincaid was the sort to trap stray females with his wheelchair, he'd never allow me to visit the Kincaid place again.

When we traipsed through the service porch into the kitchen, I saw Aunt Vi kneading dough. She glanced up, and I noticed that she looked worried, too. Aunt Vi was a light-hearted lady under normal circumstances, and she, too, was very kindly disposed toward Mrs. Kincaid, and this scandal had clearly rattled her. I hurried over and kissed her cheek. Aunt Vi was as plump as a Christmas pudding, which made sense. After all, who'd want a cook who didn't like to eat her own food?

"Whatcha cookin', Aunt Vi?" I smiled, hoping to make her feel better.

"Parker House rolls." She didn't stop kneading, but her glance was intense. "Do your best for the poor thing, Daisy. She's in a terrible taking."

"Yeah, she was crying over the phone."

A tear dripped down Vi's cheek, carving a pink path through the light dusting of flour on her cheek. I wiped it away for her, since her hands were occupied. "Try not to worry, Aunt Vi. I'll do my best."

"I know you will, Daisy. You're a good girl."

I supposed I'd always be a girl to Ma and Aunt Vi. That was okay with me. I gave her a cheeky grin and braced myself to meet with Mrs. Kincaid.

"I'm not going to go with you, Daisy, because I don't want to see that awful man."

By which, I presumed Edie meant Mr. Kincaid. That was okay with me, too, since I knew my way around the house. "Sure, Edie."

I found the Kincaids in the drawing room. Mrs. Kincaid had a handkerchief pressed to her brow and sure enough, she was pacing in circles before the huge fireplace. Mr. Kincaid sat in his wheelchair glowering out a window overlooking a magnificent rose garden and vast acres of scythed green grass. I wouldn't have guessed from Mr. Kincaid's expression that he was looking at anything more interesting than mud. In short, he appeared extremely irritable. He turned around when I entered the room and transferred his glower my way. I didn't take it personally since I'd never seen him do anything else.

As soon as Mrs. Kincaid saw me, on the other hand, she wheeled around and dashed straight at me, her arms outstretched. I caught her in a hug. What the heck. Even rich people need someone to hug them every now and then, and I doubted that Mrs. Kincaid received many hugs from her husband—or if she even wanted them from that source. I did wonder where Featherstone was, but didn't think too much about it. He was probably off doing something butlerish.

"Oh, Daisy! It's so awful!"

As if to answer my unspoken question, Harold Kincaid

and Featherstone entered the room. Harold had clearly been driving, because he hadn't removed his goggles or scarf, and looked like some dangerous creature from under the sea. "I'm back," he said unnecessarily, throwing his hat at Featherstone and going to work on the rest of his driving gear. Featherstone stood like a statue, as if he was accustomed to being used as a coat rack.

Mrs. Kincaid left off hugging me and veered over to her son. She threw herself into his arms next and cried, "Oh, Harold! What's happening with her? Did you see her? Is Mr. Pearlman with her? Is she all right? Did they hurt her?"

Throwing his goggles atop the pile of clothes in Featherstone's arms, Harold began patting his mother's back. He tried to shrug, failed, and said, "Nobody's hurt her, Mother. She was being interviewed by a policeman when I got to the station. Mr. Pearlman is there. Try not to worry. I'm sure it will turn out all right."

I was impressed with Featherstone yet again. Although he must be dying to learn the dirt on the Stacy situation, he turned around and left the room, carting Harold's stuff off. Now there was dedication for you. If it had been me, I'd have stood outside the door and listened, but I'll bet anything that Featherstone didn't. He was a pro at butlering, by gum.

"For the love of God," grumbled Mr. Kincaid. "The child ought to be horsewhipped."

Gee, I hated having anything in common with Mr. Kincaid. Too late now.

"Probably," said Harold dryly.

"No, no!" cried Mrs. Kincaid. "Oh, no! The poor child! How can you say such a thing?"

Oh, brother. Fortunately for me, she didn't expect an answer from the hired help. Harold muttered that he didn't mean it, his tone belying his words. Mr. Kincaid only growled some more.

Guiding his mother over to the sofa, Harold said,
"There's a police detective coming to visit us soon,
Mother, so try to get yourself under control. You don't
want to be crying when he gets here."

I didn't know why not. I mean, if a kid of mine were
arrested, I don't think I'd care if a policeman saw me cry.
Yet another difference between rich people and the rest
of us, I supposed.

Sniffling into her hankie, Mrs. Kincaid whispered,
"Yes. Of course. Thank you, Harold."

After ridding himself of his mother, Harold grinned at
me. "Hello, Daisy. How nice to see you again so soon.
Sorry for the circumstances. I never made it to Mojave."

Mrs. Kincaid sobbed again, dabbed at her eyes, and
said, "I asked her to come, Harold. I need some sort of
comfort."

"Ah, I see," said Harold, who plainly didn't.

I didn't either, if it came to that, but I'd do pretty much
anything Mrs. Kincaid asked me to do since she was by
far my best customer.

Harold's mother lifted tear-dampened eyes to her son.
"Will you please go fetch my Ouija Board, Harold
darling? Daisy said she'd help me by consulting Rolly
for me." She turned the eyes my way. "Did you bring the
cards, Daisy dear?"

I held up the deck. "Right here."

"Swell," said Harold brightly. He definitely didn't
share his mother's fear for his sister's overall welfare,
and I wondered if he was as sick of her outlandish
behavior as I was. "Be right back." He winked at me as
he dashed out the door.

"Um, would you like me to deal the cards while he
gets the board, Mrs. Kincaid?"

"Oh, yes, dear. Thank you so much."

Mr. Kincaid sneered at both of us, which was nothing
new. I ignored him and dealt out a Celtic Cross pattern
with the Tarot cards. I'd brought my best deck, bought

from a lady I'd met in Chinatown in Los Angeles when I was doing some research. She (the lady) claimed to be a Gypsy, but they all did. I never took claims like that seriously.

As I'd half expected, the cards decided not to cooperate with me that day. The very first hand I dealt contained more swords than I'd ever seen, bless it. I sighed inwardly, not wanting to upset Mrs. Kincaid by letting it show. Darn the swords, anyhow. They were the scariest cards in the whole blasted deck.

Evidently I didn't hide my distress well enough or didn't speak quickly enough or something, because Mrs. Kincaid gasped. "Oh, Daisy! Please tell me they don't predict disaster."

I ignored Mr. Kincaid's snort of disgust. "Disaster? Why, no, Mrs. Kincaid. No such thing." Thinking fast, I said, "They do indicate that you're facing a time of uncertainty." That was good. "There's going to be a period of...chaos." Was that too strong a word? Glancing at my victim—I mean my subject—from under my lashes, I saw that the poor woman had gone pale, so I hastened on. "This is to be expected, of course, under the circumstances." Her lips lost their straight-line rigidity, and she nodded. Good. That had worked pretty well, so I played up the temporary aspect of the period of chaos. "We all go through difficult times." I gave her one of my stock of gracious smiles, and she seemed to appreciate it.

"Yes. Of course."

I kept dealing, hoping a couple of wands would show up soon. The darned swords predominated, though, and failing wands, I hoped Harold would jog back into the room with the Ouija board.

At last the Empress landed face up on the coffee table. Thank God for small favors. I smiled harder. "Oh, there. You see? It will all work out in the end." Which was a silly thing to say. I mean, everything works out somehow in the end. Fortunately, people like Mrs.

Kincaid didn't ever stop to consider the nonsensical nature of fortune-telling, or I'd be out of a job.

"I'm *so* glad," she breathed.

Bless his heart, Harold trotted into the room, holding his mother's Ouija board under his arm. I gathered the cards together without further explanation of the dismal nature of their predictions and smiled at Harold, who winked back at me. "Let's consult Rolly, shall we?"

"Oh, yes! Let's do." Mrs. Kincaid clasped her hands at her bosom and beamed. "Oh, Daisy, I can't even begin to tell you how this is helping me cope with this tragedy."

She said no more, which was probably just as well, since I got embarrassed easily.

Harold grinned harder.

Her husband snorted again.

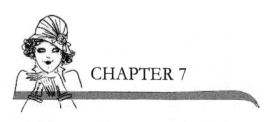 CHAPTER 7

Rolly had just told Mrs. Kincaid that the Stacy problem would, after a period of strife and confusion, resolve itself happily (something I myself didn't half believe, given Stacy's snotty nature) when Featherstone appeared at the drawing-room door. Nobody heard him until he was there, and my admiration for him swelled anew. The guy should have gone in for spiritualism instead of butlering, he was so good at appearing and disappearing silently. When he saw that we were all staring at him, he announced that the police had arrived.

"Detective Rotondo," Featherstone announced in a voice that would have sounded right at home on the Grim Reaper.

Harold jumped to his feet. Mrs. Kincaid looked as if she might faint. Mr. Kincaid scowled at his butler, who didn't look down his nose far enough to see. I just sat there, trying to be as invisible as possible. Not possessing Featherstone's skill at the art, I imagined anyone coming into the room would see me just fine.

A large, dark man in a brown tweed suit loomed up behind the butler. Flanking him were two uniformed police officers. I recognized one of them as Johnny Liljenwall, son of the woman who made Mrs. Kincaid's clothes. We'd gone to school together. I smiled briefly at him, but I wasn't sure he saw me. He looked as if he'd rather be somewhere else. Couldn't say as I blamed him, since I felt the same.

Featherstone stepped aside, allowing the police contingent to enter the room. The man I assumed to be Detective Rotondo, the large, dark man in the tweed suit, appeared to feel right at home. I was impressed. Heck, even I, who'd first entered these hallowed portals at the tender age of ten, had been vaguely intimidated during my first several visits.

Detective Rotondo nodded at the assembly without visible pleasure. He glanced at the Ouija board, passed over it, and jerked his gaze back to it. From the board, he squinted at me. I thought I recognized disfavor, so I lifted my chin a little to tell him he could lump it if he didn't like it.

He spoke first. "How do you do?" Training his dark eyes on Mrs. Kincaid, he said, "Mrs. Kincaid?"

Mrs. Kincaid lifted a trembling hand to her mouth, let it drop to her lap, and whispered, "Yes."

"I'm sorry to have to disturb you, ma'am." He glanced at the man in the wheelchair and his eyes narrowed. "Mr. Kincaid?"

"I'm Kincaid," said he grumpily. "This won't take long, will it?"

Detective Rotondo cocked his head slightly. "As to that, sir, I can't say until we get started."

"It had better not take long. I won't stand for being bothered."

Ignoring Mr. Kincaid, which I considered a sensible reaction, the detective turned to Harold. "And you are…?"

Harold, evidently opposed to his parents' not-awfully-polite welcome of this officer into their home—after all, it wasn't the police department's fault his sister was a nitwit—walked over to Rotondo, his hand outstretched. "I'm Harold Kincaid. Stacy's brother. Have a seat."

Mr. Kincaid looked as if he'd have objected except that he didn't want to make a fuss. Detective Rotondo seemed to relax under the benevolent beam in Harold's light hazel eyes. Rotondo's eyes were as dark as the rest of him. He looked like he ought to be posing for statues in parks somewhere in Europe. He'd removed his hat, and his hair showed black, glossy, short-cropped curls. He hadn't spoken much yet, but I thought I detected the kind of accent Mrs. Barrow had, only not as extreme. From this, I gathered he'd originated somewhere back East, perhaps even New York City.

"Thank you, Mr. Kincaid." Detective Rotondo bestowed a fleeting smile upon Harold, nodded to his two police cohorts, and sat on a chair across from the Kincaid congregation. And me. He eyed Mrs. Kincaid's Ouija board suspiciously, then eyed me the same way. "And you are?" He was no longer being as polite as he'd first been, probably because he could tell I didn't belong there.

"My name," I said with frigid diction, "is Mrs. William Majesty."

"She's a friend of the family's," Harold rushed to supply.

"Oh, yes," agreed Mrs. Kincaid. "Daisy's a wonderful friend to us all."

Mr. Kincaid snorted. He did that a lot.

"I see," said the detective. He didn't look as if he believed it. Pointing, he asked, "Is that one of those spirit board things?"

I answered. "Yes."

"Hmmm."

"Daisy's been trying to help me through this terrible tragedy," supplied Mrs. Kincaid, smiling tremulously at me. "She's such a sweetheart to come when I need her."

"Fortune-telling's illegal, you know, Mrs. Majesty."

Of course, I knew that. The law didn't bother me, since I never advertised my services. People just asked me to do my act, and then they gave me money. "Yes," I said, even colder than before. "I know."

Mrs. Kincaid rose nobly to my defense, which I thought was mighty keen of her, since she had plenty of her own troubles. "Daisy's not a fortune teller!" she cried. "She uses the gifts God has bestowed upon her to help us who don't have her...her gifts."

I smiled at her to let her know how much I liked and appreciated her. In fact, I thought she was a peach.

The detective shot me another frown and opened his mouth, presumably to rebut Mrs. Kincaid's assessment of me. The good lady drew herself up in a pose of indignation and didn't give him a chance, bless her heart.

"Daisy does absolutely nothing illegal, I can assure you, Officer. Why, she's a God-send!" Mrs. Kincaid, who was a mild-mannered woman, sounded about as offended as she possibly could, which wasn't a whole lot, but she got her point across.

The detective graced us with another "Hmmm," as if he knew what was what even if Mrs. Kincaid chose to allow herself to be fooled. Then he nodded at Johnny Liljenwall, who took out a pencil and a notebook. The other policeman stood at the door, as if he wanted to be sure nobody'd make a bolt for freedom. I crossed my arms over my chest, sat back in the chair I'd chosen, and frowned at the detective. I decided I didn't like him very much, mainly because he didn't seem to like me. I really hated it when people assumed I was a cheat and a humbug, even though it was true. At least I was a good charlatan, and my heart was in the right place, and I never made anyone feel bad, which I'm sure is more than *he* could say about *his* job.

Detective Rotondo asked questions of Mrs. Kincaid, who answered them to the best of her ability. It was clear to me, and I'm sure it was also clear to the detective, that the poor dear lady didn't have a clue what her daughter was up to most of the time.

The detective seemed incredulous. "You mean to say you didn't know Miss Kincaid was accustomed to visit speakeasies, Mrs. Kincaid?"

Before she could answer, Mr. Kincaid butted in. "Of course, we didn't know Stacy went to the speaks! Do you think we'd allow her to go if we knew?"

He probably would, actually. I don't think Mr. Kincaid gave a hoot what his kids did.

Rotondo eyed him with disfavor. "I'll ask you a few questions in a minute, sir. Right now I'd like to get an understanding of Mrs. Kincaid's knowledge of your daughter's friends and practices."

"This is ridiculous!" Mr. Kincaid snapped. "And it's offensive. I plan to talk to the chief about this, Officer."

"Detective," said Rotondo, who didn't seem to care much who Mr. Kincaid talked to. I began to think maybe he wasn't such a bad guy after all, although it was too soon to tell.

"You have no right to invade our home," insisted Mr. Kincaid.

"Actually, we do, sir. We have every right when a crime is involved. But we don't mean it to be an invasion," said Rotondo stonily. "We need to find out everything we can about your daughter's activities. She was arrested while breaking the law. Actually, she broke two laws. Even if it were legal to drink alcoholic beverages in saloons, she's too young to do so. You do understand that, don't you?"

Mrs. Kincaid sobbed at this harsh litany regarding her daughter, and Detective Rotondo lost some ground in my estimation. There was no need to be brutal in the poor lady's presence, even when he was talking to her husband, who deserved it.

Mr. Kincaid muttered, "Balderdash," wheeled himself

around, and commenced staring at the wall. "The girl deserves whatever she gets."

While I agreed with him regarding Stacy, I got the feeling he was more angry with her for getting caught than for breaking the law in the first place. I also thought it was mighty mean to say so in front of Stacy's mother, who clearly loved her daughter even if Stacy wasn't worth it. In fact, if I weren't an adult, professional woman, I might have stuck my tongue out at the old geezer. What did he expect, anyhow? That the police would go away and not bother him because his wife was rich? Or did he think the sons and daughters of millionaires ought not be arrested when they broke the law? Probably.

The detective questioned Mrs. Kincaid for a few more minutes. He wasn't as gentle as I thought he should have been, given what I knew about the fragile nature of her personality and her present state of nervous distress, but maybe he thought she was like her husband and deserved to be bully-ragged. I don't know how he could have thought that since she'd already gone through two hankies in his presence. Maybe he was just a stinker.

Finally Mrs. Kincaid broke down completely and could no longer speak to the detective. I rushed over to her, held her close as she cried on my shoulder, and glared at Rotondo, who stared back coldly. My uncertainty about him tilted toward dislike again. Harold sat down on the other side of his mother and patted her on the back. He didn't glare at the policeman, and it occurred to me that he might think the man was attractive in the same sort of way that I thought he was attractive, if one discounted his cold nature and gruff attitude.

Then I told myself not to be depraved, and I wondered if Billy had been right. I hated to think it. It did seem, however, that my association with Harold, now that I knew what he was, was having a deleterious effect on my innermost thoughts. I tried not to dwell on the possibility, but applied myself to comforting Mrs. Kincaid.

Detective Rotondo started in on Mr. Kincaid then. Mr. Kincaid wasn't having any of it. He answered approximately four of the detective's questions, shouted at him that he didn't have to put up with "this sort of thing," propelled his wheelchair around, and aimed it at the door, causing the poor uniformed man standing there to leap aside or get run down. I hoped to heaven Edie was hiding somewhere, because the notion of the beast cornering her gave me a stomachache.

Detective Rotondo sighed heavily, brushed his curly hair back from his high forehead, and leveled a glance at Harold. Fortunately Mrs. Kincaid had stopped blubbering, so I was able to concentrate on the questions and answers exchanged by the two men.

Johnny was still scribbling madly in his notebook. I wondered if policemen had to learn a form of shorthand, then decided they'd have to if they expected to take down what everyone said during an interview verbatim. Or maybe they just did their best. You'd run the risk of getting a lot of things wrong that way. Then again, I've heard that policemen often got things wrong in their reports.

Was that thought a result of my declining morals? This was getting too darned complicated.

Featherstone appeared as if by magic again, this time to announce the arrival of Father Frederick. I was glad to see him for Mrs. Kincaid's sake. She uttered a small cry of welcome and burst into tears again. Father Frederick hurried over to the sofa and, smiling at Harold, commenced comforting his friend, thus leaving Harold to the mercy of Detective Rotondo.

Harold didn't seem to mind. In fact, he initiated the conversation. "I'll be happy to talk to you, Detective, although I have to say I'm ignorant of most of my sister's more outrageous behavior." In a tone of subdued confidence, he added, "We've never been close."

All of my worries about Harold went up the chimney, and I decided he was a shrewd judge of character and of sound moral fiber. What the heck. Maybe this men-loving-men stuff was something he couldn't help.

Billy would tell me I'd gone beyond the point of no return, I'm sure. But darn it, Harold was a good man. He was a whole lot nicer than most of the other men in his social class whom I'd met.

Since Mrs. Kincaid was in the helpful hands of Father Frederick, and since the detective was occupying Harold, I didn't see any need for me to stay there any longer. My Tarot cards still lay on the table next to the Ouija board. I gathered them together, shuffled them once, and put them in the little cloth bag I'd made for them. It was a nice bag, made of a black silk-and-cotton blend. I'd embroidered silver stars and moons on the neck. When I pulled the drawstring tight, the stars and moons bunched together into a cluster of glittery silver. I'd found some black velvet cord at Nash's Fabrics, and the overall effect suited my business to a T.

Trying to be as discreet as possible, I rose from the sofa and tippy-toed toward the door, giving Johnny a wink as I passed. He grinned and kept writing. I'd almost made it to the door, wondering if I was going to have to bump smack into the policeman barring it before he'd step aside, when a voice behind me stopped me in my tracks.

"Mrs. Majesty." It was Detective Rotondo.

I turned slowly and gave him a stony stare. "Yes?"

"I'd like to ask you a few questions, too, if you don't mind."

I did mind. What the heck did I know about Stacy, except that she was a spoiled brat? I decided to say so, leaving out the brat part. "I don't know a thing about Miss Kincaid, Detective. I've only met her twice. Maybe three times."

"Nevertheless, please take a seat here." He gestured at a chair across from him. He also sounded irked, annoyed, and as if he didn't like one single thing about me.

I resented that. I also didn't think I had to take it. After all, I was only here because Mrs. Kincaid had asked me to come. I wasn't involved in Stacy's misdemeanors. Or felonies. Gee, I hoped it was a felony. That was mean of me, I know, but she was such a skunk. Also, I wasn't exactly your typical shrinking violet, having been reared a good Gumm, so I told the man what I thought of him and his manners and his taking a seat.

"Listen, Detective Rotondo. I'm only here at Mrs. Kincaid's request. I don't know Stacy. I don't know what she does for fun. I don't *care* what she does for fun." I offered Mrs. Kincaid an apologetic glance, but I don't think she took it in. She looked as if she were in shock at hearing me talk to an officer of the law as I was doing. "I didn't know there were any speakeasies in Pasadena, and I assure you, I wouldn't frequent them if I had known. Furthermore, I don't like your attitude."

If his mother was in shock, Harold was tickled pink. I could tell. He even gave me a victory salute with his thumb and forefinger pressed into an O. Bless his heart, too.

Rotondo's dark face got darker, either with embarrassment or fury. I suspected the latter. Nevertheless, when he spoke to me again, his tone was conciliatory. "I beg your pardon if I was peremptory, Mrs. Majesty."

I sniffed. "Peremptory, my foot. You were rude."

I could see his jaw clench. He had a good, square jaw and would have made a good cowboy in the pictures. Or, better yet, a pirate. Nobody cared if pirates looked sort of exotic. Not that Rotondo was exotic exactly. He was more...Oh, heck, I don't know. Turned out he was

Italian, so I guess that's what he looked like. Whoever heard of an Italian cowboy?

"Please," he said, shoving the words out through his teeth, which I could hear grinding, "forgive me and take a seat. I'd like to ask you some questions, even though you aren't acquainted with Miss Kincaid."

"Oh, I'm acquainted with her," I said to be annoying, and it looked as if I were succeeding admirably. "I just don't run around in her social circles." Since there were two Kincaids present, I didn't say that unlike Stacy, I had to work for a living, but I felt like saying it.

"I'm sure." I think he was trying to insult me, but I'm not sure. "Nevertheless..." He gestured again at the chair.

After gazing at the chair and at him and then at the chair again, I sighed as if this whole thing were more trouble than it was worth. Which was true, actually. But I sat in the chair, primarily because I'm a snoop. Can't help it. And, in justification, snoopery does come in handy in my work, although I was mostly just interested in this situation.

Besides all those excuses, wouldn't Ma and Aunt Vi want to know the dirty details? Yes, they would, in case you couldn't guess the answer to that one on your own.

I still wore my hat, so I plopped my small handbag in my lap, folded my hands—sans gloves. You can't work the Ouija board with gloves on—on top of it, sat up straight, lifted my chin, and gazed pointedly at Detective Rotondo. "Yes?"

He rolled his eyes, an action to which I took exception, although I didn't say so. Darn it, though, I hated it when my struggle to attain the dignity that should by right be mine if for no other reason than because I made a good living, fell flat. "When did you last see Miss Anastasia Kincaid?" Rotondo asked as his first question.

And that brought up another point. Why couldn't I have been named something elegant like Anastasia? It was hard enough fighting off the laughter of kids when your last name was Gumm. Anastasia at least had a little class. But that wasn't the point here. "The day before yesterday."

"What were the circumstances?"

"It was here, in the Kincaids' house. Some of Mrs. Kincaid's friends had gathered here that evening."

"To what purpose?"

"I conducted a séance for Mrs. Kincaid and her sister, Mrs. Lilley."

He smirked as if he'd caught me committing some embarrassing crime. "Fortune-telling is illegal, Mrs. Majesty. You said you knew that."

"Of course, I know it," I snapped back. I was ready for this one. "When I conduct a séance, I assure you, I am not telling fortunes. Quite the reverse, in fact."

"No, indeed." Mrs. Kincaid had perked up. Her words were as crisp and hard as little green apples. "There was absolutely no fortune-telling involved."

"Daisy works within the law, Detective," Harold added, sounding irate on my behalf. I loved these people. If we could only get rid of Mr. Kincaid and Stacy, we'd all get along just fine.

"So you weren't telling fortunes." Rotondo's smirk turned into a sneer.

"Right."

"You were conducting a séance."

"Right." Let him sneer. I knew my work was important to people, whether he wanted to believe it or not.

"Just exactly what does this séance-conducting involve?"

"I don't see why that's relevant," I said, and rather imperiously if I do say so myself.

He grunted. I expected him to demand an answer to his question but he didn't, for which mercy I was extremely grateful. I mean, if this fellow thought fortune-telling was bad, what would he think of chatting with dead people? "And you say Miss Anastasia Kincaid was there?"

"I said no such thing. I said I saw her after the conclusion of the séance."

"Where?"

"In the Kincaids' drawing room."

"What were you doing?"

"Talking to people."

"After this supposed séance of yours?"

"Yes. After the séance concluded." Early, thanks to Medora Louise Trunick. "There was no supposition about it."

"That's so," averred Mrs. Kincaid.

"Indeed," supplied Harold.

Rotondo quit trying to stare me down and looked over at Harold. "You were there, too?"

"I was."

Rotondo shook his head and returned his attention to me. "So you saw her. Did you speak to her?"

Had I spoken to her? "I don't remember…Oh, yes. I did speak to her." I'd got off one of my better cutting remarks, as a matter of fact. That didn't happen often, since I'm so easygoing as a rule. Easy-goingness could be a disadvantage when you had to deal with people like Stacy Kincaid. "Just a couple of words. We aren't well acquainted."

"And you weren't involved in her activities earlier in the evening?"

"How could I have been?" I asked, exasperated. "I'd been conducting a séance here in this house, and she wasn't here."

"Right. Your séance." His sneer became more pronounced. "So you have no idea what she'd been doing earlier in the evening?"

Well, I'd sort of assumed she'd been at a speakeasy

guzzling gin and smoking since that's what her appearance had pointed at when she'd made her grand entrance, but I didn't *know* she'd been doing those things. "No."

He sighed. "Very well. Thank you for your time." The thanks were both grudging and sarcastic.

"You're ever so welcome." I rose with a huff. Because I wanted Mrs. Kincaid to know I was still available for her any time she needed me, I turned and gave her hand a squeeze. She drew me down and pecked me on the cheek, which was awfully sweet of her. I mean, it isn't often a Gumm gets kissed by a rich society lady. Then I shook hands with Harold, who gave me a speaking look—I didn't understand what it was meant to convey, unfortunately—and turned to go.

A commotion at the front door froze all of us in our tracks. Featherstone didn't even have time to do his silent-materializing act before Stacy Kincaid, in the all-too-evident flesh, stormed the room as if she were intent upon taking prisoners. After rushing past the policeman at the door, she dashed forward for about three more feet, then screeched to a halt. With every appearance of loathing, she glared at Detective Rotondo and snarled, "You!"

Mrs. Kincaid screeched, "Stacy! Oh, my darling girl!" With that, she jumped up from the couch and hurled herself at her daughter, whose arms were suspiciously slow in encircling her mother's sobbing form.

I really hated the girl in that instant. I mean, gee whiz, she *must* have known the worry and pain she'd caused her poor mother. The very least she could have done is give the impression she was glad to be home again.

Not only that, but if she'd been my daughter, I'd have been mortified to behold her. For heaven's sake! I'm no prude, as I might have mentioned before this, but she looked exactly as I'd expect a lady of the night to look. Her dress was so sheer, you could see right through it, and the hem was so short that her naked knees were exposed. Add that to the fact that she'd rolled her stockings—her *flesh*-colored stockings, for heaven's sake—and her costume revealed several inches of knee and shin, bare white and gleaming as if begging to be stared at. It worked. I stared.

The whole effect, especially when you added to it the aroma of dissipation (gin and cigarette smoke)…Well, no respectable woman, and I don't care how rich her parents are, would appear in front of other people like that. Or in *public*, even the dubious public of a speakeasy. And in front of her own *parents*. I could cheerfully have driven a stake through the little tart's heart. If she had one.

My sympathy for Mrs. Kincaid trebled. And where was Mr. Kincaid when his daughter had been busy turning herself into a public spectacle? is what I wanted to know. Reading Spanish phrase books? Trying to seduce the housemaids? He sure as heck couldn't have been paying any attention to his family. He and Stacy deserved each other.

A harried-looking man appeared at the door of the drawing room, holding an elegant hat in his hand and gazing at the not-very-touching reunion between mother and daughter with a sour expression on his face. I didn't have to wonder long who he was, because Harold hurried over and grabbed the hand not holding the hat.

As he pumped it hard, he said, "Joshua! Thank God you're on the job. I hope Stacy didn't give you fits."

Whoever Joshua was, he withdrew a handkerchief from his pocket as soon as Harold relinquished control of his hand, and mopped his glistening brow. "Ah," he said, and I could tell he was striving for some kind of diplomatic response, "Miss Kincaid can be a handful." I thought that was extremely tactful and, therefore, decided he must be some kind of lawyer.

Since Stacy and her mother were still occupied with

each other, Harold handed Joshua's hat to Featherstone, who'd appeared behind the assembly as silently as ever and also apparently unfazed by the scandalous behavior demonstrated by one of the members of his household. He must have graduated from butler school with high honors. He disappeared with the hat as silently as he'd appeared.

Harold hauled Joshua my way. "Joshua, please let me introduce you to Mrs. Majesty. Daisy, this is Joshua Pearlman, my family's ill-used attorney. At least, I'll wager he's been ill-used these last few hours." Harold laughed.

Mr. Pearlman didn't. He did shake my hand and offer me a skinny, sort of acerbic smile. "Mrs. Majesty."

"Pleased to meet you, Mr. Pearlman." I struggled to achieve an extra measure of politeness, both because I figured he deserved it after what must have been an unpleasant interlude with Stacy, and because I'd been rude to Detective Rotondo.

I hoped the brutish Rotondo was watching, because I wanted him to understand that rudeness begets rudeness. Unless you were the Kincaids' attorney, that is to say, and then I guess you got paid pretty well for putting up with the Stacy Kincaids of this world. In that instant, I was glad I'd pursued spiritualism as a career instead of the law.

I don't know what he'd have said next because Stacy, who jerked away from her mother as soon as she could, threw a fit. It was manifest that she didn't much care for Detective Rotondo, which made him a little easier to tolerate on my part.

As Harold and Mr. Pearlman tried to capture her hands, which were in the process of pummeling the detective's broad chest, Mrs. Kincaid stood with her hands pressed to her cheeks and doing nothing, and Johnny and his fellow police officer looked on in awe, I made my escape. Shoot, what a monster that girl was! If life were fair, she'd have been sent to France to get shot and gassed, and Billy would still be safe and whole.

Stupid thinking, and I didn't know why my brain insisted on contemplating such notions. I hot-footed it to the back of the house, where I aimed to tell Aunt Vi a little bit about what had happened in the drawing room and try to ease her wounded spirits. Aunt Vi had worked for Mrs. Kincaid for decades, and she was very fond of the woman.

As I passed a room I knew to be the library, the door to which was closed, I heard a scuttling, shuffling sound coming there from. Suspicious—I instantly pictured Mr. Kincaid chasing Edie around room in his wheelchair—I paused.

Bump. Slide. Swish. The thud of furniture smacking against another piece of furniture. A muffled "No!"

That was enough for me. Something was going on in there. Something wrong. I knew what it was. Because I was already angry—at Stacy Kincaid and at Detective Rotondo—I decided to heck with what might be considered trespass and eased the door open. Thanks to Edie's good housekeeping, the hinges didn't so much as whisper, much less squeak.

And there they were. The louse Kincaid had pinned Edie behind his desk and was smirking at her as if he were God's gift to womankind instead of a disgusting reprobate in a wheelchair.

"No, Mr. Kincaid! Please let me go."

"I'll let you go after you kiss me, Edie. You know you want to."

Ew.

"No!" she cried, sounding as if she weren't far from hysteria. "I *don't* want to!"

"Pshaw."

"This isn't fair," she pleaded. "What would your wife think?"

He scoffed. "My wife never thinks. She's never had a

thought in her life."

The rat! How could he, who lived well only because of his marriage to Mrs. Kincaid, say such an unkind thing? And did he honestly think a woman like pretty, competent, not to mention young, Edie Marsh could be attracted to him? Fat chance. He was evil, pure and simple.

Since the hinges wouldn't announce me, I shoved the door hard. The crash it made as it hit the plaster wall served my purpose just as well. Maybe too well. I winced at the thought of plaster dust sprinkling down upon the wildly expensive Persian rug covering the library floor.

However, my ploy worked. I had the satisfaction of seeing Mr. Kincaid's body darned near lift out of his chair in alarm. Edie uttered a shriek that was (thank God) muffled by the hand that had flown to her mouth at the ghastly noise the door had made.

"Hi there," I said inanely. I wanted to light into the rotter Kincaid and tell him what I thought of him, but Edie, who had recovered as soon as she saw who'd made the noise, had commenced grimacing at me in a way I understood.

Kincaid recovered quickly, as well. Too quickly, the villain. "What the devil are you doing here?" I got the feeling he didn't like me very well.

"Um..." Good question. "I thought I heard something in this room."

He wheeled my way, and I prudently stepped behind an overstuffed chair, just in case he was angry enough to run me over with his chair. "And are you in the habit of intruding into other people's business every time you hear things, Mrs. Majesty?"

To heck with that. While I considered discretion the better part of valor—after all, I depended on rich people for a living—I didn't have to put up with this sort of thing. "I thought I heard Edie's voice," I said deliberately. "And," I added with as much coldness as I could command at the moment, which probably wasn't much since I was rattled, "she sounded as if she was in some distress." I derived a modicum of satisfaction from his flinch. "I wanted to help my friend if I could."

"Huh!" And with that, he sped past me and out the door.

Thank God, thank God. I slumped against the overstuffed chair and stared at Edie, who stared back. Recalling the terrific crash the doorknob had made, I tentatively pulled the door away from the wall and peered with some trepidation.

I saw that no damage had been done to the plaster wall. "Shoot. Thank the good Lord for sturdy construction."

Edie giggled. I figured she was still close to hysteria. I mean, what I'd said wasn't funny, you know? I shut the door quietly and went over to her. "Are you okay, Edie?"

She nodded. "Yeah. I think so. Thanks for the rescue, Daisy."

"It's nothing."

Okay, I know Edie and Quincy's business is their own. They'd asked me to butt out—or, at least, Edie had. She was a grown woman. So was Quincy—a grown man, I mean. They were both smart people who knew what they wanted out of life and also knew how to get it.

But, darn it all, I was angry! And, however much it pains me to admit it, I'm not good at minding my own business. I walked over to Edie, grabbed her by the shoulders, and shook her. "If you don't tell Quincy about this now, *I'll* do it! Darn it, Edie, that man is evil!"

Unfortunately, Edie's no shrinking violet, either. She grabbed my wrists and yanked my hands off her shoulders. "If you do, I'll never speak to you again, Daisy Majesty! I can take care of myself!"

"You weren't doing a very good job of it when I came in here!"

"Fudge." Edie sank into the big desk chair with a *whump* that wrinkled her tidy black uniform skirt. She looked up at me and gave me a shaky smile. "I would have triumphed over that cripple if you hadn't come in. I was trying not to make a lot of noise and fuss."

Resting my hands on my hips, I tilted my head, stared at Edie, and sighed. She was right. Well, she was right in that she probably could have solved the problem by herself. And she was also right that she hadn't been making much noise.

I still didn't like it.

And it still wasn't my business. So, after smoothing things over with Edie, I went to the kitchen, told Aunt Vi what had happened regarding Stacy, and toddled out to the Model T.

Quincy, bless his heart, started the thing for me. I drove home alternately worrying about Mrs. Kincaid and Edie and dreaming about buying a closed-top Hudson. I'd heard they were starting to put batteries into automobiles now, so you didn't have to be so careful with the clutch wire when you started it. It was about time, if you ask me, since I didn't fancy breaking my arm on the darned crank if I happened to do it wrong one morning.

I still burned to tell Quincy what Mr. Kincaid was trying to do to his lady love.

CHAPTER 8

The day following the Stacy debacle was the first Sunday in June and we were all going to church. June had always struck me as a cheerful month, so I'd put on my favorite summery dress. I'd made this one, too, out of a sprigged blue-and-white georgette. It had a dropped waist with a pretty blue sash encircling it, and was no more than five inches from the straps of my low-heeled shoes. I'd trimmed my straw hat with a ribbon crafted from the scraps left over from the dress. Naturally, I wore plain cotton stockings. Not for me those flesh-colored horrors worn by the Stacy Kincaids of the world.

I'd have liked to wear pink, which is my favorite summertime color, but in those days redheads didn't wear pink. Well, except for my old pink-and-white checked house dress I wore now and then. The two colors were said to clash. I couldn't see it myself, but I didn't want to make a spectacle of myself. Unlike some people I could mention.

It didn't matter anyhow, since not very many people would see my lovely costume until after the church service concluded and we all moseyed over to the fellowship hall for cookies and punch, because I'd be wearing a dull blue robe during the service. For a variety of reasons, I sang in the choir.

The first reason is that I love to sing.

The second reason is that I tried in every way I could think of to demonstrate to everyone who might doubt my intentions that I was a good Christian girl and didn't truck with the devil. My chosen career put me in a somewhat equivocal position in some people's minds some of the time. All of the time, if you took Billy into consideration, and I had to since I was married to him.

I don't really think Billy considered what I did wicked, even though he said he did. As I've mentioned before, probably too often already, I think Billy's objections were based on his own pain and frustration. I'm sure that, if he were able to hold a regular job—and he was a crackerjack mechanic and could have made a mint in automobile repair—he wouldn't have minded if I'd fiddled around with spiritualism. He'd probably have been glad if I'd made some money on the side. Maybe he'd even have been proud of his little wife, who supplemented the family income doing something so interesting.

As things stood, well…Life was complicated, and singing in the choir slightly mitigated the tensions I occasionally perceived in our home and in the community.

I even have a pretty good voice, although I have no ambition to sing on the vaudeville stage or in the grand opera. My voice doesn't vibrate enough for opera (and I'm not fat enough), and I'd have a heart attack and die if I ever had to sing a solo on a vaudeville stage.

My voice was good enough for our choir director, though, and that's what mattered. This morning, Lucille Spinks and I were going to sing a duet, in fact. I don't mind singing with other people. It's when they're on their own that my vocal chords shrivel up and begin croaking.

My family has always attended the First Methodist Episcopal Church (North) on the corner of Marengo and Colorado. It was approximately two and a half blocks down from the Chinese Methodist Episcopal Church which I'd always wanted to attend just to see, but have never quite dared, since I obviously wouldn't exactly blend in, if you know what I mean.

Our church was only a few blocks from where we lived. When the weather was fine, as it was this Sunday morning, we liked to walk. The whole family attended, including Ma and Pa and Aunt Vi. Mrs. Wilson from next door with Pudge in his Junior Boy Scout uniform and looking neater than usual, often walked with us. They did so that day.

Billy was in a good mood. I'd told him about the Stacy affair, placing special emphasis on how she'd attacked Detective Rotondo, and he'd laughed about it.

You never knew how he'd take anything. He could easily have used Stacy's deplorable behavior as another stick to beat me with, but instead he chose to find the incident amusing. I wondered if it was the morphine laughing, but didn't dwell on the possibility. My poor broken husband needed the pain relief morphine afforded him—and I needed it almost as much as he did. Pitiful, but there you go.

"What are you and Lucy singing today, Daisy?"

Billy had acquiesced when Pudge had volunteered to push his chair. I'd shrieked inside when the boy had asked but Billy took it in good temper, for which condescension I was infinitely grateful. Pudge, as a Junior Boy Scout, put a lot of emphasis on doing good deeds. Billy, as a ruined ex-soldier, didn't often appreciate his enthusiasm.

Lucy had wanted us to sing "Alas! and did My Savior Bleed," and the choir director, Floy Hostetter, had liked the selection. I'd objected. Easter had fallen on April 4, sort of mid-way through the season. That was almost two months ago, and I'm sure most of the congregation wouldn't have cared what we sang. But it seemed to me as though we'd been singing Easter songs until the day before yesterday. Besides, summertime was right around the corner.

So what, you ask? Well, I'll tell you.

"Alas! and did My Savior Bleed" is a beautiful old hymn. We always hauled it out at Easter time, which is totally appropriate, and I sang it with all my heart during the Easter season. But it seemed a trifle dismal to me with springtime over and summer hurtling toward us as fast as it could. I'd suggested a bouncier tune, "Onward Christian Soldiers."

Mr. Hostetter had visibly paled, winced, and wrinkled his nose. He equated my choice with the Salvation Army, which I had to admit made sense. In those days you could hardly pass a street corner that didn't have a Salvation Army band on it playing "Onward Christian Soldiers" with women jangling their tambourines to the rhythm, trying to get people to cough up their pennies and nickels to help feed the poor and dry out the drunks. But I still liked it. I did, however, offer an alternative which was eventually approved of by all parties.

Therefore, Lucy and I aimed to sing "Stand Up, Stand Up for Jesus." I liked it pretty well, and it was nice and soldierly, which I sanctioned. Ever since the war started, I'd been feeling militant. After it ended and Billy came back to me, I'd been downright bloodthirsty.

Lucy had a much prettier voice than I. Not only that, but she was a soprano and perpetually took the melody. Next life, if there is one, I want to come back as a soprano because they always get the good parts. As luck would have it, I'd learned to read music when I was a kid (some rich picture star had given Pa a piano when I was seven. Heck, I could read music before I could read Tarot cards), so I never had much trouble picking up my part.

"We're going to sing 'Stand Up, Stand Up for Jesus' right after the Doxology. Wish us luck."

"Aw, you'll do swell, Miss Desdemona."

When I glanced over, I saw Pudge gazing at me with adoring eyes. God bless the child. "Thanks, Pudge." I smiled, but felt obliged to point out that we were approaching a street corner. I could just imagine what horrors would ensue if Pudge managed to dump my poor husband out of his chair because he was staring at me. "Corner," I mouthed at him.

Pudge gave a start of surprise, but managed to avert the approaching calamity. He said, "You're welcome."

"You and Lucy sound good together."

This kind and pithy statement had emerged from my own husband's mouth, and it shocked me nearly out of my georgette-covered skin. He didn't generally offer compliments, being more apt to criticize.

"Thanks, Billy. I hope I don't go flat during the chorus. The alto part drones a little bit there, and sometimes I sag."

"You don't sag yet," murmured my husband with a grin and a wink.

The wink nearly did me in. As often as Billy drove me crazy with his crankiness and whining, there were other times, like today, when he could drive me to the brink of tears by acting like the Billy he used to be. Since I'd never, ever, in a million years, demonstrate how much pity I felt for him, I winked back. "Thanks, sweetie."

I did sometimes worry that my voice would deepen as I got older. It would be mortifying to have to sing with the men in the tenor section. If that ever happened, I'd just have to garner good will through some other church activity, I supposed. Maybe I could work in the kitchen, feeding the poor. If somebody was poor enough, he probably wouldn't cavil too much at eating my cooking. It was a sad fact, but I hadn't inherited my aunt's culinary talents.

We arrived at the church in a good mood, communally speaking, and greeted friends and neighbors with gusto. I love people. Billy used to be a friendly fellow, too, although his cheery nature had suffered debilitating injuries along with his body in late years. Today, though, he smiled and chatted with as much evident pleasure as I did.

I had to leave him in Ma's care while I nipped to the choir room to don my robe. I was looking forward to singing the duet with Lucy because, truth to tell, I'm kind of a performer at heart. That's undoubtedly another reason I enjoyed my line of work so well and was so good at it.

Lucy, a blue-eyed blonde who was pretty enough to make up for her lack of brain power, claimed to be as nervous as a sparrow being eyed by a hawk. She sure fluttered around enough to prove it, although I didn't buy her act. It was my opinion, and I'll bet I'm right, that Lucy had been taught from the cradle how to act like a helpless female. She'd been a good pupil, too. She was about my age, maybe a year or two older, and I swear to goodness, the woman couldn't walk across the street without a male escort.

I'm sure she figured some nice man would marry her and take care of her for the rest of her life. I wished her luck. Although my parents were too smart to have taught me to be helpless, I'd harbored the same fantasy about marriage once. Show's how much anybody can tell about life before it happens. If I ever had children, and the prospects looked mighty dim back then, I aimed to teach them all, male and female, how to get by in the world with or without help, because you just never knew what life had in store for you.

There I go, rambling again. Sorry.

Anyhow, Lucy and I and the rest of the choir members put on our robes. To the strains of "O For a Thousand Tongues to Sing" (I learned later that this is traditionally the first hymn in all Methodist hymnals, although I still don't know why), the choir climbed the stairs to the loft above the pulpit. I loved sitting there, because I could see everyone in the congregation and study the ladies' best clothes.

Apparently I'd been paying too much attention to the new summer fashions that day, because I didn't see Detective Rotondo lurking in the congregation until Lucy and I descended the stairs and approached the front of the podium for our solo. I almost died then and there.

What the heck was *he* doing here? I couldn't think of any answer to that question that might auger good for me. It was all I could do to subdue my shock and nervousness enough to start my part of the duet on the right note. I think I did okay, in spite of the detective glowering at me from the third pew from the back, but it was hard.

After our pastor, Reverend Merle Smith, spoke the last "Amen" of the day and the choir had sung a parting benediction hymn, I raced down to the choir room and threw off my robe. I prayed like mad that I could get to my family and the other hungry Methodists munching cookies and punch and hide amongst them well enough so that Rotondo wouldn't be able to find me.

No such luck. I'd even positioned myself with my back to the door, behind Billy and his wheelchair, and had begun an animated (on my part, at any rate) conversation with Mrs. Smith, our pastor's wife, about the relative merits of cherry punch versus lemonade, but it was no good. I sensed Rotondo approaching, kind of like I imagine a field mouse senses the approach of a hungry fox. I gave up, turned around, and saw him looming over Billy, staring directly at me. Billy was gazing up at him, and he appeared puzzled. Small wonder, as the detective was frowning pretty fiercely.

Peeved, I frowned back. "Detective Rotondo." I was proud of the gritty tone of voice I achieved.

"Mrs. Majesty." He sounded about as overjoyed as I felt, which was not at all.

Billy continued to peer at the detective and still looked puzzled. Seeing no alternative, I introduced the two men. "Billy, this is Detective Rotondo. Detective Rotondo, my husband, Billy Majesty." I should have introduced him as William, because it was stuffier, but it was too late now.

"How do you do?" my polite Billy asked. I could tell he wouldn't give a wooden nickel to know how the detective did.

"Very well, thank you. And you?" By the same token, it was clear that Rotondo didn't give a rap about Billy's state of wellbeing.

I couldn't conceive of any reason for a representative from the Pasadena Police Department to appear at my church unless he aimed to arrest me for fortune-telling. That was frightening, but seemed unlikely. Didn't you have to be caught in the act for them to arrest you for that sort of thing? Nobody from the police department had been present at the séance. And that wasn't fortune-telling anyway.

The memory of my Tarot cards and the Ouija board lying on the Kincaids' coffee table when Rotondo entered the parlor wormed its way into my brain, and I went cold. I'd never let on. "Detective Rotondo is investigating the problem with Miss Kincaid, Billy."

"Oh?"

My husband was clearly annoyed that the police had pursued me all the way to church to talk about Stacy Kincaid. I was, too. No money had changed hands during the Tarot episode. Or the Ouija board one, either. I'd only been at the Kincaids' out of a sense of goodwill and fellowship. They couldn't arrest me for that, could they? My palms started sweating.

"May I speak to you for a moment, Mrs. Majesty?" Rotondo sounded stern, which scared me.

He'd never get my goat if I could help it. "Of course." I waved a hand, gesturing at the milling throng of Methodists. "Be my guest. Speak to me."

I saw his jaw bunch as he gritted his teeth. "In private?"

"Why on earth do you want to talk to my wife in private?" demanded Billy. Bless his heart.

"Yes," said I. "Why do you need to talk to me in private?"

I figured that if his teeth ground together any harder, his jaw would break. I wondered if I could annoy him enough to achieve that result. Probably not. He must be used to dealing with tougher cookies than I could ever be.

"It's about the Kincaids," Rotondo said. He didn't want to say that much; I could tell.

Billy and I exchanged a glance. He shrugged, as if to give me his blessing. I turned back to Rotondo. "All right, but I don't want to leave my family for long."

"This won't take long," he promised.

"I'll make sure of it." I know I sounded kind of snotty, but I didn't care. "I guess we can talk in the kitchen." A glance at Mrs. Smith confirmed my guess. She looked as if she'd like to come along and eavesdrop, but I whispered that I'd explain everything later, and started for the kitchen. I felt Rotondo behind me like a bear about to swat me with a paw and eat me for lunch.

I waited until we were both inside and Rotondo stood next to the wood-burning stove (we were collecting money for a new stove, but you know how church projects go. We'd probably have enough money for a new stove by 1930) before I closed the door. I didn't even slam it, and was proud of myself.

I did, however, slam my hands on my hips when I turned to face him. "Okay, what the heck do you mean by following me to church?"

He wasn't intimidated. Figured.

"Frankly I'm surprised to see you *in* church, Mrs. Majesty. I shouldn't think church would be compatible with your occupation."

I think I sneered at him. I strove for a sneer at any rate. "I'm not surprised that you're surprised. So many people have no understanding of my work. Unless that's what you want to talk to me about, let's drop it."

"Very well."

Thank God. "How'd you find me, anyhow? Don't tell me you have spies watching me."

"Why the devil should I put spies on you?"

"That's what I want to know."

He huffed. "I asked one of your neighbors. Mr. Wilson said you'd gone to church, and which church, so I came here."

"Huh." I glared at him.

He glared back.

Because I wanted him to know how much I resented what I considered an intrusion into my private life, in case he'd missed it from my reaction so far, I added, "I don't appreciate being accosted by a police detective at church."

"I needed to talk to you."

"Be that as it may, I don't know any more about Stacy Kincaid this morning than I did yesterday, and I already told you that much. I don't know anything about her. What's more, I don't want to." Now that I was confident that he didn't aim to arrest me, I felt comfortable getting mad at him.

"I'm not here about Miss Anastasia Kincaid," Rotondo said, sounding something like I'd always sort of figured the Oracle at Delphi might sound—like a portent of ill fortune, if not death and destruction. "This might be said to concern Mr. Eustace Kincaid, Miss Kincaid's father."

I perked up. "Oh! Do you mean to tell me Edie finally complained?" What a brave woman, to tell the cops. I was impressed.

"Who's Edie?" Rotondo asked, bursting that happy bubble.

Shoot. Maybe he *was* going to arrest me. "Never mind. Why'd you chase me down here? What have I done wrong? I am *not* a fortune-teller."

"No? What are you, then?"

"A spiritualist. I am a spiritualist, Detective Rotondo. Many people appreciate the work I do. If you don't, that's not my problem, and I don't relish having you suspect me of being a crook."

"I don't suspect you of being a crook, for the love of God!"

"Huh. You look as if you suspect me of any number of awful, illegal things."

His lips tightened. It was an interesting phenomenon to watch since his skin tone was olive and when his lips pinched like that, the wrinkles were kind of yellowish. When I got home from church, I was going to see what color my wrinkles were. I suspected they'd be more white than yellow, which pointed out fascinating differences in people's diverse ethnic backgrounds. Which was totally irrelevant.

"The fact that I disapprove of your business isn't at issue at the moment," he said, plainly irked, which pleased me doubly. "The reason I came here today is that you seem to be friendly with the Kincaids."

"I told you everything I know about Stacy Kincaid last night."

"You didn't tell me anything about Stacy Kincaid. You only related what happened after your séance."

I watched him when he said the word "séance," but didn't detect any signs of derision. Good thing.

He went on. "I need to know as much as you can tell me about the Kincaids as people. The family. All of them."

I didn't want to tell him anything. Since I didn't know much, however, I figured it wouldn't hurt. "I don't know a single thing about the Kincaids except that Mrs. Kincaid is nice and Mr. Kincaid isn't, their daughter's a pill and their son's a peach, and that they all seem to have more money than sense. If you want me to tell you anything else, you're going to have to tell me why." That was good. I was getting better at these verbal sparring matches with Detective Rotondo.

Rotondo didn't want me to get any better at them. He looked as if he'd like to turn around and march out on me, but couldn't because of his job. That made me feel much more cheerful.

"Mrs. Majesty, irregularities have been reported to us regarding the records at Mr. Kincaid's bank."

I'm sure I looked as blank as I felt. "So what? I mean, you can't possibly suspect me of stealing from the Kincaids' bank? How the heck could I do that?"

"No, no, no. I don't suspect you of banking irregularities. I'm not accusing you of anything. Will you please get that through your head?"

"Huh."

"The reason I'm here today is to ask you to listen and watch when you visit the Kincaids. I want to know if any of them mention anything about the bank."

"What? I'm not going to spy—"

"I'm not asking you to spy!" he interrupted. "All I want you to do is keep your eyes and ears open when you visit the Kincaid home. There are problems at the bank, and Mr. Kincaid is the bank's owner and president. He might mention his worries at home. Right now, we're looking at Mr. Farrington—"

It was my turn to interrupt. "No! He's too nice to do anything illegal."

Rotondo's response was a pitying smirk. Okay, so I know that nice people can steal things as easily as mean people can, and probably do from time to time, but I didn't want Lieutenant Farrington to be guilty of theft. I wanted Mr. Kincaid to be acknowledged as the villain I knew him to be. Discovering and proving that he was a thief as well as a lecherous old goat would be a perfect way to do it. "All right, I know his being nice doesn't mean anything. But I really don't believe Mr. Farrington is a criminal."

"You never know what motivates people to do the things they do. Perhaps he's had financial troubles. Maybe he's been gambling. You can't know everything that goes on in a person's life."

"I suppose not." Betcha I could tell Rotondo more about Mr. Farrington's life than he knew already, but I'd never do it. I liked Mr. Farrington too well.

"So, are you willing to do this? I'm not asking much of you, Mrs. Majesty. And if you really want to save Mr. Farrington's skin, maybe you can discover something to his credit."

He said it as if he didn't believe it, but I knew he was wrong about Farrington. Darn it, I made a living out of studying people, and Delroy Farrington was no thief. He might be a depraved fiend, according to my husband, but I'd bet money that he was an honorable one.

"I don't know. Why don't you raid the bank or something? Or go talk to Mr. Kincaid?"

Again I saw the phenomenon of an olive-skinned man wrinkling his lips. And his nose. I got the feeling Detective Rotondo didn't like me much, which suited me fine. "The Kincaids are a prominent Pasadena family, Mrs. Majesty. We don't want to ruffle their feathers if we don't have to."

I know I managed a sneer that time. "Yeah. Money talks. Even to the police."

He didn't like that at all. "I can assure you that we don't play favorites, Mrs. Majesty. But even you must realize that we have to tread softly in this situation."

"Right." I sounded completely disgusted, which is what I'd intended.

"Besides, their daughter is giving them enough trouble.

We don't want to add to their troubles."

I squinted at him. "Darn it, you already know that's the only thing you could have said that would make me go along with spying on the Kincaids, don't you?"

"I'm not asking you to be a spy!"

"That's right. I forgot, I'm only supposed to be a sneak and an eavesdropper."

He sucked in a deep breath and held it, probably to keep from bellowing at me. All in all, I was quite gratified that I'd managed to upset him. I still resented the way he'd bully-ragged Mrs. Kincaid the other day. Not to mention the way he overtly disapproved of my line of work. And chasing me down at church was pure-D mean, if you ask me.

"So you agree to keep an open mind about this, and to let me know if you hear anything that might be of interest to the police regarding the banking problems?"

I shrugged. "Sure. I guess so."

"This matter needs to be kept quiet, Mrs. Majesty. I'm sure you can imagine how many people might be affected by problems with this bank, and many of them aren't in any shape to swallow monetary losses. We need to keep it under our hats until we know what's going on. Can you keep this matter to yourself? The alleged bank irregularities? It won't do to broadcast anything too soon, and might even be considered slander, if no irregularities are discovered."

Oh, brother. This was just swell. I wouldn't be able even to tell Billy about it. Feeling beleaguered, I snapped, "I don't gossip." That was a lie, but Rotondo didn't have to know it. "Anyhow, I can't imagine the Kincaids yakking about bank problems in my presence. We aren't exactly bosom buddies, you know."

"I thought you were a friend of the family."

"I *am* a friend of the family, but they don't blab to me about their deepest, darkest secrets, for heaven's sake!"

"We'll see." It looked like it cost him a lot to tack on a

surly, "Thank you."

I huffed and retreated to the security of my family. They were all huddled together along with Mrs. Smith, glancing at the kitchen and muttering with each other. I knew they could hardly wait to hear whatever our conversation had been about. And I couldn't tell them a single thing. Nuts.

Oh, but the homes were something special. Henry Huntington, the railroad robber baron, had a place there with acres and acres of gardens and rolling lawns, fancy lights and exotic plants. He even had peacocks wandering around to give the place atmosphere. Not that it needed them. Shoot, even without peacocks, the Huntington place had atmosphere enough for me.

I knew about it first-hand because Mrs. Huntington had hired me to play fortune-teller at a Halloween benefit she'd given to raise money for the hospital they were building. Gladys Millbrook, one of my friends, had graduated from Pasadena's Sawyer Business School, and worked there as her secretary. Gladys had taken me all through the house and over the grounds. You could get lost there if you wanted to, which didn't sound like a half-bad idea.

Not long after that, the Huntingtons donated their house and grounds to the city of Pasadena to be used as a museum and art gallery. I thought that was a very generous thing for them to do, although I also wondered what they were getting out of it. Probably because I was born and reared a Gumm, I tend to be skeptical about rich people doing charitable deeds for no reason.

Harold's house wasn't a mansion like his mother's or Mr. Huntington's. It was a swell place, though: two stories, Mediterranean style, huge lawn, gorgeous garden with tons of roses, and a little orange kitty cat named Marmalade. Harold said peacocks squawked more than cats, and he didn't like the racket. I suppose he was right.

Marmalade was okay as cats go, but she made me want a dog. Not a big dog; a smallish dog that would sleep on Billy's lap and give him something to pet. I know Billy got bored sitting in his wheelchair all day. He and Pa got along fine, but Pa was much older than Billy. Also, Pa could still get around, even though his ticker wasn't so good anymore. He had his friends and clubs and card games, and made the most of them.

Although he generally asked Billy to join him when he went out and about, Billy's interests ran more towards baseball and automobiles than cards and old men's chatter.

Poor Billy had such a difficult time getting around that he was stuck at home most of the time, a lot of it by himself. I'd always thought it was a shame that he didn't like to read more, although he did enjoy some of my detective novels. Which made one thing he didn't complain about regarding my personal self and habits.

A dog would be company for him. Besides, I've always wanted a dog. Lots of the rich people I worked for in Pasadena had special, fancy dogs. Mrs. Longworth had her poodles that were pampered, groomed, and better cared-for than most of the people I knew. Mrs. Frasier bred little high-strung dogs called miniature pinschers that were incredibly light on their feet. They also yapped a lot and made me nervous. Mrs. Frasier was on a rampage to have her chosen breed of dog recognized by the Westminster Dog Show, whatever that was.

And then there were Mrs. Bissel's dachshunds. They were my favorites, because they were so...I don't know. They had these noble, expressive faces, and fiercely protective instincts, and all of those characteristics were attached to those ridiculously long bodies on teensy, weensy legs. I think I loved them so much because they were so funny looking. Anything that can make me laugh is okay in my book.

Shoot, how did I get on the subject of dogs? I'm supposed to be talking about Harold's séance and the conversation I overheard. Actually, I don't need to say much about the séance, because it was just another séance.

When I pulled up in front of Harold's house, I was surprised to find Quincy there, parking cars for the rich folks. And even me. He grinned broadly as he raced over and opened my door.

"Hey, Quincy. What are you doing here?"

"Mr. Harold Kincaid borrowed me from his mother for the evening." Bowing smartly, he swept the cap from his head and darned near brushed the sidewalk with it. When he recovered from his bow and plopped his cap back on, he gestured at his snappy uniform. "Pretty keen, huh?"

"I'll say."

Leaning closer, he whispered, "I wouldn't have done this if I had to be inside with all the faggots, but I can stay outside, enjoy the moon and the stars. Plus which, I get to drive a whole lot of fancy cars, even if it's only up the driveway."

The word he'd used to describe Harold and his friends caught my attention. "Were you in the army, Quincy?"

He shook his head. "Naw. I wanted to enlist, but my mother'd already lost two of my brothers, and she begged me not to. Besides, she needed help on the ranch until the rest of the family got home."

I sighed. "Yeah. There was a lot of that going around, I guess."

Quincy saluted. "Have fun."

"Thanks." I walked up the front walk to the porch, which was dripping with bougainvillea blossoms, and grabbed the brass knocker, which hung from a brass elephant's trunk. When you're rich, you can do all sorts of things you couldn't get away with if you were poor. I mean, an elephant?

After Harold introduced me all around, he led me to what he called his "den," which would have been anyone else's back parlor. It was a cozy room, and Harold had it set up just right, with a big round table and seven chairs. I positioned my cranberry lamp in the middle of the table, and prepared to do my job.

As a séance, it was nothing unusual. Oliver Pittman, the dead uncle of one of Harold's friends, spoke to

Harold's friend through Rolly and assured the young man that he (the uncle) was doing well on the Other Side.

One of Harold's dead ancestors from the 1500s popped up to tell Harold that he loved what he'd done with the front room (there had been lots of ooohs and aaahs about the front room among Harold's friends before the séance. Those guys really enjoyed interior decorating). A deceased sister of another man made the poor fellow cry, and I felt terrible until afterwards, when the man rushed up to me, wrung my hand nearly off, and told me I'd eased his mind.

"I was so afraid Cissy would hate me, you know, because of—well, because of what I am, you know, and I can't *tell* you how overjoyed I was to hear that she doesn't!"

Then he kissed me on both cheeks and rushed off to tell somebody else how wonderful I was. That was sweet of him, although I wasn't used to men gushing quite so much. I didn't mind it, though. These men were very congenial, and they were much more polite and friendly than most of my clients' husbands. I was also encouraged to know I'd made the poor fellow happy. It didn't make any sense to me that people didn't like men of his ilk just because they were a little different. They sure didn't hurt anybody that I could see.

Harold was so good to me. I have to admit to thinking it was a shame he didn't like women, because he'd make some girl a swell husband. Then again, maybe if he was like other men he'd be...well...like other men. If you know what I mean.

I noticed that Mr. Farrington (I really oughtn't to call him Lieutenant Farrington any longer, since he'd been out of the army for years) seemed more subdued than he'd been the first time I'd met him. He was as courteous and considerate as ever, and as handsome, and I didn't think much about it until long after the séance was over, when I was fetching my hat and coat from the room where I'd left them.

Two men were speaking to each other in a room next to the coat room. I didn't pay any attention, not being an eavesdropper by nature, even if I am a snoop, until I heard the word "bank" plunk itself into the conversation. Then I started listening with both ears.

"I know there's monkey business going on, Harry." I recognized Delroy Farrington's voice, and he was obviously worried.

"You're probably right. Banks contain money, people always need money, and they're apt to perform monkey tricks to get it."

This pithy comment had been uttered by Harold, who didn't seem worried at all. In fact, he sounded quite chipper. That's probably because he didn't have to worry about money. Most of the time, I found it difficult to find anything at all funny about money.

"When I was auditing the books—you know, we do periodic audits in order to make sure things are running smoothly…"

"No, I didn't know, but I'll take your word for it, Del. I don't know anything about banks, and I care even less." Laughter from Harold, not joined by Del.

"It's not funny."

This attitude undoubtedly accounted for Mr. Farrington's shortage of good humor.

More serious now, Harold said, "I'm sorry, Del. Go on. What's the trouble?"

"I know the books have been doctored. When I tried to reconcile the books with the assets, I couldn't find thousands of dollars worth of bearer bonds."

"That sounds bad."

"It's worse than bad, Harry. It'll be catastrophic if the bonds don't turn up. Those bonds can be cashed by anyone. Anyone, Harry! I can't even stand to think about what's going to happen to the bank when news of this gets out."

I couldn't catch the next several exchanges, because the two men had lowered their voices or shut a door or ducked behind a curtain or something.

"What's worse," I heard Mr. Farrington say a few moments later, "is I...God, I hate to say this, Harry."

"Spit it out, Del. You know you need to get it off your chest, and if you can't talk to me, whom can you talk to?"

"I love you, Harry."

"I love you, Del."

I really wish I hadn't heard that part. And the next almost-quiet, smoochy seconds didn't do much for my peace of mind, either. All right, so I know the two men were—I guess they were lovers, actually—but I didn't necessarily want to hear about it first-hand. I wouldn't want to overhear such carryings-on between a male-female couple, for that matter. Fortunately, the kissy interlude didn't last long.

"But, Harry, I...Oh, God, I hate to say this! But I'm afraid your father is involved."

I was shocked.

Harold manifestly wasn't. "Wouldn't surprise me, Del. The old man's a dedicated scoundrel. I thought Mother ought to have left him years ago."

I was even more shocked.

"I don't know what to do, Harry." I could picture poor Mr. Farrington sinking his head in his hands and running his fingers through his pretty blond curls.

"You're doing all you can, Del."

"I'm afraid it's going to be a matter for the police pretty soon, though, Harry, and then what will happen? The outside auditors are scheduled to come to the bank for three days the week after next. If those bonds don't turn up, I'm terrified of what's going to happen to the bank. And me. They'll blame me, as chief cashier. I know they will."

"I'll protect you, Del."

"I love you, Harry."

That was enough for me. I didn't want to hear any more lovey-dovey stuff from a couple of men. I grabbed my coat and hat and scrammed out of there.

Harold gave me twice what we'd agreed upon as my fee for conducting the séance. I tried to refuse the money—not that I didn't need it, but I didn't think I'd earned it—but he wouldn't let me. Taking my hand and pressing the bills into it, he said, "Daisy Majesty, you're the best medium I've ever met in my life."

I laughed at that. "And exactly how many mediums have you met in your life, Harold?"

He laughed, too. "One so far. But I'm sure you're the best in the world. If I really believed in this stuff, I swear I'd have you contact my dead Uncle Pete. I'd love to know why he never married." Harold winked. "I have my suspicions, but nobody in the family will talk about it."

"Oh." Shoot, what does a person say to something like that? "Well, I'm glad you were satisfied."

"More than satisfied. Enchanted. And I'm so glad you like my front room. I did it myself, you know."

"It's beautiful, Harold." It was, too. Maybe I could get Harold to help me if I ever had enough money to redo our living room. The possibility was remote, but if I could get enough of these guys to have me conduct séances for them, who knew? They all seemed to have good jobs and no kids, so there was a lot of money in that quarter to throw at spiritualists.

"Indeed, you were smashing, Mrs. Majesty." Mr. Farrington had come up and was smiling down upon me like a benevolent godlet. He'd have made a keen preacher, except that I'm not sure churches approve of people like him being ministers. But he had a soothing way about him, a tenderness I guess you could call it, that would have sat well on a pastor. I could feature being ministered to by so kind and caring a man.

Lord, wouldn't that give the Methodist Episcopals conniption fits? Life absolutely baffles me sometimes. Most of the time, actually. But enough of that.

Harold walked me to my automobile, which embarrassed me a little, since it was only a junky Model T, and all the other cars parked in his huge back yard were wildly expensive, fancy machines. But Harold was so at ease about everything, I stopped worrying almost immediately. I sensed that he wanted to talk to me about something.

"Harold, do you want to talk to me about something?"

He grinned. "Actually, yes, I do, but I'm not sure how to do it."

What did this mean? Beat me. "Just spit it out, why don't you."

Sticking his hands in his pockets, thereby ruining the line of his gorgeous Palm Beach suit, he pursed his mouth, then said, "Why not?" His gaze became intense. "Daisy, have you ever noticed anything not quite right about my father?"

Huh? Did Harold think I was in cahoots with his father in cleaning out the bank? I only wish. However, as long as he'd asked, I figured I might as well hint at the Edie problem. "Er, not exactly. I mean, he's never done anything to me, but—" I'd promised Edie I wouldn't tell. Darn it. "I believe he has bothered at least one of the housemaids." There. That wasn't telling, was it?

"Aha. That wouldn't surprise me in the least. The man's a monster."

Good Lord. I'd never heard anyone talk about a parent this way. "Oh."

"He's always been a nasty old man." Harold's sudden grin caught me unawares. "To tell the truth, I'd always hoped I'd one day discover that my mother had been playing around on him before I was born and he wasn't really my father at all."

Good *Lord*! If I was surprised before, I was flabbergasted now.

"Oh, dear, I've shocked you."

"No, no. Not really. I mean…" He'd shocked me, all right. The worst part, though, was that he'd also tickled me so much, I couldn't suppress my laughter. I was still giggling when Harold handed me off to Quincy, who'd run to get my car as Harold and I had said our farewells.

"What's so funny?" Quincy wanted to know.

I wiped my eyes, which were streaming by that time. "Nothing, really. Harold's funny, is all."

"Yeah? I've never talked to him much." Quincy gave an expressive shudder, and I knew the reason for his reticence with Harold. I didn't think it was fair, either.

"He's a great guy, Quincy. You'd like him."

"I doubt it."

"He's ever so much nicer than his father."

"That wouldn't take much."

I laughed again. "And he never chases women, either, so he wouldn't give Edie a bad time." I could have kicked myself as soon as the words left my mouth.

Quincy stiffened up like one of Mrs. Garland's spotted pointers eyeing a duck. That's another dog I liked, but not as much as the dachshunds. "What are you saying, Daisy?"

I waved it away. "Nothing. I just meant that Harold isn't the sort of man who'd chase women."

"That's not what you meant, and you know it."

Nuts. "I didn't mean anything, Quincy."

He glared at me. "Is that bastard Kincaid bothering Edie?"

Darn my big mouth, anyhow. "How should I know?" I put on an act of annoyance, hoping Quincy would stop questioning me. It worked, but I sure didn't like the expression on his face when he cranked up the Model T for me.

* * *

The next day, I did my duty and visited Detective Rotondo at the Pasadena Police Department. I'd thought about calling him on the telephone but decided a visit would be more discreet. You never knew about Mrs. Barrow. I always tried to shoo her off the party line, but I didn't think it would be prudent to convey confidential information of a police nature over the telephone wire.

Before the end of the decade, Pasadena City Hall was going to be replaced by a splendid new building on Garfield Avenue, just north of Colorado Boulevard, and the Police Department would take up new quarters on Walnut and Raymond. In 1920, City Hall sat on Fair Oaks Avenue at Union, and the police station occupied space at the rear of the building.

I parked the Model T at the curb and felt funny walking up to the door of the police station. I hate to admit it, but I even glanced around to see if anyone I knew was watching. As far as I could tell, nobody was. A few of the old cats in Pasadena would have loved to see me heading into the police station, and would assuredly have the news all over town before my business with Rotondo had concluded.

It goes without saying that Detective Rotondo was nowhere in sight when I entered the building. I should have expected as much from the disobliging man. A uniformed officer sat at a desk and looked up when I entered. He smiled at me, which was nominally encouraging. I smiled back.

"May I help you, ma'am?"

"Um, I need to speak to Detective Rotondo." I glanced around uncertainly. I'd never been in a police station before, and it made me nervous, like I was a crook or something. It even crossed my mind that this might be some kind of ruse on Rotondo's part to lure me into his clutches so that they could clap the cuffs on me and fling me in a cell to rot for telling fortunes.

I gave myself a mental shake. There was no sense getting hysterical about this. I was only doing as Rotondo had asked me. He ought to be glad of my cooperation, not yearning for my capture, for heaven's sake.

Still smiling, the uniform said, "Yes, ma'am. If you'll follow that hallway, Detective Rotondo's office is the second one on the right."

He had an office all to himself? Shoot, I was impressed in spite of myself. "Thank you."

I followed the man's instructions. As soon as I knocked at the second door on the right down the corridor, I rescinded my impressedness. A chorus of voices, some sounding cranky, shouted, "Come in!"

Pushing the door open, I saw that this office contained several occupants. Rotondo's desk was the largest, and it sat against the far wall, beneath a window. That looked to me like the best place to be if you had to share an office, from which I deduced that Rotondo was in charge of this particular mob. A shiny wooden plaque on his desk said in gilt letters "Detective Samuel Rotondo." So. He was a Sam. I supposed he looked as much like a Sam as anything else.

When he looked up from whatever he'd been reading at his desk and saw me, he frowned. Not a particularly auspicious greeting and one that irked me. It hadn't been my idea to spy on the Kincaids.

The other three men in the room rose from their chairs politely. Rotondo did, too, eventually. "Mrs. Majesty." He didn't move.

I didn't, either. "You told me to tell you if I heard anything." I said it loudly, from the open doorway. Detective Sam Rotondo wasn't the only one present who could be rude.

His dark eyebrows lifted. "You mean, you *did* hear something?"

"Yes. And I came here to tell you about it." I'd have

liked to try to make him feel guilty about making me trek all the way to the police station to do him a favor, but since I lived only a few blocks away I didn't think I could carry that one off with anything akin to aplomb.

"Please," he said, at last sounding courteous if not friendly, "come over here and take a seat. I appreciate you coming."

I swished over to the chair he pulled out. It was old and shabby, I couldn't help but notice, from which I deduced the police department didn't spend money on inessentials. I guess I approved of that. I sat with a deliberate flounce, for which I was clad appropriately (my dark blue skirt had a small, tasteful ruffle around the bottom), laid my tiny handbag in my lap, and folded my gloved hands upon it. I felt quite dignified. "I was right."

One of Rotondo's dark eyebrows twitched. He was a darned good-looking man. I tried not to notice. "About what?"

"It's not Mr. Farrington. It's Mr. Kincaid."

Silence. Rotondo scratched his nose. "Ah, I think you'd better explain that one to me, Mrs. Majesty."

Probably. I cleared my throat. "There are bonds missing."

"Bonds?"

"Bearer bonds. From the bank." Was the man being deliberately obtuse? "And Mr. Farrington thinks Mr. Kincaid is the culprit."

"The culprit?"

I nodded, wondering if he was going to question every other noun I uttered.

"Cute word." He didn't sound as if he meant it. "Did Mr. Farrington tell you this?"

"No." Bother. I was going to have to confess to eavesdropping. "I overheard a conversation between him and Mr. Harold Kincaid."

"Where? I mean, where did this conversation take place?"

"What does it matter?"

He rubbed a hand over his face. You'd have thought he thought I was trying to be difficult, and I wasn't, darn it all.

"I need to know the circumstances. Often circumstances mean a lot when it comes to conversations. Believe it or not, sometimes people tell us what they think we want to hear instead of the truth."

"You can't say that about this conversation, because I wasn't a participant in it and they didn't know I was listening." That didn't sound very good, but it was true.

"I see. And when did this conversation take place?" he asked, trying again for an answer.

"Last night."

"And where did it take place?"

I was beginning to feel stupid, baiting him this way. But he was *such* an aggravating man. "Mr. Harold Kincaid's house in San Marino."

Rotondo's eyebrows lifted. "You were at Mr. Kincaid's home? And why was that, Mrs. Majesty?"

I braced myself for his sarcasm. "I was conducting a séance for Harold and some of his friends."

"Oh." Not a sneer in sight. I took heart. "You say he owns his own house in San Marino?"

"Yes. He has a beautiful home there."

"I can imagine." His tone was dry. I couldn't fault him for that. When I talked about rich people, I was apt to be a little dry, too. "Who was there?"

"What does *that* matter?"

He sighed heavily. "This matter is one of great importance, Mrs. Majesty. I'm not asking these questions for my own amusement. We're trying to get to the bottom of a potentially ruinous financial situation; one that will affect hundreds of people, if the rumors are true. In order to determine the value of your information, or of any information, I need to get all the facts. Surely you can understand that?"

I could, although I didn't want to. I just *hated* having to capitulate to common sense when it came from someone who didn't like me. "I don't remember all their names. They were Harold's friends."

"I see. Ladies and gentlemen?"

I eyed him suspiciously. He didn't look at me, but concentrated on taking notes on a lined pad with a pencil. "They were all men."

That caught his attention. His head jerked up and he squinted at me. "I'm surprised your husband allows you to work for men, Mrs. Majesty."

I shrugged. I'd be darned if I'd tell him how much Billy disapproved of my conducting a séance for Harold. "These men are not any sort of threat, Detective Rotondo. They're all perfect gentlemen."

He grunted. "They're faggots, is what you're telling me. I'd suspected as much."

"Were you in the army?" I asked, genuinely curious—because of that word, you know.

"No." He seemed a little uncomfortable, probably because there'd been a lot of abuse heaped upon men who hadn't volunteered when the Great War began.

I have to admit that I shared some of the general contempt. It was probably unfair of me, but you have to remember what had happened to Billy. If more men had volunteered, maybe it would have happened to one of them and spared my husband. The phrase "chocolate cream soldier" flitted through my brain. Rotondo seemed to read my mind.

Roughly, he said, "I was unable to enlist because my wife was too ill at the time to be left alone. I had to take care of her."

His *wife*? For some reason, I'd never, ever, not once considered the possibility that Sam Rotondo might be married, although I don't know why. I suppose he was in his early thirties at the time, certainly old enough to be married and have a dozen kids, and I felt a vague and entirely inappropriate stab of disappointment.

But his wife was sick. Since I knew what that was like, some of my hostility toward the man softened, albeit not a whole lot. "I'm sorry about your wife. I hope she's better now."

His expression hardened. I went stiff, anticipating the worst. "She passed away shortly after we moved to California."

I swallowed, sorry to have had my anticipation confirmed. "I'm very sorry. What was the trouble?"

"Tuberculosis." Short and sweet. And almost always deadly.

And not unusual, unfortunately. The white plague was rampant. What with wars, influenza, and consumption, a body didn't stand a chance in those days. You had to be tough to grow up and live to a ripe old age. I shook my head. "I'm really sorry, Detective Rotondo. It's so hard to see someone waste away like that." I knew it for a fact.

He peered at me suspiciously. I tried not to resent it. "Yeah. Thanks. But you're not here to talk about my wife."

True, if rude. "Of course not."

He cleared his throat. "So, you overheard Farrington and Kincaid talking about the bank. What exactly did you hear?"

"Mr. Farrington said he'd conducted an internal audit and discovered some bearer bonds missing. I don't know how many, but he said they amounted to thousands of dollars and could be cashed in by anybody." I wish I could find a couple of those bonds in the street one day. Finding something and rescuing it from being run over couldn't be considered stealing, could it?

"Hmmm."

I waited, but that was it. He was scribbling madly in his notebook. Impatient, I said, "Well? Is that what your own information has turned up?"

He didn't look up. "Did you overhear anything else?"

I was offended, both because he didn't answer my question and because he wouldn't look at me. "I'll tell you more when you answer my question."

At last he lifted his head. He was frowning again. No surprise there. "Mrs. Majesty, surely you can understand that I can't discuss the case with you."

"You *what*?" I jumped up from the chair, which precipitated a reaction from the rest of the men in the room, which disconcerted me. But...Gee whiz, this wasn't fair. I sat down again and decided I'd better whisper. "Darn it, you expect me to be your little spy, but you won't tell me anything!"

He heaved another one of those irritating sighs that tell a person how annoying she's being for no reason at all, even though there was a very good reason, and I wasn't trying to be annoying. I was trying to *help*. And I really hoped my assistance would lead to Mr. Eustace Kincaid being locked up for a hundred years or so. Then I could have Rolly advise Mrs. Kincaid to divorce the miserable man and marry somebody nice.

Okay, so I know divorce is scandalous and bad and evil and all that, I still think it's better than being tied to a criminal—and an unpleasant one at that—for decades without recourse. I also knew Mrs. Kincaid was an Episcopalian, because of the Father Frederick connection, and they were pretty stuffy about most things. But I didn't think they'd excommunicate a person like the Catholics do if she got divorced. Maybe I was wrong.

"Listen, Mrs. Majesty. I *do* appreciate your help. But I still can't divulge particulars of the case with you. The information we have is confidential. We can't chat with every Tom, Dick, and Harry about it."

"I'm not any Tom, Dick, or Harry, blast you! I just spied for you! Against my better judgment, too, darn it, and I'll bet I gave you valuable information. And you won't tell me anything! I don't blab, if that's what's worrying you." I felt like calling him names, but didn't think that would suit my dignified demeanor.

I could tell he'd started gritting his teeth because his jaw protruded. "I should think," he said in a disagreeable, measured voice, "that any right-thinking citizen would be happy to assist the police in their work and in the apprehension of criminals. This case is important, Mrs. Majesty. It involves a lot of money and may well affect a lot of people if we can't stop whatever's happening in the bank."

"I know that! That's the only reason I agreed to spy for you!"

"Will you stop calling it spying?" His voice had risen.

"No!" So had mine. "That's what it is! And you're expecting me to spill my guts to you when you won't tell me a thing."

"Pipe down, will you?"

Now that was unfair. He'd shouted first. I didn't point it out, because it had occurred to me that if I riled him too much, he'd stop asking for my help, and I'd be out of the picture entirely and never learn all the best dirt about this situation. I was still incensed, though.

He spoke first, so I didn't have to think up another good reason for him to tell me what was going on. "All right. I'll tell you as much as I can."

Success! Boy, that didn't happen often.

He leaned over his desk. I leaned over from the other side until our heads almost touched. I knew how to be confidential. Shoot, my entire livelihood was based on confidences and keeping them.

"The information you've supplied today confirms what we'd expected. A teller at the bank came in to the station last week, almost shaking with worry and fear, claiming he'd been unable to find some bearer bonds." His dark eyes narrowed into a squint that he directed at me. I tried not to react, although his eyes were really beautiful, which I considered (and still consider) unfair. His eyelashes were dark and long. Stacy Kincaid would kill for lashes like that. "The teller seems to think your Mr. Farrington might be to blame."

"He's *not* my Mr. Farrington, and the teller is wrong."

I knew it. It burned me up that Rotondo didn't. I suspected, too, that his doubt about Mr. Farrington was based not on anything real or tangible, but because poor Mr. Farrington was a "faggot." Nuts. I guess being a spiritualist broadens your mind, because I didn't think it was fair to judge people just because they were different from you. Heck, Mr. Kincaid wasn't one of "those" people, and he rotten to the core. Mr. Farrington *was* one of them, and he was a sweetheart. Just went to show that you never could tell.

"We'll see," said the detective unconvincingly.

I wouldn't let him get away with that. We were still hunched together, so I whispered as harshly as I could without being overheard, "Mr. Farrington is *not* guilty. You'd better not try to railroad him, either!"

That got to him with a vengeance. His voice actually shook when he growled, "We are servants of the public, and we do not *railroad* people, Mrs. Majesty. I'm trying to get to the bottom of the bank mess."

Glad I'd riled him, I settled back in my chair and sniffed. "We'll just have to wait see about that, won't we?"

I'll bet he'd have run his hands through his hair or jumped up and stamped his feet if we'd been in a private place. His fellow policemen were in the room (and surreptitiously watching us, if I'm any judge of these things—and I am) so he couldn't.

His jaw bunched some more. "Did you hear anything else that might be of use to us, Mrs. Majesty?"

I thought hard. "I don't think so. Only that Mr. Farrington is sure Mr. Harold Kincaid's father is behind the disappearance of the bonds, and Harold agrees with him."

Rotondo's eyebrows arched like little fuzzy caterpillars over his pretty brown eyes. "Why would the younger Mr. Kincaid say something like that?"

"Probably because he knows his father." I sniffed again.

He cocked his head at me. "You don't seem to care much for Mr. Kincaid, Mrs. Majesty."

"Perceptive of you."

"May I ask why?"

"Sure, you can ask."

It pleased me to see his jaw bulge again. "Would you mind answering?"

Well, now, that presented a problem. I'd promised Edie that I wouldn't say anything about Mr. Kincaid's pursuit of her. It galled me that I never broke my promises. Every now and then honor and ethics can be a pain in the neck. "He's rude, mean, insensitive, and he treats his wife badly." There. That took care of it all, although not as specifically as I'd have liked.

"In what way does he treat his wife badly?"

Trust this man to pry. "I'm not at liberty to say." I thought for a second and added, "Although the word 'liberty' might offer a clue."

After a minute, it did, and I saw the light dawn in Rotondo's eyes. I might not have liked him much, but I couldn't say he was a stupid man.

I left the police station feeling as though I'd done my civic duty. Now I only hoped the Pasadena Police Department in general, and Detective Samuel Rotondo in particular, would use my information, cast aside their prejudices, and arrest the right man.

 CHAPTER 10

They didn't. I might have expected as much. I also had a sinking feeling that at least part of the disaster ensuing from this failure had its roots in my spilling the beans to Quincy.

The telephone rang about 8:30 the next morning. Ma and Aunt Vi had already gone off to work, Billy was on the sun porch enjoying the late spring weather, and Pa was God knew where. Probably having breakfast at a café with some of his cronies or walking Brownie around the neighborhood. Pa loved to ride horses. Even though he'd always made his living with automobiles, he rued the day the horse had become passé as a means of transportation in the city. Needless to say, Brownie didn't share his opinion.

I'd been in the living room dusting the furniture and sweeping the carpet with the old carpet sweeper Aunt Vi had brought home from Mrs. Kincaid's house a couple of years earlier. As soon as I heard the telephone, I raced from the living room to the kitchen, knowing that everybody else on the party line would already be there even though it had been our ring. I harbored a faint hope that I could forestall the calling party from hanging up from sheer bewilderment.

Sure enough, when I picked up the receiver, I heard Harold Kincaid's voice communing with Mrs. Barrow and Mrs. Lynch and Mrs. Pollard and Mrs. Mayweather, all of whom were on our line and all of whom were probably already busily plotting gossip about Daisy Majesty getting a telephone call from a man.

I sighed and butted in. "Hi, everyone. It's for me, Daisy Majesty." The clicks of three receivers being hung up sounded like a telegraph message in my ear. I waited for Mrs. Barrow's click in vain. "Mrs. Barrow? This call is for me." Mrs. Barrow's click was perniciously loud. But she was off the wire.

"Harold? Is that you?"

"Oh, God, Daisy, you've got to come over to Mother's right away!"

I did? "What's the matter? Is your mother sick? Oh, Harold, she hasn't had a stroke or anything, has she?"

"A stroke? No. Why would you think that?"

Thank God. I'd hate it if Mrs. Kincaid got sick. "Well, you sound so upset. I just wondered."

"You can rest assured about her health. It isn't that bad. At least I don't think it is. The fact is, my father has disappeared."

I was so astonished, my mouth fell open and I couldn't think of a single thing to say. *It's about time* didn't seem appropriate, even if neither Harold nor I liked his father much.

"Daisy? Are you there? Don't you disappear on me, too."

I swallowed hard. "Er, yes, I'm here. I'm sorry, Harold. I was just so—so shocked. What do you mean he's disappeared?"

"Just what I said. He was here last night, and he isn't here this morning."

"But where'd he go?" I'd have bet, if anyone cared, that

the villain had taken off with the bearer bonds.

"If I knew where he'd gone, he wouldn't have disappeared, would he?"

I could tell Harold was getting exasperated, but I didn't know what to do about his present problem. "But...but, Harold, people don't just *disappear*."

"My old man did. What's more, he's evidently taken a lot of assets from the bank with him."

Aha! I'd been right.

"But it's worse than that, Daisy."

"What could be worse than that?" Sweet Lord in heaven, he hadn't kidnapped Edie, had he? I couldn't ask.

"Quincy Applewood has disappeared, too."

I thought my ears had deceived me. "Um, I beg your pardon?"

"Quincy Applewood. You know, the lad who parked cars for me last night. He's gone, too."

"He's gone where?"

"How the hell should I know?" Harold's voice had risen. I pictured him mopping his damp brow with a fine embroidered handkerchief.

"I'm sorry, Harold. But...Quincy? I can't feature Quincy just disappearing. What about Edie?"

"That's another thing. I presume it was Miss Marsh whom my father had been bothering." He must have heard me suck in air, because he went on, "I don't want to go into it right now, Daisy, but Father and Quincy had a huge fight last night. They're both gone this morning, and everyone seems to think Quincy had something to do with Father's disappearance."

"Good heavens." I could scarcely take it in. Since I was feeling faintish, I grabbed one of the chairs shoved in at the kitchen table and hauled it over to sit in. Then I sat.

"You might say that," Harold said dryly.

"But, Harold, I can't imagine Quincy doing anything to

your father."

"Truth to tell, I can't, either, but Stacy's hysterical and keeps screeching that he murdered Father and buried the body in the foothills."

"She *what*?"

"You heard me."

I'd heard him, all right. What's more, I believed him. If there were any justice in the world, and we all know there isn't, Stacy Kincaid would have been drowned at birth, before she'd had a chance to grow up and spread. "Good Lord."

"Yeah. And then there's your friend Detective Rotondo—"

"He's not my friend!"

"Whoever he is, he's here and he's got ideas of his own that sound mighty similar to Stacy's. Mother's hysterical, Stacy's throwing fits and tantrums and being a general nuisance, poor Del is out of his mind with worry about the bank, Father Frederick is wringing his hands, and poor Algie Pinkerton is in the drawing room crying with Mother. I need you, Daisy! You're the only sane person I know!"

That was a nice thing to say. I glanced down at my pretty-but-almost-worn-out pink-checked house dress, covered at the moment with a white apron. I had a scarf tied around my hair to keep the dust out, and was wearing low-heeled tie-up work shoes with black stockings. I looked exactly like a hotel maid, in actual fact. I could just see myself dashing into the Kincaid mansion looking like this. Featherstone would probably bar the door against me.

"Give me half an hour, Harold. I need to tidy up."

He agreed to it, urged me to greater speed, and we disconnected the wire.

Oh, boy, wasn't Billy going to love this? With a heavy sigh and a heavier heart, I hung up my apron, put the feather duster back on the hook after shaking it out over the rose bushes (I had planned to water them to get the dust off but would have to postpone that chore), and went into the bedroom.

Billy had been reading the newspaper, but he'd also been watching the bedroom door and saw me come in. The paper crinkled to his lap. "What's up, Daisy?" There was an edge to his voice already.

I could see no way to avoid the truth, so I went over and kissed him. "That was Harold Kincaid. There's trouble at the mansion." Hoping to ease Billy's mind, I gave a huge tragic gesture that was so big and so dramatic, I'd hoped he'd think it was funny.

He didn't. "Yeah? What kind of trouble?"

Sensing that he wasn't going to be mollified no matter what I did—sometimes he got that way; you know, he took exception to everything because he was already in a bad mood and wasn't going to let anybody or anything cheer him up—I unbuttoned my dress and hung it up. "His father's disappeared."

"What?"

Glancing at my husband from over my shoulder, I realized that my explanation had been so abrupt and outrageous that it had knocked his bad mood for a loop. I decided to keep this approach in mind for future use. "Harold said his old man's done a bunk. Poor Mrs. Kincaid is fit to be tied, of course." I opted not to mention the Quincy angle. That was too—too—I don't know. Outrageous, I guess.

"How can anybody just up and disappear?"

I'd have shrugged, except that I'd already slipped my light-blue seersucker summer dress over my head and my shoulders were occupied in getting it on. "I don't know, but I aim to find out. Harold asked me to go over there because his mother claims she needs me." That wasn't too much of a lie.

"And I don't?"

Here we went again. I turned, trying to keep my voice

at a placating tone. "Billy, I love you more than anything or anybody else in the entire universe. You know that. I've loved you all my life. But I'm wildly curious about what's going on at the Kincaids'. Besides, Mrs. Kincaid's my best customer. She's always been very generous to me, and I'd like to be there for her when she's in trouble."

He grunted and went back to his newspaper. I decided it wouldn't get any better than that, so I finished dressing, fixed my hair as well as it could be fixed, considering it had been smashed under a scarf since I woke up. It was lucky that all proper ladies wore hats in those days, since hats covered a multitude of sins. I selected a perky straw number with blue flowers on it.

Then, of course, I had to start the darned Model T. Pudge was in school. Billy couldn't crank from his wheelchair. Well, he could, but I wouldn't let him because it was too dangerous. Too many people had broken their arms cranking automobile engines, and Billy's lung power was unpredictable. If it gave out when he was cranking, there was no telling what disaster might ensue. It was my great good luck to spot Pa walking down the street, sans Brownie, and whistling. God bless my parents. They were so wonderful.

"Pa!"

He waved. "How's my girl?"

"Fine, but I need you to crank for me!"

He did it. He was such a good sport, especially when I told him about Mr. Kincaid's disappearance. Now Pa, unlike Billy, could appreciate a good piece of gossip when it presented itself. I promised I'd fill him in on all the dirt as soon as I could.

It wasn't much longer than half an hour later that I drove through the Kincaids' gigantic black iron gates, waved a hello at Jackson, and guided the Model T to the garage/stables in the back.

James, Quincy's fellow stable boy, ran out to greet me.

He opened the door and didn't even wait for me to get out of the machine before he said, "God, Daisy, you won't believe what's going on here today!"

"Yes, I would. Harold called me and asked me to get here as soon as I could. What's this about Quincy?"

Shaking his head and looking more worried than I'd ever seen him, James said, "Search me. He's gone. And so's the old man." James lowered his voice. "I hear they had a hell of a spat last night. Edie said you could hear them yelling all over the house. I know the old man fired Quincy, too. Edie told me first thing this morning." He wiped his forehead with a bandanna. "Brother, is *she* upset."

"I can imagine." This sounded even worse than I'd expected it to. "I'll see what I can find out, James."

He saluted. "Thanks, Daisy."

I entered the house through the back door because I wanted to see if Aunt Vi knew any more than James did. She didn't. She was in an even worse state than she'd been in when Stacy'd been arrested, however.

"Oh, Daisy!" Floury hands and all, she dashed over and hugged me hard. "It's just awful!"

It was going to be awful trying to get the flour off my blue summer frock. I couldn't be angry with Aunt Vi, though. Heck, she was responsible for my current pretty good income, in an odd way.

Gently attempting to disengage her hands before they'd done too much damage, I said soothingly, "I'll do what I can, Aunt Vi. I'd better get in there now."

She took the hint about letting go of me, although not about ceasing to touch me. Patting me on the back, spreading flour dust everywhere, she whispered brokenly, "You're a good girl, Daisy. You mean so much to Mrs. Kincaid. I'd say good riddance to that louse of a husband of hers, except that she's so upset about it." She sniffled hugely. "And *Quincy*! Oh, Daisy, I can't imagine that he had anything to do with Mr. Kincaid's disappearance."

"Neither can I, Vi. I'll let you know what I find out."

I managed to escape not too much later, but had to duck into the servants' bathroom to repair the flour damage to my person. My face didn't actually look all that bad, since the flour made me appear even more ghostly than usual, and that was a good thing. My poor dress was another matter, although I eventually decided it would have to do. It was about a shade lighter than it had been before Aunt Vi's attack, but the flour had pretty much sunk in and I didn't think it would shed on the furniture.

As soon as I opened the bathroom door, Edie jumped me.

"Oh, *Daisy*!"

At least Edie wasn't covered in flour. She'd been crying, though. Still was, for that matter, and I envisioned my shoulders turning stiff with glue made from salt tears and bread flour. I hugged her. "It'll all work out, Edie. I'm sure Quincy didn't do anything wrong."

"Of course he didn't!"

She sounded angry that I'd even mentioned it, evidently taking my reassurance as an indication that I thought Quincy was a killer, which it wasn't. Heck, I was only trying to make her feel better. "I know, I know. Here, Edie, try to calm down. Harold asked me to come over. I guess I'd better get to where he and Mrs. Kincaid are."

Gripping my hands so hard I feared my bones were going to break, Edie gasped out, "Come to see me later, Daisy. You have to tell me what the police are saying about all this. And what they're going to do."

"Sure. I'll be happy to, Edie." Thank God, she let my hands go.

"I'll be making beds upstairs for the next hour or so. After that, I'll probably be working downstairs."

She wiped her eyes, spun around, and charged up the back staircase, presumably to make beds and dust furniture. I was beginning to think everyone in the Kincaid house that morning had gone crazy.

The commotion hit me before I was halfway down the hall to the drawing room.

"He's dead! I know it! He killed him! I know it!" Stacy's voice had squealed this incomprehensible sentence (I mean, what "he" was she talking about?), and it sounded as if she was enjoying herself.

"Shut up!" Harold's voice. He clearly wasn't enjoying anything at all about this latest wrinkle in the fabric of family life. He also sounded powerless, as if he didn't anticipate anything he did or said to have an effect on his pill of a sister.

"Oh, oh, oh!" Mrs. Kincaid's voice. She was obviously on Harold's side, although she'd never scold her daughter, which was a dirty shame in the opinion of my humble self.

"Please, Miss Kincaid. Try to keep your voice down." Father Frederick to Stacy, sounding exasperated.

"How can you even ask me that? He's *dead*, I tell you!" Stacy. Screeching at full volume.

"Oh, God! Oh, God!" I think that was Algie Pinkerton, but I wasn't certain.

"Can we all calm down for a minute? I have to conduct an investigation." And *that*, I'm sure I need not say, was Detective Samuel Rotondo. His voice was deep and icy and reminded me of granite and steel and other hard, impervious things, coated with a layer of frost.

Pausing before the door, I braced myself. While I really wanted to hear the dope from the horse's mouth, as it were, I hated scenes and wasn't looking forward to witnessing Mrs. Kincaid's honest grief or Stacy Kincaid's dishonest hysterics.

Bracing didn't work, so I decided what the heck and pushed the door open. Everyone inside the room froze, then turned to see who'd interrupted the fun. The reactions were interesting.

Mrs. Kincaid gasped and bounded to her feet, clasping her hands to her bosom, and looking at me as if I were part of the second coming.

Harold's chin dropped to his chest and I thought I heard him whisper, "Thank God."

Mr. Farrington gaped as if he'd never seen me before. He looked almost as good gaping as he did when he wasn't.

Father Frederick smiled. I think he crossed himself, but I don't really remember.

Algie Pinkerton blinked at the door. Tears rushed down his cheeks and dripped from his chin.

Stacy Kincaid looked as if she was offended about being interrupted during one of her more stimulating performances.

Detective Samuel Rotondo turned, saw me standing there, and barked, "Mrs. Majesty. Do you *live* here?"

That broke the ice for me, darn the man. I stepped into the room and would have slammed the door behind me except that I didn't want to upset Mrs. Kincaid any more than she was already upset. "I was asked to come."

He grunted and turned back to Harold, whom he'd presumably been harassing. As I walked toward the sofa, I recalled the last time I'd been here. It hadn't been very many days ago, and I vividly remembered the tarot cards predicting chaos in Mrs. Kincaid's life. Almost made me believe in the cards.

At the moment, however, I only wanted to be of some comfort to her, so I ignored Rotondo's black look and sarcastic comment and took Mrs. Kincaid's hand. "I'm so sorry, Mrs. Kincaid. Please let me help in any way if I can."

She threw her arms around me and cried on my shoulder. Again, I featured my dress turning into paste, but didn't let her go. Poor woman needed some kind of comfort, and obviously her daughter wasn't going to be of any assistance in that quarter. In fact, Stacy had resumed pitching her fit as soon as I'd entered the room. I'd have liked to slap her across the face but didn't dare. Besides, my hands were occupied in patting Stacy's mother on the back.

"It will all be all right, Mrs. Kincaid. I'm sure it will."

"Oh, Daisy! The cards told me this would happen!"

My thought precisely, although I didn't say so. "They predicted peace in the future, though. Try to focus on that."

"Oh, for God's sake, give it up, Daisy!"

This precious tidbit came from Stacy, naturally. I glanced over to find her with her hands planted on her hips, as mad as a wet hen, probably because I'd interrupted her act.

"You give it up, Stacy," said her not-so-fond brother. To no avail.

She turned on her heel—her high heel, supported by a strap around her ankle, which also sported a gold chain—and screamed at him, "How can you *say* that? Our father has been *murdered*! You cruel, unfeeling brute!"

Stacy's ill-advised shriek caused Mrs. Kincaid to sob, "No! No! Stacy, don't say it!"

"It's true!" wailed the girl, working herself up into another frenzied exhibition. "Our father is gone, and Quincy Applewood murdered him!"

"I don't think so," I slipped in between cries of woe from various parties. I don't think anybody heard me but Stacy.

She turned on me like a whirlwind, and I couldn't get out of her way because Mrs. Kincaid was too heavy. Not that I'd have pushed Mrs. Kincaid away or used her body as a shield or anything, but I felt extremely vulnerable just then.

"What do *you* know about it?" Stacy squawked.

"You're nothing but a two-bit shyster!"

I noticed that Detective Rotondo had shut his eyes and appeared pained. Fat lot of good that did.

God bless Harold, who'd apparently taken all he aimed to take from his darling sister that morning. "Don't you *ever* talk to Daisy like that!" He delivered a resounding slap across Stacy's face along with his message, and I was deeply touched. Not to mention gladdened beyond all mercy. All right, I know it wasn't very Christian of me, but how much abuse is one smallish, youngish spiritualist expected to take, anyway?

Clapping a hand over her stinging cheek, Stacy gaped with bulging eyes at her brother, clearly not having anticipated anyone ever going this far in an effort to subdue her. Too bad, if you ask me. If she'd been thwarted more when she was young, she probably wouldn't be such a pain in the neck now.

She cried, "Oh!" and turned and raced out the door.

Harold sighed and faced Rotondo. "Sorry, Detective. Do you need her here? I can get her back if you need her."

Rotondo shook his head. "No. We're probably better off without her. She's a trifle…disruptive."

"You're a true master of diplomacy," muttered Harold. He came over to me, who was still being almost smothered by his mother. Disengaging her clinging arms with remarkable gentleness—more gentleness, I'm sure, than a so-called "real" man would use—he said in a soothing voice, "Here, Mother. You're drowning Daisy in tears. Come over to the sofa and sit down. Daisy will sit beside you."

I nodded when he glanced at me. What a great guy he was. "Absolutely," I said to Mrs. Kincaid. "I'm here for as long as you need me." I was sure glad Billy wasn't there to hear that one.

"Oh, Daisy, you're such a comfort to me!" Mrs. Kincaid fairly collapsed on the sofa. I patted her left hand which is the one that had been gripping my right hand painfully. I didn't complain.

I resented it when I looked up and saw Detective Rotondo eyeing the ceiling in obvious exasperation.

Harold expelled a huge, relieved sigh. "All right. Now that Stacy's not here to throw tantrums and interfere with everything, let's get this show on the road. Detective, you were asking about Father?"

Rotondo, beyond a doubt, hadn't expected such a take-charge attitude from Harold, a "faggot." I did. I thought Harold was a true gem among men. "Er, yes. Thank you, Mr. Kincaid." He cleared his throat. "So, you say that an argument was overheard taking place between Mr. Eustace Kincaid and the stable boy? Quincy Applewood?"

"Yes."

"Approximately when did this transpire?"

He looked at Harold, who shrugged and said, "Darned if I know. I wasn't here. Mother?" He eyed his mother in some concern.

Mrs. Kincaid had calmed down since my entrance. Take *that*, Detective Samuel Rotondo!

"I, ah, don't recall exactly. It was after midnight. I think it was after midnight."

"I see. And who was present during the argument?"

"Nobody. I mean, my husband and Mr. Applewood were the only ones there. The rest of us only heard it when the two men started yelling at each other." She sobbed. I squeezed her hand and glared at Rotondo, who wasn't impressed. As usual.

"Who else was in the house at the time?"

Mrs. Kincaid looked blank. "Who was in the house? Why, um, I..." Her voice trailed off, which was just as well since it didn't seem to be doing her any good.

"Were the maids and Featherstone here, Mother?" Harold asked, trying to be helpful.

"Oh. Oh, of course. Yes. I see what you mean."

She sat up straighter and the gears in her brain started a slow crank into thought. You could practically hear her brain gears scraping against each other, since they hadn't been greased since God knew when. I got the feeling Mrs. Kincaid had never been forced to do much thinking in her life, and that she was frightened when asked to do some now. Truth to tell, and I know it's not a very respectful thing to say, but she was a scatterbrained woman. I'm sure it's because nobody'd ever expected her to be anything else.

As a rule, I don't much care for scatty women, probably because I've had to work so hard and think so much all my life. But Mrs. Kincaid was one of the world's kindest, most generous people, and I liked her for it, even if she wasn't the brightest person in the world.

"Um, well, I'm sure Featherstone was here, because when I went downstairs to see what the matter was, he was there, too, in his bathrobe and slippers."

Boy, wouldn't I have liked to see *that*. Imagine: Featherstone in human clothes. The mind fairly boggled.

Mrs. Kincaid strained to think some more. I almost felt sorry for her, because I could tell how difficult the process was for her. "Um, Edie Marsh was here, I'm certain, because she sleeps upstairs in the maid's room. James Howard, the other stable boy, must have been here. He and Quincy sleep in the loft over the stables. Slept, I mean. Oh, dear!"

She started crying again. Again I glared at Rotondo. Again, he ignored me.

"So no one else was on the premises during the argument?"

Mrs. Kincaid shook her head. "N-n-no. I don't think so. Jackson, the gate keeper, goes home at night."

"Is the gate locked before he leaves?"

Mrs. Kincaid's vacant stare answered that question, so

Rotondo aimed the same question at Harold. Harold said, "I have a key. Jackson makes sure the gate's locked against intruders."

"I see." Rotondo appeared to contemplate locked gates for a moment. Now he, I judged, thought all the time and the process didn't hurt his brain as it did poor Mrs. Kincaid's. "How many people have keys to the gate?"

Again Harold interpreted his mother's vacant expression. "I have one. My father has one. I'm sure Jackson has one, since he mans the gate during the day. Don't know about anybody else, except Stacy. I'm sure she has one, although I don't think she ought to." He glanced at his mother and decided not to explain his reason for wanting to rescind Stacy's key privileges.

"So," said Rotondo, sounding as if he didn't approve, "that makes four keys and possibly more."

Harold shrugged. "I guess."

Rotondo decided to drop the key issue for the nonce and returned his attention to Mrs. Kincaid, who flinched as if he'd struck her. I squeezed her hand to let her know I'd protect her from the big, bad policeman. "You said that you went downstairs when you heard the commotion?"

"Yes. By the time I got my robe and slippers on and— and did some other things—"

I'd have been willing to wager that she'd had to wipe off her face cream and remove her wrinkle eradicators and perform other tasks of a like nature, which she didn't want to talk about. I can't imagine that any woman would.

"What other things?" Trust Rotondo to pry into things that were personal and didn't matter.

Mrs. Kincaid flapped a hand in the air. "Oh, just things."

Irked, I snapped, "What difference does it make? She probably had some personal matters to attend to before leaving her room."

"Yes. That's it," Mrs. Kincaid sniffled. "Personal matters."

This time it was Rotondo glaring. At me. I tried to ignore him as well as he'd ignored me, but don't think I succeeded. I'm too emotional to ignore people properly, being more apt to holler at them. I did, however, glare back, which had about the same result as it ever had.

"I'd prefer Mrs. Kincaid to answer my questions, if you don't mind, Mrs. Majesty."

"Darn it, no woman likes to talk about personal things with the police, Detective!"

His nose wrinkled, but he didn't take me up on my offer to quarrel. Rather, he returned his attention to Mrs. Kincaid. "So, did your husband tell you what the argument was about?"

Good Lord in heaven, I hoped he hadn't. This dear, stupid woman didn't need the agony of discovering her husband was an unfaithful satyr while she was trying to digest the fact that he'd taken it on the lam with assets from the bank he'd been charged with protecting.

"No." She shook her head hard.

"But you went downstairs to ask him about it?"

"Well, yes, but his office door was locked. He...he didn't tell me why they'd been shouting."

"Did it look as if there had been a physical fight as well as a verbal one?"

"Um, I didn't see him."

Rotondo squinted at her. This time I acquitted him of cruelty, since I didn't understand her answer either. "Ma'am? I thought you went downstairs to talk to him."

"I did, but he didn't unlock the office door, so I didn't go inside. Therefore, I don't know if they'd fought, although I doubt it."

"No? Why not?"

"For heaven's sake, Officer, my husband is forty years older than that poor Applewood boy, and is confined to a wheelchair. Mr. Kincaid wouldn't have stood a chance, and I don't believe for a minute that Mr. Applewood is so lost to honor that he'd attack a crippled man!"

Good for Mrs. Kincaid! She might have married a monster, but at least she could recognize goodness when she saw it. I could have sworn she smiled, but it didn't last long enough for me to tell for sure.

"I see. Did you at least ask him why their voices had been raised?"

"Oh, yes. He told me it was nothing."

"It was nothing? Shouting that was heard in the servants' quarters was nothing?"

Slumping tragically, Mrs. Kincaid sobbed, "Mr. Kincaid told me it was none of my business!"

I hugged her again, feeling honestly miserable on her behalf.

"I see. But you heard what the two men were yelling about?"

"Not exactly. Eventually, Mr. Kincaid shouted at poor Mr. Applewood to leave the house and never return."

"I see. And did Mr. Applewood respond to that?"

"Oh, yes. He—he—he—" Mrs. Kincaid had to pause and blow her nose. It killed me to see such a glorious piece of silken fabric used for such a purpose, although I didn't intervene. "Mr. Applewood shouted that he'd leave, but he'd be back, and Mr. Kincaid had better watch out." She couldn't continue. I remained hugging her and shooting killing glances at Rotondo, who didn't care as much as he'd ever cared about my killing glances.

"Those were his words?" Rotondo asked, totally ignoring Mrs. Kincaid's distress. "He said, 'I'll go, but I'll be back'?"

The poor woman nodded.

"You're sure he said, 'I'll be back'?"

Another nod.

"And you recall your husband telling him to get out of the house?"

"Yes. He told him he was dismissed, too, and that his services were not merely no longer needed, but totally unwanted as well. Mr. Kincaid demanded that he clear his belongings out that very night. He was very angry," Mrs. Kincaid said thickly. "Not at me. At Mr. Applewood. At least, I think he wasn't angry with me."

I caught Harold's eye. He shrugged, as if he didn't understand his mother's loyalty to a man who treated her so shabbily any more than I did. Mr. Farrington, standing at Harold's side, looked as if he might burst into tears any second. I sure hoped he wouldn't, because I was positive Rotondo would sneer at a man who cried— a man who wasn't as rich as Algie Pinkerton, that is.

"Has there ever been any animosity observed between the two men before last night?"

"No. I mean, I don't think so. Harold?" Mrs. Kincaid glanced to her son as if she expected him to throw her a life preserver and haul her to the shore.

"I'd never observed any animosity," Harold said.

"No," agreed his mother. "I'm sure there wasn't."

Since Rotondo's gaze had landed on me, I shook my head.

The detective opened his mouth, closed it again, and seemed to change his mind. "I see. Is it your opinion that Mr. Kincaid was physically hurt by this stable boy? Quincy Applewood?"

"Oh, no!" Mrs. Kincaid's huge, drowned brown eyes looked as innocent as a doe's. "I'm sure Mr. Applewood wouldn't do anything to hurt Mr. Kincaid. He's such a nice boy."

"But he and your husband shouted at each other last night," Rotondo reminded her. "And Mr. Applewood threatened your husband."

"Threatened? That wasn't..." But I thought better of my outburst and shut up. It was just as well. Rotondo looked as if he'd take great joy in flinging me in the clink for obstructing justice or something. As far as I was concerned, I wasn't obstructing anything at all. I was merely trying to make this policeman see reason.

"Yes, but...but...Oh, dear, I don't know what happened."

"Why don't you stop badgering her?" I blurted, surprising myself. I thought I was all blurted out. "Can't you see how upset she is?" It had also occurred to me that I could supply the information Rotondo needed as to why Quincy had dared confront his employer so vociferously, although it might not put Quincy in the best light. I'd be darned if I'd do it in front of Mrs. Kincaid.

"I'm sorry if my questions are perceived by some as badgering," Rotondo said through clenched teeth. He also wasn't sorry.

Thank God for Harold, who interrupted the scene at that point. "Detective, I really think my mother ought to rest now. Ah, I believe Mrs. Majesty and I might be of help to you." He waved his arms in a vague gesture. "As to...er...about Quincy Applewood and my father, I mean."

I didn't want to be of help to the man, but I didn't say so. I knew Harold was right.

Detective Rotondo must have perceived some kind of hint in Harold's suggestion, which led me to believe yet again that he wasn't as thick-headed as I'd hoped. After peering at Harold with eyes slitted up, Rotondo nodded. "Very well." He turned to Mrs. Kincaid. "I'm sorry this is so distressing for you, ma'am. I'll probably have to talk to you more later."

"Yes. Yes, thank you." She began struggling on the sofa. It didn't take me more than a second or two to understand she needed help getting up. Poor thing. So I took her arm and assisted her to her feet.

"I'll see you upstairs, Madeline." Algie Pinkerton

appeared at my side and took Mrs. Kincaid's right arm. He'd stopped crying, thank heavens.

"And I'll go, too. You don't need me here, do you, Detective? I'm sure I can be of more assistance to Mrs. Kincaid than the police."

Detective Rotondo gave Father Frederick his okay. Father Frederick fell in beside Mrs. Kincaid on her other side. "I'm sure prayer will help," he said in a well-oiled, preacherly voice. He might even have meant it. He looked sincere enough.

Thus supported on either side by men who appreciated her, unlike her sneaky-mean lizard of a husband, Mrs. Kincaid tottered out of the room. As for me, I was pondering the nature of a marriage that would lead a woman to call her husband "Mr. Kincaid" even after thirty-odd years of marriage. I know she called her friends by their first names. I'd heard her call Algie Pinkerton Algie many times, and I'd heard her call Father Frederick Freddy once or twice. But Eustace Kincaid was always "Mr. Kincaid." You figure it out. I sure couldn't.

I was extremely glad to see the three of them leave the room, though. I think I even sighed inside with relief. It didn't last long.

CHAPTER 11

As soon as the door shut behind Mrs. Kincaid, Algie Pinkerton, and Father Frederick, Rotondo focused on me as if I were a criminal he was trying to nail. I sat up straighter. "What? Why are you looking at me like that?"

"I might have known it would come down to you," said he in a nasty tone.

"What's that supposed to mean? Darn it, none of this is my fault!"

"Never mind."

"I don't know a single thing about any of this," I said coldly. "The only thing I might be able to help with is the reason Quincy Applewood and Mr. Kincaid were fighting. Er, arguing, I mean." I glanced toward Harold, silently asking his permission to tell all. Not that I knew all. He nodded, bless him.

"Oh?" I could hear the sneer in Rotondo's voice and took exception to it. There was no reason I could see why he should dislike me. Heck, he didn't even *know* me. "And why do you think they were arguing, Mrs. Majesty?"

"Because Mr. Kincaid was always trying to trap

Edie—Miss Marsh, I mean. That's Quincy's fiancée—with his wheelchair and—and touch her. I interrupted them once when he was trying to get her to kiss him." I couldn't repress a shudder.

One of Rotondo's eyebrows lifted. "Is that so?"

"Yes," I snapped, sensing his disbelief. "It is."

"Ah." He tapped his notebook with his pencil. His brow was furrowed as he stared at me, making me uncomfortable. "You say Mr. Kincaid pursued Miss Marsh in his wheelchair?"

"Yes." I didn't like the way he'd asked the question, so I lifted my chin and dared him to doubt me. Not that he needed a dare. He seemed to doubt me no matter what.

Still tapping, he said, "Mr. Kincaid needed his wheelchair to get around?"

I shrugged. "I guess so."

"And he used it in pursuit of housemaids?"

That tore it. Jumping up from the sofa, I fairly shouted, "Darn it, this isn't my fault! I'm only telling you what Edie told me and what I saw with my own eyes!"

"Calm down, Mrs. Majesty. I'm not doubting your word."

"Like heck." I sat again, though, knowing I'd spoil my family's fun if I left before I'd gleaned every tidbit I could about this latest Kincaid scandal.

"Out of curiosity, where were you last night, Mrs. Majesty?"

He already knew that, but I guess it was better that he didn't let on, since I didn't want everyone in the room to know I'd blabbed to the police. "Conducting a séance at Mr. Harold Kincaid's house."

"And where did you go after the séance concluded?"

"Home."

"Did you make any stops on your way home?" Rotondo's brow beetled.

Did this man honestly think I might have killed

Kincaid? "No!"

"No need to shout, Mrs. Majesty."

"The heck there's not! If you think I killed that old goat, you're crazy!"

"I accused you of no such thing," Rotondo said.

"You thought it."

"Nonsense."

"Nuts."

"Where did you go after the séance at the younger Mr. Kincaid's house?"

"Home. Without stopping anywhere else."

Rotondo didn't pursue my pique or his doubt about my complicity in a crime. Good thing, or I might have felt compelled to take a stand, leave in a huff, and then I'd never learn anything.

"And you say Mr. Kincaid needed a wheelchair in order to get around?"

"I don't know," I said with a crisp snap to my voice to let him know I wouldn't put up with any more guff from him, even though I planned to. "All I know is that I never saw him out of it."

"Father's health has been extremely poor these past few years, Detective," Harold slid in. "He could walk a little bit, but almost always needed his wheelchair. We installed the lift so that he wouldn't have to climb stairs."

A lift would be nice for Billy to have. Unfortunately, the Gumms of this world couldn't afford such luxuries. Anyhow, Billy'd probably pooh-pooh such a convenience. He was like that.

"I see." Rotondo hadn't removed his gaze from my humble self. "And you think Miss Marsh found Mr. Kincaid's advances unwelcome, Mrs. Majesty?"

"*What*?" I gaped at him. "Of *course* she found them unwelcome! Wouldn't you? Anyhow, she and Quincy were planning to get married as soon as Quincy had saved up enough money. Why would she welcome

advances from a miserable, ugly creature like Mr.
Kincaid?" I darted a glance at Harold, sorry that I'd
exclaimed so loudly something so unfortunately true.
Harold only grinned at me. Manifestly, he had known
his father well.

"And you think that Mr. Applewood found out about
this pursuit of Miss Marsh by Mr. Kincaid?"

I lowered my gaze and would have inspected my
fingernails, except that I was wearing gloves. "Um, I
know he found out."

"Oh? And how is that?"

With a heartfelt sigh, I admitted culpability. "Because
I let the cat out of the bag and told him. I didn't mean to.
It happened sort of by accident. At Harold's séance."

Rotondo mouth pursed into a grimace, I presume at the
word *séance*. "Oh?"

"Quincy was parking cars there. Harold and I got to
talking afterwards. That's where I found out—" Whoops.
I'd almost gone and done it again: blurted out something
I didn't want to admit. I really, really didn't want Harold
to know that I'd blabbed to Rotondo about the
conversation between Harold and Mr. Farrington that I'd
overheard at his house.

The notion that Harold might find out made me feel
defensive. Nobody wants people to think she's a sneak
and a spy. In reaction, I jumped all over Rotondo some
more. "But what I want to know is why are you asking
so darned many questions about Quincy? I thought it
was Mr. Kincaid who'd robbed his bank and run off, and
that's why we're here."

"We don't know what happened to Mr. Kincaid. And
we don't know what, if anything, has happened regarding
the bank's assets."

"Are there bearer bonds missing?" I asked loudly and,
I fear, sarcastically. If this man was going to tell me that
nothing had gone wrong with the bank after I'd spied for
him…Well, not spied, exactly, but…Oh, nuts.

"There appear to be some irregularities at the bank," Rotondo admitted.

"Involving bearer bonds." Only then did I recall that I wasn't supposed to know anything about the bearer bonds and the only reason I *did* know was because I'd overheard Harold and Del's conversation. Fiddle. I was getting very confused. When I glanced at Harold, his face appeared about as blank as a clean sheet of paper, so I guess he didn't suspect my part in anything. Rotondo's expression didn't undergo much of a change as a result of my sarcasm. In fact, he didn't seem to give a hoot. Figured. Even at the most intense of times I don't look particularly formidable. The best I can ever seem to manage is mystical.

"The fact that there might be irregularities at the bank," Rotondo went on, "doesn't negate the fact that Mr. Eustace Kincaid is missing after having had an apparently violent argument with Mr. Quincy Applewood."

"Nobody said anything about it being violent," I grumbled, expecting no one to accept my amendment. I was right.

"It is always possible that Mr. Kincaid, in an attempt to get away with bank assets, was set upon by Mr. Applewood."

"Oh, yeah? That's nonsense. Anyhow, if that happened, what happened to Quincy? Where's the money? For that matter, where's Mr. Kincaid? Corpses don't generally get up and mosey off on their own, you know."

Looking as if he'd like to swat me like a fly, Rotondo said, "If there were illicit bank assets in Mr. Kincaid's possession at the time Mr. Applewood accosted him, who's to say but that Mr. Applewood found them, realized he'd hit the jackpot, and has taken off with them."

"That's ridiculous. Quincy would never do anything

like that." And if he *had* discovered himself in sudden and illegal possession of a lot of money, he'd at least have gone back for Edie. It goes without saying that I didn't voice my thoughts.

Suddenly it occurred to me that I was defending someone I didn't really know very well. What did I actually know about Quincy Applewood? I knew that Edie Marsh was in love with him, and I trusted Edie's judgment. On the other hand, maybe her judgment was sound regarding everything but men. That sort of thing had been known to happen to other girls. Sometimes I wondered if it had happened to me, actually, although that wasn't fair. It was the war that had ruined any chances of marital bliss that Billy and I might have had.

Then I told myself to stop thinking so hard. I could almost always undermine myself if I thought too hard. "Quincy Applewood is a good man. A moral man." I hope my implied message, that Mr. Eustace Kincaid was neither of those things, came across.

Rotondo grunted, so I guess it did. "I suppose I should talk to Miss Marsh."

Oh, boy. Edie was going to kill me when she learned that it had been I who'd spilled the beans on her and Mr. Kincaid. Nevertheless, I stood up, feeling noble and willing to sacrifice myself to the cause. "Would you like me to get her for you?"

Eyeing me as if he were trying to decide what sort of evil business I was up to, Rotondo didn't answer for a minute. Then he said, "Yes. Thanks. Please let me ask any questions of Miss Marsh, Mrs. Majesty. You needn't contribute any of your own."

After shooting him a glance of withering scorn, I skedaddled out of there as fast as I could. Since I couldn't remember where Edie'd said she was going to be, but recollected something about bedrooms, I went upstairs to look for her. I was glad I'd done so after I'd peeked into the first couple of rooms. What a place that was! Suites of rooms, and lots of them. Boy, wouldn't it be something, to live in a house like that?

When you got to the head of the staircase, which branched off in both directions, there was a hallway like another entry hall, only on the second floor. Pictures of everything from the Kincaids themselves to what looked like all the lords and ladies in England, not to mention landscapes roaming with cows and horses that were so gorgeous they made me drool, graced the walls. From this picture-lined hallway to the right was a sitting room with tons of books and lots of easy chairs and a fireplace that might have been cozy had it been about a quarter of its size.

A hallway on either side of the book room led to the bedroom suites, which were arranged sort of like this: Sitting room, dressing room, bathroom, dressing room, sitting room, bedroom. There were at least three of those. There might have been more on the other side of the staircase, but I found Edie before I'd come to the end of the elegancies afforded by the Kincaid mansion's second story.

Truth to tell, any one of those upstairs bedroom suits could have swallowed our little Gumm-Majesty bungalow whole. Our entire block could have fit inside the upstairs of the Kincaid place.

Which is neither here nor there. I only mention it because it was so interesting a phenomenon to me, a Gumm.

"Edie!" I'd begun to feel lost, so perhaps my greeting was a little louder than I'd planned.

Edie screamed and spun around, her father duster clasped to her chest, her eyes wide, and her cheeks as pale as chalk. "Daisy!"

"I'm sorry, Edie. I didn't mean to scare you. But the detective wants to talk to you downstairs."

"Oh." She deflated, reminding me of a spring lily wilting on its stem. "Does he think Quincy did it?"

I didn't have to ask what "it" was. "Naw. He's only blowing smoke. We both know Quincy didn't have a thing to do with Mr. Kincaid's disappearance."

"But where is he, Daisy?"

The expression on her face was eloquent. I sure wished I had an answer for her. "I don't know, Edie, but you don't really think Quincy had anything to do with Mr. Kincaid's disappearance, do you?" She, of course, knew her boyfriend better than I did.

"I can't believe it of him."

"Well, then." Darned if I could think of anything else to say after that, so I took Edie gently by the arm and led her downstairs, relieving her of the feather duster before I opened the door to the drawing room. "I'll just put this away in the service porch," I whispered as I drew the door closed, hoping to escape before Rotondo noticed me.

I should have known better.

"Mrs. Majesty!"

Darn. Cracking the door open an inch or so, I peered into the room. Harold tossed me a wink and a grin, which was nice of him, I guess. "Yes?"

"Please don't be out of reach. I'll probably want to talk to you some more."

"I don't know why," I growled. But I added an "Okay" before he could tell me. Then I shut the door and fled to the kitchen. There I flopped into a chair and started fanning myself with the feather duster until I saw the dust fluttering therefrom. Before Aunt Vi could yell at me, I took the duster outside, shook it, and hung it on a hook on the wall of the service porch, where the iceman and the grocery people made their deliveries.

Anticipating my needs, God bless her, Aunt Vi set a nice hot cup of tea in front of me, along with two of her most delicious culinary treats in the form of buttery slices of Scotch shortbread. "Thanks, Vi. I need this."

"I expected you would." She sat across from me,

poured herself a cup of tea, and grabbed a piece of shortbread. "So what's going on, Daisy? I'm so worried about the missus."

The first bite melted in my mouth so I followed it up with another. I paused to savor both bites before answering my aunt. Aunt Vi's Scotch shortbread seemed at that moment ever so much more important than anything else that was going on in that huge, expensive house.

"Well," said I after I'd swallowed and forced my mind back to the present, where it didn't want to go, "it looks as if Mr. Kincaid's taken it on the lam with money from the bank. The detective thinks Quincy Applewood knocked Kincaid off, snatched the money, and blew town."

Aunt Vi eyed me skeptically. "Have you been reading crime novels again, Daisy?"

I gave her a toothy grin. Nobody but me appreciated my taste in literature. "Ring Lardner. Sorry, Aunt Vi. But it looks as if Mr. Kincaid's taken off with bank money—"

"*And* without his wheelchair," Aunt Vi plopped into the conversation.

I sat up straight. "He what? You say he didn't take his wheelchair?"

She gestured toward the service porch. "There it is, big as life, beside the back door. As if he'd just hopped out of it, opened the door, and escaped outside and into a waiting car."

I goggled. I'd walked right past that wheelchair as I'd gone to shake out the feather duster and hadn't even noticed it. I noticed it now. "Good heavens. Does the detective know about this?"

"Humph. What that man knows and what he doesn't know are two things *I* don't know. Nobody's bothered to ask me questions. Why ask the hired help? Do we ever know anything?"

I understood her peevish attitude, although I was sure her time was coming, and probably soon. The truth of the matter was that most of the time the hired help knew a good deal more about what was going on in these big mansions than the people who lived in them, and I'd be surprised if the police didn't know it. "I wonder if I should tell him about the wheelchair." I took another bite of shortbread to help me think.

Aunt Vi shrugged and took a big glug of tea. Glugging tea is about the only thing a hired cook can do when it comes to demonstrating displeasure; otherwise, she'd be fired. As usual, life wasn't fair.

A fuzzy memory slid into my shortbread-happy brain and floated around there for a minute before it sank into a recognizable image. It shocked me so much, I darned near dropped my second piece of shortbread. Rescuing it, I popped it into my mouth and stood up again. "I've got to go back there and tell them something. And tell them about the wheelchair, too."

"What?" Aunt Vi clearly had no idea what had gotten into me.

"I just remembered something they probably ought to know, even though they won't know what to do with it." *I* knew what to do with it. And I'd wager Mary Roberts Rinehart would know what to do with it, too. I didn't trust Detective Sam Rotondo as much as I trusted Mrs. Rinehart. However, I could but try.

She sniffed. "I hope it won't bring any more grief down onto the missus. What with that dreadful daughter of hers and that miserable husband, the poor woman can't take much more."

I thought about all the tragedies Aunt Vi had been forced to endure, and internally commended her for her big, inclusive heart. I'd wager Mrs. Kincaid didn't even know Vi had lost a son and a husband within the past couple of years. "I don't know about that, but I think they ought to know what I remembered."

"Tell me about it before you leave to go home, Daisy." The words were pleasant, but I knew a command when I heard one

"Don't worry, Vi. I won't leave you in the dark." And with a wave, I took off through the pantry and down the hall to the drawing room.

I probably didn't really need to knock, but I did. Nothing happened for a moment, then the door was yanked open from within by none other than Detective Rotondo, who looked furious. I was used to it, so his expression didn't disturb me.

"What do you want now?"

That disturbed me. I gave his outrage back to him, with interest. "For your information, I just found out something and remembered something else that might be useful in your investigation. If you're too busy to hear it, I'll just take myself off." I turned, pretending that I'd march off if his manners didn't improve.

He didn't sweeten up, but he did grab my arm to stop me from walking away. "No need for sarcasm," he muttered, opening the door wider and more or less thrusting me into the room.

Rubbing my arms pointedly—they didn't really hurt, but I'd be darned if I'd let *him* know that, I said snippily, "I'll be the judge of that."

At once I saw why he was in a twit. Harold and Mr. Farrington had left the room, so the only people there were Rotondo and Edie. Poor Edie had broken down and was weeping huge, gusty sobs into her apron. I rushed over to her, casting accusing glances at Rotondo as I went. "Edie! Has that hateful man been bully-ragging you?"

"Yes!" she whimpered.

I glowered at Rotondo who gazed at the ceiling as if he'd never understand women as long as he lived. I agreed with him on that point; I was dead-bang certain he'd never understand us, too.

"I'm not bully-ragging her. I'm trying to get some information out of her."

"You don't have to be mean about it," I pointed out.

"I'm not being mean." I heard his teeth clank together.

"I just bet."

It took a while, but at last Edie stopped crying. She subsided into painful hiccups, still holding her apron to her face, which was flushed and blotchy. Her eyes would probably take several days to un-puff.

"Do you really have to question her more now, Detective Rotondo? She's as upset as everyone else about this. You let Mrs. Kincaid off the hook. Why not Edie? Is it just because she's a maid?"

"Don't be ridiculous!"

Glad that I'd found a raw nerve, I tweaked it some more. "I don't think it's ridiculous to expect fair treatment for all citizens of the United States. Even the Supreme Court has finally recognized that women are citizens, you know."

"Good God, what are you talking about now?"

I was talking about the vote and he knew it. I didn't press the point, but sniffed significantly.

He threw his arms out in a gesture of frustration that I found gratifying. "All right, all right. Take her out and give her a posset or something. But come back. I suppose I have to listen to what you just *remembered*." He put an undeserved emphasis on the word, drat him.

Wondering if any of the unhappy people in this household would ever recover from their recent blows, I helped Edie up from the sofa and kept my arm around her as I led her out of the room. Because I knew Aunt Vi to be one of the world's most comforting human beings—and then there was that fresh batch of Scotch shortbread—I guided Edie to the kitchen.

As soon as I opened the kitchen door and staggered through with Edie, Aunt Vi's hands flew to her plump cheeks. "Good Lord, child, what's happened?"

"The detective is what's happened," I said grimly. I led Edie to a chair and pulled it out for her. She sank into the chair and drooped there like a morning glory going on towards midnight. "She needs some shortbread, Vi, and some strong tea. Pronto."

"Of course, she does." It never took Vi long to recover her composure when it had been rattled, and she invariably headed toward foodstuffs to cure all the world's ills. What's more, she was usually right about food easing problems from heartache to broken bones. She knew her way around a kitchen better than any other woman of my acquaintance, too—and she was *mine*, thank the good Lord. Sometimes I didn't know what I'd do without her. In a jiffy, Vi had set a cup of strong, sweet tea and a plate of shortbread in front of Edie, who looked at it as if she didn't know what it was or what to do with it.

"Eat," I commanded her. When she didn't move, I picked up a slice of shortbread and held it to her mouth. She took the hint at last, and thank the good Lord I didn't have to feed her more than one bite.

When she seemed to be on the way to temporary recovery—I supposed full recovery would only occur when all the mysteries had been cleared up—I sighed and stood up again. "Gotta go back to the torture chamber. I'll be sure to let you know what's up."

I left them to each other and realized I felt Edie was in better hands than Mrs. Kincaid, even though the latter had a rich friend and her preacher at her side. Neither Algie Pinkerton nor Father Frederick, even though they were both well-intentioned gentlemen, could come close to matching Aunt Vi and her Scotch shortbread.

This time I didn't bother to knock when I got back to the drawing room. Of course, this was the one time I should have, because Rotondo was in deep discussion with another policeman, and Harold and Mr. Farrington had returned to the room. They were conferring, too, and

I felt like an intruder. Oh, well.

Rotondo looked up and frowned at me. I frowned back, feeling as though we were back on familiar territory. Harold and Mr. Farrington broke off talking, and Harold gave me a thin, strained smile. He walked over, holding out both hands, which made me feel a little better.

"What's up, Daisy? The detective said you remembered something that might be helpful."

"I don't know how helpful it will be, but yeah, I remembered something. And I also just found out that your father left his wheelchair on the service porch last night, I presume before he disappeared."

Harold's rather protuberant, light-hazel eyes bulged appreciably. "He what?" His voice was kind of blankish.

"What's that?"

At Rotondo's sharp bark, I jumped and turned. "No need to shout," I said as frostily as I could.

"What did you say about Mr. Kincaid's wheelchair?"

I cleared my throat. "I said," I said, "that Mr. Kincaid's wheelchair is presently sitting on the service porch. Next to the screen door leading into the back yard, where, one presumes, he left it as he lammed it out to a getaway car."

"I thought you all said he needed the wheelchair to get around."

Harold and I exchanged a glance, then we both shrugged. "I thought he did," I said.

"So did I," said Harold.

"He used it at the bank," Mr. Farrington said. When I glanced at him, he seemed as puzzled as the rest of us. He also looked as though he'd just as soon disappear into the woodwork but knew such a happy occurrence wasn't in his future. "I never saw him walk. He'd even had a ramp built at the back of the bank, on Green Street, so that he could roll himself up and into the building."

"I see." Rotondo offered an all-around, general glower,

which made me feel as if he wasn't necessarily picking on me alone, but that his enmity was universal. Small comfort. "Of course, this may mean anything or nothing."

"It means he went away without his wheelchair," I offered incisively. "So, in spite of what we all believed, he apparently could get along without it." I thought I was building a pretty good case against Mr. Kincaid as a dyed-in-the-wool villain, although I didn't expect Rotondo to agree with me.

"Unless someone else lifted him out of it, perhaps rendering him unconscious first, and carried him out of the house to an automobile," Rotondo pointed out.

Meaning Quincy, of course. "I hadn't thought of that." I hated to admit it. Then I remembered what else I'd been going to tell them. "But I'm sure Quincy didn't do anything of the sort. I'll bet you anything that Kincaid didn't need the chair, but was only trying to fool everyone into thinking he did. I think he was faking being crippled."

The dirty rat. My poor Billy would have given anything to have his legs and lungs working again, and it made me furious to think that a stinker like Kincaid would actually fake such a terrible injury.

Rotondo gave me a look that pretty much told me he thought I was grasping at straws. Maybe I was. "But that's not the important part. What makes it interesting is that I saw Mr. Kincaid with a Spanish phrase book the night of Mrs. Kincaid's séance," cried I. "That's what I just remembered, and I'll bet you anything, he was brushing up on his Spanish because he was going to clean out the bank and scram to Mexico with the money."

Okay, it sounded thin when it popped out that way, but I really thought I had something here.

From the look on Rotondo's face, he didn't. I pressed the point. "Darn it, don't look at me like that! It's a better clue than anybody else has been able to come up with, and it makes more sense than that Quincy Applewood would murder the man! Quincy's a prince of a fellow, and I know good and well he didn't do anything to Mr. Kincaid! It makes more sense to me that Kincaid had been planning this bank raid and escape for a long time."

"How do you account for the argument?" Rotondo asked.

"I don't, except that Quincy was irate when he found out that Kincaid had been bothering Edie. Wouldn't you be mad if you found out some rich louse was harassing your girlfriend?" I thought for a second. "It was probably just a coincidence that the two things happened on the same night."

"I don't believe in coincidences." Rotondo smirked. "In police work, you find that coincidences are generally orchestrated events."

"Yeah? You ought to tell that to Charles Dickens," I said testily, not that I expected the man to have an education that included Dickens. "Anyhow, why not? It makes more sense that it was a coincidence than that Quincy could actually murder somebody."

"I'm sure your heart's in the right place, Mrs. Majesty," Rotondo said, sounding as if he were lying through his teeth, "but believe me, stranger things than jealous boyfriends killing their girlfriends' lovers happen every day."

"He wasn't her lover!"

"Her pursuer, then." I could tell Rotondo was hanging on to his patience with a great effort, drat the man. "Although I'm sure even you will admit, if you'll allow yourself to think clearly, that Miss Marsh wouldn't have been the first young woman to succumb to the lure of a man with money."

"Maybe the girls in New York City are degenerate strumpets," I bellowed. "But around here, girls have morals! Besides, I *know* Quincy didn't kill Mr. Kincaid.

Mr. Kincaid's taken it on the lam to Mexico!"

I'd finally succeeded in wiping the sneer off Rotondo's face. I'd also succeeded in producing shocked expressions on the faces of Harold Kincaid and Del Farrington. I was, in fact, rather pleased with myself.

As I might have anticipated, it didn't take Rotondo long to get over his amazement. Although he thought better of producing another sneer, he did sound dubious when he said, "How do you figure that?"

"I saw him with a Spanish phrase book on the night of Mrs. Kincaid's séance. It looked to me as if he'd been trying to keep it hidden under the blanket he always tossed over his legs, but the blanket had slipped and I saw it clearly. It said *Espanol Para Los Turistos*. I thought at the time that reading a Spanish phrase book was an odd way of having fun, but what do I know about how rich people amuse themselves?"

Rotondo uttered a gurgling sound and muttered, "You, of all people, ought to know that many rich people are as gullible as geese."

He was talking about my business, the demon. "Darn you! That's not fair!"

"Wait a minute, Detective." Harold stepped forward, leaving poor Del Farrington gaping in the background and looking as if he'd like to wring his hands but didn't dare since "real" men didn't do things like that. "I think Daisy might have something here."

I absolutely adored Harold Kincaid. Even if he didn't like women. Maybe *because* he didn't like women. I mean, when it came to Harold, a girl could always be sure he had no ulterior motives, if you know what I mean. That being the case, I gave him my most winning smile, which differed from one of my gracious smiles in that there was no mystery behind it, but only honest gratitude.

Without bothering to ask if it was all right with Rotondo, Harold sat next to me on the sofa. I threw a look of triumph at the detective, who apparently didn't care. As usual. "Are you sure about the nature of the book, Daisy? You're sure it was a Spanish phrase book?"

"Yes. I even remembered the title. I noticed it in particular, because I thought it was so strange. I mean, unless you were planning a family jaunt to South America or something, why would he be boning up on Spanish phrases?"

"Believe me," Harold said drily, "my family doesn't go in for family jaunts." He looked up at Rotondo. "There's got to be another explanation for that book, Detective. My father never reads anything but the newspaper, and he never does anything for no reason. I think Daisy's is a very good one."

Rotondo was clearly unconvinced. "Now see here, you two. There might be a million reasons for a gentleman to be studying Spanish. There are lots of Spanish-speaking people around here. Maybe he wanted to be able to talk to them."

"My father?" Harold laughed. It wasn't a pleasant laugh. "Believe me, Detective, my father had no interest in communicating with anyone at all, and especially not with people he considered beneath him."

"Beneath him?" Rotondo's black eyebrow lifted in that way I wished I could emulate. It was such an effective tool for quelling the opposition.

"Right. And, since he believed almost everybody was beneath him, and especially the Mexican laborers who work around Pasadena as gardeners and such, I can conceive of no earthly reason for him to be learning Spanish."

"Unless," I said before Rotondo could interrupt, "he was planning a dash to the border or overseas to Spain or someplace like that with a cartload of stolen money."

"Exactly." Harold squeezed my hand. Before Rotondo could shoot my theory out of the water, Harold continued, "I have to agree with Mrs. Majesty about the man who is, unfortunately, my father, Detective. I'd never say so in front of my mother or my sister, but my father is a bad man. A *very* bad man" I saw Mr. Farrington slap a hand over his mouth, for all the world like a woman might have done. "Frankly, I wouldn't put anything past him."

Even Rotondo was taken aback by Harold's candor. He cleared his throat. "Er, is that right, sir? Do you have any facts to back up this claim?"

"I don't even have a claim," Harold said with a humorless laugh. "Although, as I once mentioned to Mrs. Majesty, I'd always rather cherished a hope that my mother had been fooling around on my old man nine months before I was born."

Farrington gasped. I suspected Rotondo wanted to, but was too well-versed in policemanship to let a gasp slip past his rigid guard.

Harold went on, "I fear there are no facts I've ever been able to discover to support that fortuitous fantasy, since my mother always was and still is a woman of the highest moral principles. But I do know my father has no principles at all and even fewer scruples. He married my mother for her money and has been living on the proceeds therefrom ever since they got together. When my grandfather died, the old man started putting on a show of running the bank, but Del can tell you he's an incompetent ass. It's Del who's been doing all the work, and it was Del who first suspected something was amiss with those bearer bonds."

Mr. Farrington made a gurgling sound and waved his hand in a gesture of denial. I believed Harold, though. I think Rotondo did, too, although he'd probably never admit it.

 CHAPTER 12

Detective Rotondo gazed at Harold, Del, and me for approximately twenty-five seconds, during which time I could swear I heard the hamsters getting dizzy trotting on the wheel that ran his brain. The three of us (Harold, Del, and I) gazed back, looking as sweet and innocent as any trio of human beings who ever graced the earth.

At last Rotondo muttered, "Do you have a telephone room, Mr. Kincaid? And if so, may I use the wire? It might be a good idea to report the latest twist in this case to the police department. That way we can spread the word to Los Angeles and other outlying counties."

"The Spanish twist, do you mean?" I asked in a voice dripping with treacle and honey and other disgustingly sweet and gooey things.

He frowned at me. "I don't suppose it would hurt to mention the Spanish angle."

"I don't suppose so," I agreed. "You might even want to post guards at the border crossings into Mexico." I offered him another cherubic smile, which he deflected with his usual skill. "And perhaps the United States Life Saving Service might be notified as well. People do occasionally travel by water, don't you know. Especially rich people who can afford yachts and big boats with motors and speedy machines like that."

"The United Stations Ocean Rescue Service has been called the United States Coast Guard for three years now, Mrs. Majesty," Rotondo said in something of a snarl. "And I consider that possibility slight at best. I'm certainly not going to call on the Coast Guard, at great expense to the public, without more proof than your harebrained theories."

I sniffed. If money was the best reason he could come up with to denigrate my knowledge of American oceanic protective services, he was a bigger oaf than I already thought he was. Harold patted my hand to show me he thought so, too.

Turning to give us all a good glower, Rotondo said, "I'll be sure to have them watch out for Mr. Applewood as well, you can be sure. I think it's much more likely that Applewood had something to do with Mr. Kincaid's disappearance and has taken the money. There's no good reason to believe he might not make use of a Spanish phrase book, either, as I'm sure you can understand, if he got the notion of running off to Mexico." He sneered at me, darn him.

"Nuts," I said. It wasn't much, but it was the best I could come up with at the moment. Did that make me an oaf, too? Naw. I'm never spiteful to people unless they're hateful to me first.

"I'll take you to the telephone room, Detective Rotondo." After squeezing my hand once more, Harold rose, gave me a quick grin, and walked off with the policeman.

As soon as the door closed behind them, I turned to Mr. Farrington. "I can't stand that policeman."

Mr. Farrington sighed heavily. "He's only doing his job, I guess."

"You're too nice, Mr. Farrington. Did anyone ever tell

you that before?"

He grinned. "Please call me Del, and yes, Harry's been telling me that forever, as a matter of fact. But I think it's probably better to be too nice than too much the other way."

"Right. Just look at Mr. Kincaid if you need proof of that one."

"My word, isn't that the truth!"

The door to the drawing room burst open, making both Del and me jump at least a foot and a half. I popped up from the sofa, ready to do battle, propelled by a vague understanding that Del Farrington needed protection. Del seemed to shrink back against a sofa cushion. I didn't hold it against him. Heck, I was accustomed to fighting battles for other people against the vagaries of life. I got the feeling Del had been pretty well pampered during his growing-up years, the lucky stiff.

As I should have expected, given recent events, it turned out to be Stacy who'd crashed through the door, whatever demons possessing her having catapulted her into another dramatic role. She scanned the room, wild-eyed. "Where's Mother? Where's Harold? What are *you* still doing here?"

This last question, typically rude, had been directed at me. She'd never have asked the question of Del, since she had a crush on him. Little did she know how much luck she'd ever have in that direction, and no matter how much I'd like to clue her in, I'd never do anything so vicious to Del or Harold.

Since Del had picked up the cushion and looked as if he were trying to hide behind it, I guessed I had to answer the bitch—I mean the witch. "Your mother went upstairs to lie down. Father Frederick and Mr. Pinkerton are with her."

"In her *bedroom*?" she shrieked, as if she'd never heard of anything so reprehensible in her life. "With two *men*?"

I thought about telling her that, personally, I considered young women smoking and drinking and taking drugs and hanging out at illegal speakeasies was infinitely more reprehensible than a poor bereaved woman being administered to by good friends even if they were men, but didn't. See? Sometimes I can control myself. I said, "Yes."

"I can't *believe* this! First my father is murdered by that horrid stable boy—"

"He was not!" I shouted, furious.

"Oh, shut up! What do you know about anything?"

"I know your father's a nasty old lecher who stole bearer bonds from his bank and took off to Mexico without any help from Quincy Applewood! That's a lot more than you know!"

"How *dare* you speak of my father to me like that?" she screeched.

"Because you're a spoiled-rotten brat, is why, and somebody should have told you so years ago!"

"Good God, what's going on in here now?"

Thank the merciful Fates, it was Harold, standing in the open doorway and looking bewildered. I sighed and told him. "Your sister decided to throw another tantrum. Unfortunately, her audience hasn't been receptive."

"Why, you *bitch*!" Stacy made a run at me, her sharpened, brilliantly painted fingernails scrunched into claws. Harold, God bless him for a saint on earth, stuck out a leg and tripped her.

When she went down, she banged her head against a soft-ish chair, so I didn't think she was hurt much. I regretted it, too, which just goes to show how mean-spirited some of us can be without half trying. When Stacy lifted her head from the fancy Oriental carpet upon which she lay, her mouth fell open and stayed that way, which I considered a distinct improvement over her former shrillness, and it made me feel pretty good.

Then, I guess because she didn't want Harold or me

getting the better of her, she fainted (or pretended to faint). Right smack in the middle the floor between a pie-shaped table and the elegant red velvet Louis the Whateverth chair against which she'd bumped her head.

Because I didn't like her, I left her there. I got the feeling that neither Harold nor Del felt like picking her up, either, so we all sat back down on the sofa and waited for somebody else to show up, pretty much ignoring her altogether. Although I doubted our luck would be that good, there was always a chance she'd suffer a heart spasm brought about by overuse of cocaine or morphine or some other illegal substance and would die before Rotondo returned to us.

No such luck. Rotondo opened the door a second later and darned near stepped on Stacy's leg, which might perhaps have broken it. Unfortunately, he spotted her, thereby preventing a providential and well-deserved punishment for the spoiled little rich girl. He frowned down at her. "What the hell's wrong with her now?"

I shrugged. "First she threw a tantrum, then she tried to kill me, and then she fainted. Or pretended to faint." It wasn't much of a lie, and I didn't want Rotondo to think Harold wasn't a gentleman just because he'd tripped her, since he was quite gentlemanly as a rule.

Del nodded his agreement.

Harold said, "That's it, all right."

Mrs. Kincaid, who doubtless believed she'd chickened out earlier in the day when she'd gone upstairs and rested, must have felt stronger now, because she'd come downstairs again and was standing behind Rotondo, who stood aside politely.

She still looked mighty shaky, but Father Frederick had her by the right arm and Algie Pinkerton, who'd finally stopped crying, held her left arm, and they guided Stacy's mother around her fallen child, depositing the woman on one of the red-velvet chairs. They stood beside her like knights of old guarding their queen. It might have been sort of cute and courtly if the circumstances had been different.

Eyeing Stacy with what I could only term curiosity tainted with disapproval, Mrs. Kincaid asked, "What happened to Anastasia? Is she ill? Shouldn't someone pick her up? Or something?" Her face took on an expression of consternation. "Good God, she's not been drinking, has she?"

"I don't think so," Harold said doubtfully.

Only because I liked Mrs. Kincaid, I said, "I'm sure she hasn't, Mrs. Kincaid. I'm sure she was just upset by—by—" I waved my hand in a vague gesture. *Because she was a brat, was why she was upset.* Which, naturally, I couldn't say. Nor had Stacy been drinking tea and eating shortbread with my own beloved aunt Violet, which might have sweetened her disposition a good deal had she done so earlier in her misbegotten life, not that she deserved any of Aunt Vi's shortbread.

Since nobody else made a move to do so, Detective Rotondo knelt beside the fallen girl and tried to get his arms around her in a way that wouldn't shock the onlookers. Stacy's mother might have been dismayed had one of her daughter's breasts been touched, even inadvertently, by a policeman. I'm sure Stacy wouldn't have minded one little bit.

Rotondo finally got her on her feet, which wobbled suspiciously—I study things like that as a profession, and I can tell a fake performance when I see one—and dumped her ungently on a sofa at the far side of the room. I suspected he wanted her as far away from the important questionings as possible.

"Do you think she needs anything?" he asked as if he didn't care much.

Mrs. Kincaid pressed a hand to her forehead. "Oh, dear, oh, dear, I just don't know what to do. What does one do in emergencies? Administer tea? Brandy?" She realized what she'd said, and her face turned purple.

"No! No! I didn't mean brandy!"

"Naw," I said. "She'll be fine in a minute." Again, I thought about Vi's shortbread and decided not to waste any of it on Stacy. If Stacy ever left the room again, I might get some for everybody else, though. Even Rotondo probably deserved a bite of something good to eat every now and then.

"Don't worry about her, Mother," Harold said in a voice harder than his usual dulcet tones. "You know she only does these things to get attention."

"Oh, Harold!" Mrs. Kincaid started to cry, and I thought, *God save me from wealth, if this is what it does to people.* I didn't mean it, of course.

"I'll take care of her, Madeline," Father Frederick offered, which I thought was awfully nice of him considering the obstacle facing him. Heck, I wouldn't want to tackle Stacy, even if I were God Almighty Himself. Also, I doubted very much that Stacy Kincaid ever went to church of a Sunday. Probably not even on Easter or Christmas, which just went to demonstrate how good a man Father Frederick was.

"Thank you." It was the first time I'd heard Rotondo sound honestly grateful to anyone for anything.

Father Frederick went to the couch, sat on the edge as far away from the girl's body as he could get, took one of Stacy's hands and began chafing it and speaking softly to her. Praying, maybe. I hoped so. The girl needed as many prayers as she could get, and as good a Christian girl as I tried to be, I couldn't force myself to pray for that demon-spawn-child of Satan.

"I appreciate you coming downstairs again, Mrs. Kincaid," Rotondo said, again surprising me by using good manners.

"I felt I should," she said, her voice hushed and shaky. "After all, it appears that my husband has perpetrated a dreadful crime." She began crying softly. "And what if it turns out that poor Mr. Applewood killed him? Oh, poor,

poor Eustace! I don't know what my friends will think! But what if he isn't dead, and has to go to prison? Can you imagine *me*, Madeline Kincaid, with a jailbird for a husband? Think of the horror! Think of the scandal! Oh, my goodness! Whatever will we do? My God, we might have to move back to New York and live in all that horrid snow!"

Algie Pinkerton, who hadn't said much so far, having been weeping almost ever since I showed up as far as I knew, patted her shoulder consolingly. "It will be all right, Madeline. Don't forget that a little crime and scandal, and especially an interesting murder, will only add cachet to your reputation. People will be falling all over themselves to ask you to attend their soirees and parties and theater outings. Don't you ever read Mrs. Christie's novels, darling?"

I had occasionally been inclined to think it was a shame that Mrs. Kincaid hadn't married Algie Pinkerton instead of Mr. Kincaid, but I wasn't so sure any longer. Although I believe everyone's entitled to one or two *faux pax* in their lives, I thought that one had come mighty close to insanity. Then again, come to think of it, I'd committed more than one or two verbal mistakes and that was only today, so I forgave Algie. Besides, he was probably right.

"Algie! How can you say such things?"

Algie shrugged as if he couldn't think of a good answer.

"And to think that Mr. Kincaid stole those bonds from the bank!" Mrs. Kincaid went on, sounding as if she were working up to another hearty hysterical fit. "People might condone murder, Algie, but *nobody* condones theft, and I'll be married to a *convict*!"

Now that, to my mind, was a curious way to look at things, but, as I've mentioned several times already, I'm not rich and, therefore, have a different outlook on life, I'm sure. By my way of thinking, murder's a good deal more heinous than theft, but I guess it depends. On what, I don't know.

I did say, meaning it sincerely, "It's a good thing the theft was discovered on a Saturday, though, don't you think? I mean, whatever would people have thought if the newspapers leaked the news that the auditors had discovered the theft of the bonds? It would have been a terrible shock, and they'd probably blame the whole family for the actions of the one." I shook my head. "Imagine all those poor people in Pasadena who'll have lost their savings. With today to work on the problem, maybe this will give your bank people some extra time to get things under control before Monday. Maybe the bonds will be rediscovered before the bank is forced to close."

That, it became instantly clear to me, wasn't the right thing to say, either, because Mrs. Kincaid's eyes went as round as chocolate cupcakes, Harold sucked in enough air to float a balloon, and Del Farrington slammed a hand over his heart and uttered a syllable I don't think I heard correctly. At least I hope I didn't, because it would astonish me if Del knew words like that.

Unfortunately, Stacy recovered in time to hear what I said. "What kind of comfort is that for my poor mother, you idiot fool? If that's not the stupidest thing I've ever heard, I don't know what is!"

Strange as it sounds, it was Algie Pinkerton who came to my rescue. Algie had never before seemed to me like the rescuing type. "No," he said in a peculiar voice and in direct contradiction to Stacy's insulting comment. I'd never heard him contradict anybody, and it made me happy that it had been Stacy who'd been his first. "It's not stupid at all. In fact, I believe Mrs. Majesty has perhaps hit on a miracle cure for the bank's ills, if not those of Mr. and Mrs. Kincaid."

Del gasped and opened his baby blues as wide as a robin's eggs. Shoot, the man was gorgeous. "What—

what do you mean, Mr. Pinkerton?"

Algie blushed. "Ahem. I'm sure nobody knows this, but I'm quite a hand with investments." He bowed his head as if he'd just admitted to committing a salacious and distressing crime. "It would be my pleasure"—he directed a lover-like glance at Mrs. Kincaid. Aha! I knew he cared for her!—"to assist a friend in distress. Especially such distress as this. And such a friend."

It sounded to me as if poor Algie was getting his thoughts muddled, but apparently Mrs. Kincaid didn't think so. She clasped her hands to her bosom for no more than a second before she threw her arms around Algie's neck and sobbed onto his shoulder.

Stacy, who'd managed to sit up under her own steam since nobody was inclined to help her, said, "Oh, God," in a disgusted-sounding voice. Harold shot her such an evil look, it would have killed a lesser woman than his sister. Unfortunately, it didn't kill Stacy. It did, however, shut her up.

"Mind you," Algie continued, sounding unsure of himself, "we only have Sunday to work with, since the bank is closed this afternoon, but I'm sure we can come up with something."

Del seemed to be collecting his wits, which was a good thing since a banker without wits wasn't much good to anyone, and I'd begun to believe his were permanently scattered. "Do you really think we can do something to rescue the bank, Mr. Pinkerton? At least temporarily? Something we can build upon so that the bank won't have to close? I can't stand the thought of all those poor people losing their money and investments. Some of them have so little, you know, and their entire life's savings are in the bank. Mr. Pinkerton, if you can do something, you'll be a true life-saver!"

"Please," said Algie, blushing, "call me Algie."

If anyone called me Algie, I'd smack him. On the other hand, Algernon was worse, I suppose. This was getting interesting, especially since Mrs. Kincaid was seriously impeding Algie's intent as it revolved about saving the bank, because she clung to him like a limpet. I decided I might be of help there, so I walked to the sofa, gave Algie an *I'll-rescue-you* look, and he smiled and nodded at me.

"Here, dear, please allow Daisy to help you compose yourself. I believe Del and I ought to start working on bank business at once."

"Of course," Del said in a contemplative tone, as if he'd just had a comforting thought, "If Mr. Kincaid *has* been killed, it would be considered perfectly decent and proper to close the bank on Monday, as a show of respect. Perhaps even extend the closure to Tuesday. That would give us even more time"

It was probably a good idea, actually, but Del's timing could have been better. As soon as Algie rose from the sofa, Mrs. Kincaid let out a screech that would have shattered glass if it had been the thin kind used in our house on Marengo. Working as fast as I could, I sat next to her and threw my arms around her, relinquishing my ear drums to what might conceivably be considered a good cause.

Stacy heaved herself up from the other sofa and marched out of the room, a circumstance that caused a more or less universal sigh of relief. The only one who didn't sigh with relief was Mrs. Kincaid, who was still sobbing frantically. On my blue-floured dress that I'm sure would never recover from this day's work.

Which reminded me of the shortbread again. Oh, Lord, could I ever use a cup of tea and some shortbread. With as much alacrity as possible, I soothed Mrs. Kincaid's nerves without hurting her feelings (I hope), and said, "I think we could all use some refreshments. Would you mind if I went to the kitchen and asked Aunt Vi to fix a tray?"

"Oh, Daisy!" Mrs. Kincaid cried, her hands clasped to

her bosom in a gesture I was beginning to recognize as one she used whenever she was particularly touched by something. I'll bet she never had cause to use it on her daughter. "You're such an angel."

I'm sure the jury would be out on that one for a long time, but I didn't say so. Let the lady have her fancies; she deserved them. Because I didn't trust him not to thwart my angelic purpose, I glanced at Rotondo, who nodded his approval. It wasn't even a crabby nod, and I took heart. I imagined he could use a cup of tea, too.

I rushed to the kitchen. Edie had left Aunt Vi to resume her house-maidly duties by then, for which I was glad since I didn't want to go into details at the moment. All I wanted was tea and shortbread.

Fortunately for all of us, Aunt Vi had made plenty. "I knew I'd need lots of it," she told me. "You know there's nothing as heartwarming as Scotch shortbread and tea when a person's down in the mouth, Daisy, and if there's any woman who needs help at the moment, it's that poor dear Mrs. Kincaid."

"I couldn't agree more. Thanks, Vi. You're the real angel in this family."

"Don't blaspheme, Daisy," she said severely. But she blushed, and I knew she appreciated the complement that had been delivered to me, but should have been directed at Vi.

Since the tray holding the cups and tea was heavy, I carried that one. Aunt Vi arranged a brilliantly beautiful arrangement of shortbread cookies on another tray that she'd covered with a pretty doily, and carried that one to the drawing room. Someone—I suspect Harold, since he was the only person in the room with a functioning brain at the moment—had anticipated the need for an open door. I marched in with the tea tray, and Vi followed with the tray of shortbread. I could have sworn I heard drools commencing throughout the room.

Crying as usual, Mrs. Kincaid said, "Oh, Vi, thank you

so much! You and your niece are the kindest women in the whole world!"

Rotondo cast a glance at a ceiling fixture, but I didn't resent it. Too much.

Harold said, "You got that one right, Ma." He mitigated the use of the word "Ma" and his use of poor grammar by kissing her on the cheek. Then he turned and kissed Vi, which I considered extraordinarily diplomatic of him, and he rose another couple of notches in my book. Harold was a peach of a guy, and that was that.

Vi smacked Harold lightly on the arm, which to me spoke of many such instances in Harold's life. Bless my aunt Viola's big heart. She and my mother and father were three of God's greatest gifts to the world. It made me glad to know that people like Harold Kincaid, a rich and important man, knew it, too.

"I'll serve the tea and cookies," I said, taking over the duty since Mrs. Kincaid wasn't in any condition to serve as hostess. Harold helped. I can't even begin to tell you how soothing Aunt Vi's shortbread and tea can be.

Even Rotondo's usually grumpy face relaxed into something that looked vaguely human. "These are delicious, Mrs. Majesty. Please thank your aunt for me."

By that time, Aunt Vi had left the room, of course, so I said, "Sure will. She'll be pleased that you enjoyed them."

"They're marvelous," Harold exclaimed. He looked as if he were experiencing a holy vision. "I *must* have the recipe! Will she divulge it, do you think? Or is she one of those people who keep these secrets to themselves?"

I eyed him curiously. "Do people really do that?" I'd never heard of anything as stupid as not sharing a good recipe, but what did I know? Maybe rich people did lots of unusual things the rest of us would never even think of.

"They certainly do." This came from Del, who

exchanged a speaking glance with Harold, from which I gathered they'd been caught in a recipe-secret-keeping plot before. Shoot, life could be really interesting when you hung around with all sorts of different kinds of people.

"I think I'll leave you folks to yourselves for a while," Detective Rotondo said after consuming about three dozen shortbread cookies (okay, I'm exaggerating a little bit). "But I'm certain I'll have to return tomorrow as soon as I gather information that might have come in at the station. And please don't hesitate to telephone me at the station should anything of significance happen here."

"Of course." Harold stood and shook the man's hand, which I thought was quite egalitarian of him.

"Yes. Of course," said his mother more vaguely.

Del and Algie nodded. They were already spreading books and ledgers out on a big desk sitting under a window next to Stacy's fainting couch.

"See ya," said I to the detective, who gave me one of his better frowns in return. He didn't bother with a verbal good-bye, which was fine with me.

As Del and Algie consumed tea and shortbread, they pored over the bank's books Del had brought to the Kincaid mansion that afternoon, after it had been made clear that Kincaid had absconded. I have to admit to a certain degree of interest in the intensity they devoted to the books.

People's choices in matters of careers fascinate me. I knew my dad had been a great chauffeur and had taken delight in driving moving-picture people all over the place. He could keep a body entertained for hours with some of his stories—and I imagine I've never even heard some of the better ones.

I knew, too, that Billy had been all set to go into motor mechanics before he went to war and got himself mutilated. He'd always loved automobiles. And I knew my mother was a crackerjack bookkeeper because she enjoyed working with numbers. It went without saying (any more often than I already have) that Aunt Vi was a superb cook. And, not to sound vain or anything, I even knew I was a darned good spiritualist.

But the notion of two wealthy men sitting down together and trying to figure out how to save a bank so that a bunch of people poorer than they wouldn't go broke meant something special to me. I don't know why, unless it's because I tend to think of people who have lots of money as being uncaring about the rest of us. And this is in spite of all the evidence to the contrary that I've gleaned from many different sources, including Harold and his mother.

By the time I knew I had to be going home or Billy would be in a perfect tantrum—not that his tantrums came anywhere close to those thrown by Stacy Kincaid, and he had a better reason for throwing them—I could see Del and Algie smiling. I took the smiles as a good omen and stood up. Mrs. Kincaid had asked to have her Ouija board brought into the drawing room, so we'd been asking Rolly a bunch of questions about the future of Mrs. Kincaid's life and when or if it would ever brighten again.

Naturally, Rolly told her that her life would be full of joy and wonder after a period of chaos (chaos is always a good word to use, because it can mean almost anything). I've always been grateful to Rolly for showing up in my life, even if I'd made him up in the first place. You never know about such things. Maybe I didn't make him up. Maybe he'd made himself up.

There I go: thinking again. I really ought to stop it, because thinking only confuses me.

"I really need to get back to my family, Mrs. Kincaid," I told her sympathetically. "I'll come back tomorrow if you need me." I gave her one of my more gracious smiles, tinted with sweetness and light, in order to soften the blow she might feel at my deserting her. But heckydarn, I had a family, too. Fortunately, I was so full of shortbread, I wasn't starving or anything, but I was worried about my husband.

Mrs. Kincaid squeezed my hands so tightly, I wasn't sure I'd be able to hold on to the Model T's steering wheel. Thank heavens James was still there in the stables to crank for me. "Oh, Daisy," sobbed Mrs. Kincaid, "I can't thank you enough for coming over to help me today. I don't believe I could have survived the day without you."

All right, I know this sounds unkind, but sometimes I wish some people wouldn't cry so darned much. I liked Mrs. Kincaid a whole lot, and I appreciated her, and I valued her even if she didn't have a very useful brain or anything much in it, and had bred one offensive daughter, but blast it all, she cried every time anything at all happened, and it got to be a trial after a while. Maybe I was only tired. It had been a full day for me, too, and I still had to fill Aunt Vi in on all of it before I could go home to my husband.

Fortunately, Aunt Vi knew my situation with Billy. So to the aroma of roasting lamb and garlic-mashed-potatoes and tomato and cucumber salad, which didn't do as much damage to my self-control as it might have done had I not consumed so much shortbread, I told Vi all the interesting tidbits of the day. Never think I left out Stacy's nasty comments to me or her fainting fits, either. After all, we Gumms know what goes on in the world, and we appreciate hearing how the other half behaves itself, which it so often doesn't.

"That child will be the death of her poor mother, if her father doesn't finish the poor woman off first," Aunt Vi said, tutting as she stirred the gravy. It smelled *so* good. We Gumms and Majestys didn't eat a lot of lamb because it was an expensive meat, but I adored it when I could get it.

"But at least Del Farrington and Algie Pinkerton are

saving the bank," I said, hoping to make her feel better.

I succeeded beyond my expectations. She actually dropped her wooden spoon into the gravy pan and slapped her hands together as if she were praying. "They are? You really think they're going to be able to save the bank?"

"They think so. I guess Mr. Pinkerton is something of a financial genius." I snabbled a piece of the lamb before Vi could smack my hand. It was *so* good. "You'd never know it to look at him, would you?"

"You can never tell by appearances, Daisy Majesty, as you ought to have learned long before this."

Lectures, lectures, lectures. I suppose that's what mothers and aunts are for, but they did put a crimp in one's style sometimes. "Say, Vi, I really need to get home to Billy. Would you mind filling Edie in on what's gone on today. I promised her I would, but . . . well, you know Billy."

"Oh, Daisy, my love!"

I knew a reference to poor Billy would get her. It always did. Vi felt sorry for both of us. So did I, for that matter. This time it worked out okay, because she sliced off a large portion of lamb, added some gravy and some potatoes, handed me a small jar of cooked green beans, and I left the house with a better dinner than Billy could ever get from me. Unfortunately, I hadn't inherited the family's cooking gene, or whatever it was.

"Are you sure you can spare this?" I asked, not wanting to deprive even so wealthy a family as the Kincaids of their dinner.

"Don't be daft, child. I always make enough for an army, and there's not going to be an appetite in the house this evening anyhow."

I hadn't thought of it that way. Made me feel better as I crept out the back door with the spoils of my day.

You could have knocked me over with a feather when I tippy-toed in through the front door of our house on

Marengo Avenue, expecting to find my darling Billy in a roaring rage and my parents gone somewhere to get away from him, and I discovered him sitting on the comfy old sofa in the living room, laughing up a storm, and playing gin rummy with—hold your breath—Detective Sam Rotondo!

 CHAPTER 13

I stopped dead in the doorway, holding the jars of food Aunt Vi had wrapped up for me. "You!" I'm pretty sure I didn't sound delighted to see him.

"Hey, Daisy!" my Billy cried, unmistakably pleased as punch to have me home again and not even mad that I'd been gone all day.

What was going on here, anyway?

"You know Detective Sam Rotondo, don't you?" asked my innocent spouse. Little did he know that Rotondo and I had been mortal enemies from the moment we'd set eyes on each other. Why, the fiend had even suspected me of murder. I know he had. I'd have liked to have told Billy so, but I couldn't bear to spoil his fun since he got so little of it.

"I've had that pleasure," I said, trying not to sound sarcastic for Billy's sake, but it was a rough bicycle to ride when one wheel was flat and the other was losing air fast.

Rotondo had stood as I'd entered the room, much to my stupefaction. He was never this polite to me at the Kincaids'. "Here, Mrs. Majesty, please let me help you carry your burdens."

My "burdens" were our dinner, Billy's and mine. If I were feeling charitable, I'd have had to admit that there was plenty enough for three, but I didn't feel the least bit charitable toward this man and didn't expect I ever would. "Thanks," I said. "I can manage."

"Come on, Sam, why don't you join us for dinner? From the smell of things, Daisy's aunt Vi sent some food home with her, so we'll eat well tonight." Billy smiled up at me, reminding me of what he'd once been, and my heart broke all over again. I could never stay angry with Billy, no matter what other provocations were present, such as irascible detectives and so forth. "Is there enough for three?"

"Oh, sure," I said, resigned to my fate. I carried the stuff to the kitchen, but then went back to the living room. Darned if I wasn't going to find out what fell purpose lay behind Rotondo's sudden appearance in my own personal home, playing cards with my own personal husband. Something was rotten in the State of California, and it wasn't Hamlet or his villainous step-father.

I sat down next to Billy, who'd abandoned his wheelchair for the sofa. Our sofa, needless to say, was nowhere near as elegant as any of those residing in the Kincaid mansion, but it was a good height for Billy, who could get onto it and off of it with relative ease. Billy must have told Rotondo where the card table was (in the hall closet), because he'd set it up and currently sat on a kitchen chair he'd hauled in from that room.

I have to admit that Rotondo looked more comfortable in these surroundings than in the Kincaids' place, which probably meant his financial upbringing had been more akin to mine than Harold's. Made sense, I guess, or he'd have been a stock broker instead of a policeman. Or done nothing, like those guys in Mr. F. Scott Fitzgerald's books generally did. Or didn't. Oh, you know what I mean.

Reconciled to an evening of unpleasantness, not unlike the rest of my day, after a short, boring time during which I watched them play cards, I left the two men. They seemed to be having a grand old time without me, anyhow. I went to the kitchen to heat the food. I even made a salad to go with the lamb and potatoes and gravy and beans. Heck, even I can make a decent salad dressing. Sometimes.

I loaded up the plates in the kitchen and carried them to the living room. I figured it would be easier to eat at the card table than for Billy to get himself to the dining room.

After we'd dug in and the relative deliciousness of the food had waned as a conversational topic, I turned to Rotondo. "So, how come you invaded our house this afternoon, Detective? I thought you were going back to the police station. Don't you have enough to do without investigating the obviously innocent?"

Billy's mouth was full, or he'd assuredly have taken me to task for being ugly to someone he was beginning to consider a friend—God protect us all.

Rotondo didn't seem offended by the question or my attitude, doubtless because he was used to them both by this time. "It occurred to me that you're a smart cookie, Mrs. Majesty. It also occurred to me that your husband might be able to shed some light on the Kincaid situation."

"Yeah?" My glance slid between him and Billy, and I couldn't detect a single indication of fabrication or out-and-out falsehood on either face. Billy's handsome countenance even indicated to me, who knew it so well, that he considered the detective's reasoning...well...reasonable.

I didn't consider it any such thing. "I must admit to being surprised by this supposition of yours, Detective, especially since Billy has never met a single one of the

Kincaids and doesn't care for my association with the family."

Billy shrugged and grinned. "Aw, heck, Daisy, I don't mind the Kincaids. They just take you away from me a lot, is all I have against them. But I told Sam everything I know, which is just about nothing. You spend more time at the Kincaids' than you do here, but you make a good living at it, so it's okay. God knows, my disability pension isn't worth much more than the paper it's printed on."

Not only did the above words spouting forth from my very own and beloved husband's lips directly contradict everything he'd been yelling at me for months now, but I couldn't help but be concerned that the two men had fallen into a first-name basis at the drop of a hat. I feared for my future peace of mind.

"You can't help what happened to you in France, Billy," Rotondo said in a voice I never would have expected to hear come out of his mouth. Why, the man sounded…I don't even know how to describe it. It was as if he understood Billy's plight and, while he was sorry about it and felt like hell for Billy's sake, he'd be hung upside down from a chestnut tree and had his guts pecked out by a band of ravening jackdaws (whatever they are) before he'd admit his sympathy aloud.

Darned if I didn't start to like him, which turned out to be a stupid thing to do, as I might have predicted had I been in my spiritualist mode. I wasn't, having been disarmed by two attractive men, blast them. They're totally untrustworthy, men are. Just when you think one of them's all right in the overall scheme of things, he turns around and bites you on the butt.

"Well," I said, touched and not wanting to show it, "we all do our part."

"Actually," Rotondo said in his back-to-business voice, "your husband has been quite helpful to me, Mrs. Majesty."

"He has?" What did this mean? Nothing good, I was sure.

"Indeed. He confirmed everything you've told me regarding the Kincaids and their household." He forked up a piece of lamb. "And he also confirmed your sentiments about your aunt's cooking. Not that he needed to, since I'm confirming them right now all by myself."

"Aunt Vi's the best," I said honestly and because I couldn't think of anything vile enough to say to this louse in front of Billy, who'd apparently decided he liked him. I mean, what in the name of God did this detective think he was doing, checking up on me with my own husband? I took back all the good thoughts I'd almost started having about him.

"Anyone in the city of Pasadena can tell you Aunt Vi's the best cook in town. People try to hire her away from the Kincaids all the time," I said. "But she likes working there, and Mrs. Kincaid's a good woman who treats her staff well. And Mr. Kincaid never chased Aunt Vi around in his wheelchair." *So there and nyah, nyah, nyah.* I didn't add that part, as I'm sure I need not say.

"That's the impression I've come away with," confirmed Rotondo. "But what about that daughter of hers? And that husband?"

Good questions. "I don't know. I think Stacy's just a spoiled rich kid who's never had to do anything for herself. Harold's a great fellow who'd give you the shirt off his back. He tries to help people at every turn." I saw the glance that passed between the two men when I made the "shirt off his back" comment and knew what they were thinking. Men have such filthy minds.

"How well acquainted are you with Mr. Farrington, Mrs. Majesty? I know you believe Mr. Kincaid is behind the bank business, but don't forget that Mr. Farrington has been second in charge at the bank for quite a while now. From what the staff at the bank have told my men, Farrington's the one who knows what's going on.

Kincaid seems to be regarded as merely a figurehead."

"That's the impression I got, too, but I can tell you that Mr. Farrington wouldn't steal a penny from a fountain in Chinatown, Detective Rotondo. He's too good for this world. Kincaid, on the other hand, would steal the pencils out of a blind man's cup if he felt like it."

"His staff at the bank don't seem to care much for Mr. Kincaid. They all speak highly of Farrington."

"Sure, they do. He's a good man, and I doubt that he'd ever even think of doing anything illegal or immoral."

Billy made a face, and I knew why, but I pretended not to see it. These so-called "regular" men might not appreciate the Harolds and Dels of this world, but we women, who are much more discerning and kindly disposed toward our fellow human beings than are members of the male gender, are not so blind to other people's good qualities, no matter what…um…eccentricities, I guess is a good word for it, they might otherwise possess.

"To your knowledge has your friend Miss Marsh heard anything from Mr. Quincy Applewood since his disappearance?" Rotondo asked, getting back to business once more.

"I didn't see her again after she left the drawing room to go to Aunt Vi for a cup of tea. But I don't think so. I'm sure she'd have raced right back downstairs and told everyone if Quincy'd come home again."

"If she didn't decide to hide him from the law."

"She wouldn't do that," I said with a something of a snarl. "She only drank some tea. And she needed it!"

"Ah, tea," sighed Rotondo. "The universal cure for everyone's ills."

"Tea and Aunt Vi's Scotch shortbread," I said.

He smiled and looked wistful, so I knew he agreed.

"She made shortbread?" Billy sounded as excited as I'd heard him sound in days. "Did she send some home with you?"

I was so glad I'd remembered to beg some shortbread from Vi. By the time I got out of the Kincaid house, there wasn't much left, but Vi gave it all to me. The woman's a saint. "Yup."

"You're sure Miss Marsh hasn't heard from Mr. Applewood?" Rotondo was certainly a dogged fellow. I guess that was a good quality in a policeman, but it could be a real pain in the neck during social occasions.

"I'm sure. Besides, Edie knows, and I know, that Quincy Applewood could no more harm Mr. Kincaid— no matter how much the stinking rat of a man deserved it—than he could fly to the moon."

"Oh," said Rotondo. I was rather proud that I'd evidently been so forceful in my defense of my friends that he couldn't think of anything more interesting to say than *Oh*.

"How about some of that shortbread?" asked my adorable Billy.

I smiled benignly and rose from the table. "Coming right up."

"Aunt Vi's shortbread is a miracle of nature," Billy whispered, sounding as if he were awaiting a message from the Almighty.

"God bless us all," whispered Rotondo in agreement. *He*, on the other hand, sounded like an older, slightly overweight, New-York-Italian version of Tiny Tim Cratchit.

I cleared the remains of dinner from the table—there weren't many of them, either, Aunt Vi's roast lamb and garlic-mashed-potatoes being what they were—and took the plates to the kitchen. Then I made up a pot of tea in my favorite yellow-flowered teapot, set out some pretty cups, unmatched but that went together pleasantly, and carried the tray to the dinner table. Not long after that, I brought out the remains of the shortbread. It didn't last long enough for Pa to get any when he and Ma came home a half-hour or so later, but nobody seemed to mind.

Pa and Ma took to Rotondo almost as much and as quickly as Billy had, for some unfathomable, not to mention unfortunate, reason. I was beginning to feel left out of this picture, and I didn't like it. But there wasn't much I could do about it except wash dishes, so that's what I did. By the time I had them all dried off and put away, Pa had joined Billy and Sam in their gin rummy game. I guess Ma had gone to her room to sew or read or something, because she wasn't around. Aunt Vi had come home while we'd been eating, and she'd vanished, too. She liked to go upstairs and read after a day at work, and she always ate dinner in the Kincaids' kitchen with the rest of the staff.

Because I was feeling out of sorts with the men in my life and excluded from the happy group (not to mention deserted by my mother and my aunt), I said, "What are those pennies doing on the table, Detective, hmmm? Isn't gambling illegal? Like you told me fortune-telling is?"

He grinned up at me. "Aw, we make allowances."

"Humph. You'd darned well better make allowances for me, is all I have to say about it."

"No problem," he said. I wondered if he meant it.

Rotondo left our house shortly after that encounter. I was relieved to see him go. I also (and I hate to admit this because it sounds so petty) was feeling a good deal of annoyance that my family should instantly like a man who'd given every appearance of loathing me at first sight.

Maybe I was being too hard on Rotondo. After all, he was just doing his job at the Kincaids'. Maybe I was being too hard on *me*, for that matter. Aw, heck, I don't know. All I know for sure is that I'd never been so happy to hit the sack as I was that night.

Billy had remained in a good mood until we were in bed, too, what's more. I attributed his happiness to having met a man he liked and who was willing to talk to him and play cards with him, and treat him as he would any other person in the world. In other words, Rotondo didn't treat Billy like a cripple. I'm ashamed to admit this, too, but that upset me a bit. I didn't want Billy liking Sam Rotondo more than he liked me, for Pete's sake.

In short, I was jealous of Sam Rotondo. Please feel free to consider me a fool; you'd be doing no more than I did when I realized it.

I worried about the Sam-versus-me situation for approximately thirty seconds before I fell asleep. Didn't wake up once during the night, either, what's more, so I guess I wasn't all *that* concerned about the Sam-and-Billy situation.'

I didn't want to get out of bed the next morning. Even after a full night's sleep, I was bone tired and ever so weary of the Kincaids and their problems. Also, Billy's arm lay across my stomach, and it felt good there. Sometimes the fact that he'd been irreparably damaged by the Germans made me want to scream and throw things, two idiotic and unproductive activities. Oh, but I wanted a real marriage with my Billy. On mornings like this, I felt the loss a lot.

Reality and my emotional reactions to it, however, didn't make money, and I had a feeling I was going to be hearing from the Kincaids any second. Turning my head—I didn't want to turn my body because I'd disturb Billy's arm—I saw that it was already eight o'clock. Shoot, I almost never slept that late.

With a heavy sigh, but knowing I'd best get going or Mrs. Kincaid would catch me in my nightgown, I decided to get out of bed. I knew she was going to phone. She wasn't one to handle problems without all the help she could get. And, honestly, she really did have some tremendously big problems to deal with at the moment, and I did feel obliged to help her if I could.

Billy awoke as I tried to slide out from under his arm. I turned and kissed him on the lips. "Morning, sleepyhead."

He rubbed his eyes. "What time is it?"

"Almost eight."

"Golly, we never sleep this late."

My sentiments exactly. "I guess we both had tiring days yesterday."

"I guess so." Billy lifted his arms and made a cradle with his hands against which he laid his head. Grinning with what I could only describe as true happiness, he said, "Say, Daisy, that detective fellow is a pretty swell guy. He's easy to talk to, and he plays a bad game of gin rummy, so I get to win."

Even though my heart gave a smallish spasm when I heard the *he's easy to talk to* part of Billy's speech, I smiled. "I'm glad. I didn't like him at all when I first met him, but I guess he's okay." I think that was a lie, although I'm not entirely sure. Sam and Billy together were okay. Sam the detective, all by himself, was a louse.

"How come you didn't like him?"

I'd put on a spring frock of light-green-and-white foulard that Aunt Vi had sewn for me for Easter (*and*, I might add, that ended a tasteful five inches from my low-heeled brown pumps), and was tying the solid green sash about my waist when I answered him. "Well, for one thing, he thought I'd killed Mr. Kincaid at first. I know he did."

"Ha!" Billy laughed. I thought that a rather strange reaction from my very own husband, but I didn't take exception aloud. Inside, my indignation swelled.

"And," I went on, "he thinks all spiritualists are fortune tellers and illegal bunco artists."

"Can't really blame him for that, either, Daisy. I know, I know," he said when he saw I was heating up and about to blow, "I don't like your job either, but I know you have to do it."

"Hmmm." That was a bigger concession to reality than Billy had made in a long time. I considered thanking Sam Rotondo for it the next time I saw him, but decided it was far too soon to be thanking him for anything.

"You look swell today, Daisy," Billy said when I'd finished brushing my hair into its regulation knot in a pouf.

"Thanks. I try to look as mysterious as possible under all circumstances, you know." I said it in a sepulchral tone and made my face into one I hoped resembled Dr. Hyde in a flicker we'd seen last year (a flicker, by the by, that had scared Billy and me into leaving a night light on in our bedroom for almost a week).

"I think you'd look good in one of those short bobs," said Billy. "You know, like that picture actress everybody's talking about. She's a redhead, too, you know."

I turned around, my Dr. Hyde expression vanishing like magic. "Really? Do you really think so? You don't think it would tarnish my mediumistic image?"

"Hell, no! Anyhow, you can always wear a hat."

"Boy, oh boy, I've wanted to get a bob for the longest time."

"Do it," Billy said. "To heck with your image. Nobody's not going to hire you if you get your hair cut, are they? That would be dumb."

I made another face, this one merely a stab at a humorous grimace. "Most of the rich people who use me are dumb, or they wouldn't be hiring mediums in the first place."

It made him laugh, and I was glad. Usually, I only annoyed and irritated him. "Gotta get some breakfast," I said. "I have a sinking feeling Mrs. Kincaid's going to call any minute now, and I can't face that hell-house on an empty stomach. Want me to bring you something?"

"Naw," my Billy said. "I'll get up in a bit. It feels good

to lie here for a while."

That was because, when he'd been lying in bed for several hours, he didn't feel the pain in his lungs and legs as much as when he moved around. I thought about offering to get him his morphine, but didn't. Billy's morphine use scared me, even though I understood that he needed it. Anyhow, he knew his body better than I— which was just one more unlucky aspect of our marriage, I guess.

So I staggered out to the kitchen, feeling tired and head-achy. In fact, I felt as if I'd been hit on the head with a sledge hammer and then run over by an automobile.

Ma hadn't left for work yet, so there was coffee already made. I kissed her on the cheek. "You're saving my life with this coffee, Ma. I hope you know that. I'm sure it will cure my headache."

She laughed. "Take a powder with it, and it'll go away." Good old Ma. She always knew what a person needed. She picked up her handbag, ready to walk to the Hotel Marengo and keep their books for yet another day. "The Kincaids are getting to you, are they?"

I shut my eyes and shuddered. "I know they're going to call me to go over there today. I'm not sure I can face another day in that house."

"Sure you can," said my mother, kissing me on the top of my knot. "It's your job, and a Gumm always does her job. And so does a Majesty," she added conscientiously.

Of course, she was right. And, of course, the phone rang. It wasn't even eight-thirty yet. It was our ring, but Ma and I raced to get to it in order to forestall the neighbors. Ma got there first.

"It's for Daisy, Mrs. Barrow. Please hang up the wire." I could tell Mrs. Barrow wasn't being cooperative, because Ma's mouth scrunched up like a prune and her nose wrinkled. "Of course, Daisy is here. She's standing next to the telephone. Waiting to take her call." She put emphasis on the *waiting* part, not that Mrs. Barrow ever cared.

With a sigh, Ma handed the phone to me. "The old cow won't believe me," she said in a stage whisper Mrs. Barrow could probably have heard in her house down the street even without the telephone to help, but I took the receiver and tried to smooth over the unpleasantness.

"Mrs. Barrow? I believe this call is for me."

"Daisy? Daisy? Is that you?"

The voice belonged to Mrs. Kincaid and my heart sank, because she sounded frantic again. If Stacy had run off to some speakeasy and gotten herself arrested a second time, I was going to personally take the child to the dog pound and have her put to sleep. I could tell them she was a rum-running Rottweiler or something.

"Huh," said Mrs. Barrow. "Well, if you're so sure it's your call, Mrs. Majesty, I'll hang up. But you really must understand that sometimes the rest of us like to speak to our friends on the telephone, too. You shouldn't hog the wire the way you do."

Yeah, yeah, yeah. Nuts. I'd been away from home all day long the day before and couldn't possibly have hogged a thing on Mrs. Barrow's telephone wire. Also, I knew good and well that Billy and Pa never bothered to use the phone if they could avoid it—another male idiosyncrasy, I suppose. I didn't point that out, since I figured it was a good idea to keep conditions civil whenever possible, but said gently, "I believe this is an important call, Mrs. Barrow."

"Yes!" shrieked Mrs. Kincaid. "Oh, yes, yes! Oh, Daisy, you *must* come back here! Something awful's happened!"

Mrs. Barrow still hadn't hung up, so I decided *to hell with civility*, and said, "Hang up the wire right this minute, Mrs. Barrow, or I'll call the police!" Remembering Sam's visit from the night before, I lied like a rug. "As a matter of fact, there's a policeman sitting in my living room right this very minute!"

She hung up with a clang that nearly broke my ear drum. It occurred to me too late that Mrs. Barrow would probably already be racing out her back door to spread the gossip that something dreadful had happened at the Majestys' house because the police were surrounding the place, and wouldn't you just expect something like that from one of *them*. But at least I got rid of the old hag, and that was the point.

Working on Mrs. Kincaid, I said, "Please try to calm down, Mrs. Kincaid. What can I do for you? What's happened?" Oh, sweet Lord in heaven, they hadn't discovered her husband's body, had they? I couldn't ask.

"Quincy Applewood has come back!" she shouted in sort of a combination of a sob and a wail that would have done an Irish banshee proud. "He's saying some crazy things, Daisy! *Crazy*! And nobody can find that Mr. Rotund person who works at the police office, and I don't know what to do, and Del and Algie have gone to the bank, and Harold hasn't a clue what's going on or what to do about it, and Stacy is threatening to throw a knife at Mr. Applewood and kill him the way he killed her father, and poor Edie Marsh has just throttled Stacy with the cord from the vacuum cleaner, and—Oh, Daisy! You *must* come! *Now*!"

Golly, I guessed I did. And by gum, if I wasn't proud of Edie, I just didn't know anything. "Please try to calm down, Mrs. Kincaid. I'll be there as soon as I can be."

Someone had knocked on the front door as I was talking to Mrs. Kincaid. Ma went to get the door and by golly if it wasn't Sam Rotondo! If Mrs. Barrow had argued with me for another thirty seconds or so, I wouldn't have had to lie to her.

His arrival, one I considered suspicious in the extreme although I couldn't have said why, did make my conversation with Mrs. Kincaid easier, however. "And you'll be pleased to know that Detective Rotondo is here right this minute. Perhaps we can drive over there together." The notion didn't appeal, since I didn't want to ride anywhere with Rotondo, but it might save time. And I wouldn't have to crank.

"Oh, Daisy! I *knew* I could count on you!" She was weeping copiously when the receiver clicked down in the cradle.

Sucking in air for comfort and squaring my shoulders for strength, but still feeling more than a little bit shaky, I toddled into our bedroom. Billy was up, and I could tell the pain had started in on him hard. He was already in a bad mood when he looked at me.

"Let me guess," he said, sounding surly. "You just got a call from that insane Kincaid woman begging you to bring your crystal ball to her house and throw it at her insane daughter."

I smiled broadly at my adorable, albeit cranky, husband. "Gee, Billy, that's one I'd never thought about before. But it's good! I'll have to mull it over. There might even be some way to make it work. But I don't have to use my crystal ball today. Edie strangled Stacy Kincaid with the vacuum-cleaner cord."

"She *what*?" After staring at me, wide-eyed, for about a second and a half, Billy started laughing so hard, I knew it hurt his lungs. I'd learned a long time ago not to let him see my fear and worry about his condition, so I merely continued to grin.

"Detective Rotondo just got here, too. Want to see him? I hope he can drive me to the Kincaids' place, because I don't feel like cranking the Model T."

"Sam's here?" He sounded pleased, which made one of us.

"Yup. He's in the living room, and I guess he's talking to Ma, because I was talking to Mrs. Kincaid when he arrived."

"Tell him I'll be there in a minute."

I neither sighed nor balked, for which I believe I

deserve some sort of commendation from Above. Ha! As if.

Ma had already left for work when I got to the living room, and Rotondo sat on the sofa, his hat on his lap. I presume he'd removed it in deference to my mother, since he was seldom so polite with me. When I entered the room, he stood politely, too. "Good morning, Mrs. Majesty." He even sounded courteous. My level of suspicion soared like a lark. Or maybe like a buzzard.

"Good morning." Because I couldn't think of anything else to say, I got right down to business. "I just got a call from Mrs. Kincaid."

Before he could ask about the telephone call, Billy rolled into the living room.

"Hey, Sam!" His face was pale and pinched, and I knew the morphine hadn't begun its job yet. "Did you hear that Edie Marsh strangled Stacy Kincaid with the vacuum cleaner cord?"

"God bless Edie for a saint," I added. They probably thought I was teasing, but I meant it.

"She *what*?" Rotondo looked as if he wasn't certain we weren't simply fooling around.

Of course I wasn't either, so I couldn't very well resent his doubt. I did, however, say, "Just joking," to ease his mind. "Unfortunately, Stacy Kincaid's still alive. And probably kicking."

"Oh. You had me worried there for a minute." He grinned at Billy. "Morning, Billy. Spent all my money yet?"

Billy grinned back, in spite of his pain. "Not yet. There's still today, though."

Rotondo chuckled. So did Billy. Their levity vexed me. I'd just received an important telephone call, and these two men were joking about pennies won in a gin rummy game. I was probably only jealous, but I felt righteous at the time.

"Back to the problem at hand," I resumed tartly, "Mrs.

Kincaid just telephoned. Evidently Quincy Applewood has returned to the house and everyone's in a furor. I guess Stacy threatened to stab him through the heart, and that's when Edie wrapped the cord around her throat." Boy, I wish I could have seen it happen, too.

"What?" Rotondo, who had walked over to Billy's wheelchair to shake Billy's hand, jumped up so hard, he darned near fell onto Billy's lap. "Oh, God, I'm sorry, Billy."

Still smiling, Billy said, "That's okay. I figure I have all your money, so that's pay-back enough."

"I should say so," Rotondo said, his smile thin and concerned-looking. Turning to me, he said, "You say Applewood's returned to the Kincaid house?" As soon as he asked his question, his attention returned to Billy to assess any damage he might have done when I'd startled him.

Since I didn't want him feeling sorry for Billy, primarily because Billy *hates* for people to feel sorry for him, I spoke up. "Yes. I'm not sure when. Mrs. Kincaid was in kind of a state."

"What else is new?" Rotondo said bitingly.

"Good question," said Billy.

"Would you mind driving me to the Kincaids' place, Detective? As long as you're here, I mean." Since both he and Billy were looking at me as if I'd asked him to climb an Alp, I said, "If you're going there, that is. I assumed you were, since Quincy's returned to the place."

"Oh," said Rotondo. "Oh, certainly. I'll be glad to drive you. You're right. I need to get over there as soon as possible." He looked down at Billy. "I was going to make a date with you to win my money back, but I guess we can do that later."

Good Lord in heaven, they really *did* like each other. I glanced at the ceiling, hoping God would spot my face among the millions he saw daily, and asked Him if He didn't think I had enough burdens to bear already, and couldn't He spare me just this little one? A glance at Rotondo made me alter my prayer a bit. He was actually sort of a large burden.

It was no use. I already knew God didn't pay attention to trivial prayers, and He would without a doubt consider mine trivial. The fact that I didn't consider it any such thing was of no consequence to God.

I went to Billy, leaned over, and kissed him hard on the mouth because I loved him so much. That made him happy, and it also made Rotondo look at the two of us in a strange way. To heck with Rotondo.

"Gotta run back and get my hat and handbag," I said to Billy. I chose a dark green cloche hat and bag, which, when combined with the light green dress and my dark red hair, looked fairly dignified. When you're not even twenty, dignity's a difficult commodity to come by sometimes.

As a color, green brought out the best in me. By that I mean the combination of my skin tone and the green made me look pale and a trifle pasty. Perhaps even a little ill. I figured if I looked sick enough, maybe Mrs. Kincaid wouldn't keep me around until the earth ceased to turn on its axis or hell froze over. I really did like to be home with Billy, even if he could be a difficult and a lot of trouble sometimes. Often, even. I selected my brown gloves from the drawer because they went with my brown French-heel shoes, and thought I made quite an elegant picture for a woman about to spend a day in what might as well be a haunted mansion for all the turmoil going on in it.

I was beginning to long for the days when all I had to do was call people up from the grave to chat with, deal out Tarot cards, fiddle with the Ouija board, and gaze into a crystal ball and say pseudo-profound things to silly women. Sing in the choir. Take walks around the block, pushing Billy in his chair. Force Brownie to exercise once in a while. Things like that. Things I was used to doing. Things I understood. This Kincaid mystery nonsense was driving me nuts.

Billy wasn't overjoyed to see me stepping out with another man; I could tell. But he liked Sam, so he'd probably get over it as soon as we were out of sight. I gave him a cheery farewell, made a joke about coming back with all the latest gossip, kissed him again, and he took it pretty well. Rotondo actually helped, too, by completely ignoring me and my nice-looking costume. I swear, the man was a perfect ogre except when he wasn't.

"So," Rotondo said as soon as he'd helped me into the police car, "things are heating up."

"They are?" I didn't see how.

"At the Kincaids'."

"Oh." I wasn't a policeman and guess I wasn't seeing the Kincaid problem from his perspective. It only looked like a mess to me.

Police cars had doors on both sides, which made them much more easy, not to mention more modest, to enter and exit than my old Model T. This particular police car was a Hudson and was nice and roomy and had a closed top. You also didn't have to fiddle with the clutch cable while you cranked it, which was a distinct improvement over the Model T. Some cars were even being made with batteries in them nowadays so you didn't have to crank at all, but they were way out of my price range.

I was seriously beginning to consider purchasing a Hudson as my next car. You know, when I got rich. Ha! Sorry. Sometimes I get these silly fancies.

Although the Hudson was an improvement over the Model T, I still hoped nobody noticed me in it. My reputation was fragile enough, especially after having screeched at Mrs. Barrow this morning, without having all the neighbors seeing me driving around in a police car. Of course I was in the front seat and not behind the screened-in back seat, but I'm sure that part of the picture wouldn't be bandied about. It would be the "Did you know that Daisy Majesty must have been arrested, and didn't I just *tell* you it would happen one of these days?" part that people would talk about.

"You say Mrs. Kincaid told you Applewood came back to the house?"

"Yes. And that's all I know. She didn't tell me anything else over the telephone except about Edie throttling Stacy with the vacuum-cleaner cord." I couldn't help myself. Every time I thought about that part of the drama, I smiled.

"Did she mention anything about her husband coming back?"

I frowned at him. "I just told you every single thing she said to me. Did I say anything about Mr. Kincaid? No, I didn't. And that's because *she* didn't say anything about her husband."

"Don't get testy, Mrs. Majesty. This is a tough case. Sometimes people know more than they think they do."

"Well, I don't."

The expression he shot at the sky outside the Hudson's window made me think he believed me, darn him.

The Hudson had a smooth ride, too. If I hadn't been in it with Detective Sam Rotondo, I think I'd have enjoyed the ride a lot. Drawbacks. There are always drawbacks. Sometimes I get frightfully tired of them.

CHAPTER 14

Featherstone met us at the door with his nose in the air, his patent-leather shoes shining like mirrors, and his pristine white cravat all but gleaming at his throat. I don't know how the man did that—you know, look perfect all the time. It must have taken years of practice.

I wanted to ask him if Edie had damaged Stacy with the vacuum-cleaner cord, but knew he'd never answer me, so I didn't bother. Aunt Vi, now, she'd tell me in a second. Less than that. Aunt Vi was human. Featherstone was British. There's a big difference.

The commotion coming from the drawing room didn't leave us guessing where we'd be heading. Although we didn't really need the butler's guidance, Rotondo and I followed Featherstone down the hall to the scene of the drama. We even let him do his duty, open the door, and announce us. Talk about important. I actually felt like a queen there for a second. Maybe half a second. I hate to admit it, but Majesty can be a heck of a name to live with sometimes—or live up to, I guess I mean.

"Mrs. Majesty and Detective Rotondo, Mrs. Kincaid." Featherstone might have been announcing the arrival of the Prince of Wales.

"Oh!" Shrieked Mrs. Kincaid, vaulting up from the red velvet chair in which she'd been ensconced, and launching herself at me. Harold stood behind the chair, and it looked to me as if he'd been attempting to press her shoulders down and keep her put.

I braced myself against a heavy table with a marble top so I wouldn't fall over when she hit. I got a heck of a bruise on my bum, but I didn't mind. The poor woman was practically out of her mind with all the fuss and bother going on in her life.

"Daisy!" I heard somebody else scream, but I was at present enfolded in the rather fleshy arms of Mrs. Kincaid, so I couldn't see who it was. I think it was Edie, though. It sounded like her voice. In a way. It sounded like her voice might sound if she'd been crying and carrying on for a year or two.

It took a while, but things settled down at last. By then, I'd realized that not only was Edie in the room, sitting in another red velvet chair as if she were a normal human being and not merely a housemaid, but so was Quincy Applewood, who looked sort of like death warmed up, although it also looked as if death might claim him any second. His face was filthy and covered with bruises and welts, and his knuckles had been scraped raw. His chair and Edie's were close together and they were holding hands. I thought that was just the sweetest thing. I guess I'm a romantic at heart, in spite of everything.

After being released by Mrs. Kincaid, I went to Edie first, since she was my friend. "How are you holding up, Edie? I hope everything will clear up soon."

She started crying. Figures. *Everybody* seemed to be crying at me in those days. I patted her on the shoulder and headed for Quincy. "What the heck happened to you, Quincy? You look terrible!"

"Thanks." He grinned, which made a split in his lip start to bleed, and I felt awful. I patted the air with my hand to show him he needn't smile. Lord, I couldn't *wait* until this lousy mess was cleared up.

After I'd spoken to Quincy, I aimed straight at Harold, whom I knew to be sane and normal. Mostly normal. He greeted me warmly, and I felt better.

"All right, everyone, let's get organized here."

I was almost glad Rotondo had decided to put on his tough-copper attitude and take over. We all stood (or sat) at attention instantly. Rotondo turned to Quincy.

"Young man, tell your story. Make it quick and clean, and don't leave out any essential details."

Quincy sighed, leading me to believe he'd already told his story more than once and that it would hurt, literally, to tell it again, but he knew what he was up against. After all, the Kincaids were millionaires. Quincy worked as a stable boy. He didn't expect anyone in the room except Edie and me to believe anything he said.

"Wait! Wait!"

Before Quincy could begin, Mrs. Kincaid hurried to his chair and commenced hovering over him.

It looked to me as if Rotondo couldn't believe what he was seeing. It was sort of unusual, I suppose, since Quincy was Quincy and Mrs. Kincaid was Mrs. Kincaid, but I never have thought Rotondo truly understood people.

Quincy's expression was one to behold when Mrs. Kincaid laid a hand on his shoulder. He looked scared to death.

"Mr. Applewood, we must get your wounds attended to before you do any more talking. Do you need more carbolic? Ointment? That's such a dreadful cut on your lip, and I'm sure you ought to keep ointment on it.

"And your *head*! My goodness, I don't know what to do for that wretched lump on your head. But I have lanolin and boric acid ointment. They're both good for wounds. And I'm sure you could use a cool drink. Or would you prefer a cup of hot tea or coffee? You've endured such an ordeal." She turned in a circle, apparently seeking something (probably a maid), and then, not seeing any present except Edie, who wasn't acting that particular role today, she stopped still, confused.

I got up from the sofa I'd commandeered. "Let me get some things for him, Mrs. Kincaid. I'm sure Aunt Vi will know exactly what to do."

There went Mrs. Kincaid's hands to her bosom again. "Oh, Daisy, I knew I could count on you!"

"Absolutely." Harold. It sounded to me as if he were trying not to laugh. Couldn't say as I blamed him.

Aunt Vi knew what to do, precisely as I'd predicted. She made tea and coffee, put some little petit fours on a platter, and had the second housemaid, a twelve-year-old girl named Karen who worked at the Kincaid mansion after school except during summer vacation when she worked all day, carry them to the drawing room.

As for the medicaments, first of all, Vi gave me firm instructions on cleanliness. "I just read an article in the *Saturday Evening Post* that says germs cause infections, and infections lead to death."

I couldn't help it. I made a face.

Aunt Vi shook her finger at me. "Now don't you go getting squeamish on me, young lady. You've had practice in nursing." She was right on that count, and I'd hated every minute of it. "You have to clean wounds thoroughly so they won't grow germs. Germs are the killers. Silent killers, the article said of them."

"Germs. Right." I had no idea what she was talking about. That had never stopped me before, and it didn't stop me then.

"So I'm going to give you two bowls of warm water." She held up one bowl. "I'm putting carbolic soap in this one. Wash that bump as well as you can, whether he likes it or not."

He wouldn't like it at all. I could tell I wasn't exactly

going to be having a swell time during the next several hours.

"Then rinse it with the clean water to get all the soap out. *All* the soap, Daisy. Do you understand me?"

"Yes, ma'am."

"And then he'll need to medicate the wound and keep it clean and bound so germs can't get at it. Sanitation is what's needed here."

Sounded like a good idea to me.

Aunt Vi handed me a jar of lanolin. "Make sure he keeps the wound on his lip well greased with this or it'll never heal and he'll have a scar for life. It would be a shame for such a good-looking boy to have a hideous scar to mar him. He shouldn't be talking at all, but you know as well as I do that that dreadful policeman will make him go on until they take him down to headquarters and give him the third degree."

The third degree? I eyed my aunt suspiciously. "Have you been reading my detective novels, Aunt Vi?"

She blushed, giving me my answer. "I'll tolerate no sass from you, my girl." Aunt Vi, like Mrs. Kincaid, couldn't sound strict if someone tied her to a tree and commanded her to do so or die, so I wasn't scared. "I don't know how much you've been told so far—"

"Nothing," I broke in.

Aunt Vi nodded. "As I suspected. Well, poor Quincy suffered a vicious smack on the head and has a huge lump there. This is the padded bandage he's going to need to keep on it. And it will have to be changed daily. *I* will see to *that*."

"You will?" She'd probably have to fight Edie for the privilege, although I didn't mention it. But I was confused. "I thought he'd been fired. Will he even be here for you to change his pad?"

Her face took on an expression of fierce militancy that I myself had encountered once or twice when I'd been sick and rebelled against taking the gruesome-tasting medicine I was supposed to take. "He'd better be. I can't believe that such a kind-hearted woman as Mrs. Kincaid would turn the poor abused boy away from her door when he's so ill."

Since I couldn't come up with an opinion on the subject to save myself, I remained mute.

As she'd been talking, Vi had also been working, folding some clean white cotton material into a thick pad. After that she dunked the pad in water. Then she poured some witch hazel on the cloth, made sure the pad was well saturated, put some other kind of smelly, oily stuff on it—I think I recognized the aromas of eucalyptus and maybe mint, but can't say for sure—and handed the pad to me. "There. Now I'm going to give you some bandages, and I want you to *promise* me you'll tie this pad to the bump on his head after you've thoroughly cleaned it and before he starts talking to those miserable policemen, and I don't care how much he kicks and moans about it. Have that fat detective sit on his feet if you have to."

Fat detective? "Are you talking about Detective Rotondo?"

"Is that his name? I guess that's the one. The dark one."

"Gee, I never thought he was fat." I thought he looked pretty darned good, as a matter of fact. Muscular rather than thin, but not fat. Maybe it was his name. I mean, face it, Rotondo makes people think "rotund," and that makes people think fat. That's my theory, anyhow.

"I don't care if he's the Lord Harry, you just promise me you'll get that poor boy's head patched up before he says a single word to the coppers."

Good soldier that I was, I saluted. "Yes, ma'am"

She smacked me on the bottom as I left the kitchen, taking Quincy's cure with me. It wasn't a hard smack.

When I entered the drawing room, I could tell the housemaid had brought in the refreshments and skedaddled, because she wasn't there and the refreshments resided all by themselves on a gorgeous table in the middle of the room. Everyone was ignoring them with what I could only consider deliberate perfection. Guess when things go *really* badly, people don't care about food.

Other than that, it didn't look to me as if any of the drawing-room occupants had moved so much as an inch. It was kind of like in "Sleeping Beauty," when the good fairies put the kingdom to sleep for a hundred years.

My entrance changed all that. Mrs. Kincaid squealed, Harold said, "Daisy," in a relieved-sounding voice, Edie gasped, Quincy gave me a very small wave, apparently deeming a wave less painful than a smile, since waving didn't make his split lip bleed.

Rotondo, as might have been expected, huffed and muttered, "It's about damned time."

I gave him as good a glower as I could come up with. "You're going to have to wait to question Quincy until I doctor him, Detective Rotondo, so you might as well get used to it." I put my own tray full of ointments and bandages on the table next to Quincy, who eyed them uneasily. I looked over my shoulder at Rotondo. "Why don't you eat a few of Aunt Vi's petit fours. They might sweeten you up, although that seems unlikely."

I saw his lips pinch before I turned to doctor my victim—er, I mean, my patient—and added another point to my side of the Rotondo-Majesty sniping scoreboard.

Since I believe in getting the worst over first, I decided to start with Quincy's head. "Turn your back to me, Quince. I have to put a patch over your bump, but first I have to cleanse it."

"It hurts enough already, Daisy. You do anything to hurt it more, or I won't be very happy with you." His tone of voice was merry, but I recognized the threat behind the tone.

"Don't you dare try anything with me, Quincy Applewood. At the moment, I'm in better shape than you are and I'll squash you like a beetle if you don't cooperate. Besides, I have my aunt Vi's permission to make Detective Rotondo sit on your legs if you even think about taking it on the lam. And Harold and Edie can hold your arms down." I thought of a great idea. "And if you *really* annoy me, I'll just have you tied to chair until I'm through with you."

"Crumbs, Daisy, you can be a real shrew without half trying, can't you?" He was exceedingly unhappy with me. I could tell.

"You're wrong, Quince. I try hard." I jerked a nod at Harold, who came over to the chair. "Hold his shoulders down, Harold. Aunt Vi promised me this is going to hurt. A lot. It's going to be even worse if he tries to fight me."

I think I heard Quincy repress a whimper.

Rotondo said, "I'll hold his legs down," giving me one of the more monumental shocks of my life. I'd never have expected a civil deed to emanate from that source while he was performing his policeman act.

I peered up at him. "Thanks." I know I sounded as surprised as I felt, and I also know he didn't appreciate it. But shoot, what had he ever done to make me think he might be a nice person under his outer crust?

"All right. Let's see here." I eyed my operating theater. Harold pressed hard on Quincy's shoulders, Edie held one of his hands to the arm of the chair, and even Mrs. Kincaid joined the party, keeping his other hand still.

Aunt Vi proved to be absolutely correct, as usual. As I worked on him, I hurt poor Quincy. A lot. My heart took to squishing and quaking, and it was all I could do to keep my hands from shaking and me from bawling like a baby as I washed his wound. It was an ugly one.

Someone had belted him a good one on the back of the head with something hard and unmistakably knobby, because most of his hair had come off onto the implement and the rest was stuck in blood-clotted cuts and scrapes. He must have fallen down in an area where there was a whole lot of dirt, because there was a plethora of dust, leafy matter, and—I swear this is true— bugs. Little bugs. Ants, in fact. There weren't many of those, thank God (I hate bugs) and they were all dead, so I didn't have to fight nausea, which was the only blessing I could detect in the entire process. I felt sorry for Quincy, but I did as Aunt Vi had instructed me, no matter how much I hated doing it.

After I was through de-germing him, he looked as if he'd gone ten rounds with a gorilla. Maybe a mountain lion.

It was a truly hideous bump sitting there on Quincy's head, and I knew it must hurt like crazy. Now I had to hurt it some more by applying a pad soaked in witch hazel, which I knew from experience hurt like the very devil when applied to cuts and sores. By this time, I actually did feel a little sickish.

"Don't let go yet," I instructed my aides. "There's witch hazel on the pad, and it's going to sting like anything."

"Dammit, Daisy, this isn't fair!" Quincy shouted. I wondered if he'd ever be my friend again.

That didn't stop me, but it almost made me cry when I gently pressed the pad on Quincy's lump and, in spite of his supreme self-control, he stiffened up like a starched petticoat and tears leaked from his eyes. He'd probably be embarrassed about those tears for the rest of his life, but he had no reason to be. Tears just come on their own sometimes, you know?

My hands were shaking as if I had St. Vitus' Dance, and I longed to sit down, put my head between my knees, and regain a modicum of composure before I had to tie the pad down, but I didn't dare. I had to get this operation over with because Quincy couldn't take much more, and neither could I. And he still had to undergo a grilling from the police.

That being the case, I put on my best combative expression and picked up the first strip of cloth Vi had given me. "Okay. Now for the fun part."

Quincy gave me a scowl so vicious, I was impressed, as I didn't think he had anything of the sort in him. "Don't look at *me* in that tone of voice, young man," I said sternly, trying to infuse some humor into what was not a humorous situation. It didn't work, so my effort was wasted. Everyone in the room looked as if they were undergoing unspecified but brutal tortures.

In spite of my experiences with Billy, who had come back to me only after the worst of his injuries had been cared for and he was as well as he'd ever be, I'm no nurse. I'm a spiritualist. I hadn't a clue how I was supposed to tie the pad to Quincy's head, so I did it in the most expedient manner I could think of. By the time I was through with him, Quincy looked as if he was wearing a hat that tied under his chin in several places and was also sporting an Indian head band, if you can feature such an arrangement. In short, he looked silly.

There was nothing silly about my own state of nerves by that time. I sat with a plunk on one of the elegant chairs and, feeling faint, decided to heck with everybody and what they thought, and lowered my head between my knees until the dizziness passed.

When I glanced up at last, everyone was watching me. Oh, goodie. I just love creating a spectacle of myself. I grinned. "Sorry. I guess Clara Barton would kick me out of the nursing force, huh?"

"Are you all right, Daisy?" Harold finally lifted his hands from Quincy's shoulders.

As soon as he did so, Quincy slumped forward. I guess Edie and Mrs. Kincaid weren't certain that he wouldn't hop up from the chair and try to wallop me for hurting him, but I realized an instant later that he, too, felt faint. If Rotondo hadn't jumped out of the way (he'd held

Quincy's feet still through the entire operation), their heads would have crashed together. I felt sick again for a moment until I saw *that* particular danger had passed. I *really* didn't want to patch up any more bumps on any more heads.

"Yeah. Thanks, Harold. I'm fine. But I'm sure no nurse."

"I can vouch for that," came, muffled, from Quincy, whose head still hung forward. Made me wince to see that, since the blood was probably pounding through his head and making the lump throb like a war drum. Combined with the witch hazel and everything else, I imagine the poor boy was in truly horrifying pain.

"Sorry, Quincy. I really didn't want to hurt you."

It was only then that I remembered the lanolin. I felt faint again at once. With sinking heart, I rose from my chair, straightened my shoulders, tried to get my brain to work, and returned to Quincy, who pushed himself back in his chair and squinted at me with such evil intent, I got angry.

"Darn it, Quincy, it's not my fault you got yourself all bashed up! My aunt Vi said to put this lanolin on your lip before you try to answer any questions, and I'm going to do it, with or without your cooperation! And if you so much as flinch, I'll hit your face so hard, your cheek will match the lump on your bull head!"

Somebody laughed. I turned, irate, and was astonished to realize it was Detective Sam Rotondo. I frowned at him. "It isn't funny."

Rotondo ignored me. "Better do as she says," he advised Quincy. "She's got some really eerie connections, remember. She might turn you into a frog if she gets mad enough."

That made me so furious, I wanted to throw one of Quincy's bloody-water-filled bowls at the detective. Then I realized everyone else in the room was laughing uproariously, and it occurred to me that perhaps I was the slightest bit on edge and my threat had been a trifle irrational. Ah, well.

Quincy sat up, looking grumpy, and darned if Mrs. Kincaid didn't make a sensible suggestion, perhaps the first one in her entire life. See? She'd been without her miserable clod of a husband for a mere few hours, and already she was beginning to think for herself. I began to wonder if I was seeing a miracle in action.

"Edie, dear, will you go upstairs to my bathroom and bring down the laudanum bottle you'll find in the medicine chest? After the policeman is through with Mr. Applewood, I'm going to see that he takes some for his pain. I'm sure it will help him sleep, too."

Quincy's face was a mass of mottled bruises, but you could see his blush between the black-and-blue marks. I'm sure his nose was broken, but, since Mrs. Kincaid had threatened him with laudanum, I decided it would be prudent to wait until he'd taken the medicine before I taped his nose back into place.

"You don't need to do that, ma'am. I'm fine. Honest." Poor Quincy. He looked about as embarrassed as it was possible for a human male to look.

"Huh," said I inelegantly.

"Don't be stupid, Quincy," Edie delivered in a tight, pithy voice. "You need the laudanum and someone to take care of you until you get better."

Quincy's expression turned mulish. He crossed his arms over his chest, wincing as he did so, from which I deduced he had bruises in places other than his head. Suspicious, I asked, "Do your ribs hurt, Quincy? Because if any of them are cracked, they'll need to be bandaged. And I'll bandage them, whether you like it or not. I'll have you tied down this time for sure. Of course," I added magnanimously, "I'll wait until the laudanum takes effect."

"But I don't *want* to take any laudanum." Quincy sounded desperate.

He was also too late. As soon as Mrs. Kincaid's request left her lips, Edie bounded out of the room, pausing only to scold the man of her dreams and tell him to stop being a stubborn so-and-so. I heard her footsteps on the carpeted stairway, making me believe she was taking them two at a time (Edie works for the Kincaids; she wouldn't dare be noisy under normal household conditions).

"Nonsense, Mr. Applewood," quoth Mrs. Kincaid. "You need it."

"Yes," said I. "You do."

The scowl he gave me that time surpassed any single one of those bestowed upon me by Rotondo.

"Perhaps it would be best to tape his nose after he takes the laudanum, too."

By gum! Mrs. Kincaid was coming into her own with a vengeance, and it had only been hours since her old man had run out on her. It was enough to give you faith in the workings of fate.

"The laudanum's probably a good idea," said Rotondo. "I can help keep him still and pinch his nose shut while you dump it down his throat. Then we can strip him and you can bandage his ribs." He laughed again.

The darned man was keeping me totally off balance. One minute he was as mean as a scorpion, and the next minute he was being nice and helpful and—even more incredible—humorous.

"Doggone it, Daisy Majesty, I'm not going to take my shirt off in front of any ladies!"

"Most nurses are ladies, Quincy," I pointed out. "No matter where your ribs are checked, you're manly chest is going to be looked at by a lady."

"That's the truth, dear. Although perhaps Detective Rotondo and Harold would be willing to bandage Mr. Applewood's ribs, if that would save him embarrassment."

Both men nodded.

It was all I could do not to stare at Mrs. Kincaid in awe. "Brilliant idea. And after they bind your ribs, I'll fix your nose." I smiled broadly at Mrs. Kincaid, who smiled broadly back. I'd always liked the woman, but she might just become one of my favorite people if this kept up.

"What's the matter with my nose?" Quincy yelled, feeling said appendage and then cringing in pain. "Ow. I didn't even feel my nose because my head hurt so much." He sent me a hideous scowl. "Thanks a lot for pointing it out to me, Daisy."

"My pleasure."

"I don't doubt it," he said tartly.

"Your nose is probably broken," I said, not mincing words. "And I'm going to tape it up, whether you like it or not."

"Like hell," Quincy muttered under his breath.

I scowled back at him. "But that doesn't mean I'm not putting lanolin on your lip now. You have to get that oiled up before the detective questions you."

He'd probably have hit me if I'd been a man. He did, however, snatch the jar of lanolin out of my hand. "I can put lanolin on my own lips, darn it!"

Edie came back with the laudanum, and Quincy took a spoonful without whining.

I sniffed, turned around, and sat demurely on the sofa a couple of feet from Edie, who grinned at me. I could tell she was relieved Quincy was home, even if he wasn't out of the woods yet. She patted my knee and whispered, "Good work, Daisy."

"Thanks." Grateful to her for her commendation, tears filled my eyes, and I felt stupid. But I really, honestly and truly, *hate* hurting people. Still, I believed I had behaved in a manner befitting a Gumm. And a Majesty, too, come to think of it.

After Quincy had spread his lip liberally with lanolin, grimacing the entire time (men are such babies), he sat up straight, groaned only once, sighed, and said, "I guess I'm ready to talk now."

Rotondo took out the notebook and pencil he always carried in his pocket. Then he went to a hard-backed chair standing against a near wall, picked it up as if it weighed approximately six ounces, and plunked it down in front of Quincy.

From the novels I've read, I understand policemen like to maintain eye contact with their crooks because in that way they can determine whether or not a person is lying. I've tried staring into people's eyes with that truth-or-lie question in mind and it doesn't work for me, but I'm not a policeman. Maybe you need special training.

Quincy started the interview. Interrogation. Whatever it's called. "You've already probably heard that Mr. Kincaid and I had an argument last night."

"Yes, but please don't ask me any more questions. I'm the one doing the asking here."

Well! I'd never heard anything so rude in my life.

Apparently, neither had Quincy. He slumped back against the chair, glowered, and said, "Go ahead, then. Ask."

Animosity didn't seem to affect Sam Rotondo in any way whatsoever. Given his personality and profession, he was more than likely accustomed to people being hostile to him. He didn't even frown, which is more consideration than he ever gave me. Big dolt.

"You and Mr. Kincaid were arguing," said Rotondo, not skipping a beat. "Of the two of you, who precipitated the animosities?"

Quincy looked as if he was wondering what the heck *precipitated* meant, but he figured it out right away. "I barged in on the old bastard—" He cast a dismayed glance at Mrs. Kincaid. "Oh, ma'am, I'm so sorry…"

She only waved a hand in the air as if to say she felt the same way, took no exception to Quincy's assessment of her husband's worth, and only wished she wasn't high-classed so she could use those kinds of words herself.

Quincy cleared his throat. "Well, then. I barged into his office. Didn't even knock first. He, of course, got mad at me instantly, but I didn't care. I was too furious to care. I marched straight up to his desk and slammed my hands on it." It looked to me as if Quincy was relishing the memories.

"And why was that?" Rotondo's voice purred like that of a cat. An extremely large and dangerous, not to mention sneaky and probably treacherous, alley cat.

"The damned bastard—" Again Quincy stopped talking and glanced at Mrs. Kincaid. She waved his worry away a second time.

"He'd been chasing Edie around in his wheelchair, trying to take advantage of her!"

This time, Mrs. Kincaid didn't wave. She gasped so hard her face turned pink, stood up, swayed back and forth for a second or two before her knees gave out, and she collapsed like a popped balloon on the sofa. I thought she'd fainted dead away until I heard her whisper, "The fiend! The horrid, vicious fiend!"

Well, glory be.

Before Rotondo could continue, Mrs. Kincaid went on bitterly, "I knew it. I always suspected he was having affairs. And he was *always* chasing the housemaids, poor things. He was such a terrible man." She sat up suddenly, making me jump, and stared straight at Quincy. "I'm *glad* you killed him, Mr. Applewood! You performed a good Christian deed and rid the world of a devil!"

"Me?" Quincy pointed at his probably cracked rib cage. "Hell's bells, ma'am, I didn't kill anyone."

"Oh." Mrs. Kincaid looked disappointed.

My goodness. People constantly astound me.

Rotondo turned to me. In a harsh whisper, he said, "Can you get that woman out of here? I can't have all these interruptions."

Harold overheard Rotondo's request and stood. "I'll take Mother outdoors to enjoy the roses, Detective. I think you need Daisy here, since she knows more than most of us about the whole debacle."

"Huh," said Rotondo.

I wanted to kick him.

Harold went on, "And I know Mother needs to smell something sweet for a change. Lanolin really stinks, doesn't it?"

"Yes," said Quincy and frowned at me, even though none of this was my fault.

Then Rotondo said, "Thank you, Mr. Kincaid."

"Oh, yes, thank you, Harold! You're such a wonderful son!" Mrs. Kincaid bolted to her feet and all but fell upon her son's pudgy shoulders, weeping and moaning like a Halloween ghost. I have to admit to a sense of relief when the door closed behind mother and son.

Edie muttered, "Thank goodness," and I got the feeling she felt the same way.

"So," continued Rotondo as if nothing had happened to interfere with his interrogation, "you say you were angry with Mr. Kincaid for attempting to entrap Miss Marsh by the use of the wheelchair?"

"Yes. The filthy bastard."

"Quincy!" Edie said reprovingly.

As for yours truly, I thought Mr. Kincaid deserved all the filth and abuse anyone wanted to heap upon him. Nobody had asked for my opinion, however, so I kept it to myself.

"I was mad as hell and almost crazy when I found about it from Daisy."

You ought to have seen the look I got from Edie after that revelation. She pushed herself several inches farther away from me on the sofa. Her eyes thinned into slits and she glared at me as if I'd just killed her dog.

I tried to placate her without words. You know, I gave

her a little finger wave and a sympathetic grin, and mouthed that I'd explain everything later. She didn't seem to value my intentions, because her glower didn't abate.

Quincy resumed. "I was furious. I mean, that old geezer is disgusting. And any man who uses his wealth and power to seduce a poor working girl needs to be shot." His face between the puffy blue parts turned as red as autumn apples.

"Is that how it was done?" Rotondo asked quietly.

"Is what how what was done?" Quincy only looked confused.

"Is that how you did away with Mr. Kincaid?"

"What? Dammit, I told you I didn't do a thing with Kincaid! Well," he amended, grinning broadly (thank God for the lanolin) "I sure ripped him to hell and back verbally that night. It felt good to tell the old man exactly what I thought of miserable, not to mention married, not to mention *old* buzzards chasing around after good girls who aren't in a position to defend themselves."

"I see," said Rotondo, frowning. "So how *did* it happen?"

"How did what happen?"

"How'd you kill him?"

"Dammit, I *didn't* kill him! If you'd stop condemning me, maybe I can finish explaining what happened!"

Good for Quincy. I wanted to applaud, but since Edie had started ignoring me in a manner so pointed I felt as if she were sticking pins in me, I feared she might think I cared more about Quincy than was proper. As if. I've had enough trouble with the only man in the world I've ever loved even to consider taking up with another one. If anything ever happened to Billy, I aimed to get myself a dog.

Rotondo appeared to be under great stress. I liked that. He said, "Very well. Tell your tale from the fight on."

Quincy shut his eyes as if he were gathering his thoughts together. I hoped none of them had got stuck in the lump on his head. "All right. It must have been after eleven, because James had already gone to bed when I got back from Mr. Harold Kincaid's house." He looked around the room, presumably for Harold, but Harold had taken off with his mother. Quincy sighed. "In fact, it must have been pretty close to midnight, because I was thinking I wasn't going to get much sleep that night and was going to be bone-tired in the morning. I was too angry to sleep, though."

"And why is that?"

"I just *told* you!" Quincy declared. "That God damned bastard Kincaid was bothering my Edie! And then *he*, who'd been the cause of the trouble in the first place, fired *me*, who was only defending my girl!"

Language, language, I thought. A little bit of bad language goes a long way, and I thought Quincy had already used up his quota for one interrogation. On the other hand, I knew he must be in great pain, so I made allowances.

Edie began weeping quietly into her handkerchief, and I felt sorry for her. I didn't dare try to comfort her, since she didn't seem to like me much now that she'd found out I'd ratted on her and Quincy to Harold.

The door opened at that point, and Harold tiptoed in. In a stage whisper, he said, "Algie Pinkerton showed up, so I left Mother to him. I want to hear this."

His smile was as ingenuous as any I'd ever seen, and he reminded me of my girlfriends when we used to sit in the mausoleum at the Mountain View Cemetery in Altadena and play jacks and gossip for hours. I guess that sounds like an odd way to pass one's time. But it was so cool in the mausoleum, and during the summertime, believe me, you take relief from the heat wherever you can find it.

Rotondo looked as if he'd rather Harold had not

returned, but this was Harold's mother's house, so he only waved him to a chair. "Please don't interrupt, is all I ask," he said

Harold held up his right hand. "On my oath as a Kincaid, Officer. Or...Not as a Kincaid. Most of them are untrustworthy scoundrels. On my oath as a gentleman, then." I got the feeling his sweet smile annoyed Rotondo a lot and that made me feel much more the thing.

Rotondo produced an amazingly expressive scowl. I think it expressed disgust and disapproval, maybe mixed with a smidgen of exasperation.

I just sat back to enjoy the show.

CHAPTER 15

Rotondo transferred his attention from Harold back to Quincy. "Please go on."

Quincy thought for a minute, I presume to organize his thoughts. "All right. I went upstairs to the loft over the stable to pack up and get out of there. I was wondering where the heck I was going to sleep that night, and I was trying to be quiet, because I didn't want to wake James up."

"Did he wake up?" Rotondo asked.

"No. James sleeps like the dead. I was packing my stuff in a carpetbag, still mad as hell. I was aiming to get in touch with Edie the following day and tell her to quit her damned job and get another one, even if it meant working as a hotel maid."

He shot a guilty look at Edie, I guess because he'd cursed again, but Edie was still crying into her hankie and I don't think she even heard him. Or if she did, she didn't mind. She probably thought her love was akin to a knight in shining armor for wanting to remove her from a miserable situation.

Ah, young love. I almost remembered the emotion

from my own life, although recent years had blunted the memories considerably.

"So," said Rotondo, trying to keep Quincy on the right track, "you were packing to leave the Kincaids' employ."

"Right. The bastard couldn't stand hearing the truth, especially coming from such a low person"—he added toxic sarcasm to the "low" part of this speech—"and he fired me." He grimaced spectacularly for a couple of seconds. There's nothing quite like a bruised and battered face to add emphasis to a good grimace. "The moon was full. I remember it because you could see the rose garden from the stable loft. That doesn't happen very often."

I noticed Rotondo's knuckles whitening around his pencil and assumed he didn't care for these diversions. He didn't say anything.

"Anyhow, while I was standing there, trying to calm down and also trying to figure out how the devil I was going to make a living for Edie and me now that I'd been fired from the Kincaids', I saw a car pull up outside the door to the service porch."

"Did you notice what kind of machine it was?"

Quincy thought for a minute. "It was a big one, and black. At least, I think it was black. It was night, you know, and even though the moon was full, I couldn't make out a whole lot of details. But I think it was either a Maxwell or a Duesenberg. It was big, is all I know for sure."

Rotondo wrote it down.

"Well, when I was standing there looking out the window and thinking, I saw Mr. Kincaid walk out through the back door carrying a suitcase."

"He was walking?" Rotondo stared hard at Quincy. "Without his wheelchair or anyone assisting him?"

"He was walking," Quincy stated firmly. "As well as any man alive. That wheelchair of his was an act. It had to be, because the bastard wasn't even limping. And the bag he carried seemed heavy."

"He carried only the one bag?"

Quincy squinted at Edie, I surmise to help his memory along. "I think…No. He also carried a satchel in his other hand. That one didn't seem as heavy as the suitcase."

Rotondo wrote it all down.

"I knew right then and there that something fishy was going on. I mean, why would Mr. Eustace Kincaid sneak out the back door of his own house if he wasn't trying to hide something or get away with something? And why was he walking as if he'd never been crippled, when he'd been rolling around in that damned wheelchair for years and everybody thought he was sick?"

"You said the automobile was driven up and parked at the service-porch door. So there was a driver?"

"Yeah, the old bastard had a driver, all right. Cars don't generally drive themselves." Quincy's hand lifted to the pad covering his lump.

"The driver's the one who hit you?"

You couldn't fault Rotondo when it came to jumping to obvious conclusions.

"Yeah. He was the one, all right. But you're getting ahead of me. A lot of things happened before that."

I smiled inside. Good for Quincy.

"Of course." Rotondo didn't like being told the truth when it wasn't to his advantage. I was thinking *ha, ha, ha.* "Please continue at your own pace."

"I knew something was up, and that it probably wasn't right, because Kincaid's a real rotter, and I never have trusted him. Sneaking out of his own house carrying luggage in the middle of the night—and walking, to boot—well, it looked mighty shifty to me."

"Is there any other reason you suspected him of wrongdoing?"

Quincy looked apprehensive for a second, glanced at

Edie and me, swiveled (undergoing great pain to do so to judge by his expression) to look at Harold, then shrugged, which made him wince. I was *definitely* going to have the men bind his ribs as soon as I could get my hands on him and dump some more laudanum down his throat.

"Listen, Mr. Rotondo—"

Rotondo didn't correct him. I mean, he *could* have told Quincy to call him Detective Rotondo. I guess even smart-aleck detectives know what's important and what's not sometimes.

Quincy went on, "—servants talk. All the time. And they usually know what's going on in the family because rich people forget we're people, too." He recollected that Harold was present and almost broke his neck turning to offer an apology.

Harold held up a hand and smiled winningly. "No need to apologize for telling the truth Mr. Applewood. You're right. Most of us are awful snobs."

Visibly shaken, Quincy stuttered a bit when he said, "I…I…Er, thank you, sir."

"Let's get along here, all right?" Rotondo said through gritted teeth.

After wiping his sweaty brow with a dirty handkerchief (he hadn't had a chance to bathe or change clothes yet), Quincy continued his story. "All right, the truth is, I'd heard from everybody in the servants' quarters for weeks that people thought something was wrong at Kincaid's bank.

"When I saw him slinking out of his own house in the middle of the night carrying a suitcase and a satchel, and when I added that to the fact that he must have been faking being crippled…well, I knew he was doing something rotten, is all. Probably having something to do with the bank. I could feature that satchel full of money."

"So what did you do then?"

"I left off my packing and decided I was going to follow the machine he was in and see what was up. It wouldn't have surprised me if he'd kidnapped Edie." His scowl was a beauty.

Edie sort of yipped, slapped a hand over her mouth, and shut up.

Frowning heavily at Edie and me, Quincy added, "And that's another thing. I'd like to know why nobody ever told me about that bastard Kincaid bothering Edie before Daisy let it slip. God knows, they knew all about the bank business. I'll bet everyone in the whole house knew he was harassing Edie, and nobody bothered to tell me about it."

That was an easy one, although I didn't go into it, not wanting to incur Rotondo's wrath. But if Quincy would only allow himself to think for half a second, he'd understand that everyone was trying to prevent exactly what had happened when he *had* learned the truth. No one in the servants' quarters wanted him to be fired from his job.

"I'm sure you'll have an opportunity to ask your friends later why they kept the information from you. Right now, let's keep to the subject, all right?" I heard Rotondo's teeth grinding.

Quincy mumbled, "Sorry."

Rotondo squinted hard at Quincy. "Why was that? I mean, why did you think she might have been kidnapped? Did you ever see Miss Marsh with Mr. Kincaid?"

"Naw." Quincy shrugged once more, evidently forgetting how badly it had hurt the first time he'd done it, because he came out with a short, sharp word that I shan't repeat on these pages. "I guess I thought…Ah, hell, I was afraid he'd killed her, chopped her up, and stuffed her in the suitcase. You know, like that freak Crippen a few years back." He was embarrassed after his admission. When this session was over, I aimed to ask

Quincy if he liked to read crime novels as much as I did.

Rotondo didn't crack a smile. "And then what did you do?"

"As soon as he went out through the service porch door, the driver got out of the machine and went to the back of it. He took the bag and satchel from Kincaid and put them in the rumble seat. Then he went to the back door on the passenger's side and opened it for Kincaid." Quincy sneered, which didn't seem to hurt any of his cuts or bruises. "It was like he was the guy's chauffeur or something."

Hey, I thought, my pa's been a chauffeur for years, and he never went around whacking people over the head with blunt instruments. Or even knobby instruments.

"And then?"

Rotondo sure was a pushy fellow. I guess he had to be, given his line of work.

"Then I decided to follow the son of a bitch and see what he was up to."

"Quincy!"

Quincy shot a guilty look at Edie and muttered, "Sorry."

"If you don't clean up your language, I won't marry you."

Wow, I didn't know Edie was so tough.

Abashed, Quincy repeated, "Sorry."

"Please go on." It was getting harder and harder for Rotondo to push words through his teeth as he became more frustrated. I got the feeling he'd be really happy if Edie went somewhere and dusted something. He sure didn't care for interruptions.

"Okay. So, anyhow, I decided to follow Kincaid's machine to see what he was up to. I figured it couldn't be anything honest because of how it was happening.

"I went downstairs and stood at the barn door, making sure neither Kincaid nor his driver could see me. As soon as their car had been cranked up and was moving, I waited until it had gone quite a ways down the deodar drive before I started up the Ford and followed them."

"You kept them in sight the whole time?"

Quincy looked at Rotondo as if the detective was the biggest dimwit in the world. "How the hell could I keep them in sight? They were behind a bunch of trees once they left the circular drive."

Edie opened her mouth, I imagine to chastise Quincy for using the word "hell," but she shut it again. I think she'd caught some sort of vibration emanating from Rotondo and feared he'd ask her to leave the room if she interrupted the interview again.

"How do you know you were following the right car, then?"

It was an almost-reasonable question, I decided, but not quite, as Quincy instantly pointed out.

"Because it was past midnight and nobody else was on the damned road!" Quincy's voice had risen, but he was in a lot of pain, so he didn't keep shouting. Rather, he pressed a hand to his head, grimaced horribly, and said, "Aw, nuts."

Rotondo's tone of voice softened. "I'm sorry about this, Mr. Applewood, but I have to ask these questions. I'm sure you'll understand if you think about it."

"I guess." Quincy didn't sound convinced to me.

"You followed the car in which Mr. Kincaid was riding," Rotondo prompted.

"Yeah. I followed it. I tried to stay sort of far back, and I drove a lot with the lights off, because of the full moon, but I had to turn them on sometimes because you can't see much in the dark."

"Right."

"I followed them down Fair Oaks. *Way* down Fair Oaks, until you get to that sycamore grove they're turning into a park, past the ostrich farm. It's real rural there."

"I'm familiar with the area," said Rotondo. His pencil never left his paper.

"Anyhow, that's where I lost them. When I made that curve near the sycamore grove, I didn't see another car anywhere. I wondered if they'd driven into the sycamore grove to stash the loot somewhere, but that didn't make much sense to me."

Me neither. Naturally, I didn't say so.

"What did you do then?"

"I drove on for a little bit, then pulled over to think." He made a face, not that he had to, because the one he was sporting at the moment was enough to scare a witch off her broom. "Brother, was *that* a mistake. As I sat there thinking, Kincaid's driver snuck up on the driver's side of the Ford, opened the door, and yanked me out of it."

"Did you recognize him? Did you know who he was? Had you ever seen him before?"

"Hell, no. All I know is he was about nine feet tall and six feet wide and strong as an ox. I don't know what he hit me with, but I saw stars, believe me. I think he hit me on the head twice, although I don't know for sure, and I went down hard. He must have kicked me when I'd passed out, because—" He stopped speaking and glanced over at me, as if he didn't want me to hear the rest of his statement.

Too bad. I wasn't going anywhere. I crossed my arms over my chest and stared back at him to let him know it.

He sighed. "I guess he kicked me a couple of times, because my ribs hurt like the devil."

"Did you see Mr. Kincaid during this period of time?"

"All I saw were stars," Quincy said gloomily. "He got me good."

"So I see," said Rotondo. He didn't sound precisely sympathetic.

"I don't know how long I was out. It could have been minutes or hours. It took me a forever even to stand upright. I managed to get to my hands and knees twice, I think. Maybe three times, but every time I tried to stand, I passed out again."

Edie sobbed out loud. I noticed Rotondo's lips tighten.

"That's about it," Quincy said after thinking about it for a minute. "Thank God the Ford was still there by the time I finally managed to get my feet working. If it had been stolen, I'd have been in worse trouble than I already was." He glance apprehensively at Rotondo and corrected himself. "Am."

"True." Rotondo sounded cynical.

Quincy recognized that tone of voice as one that boded ill for his own personal future, because he said, "But I didn't *do* anything! I was trying to stop Kincaid from doing whatever he was doing! I *know* he was up to no good, dammit!"

"Yes, so you say." Rotondo perused his notes as Quincy gazed upon him with a mixture of worry and dislike.

"What did you do with the bearer bonds, Mr. Applewood?"

Quincy blinked a couple of times. "Huh?"

"The bearer bonds. You took them from Mr. Kincaid, didn't you? Where are they now?"

There was a period of silence in the room that I swear lasted a century. Then Quincy said, "I don't know what you're talking about. What's a bearer bond?"

Rotondo laid his pencil and notebook on his knee and looked straight at Quincy, unsmiling. "There's a theory—a good theory, in my opinion—that Mr. Kincaid stole the bonds from the bank."

"Well, yeah, I guess so." Quincy sounded confused. "I figured he'd stolen something. I thought it was money."

"I can well imagine," said Rotondo in his most detectival mode, "that you did indeed follow Mr. Kincaid in a car. It also wouldn't surprise me if it was Mr. Kincaid with whom you fought, and that you stole the stolen bonds from him. Where's the body, Mr. Applewood?"

"*What*? Where's the *body*? *What* body? If you think I killed that son of a bitch, you're crazy! I never touched him." He frowned sulkily. "For that matter, he never touched me. He didn't need to. He had his hired goon do it for him."

"Hmmm." Rotondo wasn't convinced.

I was. I thought Quincy had told the absolute truth. So, of course, did Edie, who had begun crying again. I can't keep away from crying women to save myself.

"So what happens now?" Quincy was scared stiff. His fingers clutched the arms of his chair as if he were trying to wrench them off.

"I haven't decided that yet," Rotondo said. "First we're going to give you some more medicine, bind your ribs, and have Mrs. Majesty tape your nose. Other policemen are questioning the rest of the servants in the household as we speak."

Golly, I didn't know that. These guys were thorough when rich people were involved.

"I don't want any more damned laudanum," Quincy grumbled.

Rotondo gave him what could only be deemed an evil grin. "Too bad. You're getting it." He turned and nodded at Harold and me.

Harold picked up the brown bottle Edie had brought downstairs. I noticed that it was more than half full, which I hoped meant that Mrs. Kincaid didn't depend on the drug too much. I knew from talking with Billy's doctors that people could become addicted to laudanum and morphine and other drugs derived from opium. The thought of Billy becoming an addict worried me during those periods of time when I wasn't worrying about other things. In other words, I worried about it approximately half my waking hours.

"Would you like me to telephone Dr. Dearing,

Detective? I know for a fact that Daisy can perform magic, but it might be wise to call in a doctor for this situation."

"That's a good idea, Mr. Kincaid. Let's get this over with first, and then the doctor can give him a thorough examination and patch anything else that needs patching."

"Good. Mr. Applewood can stay in the apartment off the breakfast room." The Kincaids were so rich, they had a dining room *and* a breakfast room. "Daisy's aunt doesn't sleep here at night, and the room is fully furnished and has its own bathroom."

"For God's sake, you don't have to do that!" Quincy was plainly undergoing tortures of humiliation and irritation.

Harold winked at him. "Too bad you're too busted up to do anything but complain, isn't it?"

Oh, my, but I *did* like Harold Kincaid.

"One minute, everyone." Rotondo stood up. He looked awfully tall, standing there when everyone else was sitting down. "I have yet to make up my mind whether or not Mr. Applewood is to be arrested for murder."

"*Murder?*" It was embarrassing, but I admit I screeched the word. "You can't arrest Quincy for murder. You don't even know if there's a body involved yet! And if there is a body, where is it?"

"If you will recall, Mrs. Majesty, *I* am the police officer in charge in this situation."

I stood up, too. I don't suppose I made a very impressive figure, since I'm only a little over five feet tall, but I was furious. "I don't care if you're the Lord God Almighty! Until you can prove that Mr. Kincaid is dead, and that his death was the result of murder, you have no business arresting anyone, and especially not Quincy, because he's *wounded*! What's more, he was wounded in action. So to speak. I mean, he was trying to figure out what Kincaid was up to, and if he'd succeeded, you'd be calling him a hero instead of a criminal!"

I think the noise I heard after I ended my rather loud speech was Harold applauding, but I didn't look to see for sure.

Rotondo stared at me as if he wished he could stomp on me and squish me like a cockroach that had invaded his larder. But I was right, and he knew it. He hated knowing it, too. After heaving a huge sigh, he said, "Very well. Mr. Applewood can stay here until the body's found."

"There isn't any body," Quincy muttered. He looked rather furious himself.

"That remains to be seen," said Rotondo in a voice filled with condemnation. "Right now you'd better take that laudanum and we'll get your ribs and nose attended to."

Quincy gave up arguing about the laudanum after that. Heck, I would have, too. It's true laudanum tastes awful, but I'd rather take it than be arrested for murder. Quincy must have felt the same way.

He did try scrunching back in his chair to get away from us, but it didn't work. Harold held his arms, Edie sat on his feet, and Rotondo pinched his nose shut. I hoped he did it gently, since the nose was broken, but I doubt it.

Quincy struggled for breath for a few moments until he either had to open his mouth or suffocate, and I thrust a spoonful of laudanum into his mouth then clamped his lips together. Poor guy. We really did treat him roughly. But, darn it, he needed the pain relief!

Making a terrible face, Quincy said a lot of things nobody could understand, which was probably just as well, given his fondness for profanity.

"Blech! Ugh! Argh! Damn!"

At that point, I decided to take charge of Edie, whether she liked me anymore or not. "Let's go visit Aunt Vi while Harold and Detective Rotondo get those ribs bandaged, Edie."

Bandages. Dang it, they'd need bandages. I glanced at the supply left over from those I'd used to bandage Quincy's head and knew we'd need more. Perhaps I'd been a trifle generous with the head bandages, but I wanted to make sure the pad remained in place.

"I'll get some more bandages from Aunt Vi. So keep your clothes on until I get back, Quincy." I did a fair imitation of one of Harold's winks.

"Daisy!" Edie was so shocked, she forgot to be mad at me and burst into giggles.

"This isn't funny!" Quincy shouted as I trotted out of the drawing room.

Gee, I thought it was. I didn't talk to Edie or try to explain how I'd mistakenly relayed the information about the relationship between her and Quincy, but hurried to the kitchen, deciding explanations could wait. Aunt Vi kept a huge supply of medicaments and bandages in the pantry, since she was used as the family's nurse as well as the family's cook, so it took her no time at all to get a roll of gauze and plenty of cotton wadding ready for Quincy's ribs.

I ran back to the drawing room with my gear and almost barged in without knocking. But it occurred to me that it would be just like Rotondo to ignore Quincy's wishes and make him take his shirt off before the bandages arrived.

Therefore, I knocked on the door and said, "Is everyone decent in there?"

"Yes!" Rotondo sounded angry, which I didn't think was fair. I mean, I was only being cautious, for crumb's sake.

So I took in the bandages and gauze, and retired to the kitchen, taking a much-needed rest. There wasn't any more shortbread left, but Aunt Vi still had some petit fours handy. Edie and I drank tea and ate petit fours until Harold meandered through the pantry and tapped on the open kitchen door.

"Intruders!" he cried jovially. "I'm here to kidnap Daisy. The ribs are bandaged, and the nose is ready for taping." He winked at Edie. "Your future husband is certainly a strong man, Miss Marsh. We had to tie his hands over his head and I had to sit on his legs before that poor detective could bind and tape the ribs."

Edie shook her head. "Quincy's just not used to being hurt and helpless," she said, being true to her love. "He's always been so strong and independent." She heaved a soulful sigh. I thought, *Oh, brother*.

Harold, nicer than I, said, "Of course. I'm sure that's the answer. But I need Daisy now." He noticed the petit fours and rushed over to snatch a couple. "Mrs. Gumm, if you ever decide to retire, please let it be at my house."

"Go on with you, Mr. Harold," said Aunt Vi, pleased as punch.

"Not on your life, Harold Kincaid," I said sternly. "Vi is *my* aunt, and I'm not giving her up."

"Pooh. You can live there, too."

I got the feeling Harold was only half joking. Harold was a man who loved his food. And it wouldn't surprise me in the least if he'd let Billy and me live at his huge house as long as Aunt Vi was part of the deal. Not for the first—or even the million and first—time, I wondered what it must be like to have money by the ton. Ah, well.

So, as little as I wanted to, I went back to the drawing room. Poor Quincy looked as if Harold and Rotondo had been torturing him with thumb screws and the rack while I was away. His expression held about as much joy as Ebenezer Scrooge's before he met the ghosts. And the look he gave *me* would have made me turn and run if I'd thought he was capable of chasing me down and pummeling me.

But he was injured, I was healthy, and Harold and Rotondo were both stronger than Quincy at the moment.

In full health, I'd still put my money on Rotondo over Quincy, but Harold was kind of a cream puff.

"Hold him down, gentlemen," I said, sounding to my own ears like somebody who was actually competent at the job she was about to undertake. What a joke.

"Damn it," Quincy grumbled, "nobody has to hold me down."

"Nuts. I don't trust you, and Billy wouldn't like it if I came home with a black eye."

I'd managed to outrage him. "I'd never hit a lady!"

"Yeah? That some sort of cowboy code or something?" I picked up the roll of gauze and cut off a strip approximately three inches long. As I did so, I was thinking that it would be really nice if I knew what I was doing.

"Yes, dammit, it's a cowboy code!"

Oh, dear. Guess I'd offended him again. In what I hoped was a placating voice, I said, "Good. I wish more men operated by it." I didn't even look at Rotondo as I said it, although it was a struggle.

"Huh."

I nodded at Harold and Rotondo, and both assumed their assigned positions, Harold holding both of Quincy's arms, and Rotondo sitting on his feet. With as much gentleness as I could, I wiggled Quincy's nose, trying to figure out exactly where it was broken. Didn't do any good. I couldn't tell a broken nose from a smashed Cadillac.

Finally, and to my infinite joy, my luck turned. And none too soon, if you ask me. Just as I was approaching Quincy with the strip of gauze, wondering where to put it and if I was going to make it worse or fix it, the drawing-room door opened and Featherstone announced, "Dr. Dearing, Mr. Kincaid."

Thank God. I was so relieved, I actually hung my head and whispered a prayer of thanks. I didn't even ask God why it had taken him so long to send the doctor, either, which I think speaks of remarkable restraint.

Apparently Mrs. Kincaid and Algie had seen the doctor's buggy draw up to the front of the house, because they rushed into the room after him. Dr. Dearing claimed automobiles were works of the devil and still rode around in a horse and buggy. He was a comfortable sort of man, a little chubby, with rosy cheeks, thin hair, and an intelligently funny outlook on life. He went to our church and sang bass in the same choir in which I sang.

He, being a medical man, inherently disdained my line of work, but he never got ugly about it. He only teased me a little bit every now and then.

"Oh, Dr. Dearing, I'm *so* glad you could get here so quickly!" exclaimed Mrs. Kincaid.

Algie nodded his head and said nothing. Sometimes I wondered if Algie Pinkerton would be happy if he never had to talk again in this lifetime. He was one of those people who preferred others to entertain him rather than to entertain others. Or maybe he was just shy. What do I know?

After greetings all around, Dr. Dearing said, "What's this I hear about Quincy Applewood going fifteen rounds with Jack Dempsey?" He had a booming voice that overwhelmed the drawing room but sounded great in church.

Mrs. Kincaid looked blank. So did Harold and Algie. My Billy would know who Jack Dempsey was. Just one more difference between the rich and the rest of us, I guess.

Quincy tried to grin. "It feels like it, all right."

"Well then, let's see what we have here." He glanced at Rotondo and apparently recognized him as a detective. "Is this a police matter?"

"It might be," said Rotondo. He jerked his head my way. "Mrs. Majesty has done a little nursing on the patient and Mr. Kincaid and I bound his ribs, but we figured you ought to check him over."

Since he didn't sound too condescending about my nursing abilities, I didn't snap at him. I didn't wait around to watch the examination, either. I'd had enough of bloody wounds for one day. "I'm going home, if nobody minds," I said, trying for chipper but achieving merely a tone of semi-jolly desperation.

"Oh, but Daisy! I need you so!" Mrs. Kincaid's hands clamped at her bosom again. Yoiks. What did this woman think I was, anyhow? Sure, I was a medium and had become some sort of spiritual healer for her, and she was my best customer, but gee whiz, I also had a husband and a family.

It was Harold who broke this news to his mother, in so subtle and tender a way that he didn't even hurt her feelings. Every day, in every way, Harold Kincaid was getting better and better in my book.

Obviously disappointed, Mrs. Kincaid said, "Very well." She rushed over to me and grabbed my hands. "But please return tomorrow, Daisy. You're such a comfort to me."

"Thank you." I think.

It was then I noticed Detective Sam Rotondo frowning hideously at Quincy Applewood, and I remembered he'd brought me here in his police automobile. I supposed I could walk home, but I didn't want to. It had been an exhausting day already, and a three-quarter-mile walk didn't hold much appeal. I sidled over to him and he transferred his frown to me. "What?"

"You know, you're such a polite and considerate man, Detective Rotondo. I can't tell you how much I appreciate your warmth and courtesy."

His mouth twisted into an ironic grin. "Yeah. I get that all the time from the ladies."

I decided to give up the sparring match. "Are you able to take me home? I'm done in. And my husband needs me, darn it."

He thought for several moments. The man wasn't one

for making snap decisions. I was about to hit him out of sheer frustration and wondered if I'd have to spend the night in jail if I did, when he said, "Your husband's a first-rate man, Mrs. Majesty. It's a shame, what happened to him."

I've seldom been more embarrassed in my life than I was at that moment, when I suddenly burst into tears. "Yes," I sobbed. "I know." Because I felt like such a fool, I rushed out of the room, trying to avoid everyone by taking one of the side doors. The door led me into a small sitting room I'd never seen before, and I stood in the middle of it, trying to get my bearings. I couldn't.

I nearly screamed when someone put a hand on my shoulder. When I spun around and discovered it was Rotondo, and that he had a sympathetic look on his face, I started bawling again. He put his arms around me awkwardly and patted me on the back. "It's all right, Mrs. Majesty. You and Billy are doing fine, even though you're going through some rough times."

The man had lost his wife from consumption not long ago, I remembered suddenly. Maybe he wasn't the rotten bum I thought he was, but only pretended to be one when he was on the job.

"Th-thank you," I said at last, when I could talk again. I was completely mortified. Never, in my whole life, had I cried on a stranger's shoulder. Only minutes earlier I was wishing I'd never have to see a woman cry again, and here I was, having a fit on the shoulder of a man I hardly knew, and one whom I didn't think liked me.

He didn't hold me for long, which was assuredly a good thing because it was beginning to feel too right. Pushing me gently away, he said, "I'll drive you home now. Mr. Harold Kincaid is going to see that Applewood is set up in a bedroom while he's laid up."

I sniffled pathetically and blew my nose on my handkerchief, still feeling stupid. "He didn't kill Mr. Kincaid. I know he didn't."

I could feel him mentally rolling his eyes, which actually helped my pitiful condition some, because it made me angry.

"We're still working on the investigation, Mrs. Majesty," Rotondo said stiffly.

"Have you posted guards at the border?"

"There are already guards at the border."

"There'd better be more of them than usual if they expect to catch Kincaid escaping." From what I'd heard, there were approximately one and a half people guarding the border between the U.S. and Mexico. In other words, not anywhere near enough.

"If it will make you feel better"—he wanted to add *and shut you up*, but didn't—"then, yes. We have asked for more guards to be stationed at the Mexican border." He didn't like admitting it, because it had been my idea. I began to feel somewhat more chipper.

"And what about the Coast Guard? Have you been in touch with the Coast Guard?"

"No. As far as I'm concerned, that's about the most far-fetched notion anyone's come up with so far regarding this whole mess."

"It is not! It makes tons of sense!"

"I guess it makes about as much sense as holding a séance."

"Oh, so you're back to that, are you?"

"Even you've got to admit talking to the dead is a grotesque thing to do."

"It is not!"

"If you say so."

"Oh, you drive me crazy!"

"Likewise, I'm sure."

In other words, we were back to normal.

 CHAPTER 16

I muttered good-bye to Rotondo when he pulled the police car up to the curb in front of my house. I still felt silly for having cried on him, but he was being nice about it and pretending it had never happened, which was more consideration than I'd have expected from this source, especially since he totally disapproved of how I made my living.

Because I felt stupid, and because I thought it was important, I turned back and leaned in through the window. "I'm not kidding about the Coast Guard, Detective. I know you think the idea is a bad one, but it *has* to be easier to slip away over water than get through a guarded land border.

"The man was studying Spanish, for heaven's sake! There are ports all down the coast of South America where he could catch a steamer to anywhere in Europe or Asia or—shoot, I don't know. Maybe he wants to buy a Greek island and live on it or something. If you don't get in touch with the Coast Guard, I'll bet you'll be sorry."

He looked exasperated. "Right. I keep forgetting you

have connections with the other realms."

"Darn you! That's not the reason, and you know it!" Totally irate, which doesn't happen *too* often due to the amount of practice in holding my temper I get daily, I stamped down the walk to our cute little bungalow, stormed up the porch steps, and would have slammed the door behind me except that I didn't want anyone inside, and especially not Billy, to know what had happened. With me, that is. The whole family wanted to hear all the dirt I could give them on the Kincaid affair.

It was way past dinnertime. I'd forgotten about food (and I suspect the petit fours had temporarily cured any hunger pangs I might have experienced without them) until I sniffed Aunt Vi's pot roast as I walked through the kitchen to our room. Then my stomach growled as if it belonged to a bear that had been hibernating all winter.

Billy sat on the sun porch with Pa, Ma, and Aunt Vi. They were all talking softly and watching the lights on Mount Wilson blink. They'd installed—not Pa, Ma, Aunt Vi, and Billy, but some scientists—a huge telescope up there the year before, and we'd sit out there at night sometimes and wonder what discoveries were being made. The Mount Wilson Telescope was the largest in the world, and we all liked to imagine what it was seeing. Talk about a Great Beyond; now the sky is what *I'd* consider a Great Beyond.

"Hey, I'm home."

I needn't have announced myself, since they'd already turned to see who was there. I was grateful for the dark, because I didn't want anyone to know I'd been crying.

"What the heck happened, Daisy?" Billy asked. He was mad as heck at me for being away so long, but he was trying to be nice about it because my relatives were with him. Do I know my Billy, or not?

"It was pretty awful. I'll tell you everything in a minute. I *have* to eat something or I'll keel over."

As I might have expected, Aunt Vi jumped to her feet.

"I'll fix you a plate, child. You look all done in."

I was all done in, but I didn't want to put Vi out. After all, she'd worked all day, too. "No, no, please don't bother. I'll just get a sandwich."

"You'd be better off taking Vi's suggestion," Billy said, a hint of a grin in his voice, for which I was infinitely thankful. "It was one of the best pot roasts I've ever tasted."

Blushing, as was her wont, Aunt Vi said, "Go along with you, Billy Majesty. You say that every time I cook a meal."

"That's because it's the truth," my Billy said.

I guess I was really worn out, because that statement, uttered in his old-Billy voice, made me feel like blubbering some more. Shoot, I had to get over this. And quick. Billy would hate it if he knew I was pitying him. I know it sounds contradictory, because he really did need sympathy and attention, but there's a fine line I tried never to cross between understanding and pity. It was my bad luck that the line seemed to move from day to day, and I was always stepping on the wrong side of it and aggravating my husband.

"Please don't bother with feeding me, Vi," said I nobly—at that point, I could have eaten the entire cow raw; to heck with the roasted parts. "I can fix myself a sandwich." And it would be quicker than her fixing me a full dinner plate and warming it up.

"Fiddlesticks. You look like you're going to drop in your tracks, Daisy Majesty. You just come right out here and plop yourself in this chair and wait five minutes. It won't take me more than that to get a real meal ready for you to eat." Aunt Vi didn't believe in sandwiches unless you were going on a picnic somewhere far, far away from your own home.

Outnumbered and overruled, I tried to be polite as I conceded the point. "Thanks, Vi. Let me hang up my hat and get comfortable."

Getting comfortable would probably have taken a week of sleep, a healthy husband, and a million dollars, but it felt good to take off my hat, slip out of my lovely foulard dress and hang it up, remove my shoes and stockings, throw on an old polka-dot wrapper, and shove my tired feet into a pair of floppy slippers that probably should have been discarded eons before, but which were so comfortable I couldn't bear to part with them.

I limped out to the sun porch, kissed Billy, and collapsed into the chair beside him. "My land, but those people have problems," I announced in a tired voice. "Quincy Applewood came back, though."

"What about Kincaid?" Billy asked.

"No sign of the old buzzard yet," said I.

"Daisy!" Ma had always tried to make me behave like a lady, but her efforts hadn't panned out very well thus far.

"But he is an old buzzard, Ma. He's a thief and a lecher. He used to chase Edie Marsh around in his wheelchair." My mother gasped. Pa chuckled. I'll never understand men. "The police think Quincy murdered him and re-stole the stolen bearer bonds."

"This is getting confusing." Billy chuckled, and my heart went all warm and gooey.

"You're telling me. What's even worse is that the man who drove Mr. Kincaid away from the mansion last night bopped Quincy over the head with a tree trunk or something and I had to doctor the poor boy." I shuddered, remembering.

"You?" Billy's eyes opened so wide, I could see how gorgeous they were even in the dark.

"Good heavens." Ma again, pressing a palm to her heart.

"That's my girl," said Pa, who was much more easygoing than Ma.

"Maybe. But I didn't like doing it. It was horrid. He had a lump on his head the size of a boulder, and there were even bugs stuck in the dried blood there."

"Good God." Billy.

"How awful!" Ma.

"Be damned. Were they alive?" Pa. Of course.

God bless him. I laughed. "Naw. They were only dead ants, but the experience wasn't one I care to repeat any time soon. I don't think I'm cut out for nursing."

Aunt Vi was as good as her word, and within five minutes I was trying to act like a lady for Ma's sake, but I'm afraid I ate too quickly to maintain a true ladylike appearance. Since I'd been in the middle of describing the state of affairs at the Kincaid mansion when the food came, not even Ma chastised me for gobbling my food. She was as eager as everyone else there to hear the scoop.

As soon as I'd downed the very last bite of pot roast, carrots, pearl onions in Aunt Vi's special and never-to-be-forgotten cream sauce, potatoes, and gravy, I sat back and sighed. "That was the best pot roast you've ever made, Vi."

Aunt Vi shook her head. "You're as bad as Billy, Daisy Majesty."

"Sure, I am." I reached for Billy's hand and squeezed it. He returned the pressure. "We're alike like that."

"Hmph. Well, all I can say is that you'd better not tell any more of your story until I get back with your piece of coconut cake, young lady."

"Coconut cake?" Awed, I stared up at my sainted aunt. If there's one thing on earth I love almost more than Billy or Scotch shortbread, it's coconut cake the way Aunt Vi makes it—white cake with fluffy white frosting sprinkled with flaked coconut. I could die happy if my last meal ended with Aunt Vi's coconut cake.

But I respected her wishes. Gazing up at the sky, I muttered tritely, "The moon's sure bright tonight. It looks kind of like a silver dollar, doesn't it?" I sighed, overjoyed to be back in the bosom of my family. And being waited on, too. Life couldn't get much better than that. Well, unless Billy were to get well, but there you go. There are always a few kinks getting in the way of perfection.

"Yeah, but you can't see the stars so well when the moon's this bright," Billy said, not complaining, just stating a fact.

"True."

"I wonder what that telescope's finding up there," mused Pa. He'd always been intrigued by gadgets, and I'm sure he'd love to visit the telescope.

"Maybe we can all take a trip up to Mount Wilson one of these days and see for ourselves," I said.

There used to be a small-gauge railway that took rich people (and their servants, although I'd wager they stayed in less opulent cars than their employers) up to the lodge at Mount Wilson, but the lodge had burned down a few years before. I think the railroad was still running, though, and I knew that somebody, probably at the California Institute of Technology (I had a hard time remembering it wasn't Throop College any longer) held guided tours through the planetarium at Mount Wilson.

"That would be swell," said Billy. "I wonder if I could go, too."

He sounded so pensive, I almost cried *again*. I was beginning to wonder if my monthly was coming early. I don't generally get weepy at the drop of a hat.

"We'd see to it that you came with us, Billy. Don't you ever worry about that." Pa patted Billy on the shoulder.

As a rule, Billy didn't like people patting him on the shoulder in exhibitions of compassion or sympathy, but he never minded when Pa did it. Pa was like that. Everyone loved him because he was, purely and simply, a good man. There was no getting around it. It was a fact of life.

And, when I wasn't feeling unjustly burdened by life, I felt honestly blessed to have been born into such a wonderful family. Heck, look at the Kincaids. They had more money than God, and their family was a total disaster except for Harold, and he wasn't exactly normal.

Aunt Vi brought me a big piece of coconut cake and a glass of milk, and the only sounds that could be heard for the next several seconds were those of my own slurping and gulping. Again, Ma didn't complain about my manners. Not being scolded by my mother was the best of all ways to conclude a ghastly day, and I appreciated it.

When there wasn't any food left for me to eat after I'd devoured the cake, I finished my tale of Quincy's unfortunate beating, my unfortunate nursing, and Detective Rotondo's unfortunate interrogation.

"The rotten policeman actually believes Quincy killed Mr. Kincaid and took the bearer bonds," I announced, vexed. "He's such an idiot."

I felt Billy shrug beside me. "I don't think Sam's anything close to being an idiot. I think he's smart as a whip and probably great at his job."

Staring at my beloved, I recalled their gin rummy game and the fact that Rotondo had visited him this morning. "You were beating the pants off him in gin rummy," I reminded him.

I heard the grin in Billy's voice when he answered my irate declaration. "Yeah, but that doesn't mean beans when it comes to police work. He told me a lot of things about the police while we were playing, too. If I were still a whole, sound man, I might even try to get into the police force."

"You? A policeman?" My mind boggled, although I think I disguised it. "I never knew you were interested in police work."

"I never knew it either, until I talked to Sam."

Sam. Sam, Sam, Sam. Foolishly, I resented the fact that the two men were into a first-name relationship. Also, I didn't trust Rotondo—Sam, to Billy—not to have been using Billy to get information in a sneaky way. Not that Billy knew a thing about the Kincaids, but I still didn't trust Rotondo. Sam, indeed!

"Brother, it sounds like that family's in a whole lot of trouble," said Billy, dropping the Sam subject, for which I could only be gratified. "What do you think happened to old man Kincaid?"

"I think he took a bolt for the ocean and aims to get a boat and hie himself off to some other country with his stolen loot. The police think Quincy stole the money from him, killed him, and hid the money and, presumably, the body somewhere." I sniffed significantly.

"Why'd he aim for the ocean when the land border to Mexico is so close?" Billy wanted to know.

It irked me that men stuck together even when they were apart. My own dear Billy was beginning to sound like Detective Rotondo, and I didn't like it.

"Because there are guards there," I said, trying not to sound as irked as I felt.

"But there aren't many of them. Heck, Daisy, face it, the border into Mexico is easy to cross. Or he could have driven to Arizona and gone to Mexico that way."

"They posted more guards at the California-Mexico border, specifically to stop Kincaid if he headed that way." Golly, Arizona hadn't once crossed my mind, and I felt I'd missed a good idea to fling at Rotondo. Sam. Whoever he was.

"Ah."

"But it's a lot harder to drive to Arizona than it is to drive to the Los Angeles Harbor," Pa pointed out. "Think of all that desert to cross. I'm sure Kincaid has a better machine than we do, but no automobile ever invented can cross a desert without getting into trouble with water or blown tires. And if he has a machine with a battery, I hear they don't do so good on the desert." He shook his head. "I sure wouldn't want to be stranded between

California and Arizona, or Arizona and the Mexican border, with no water. A man would die from dehydration before the day was out."

I leaped upon this salient point with both feet. "Exactly! That's why I think your precious Sam ought to notify the Coast Guard to be on the lookout for Kincaid's get-away boat. Or whatever it is. But will he listen to me? Of course, not." I thought *Sam* believed my ideas were foolish because I was a woman and a so-called fortune-teller, but I didn't say so for Billy's sake. If he liked the man, so be it. Nuts. "For all I know, Mr. Kincaid bought himself a yacht and plans to sail to the Hawaiian Islands."

"I've got to admit you have a point there, Daisy," Billy conceded. How generous of him.

"I think it's a brilliant idea," said Ma.

Now let me say right here and now that I adore my mother. She's an excellent accountant and a whiz when it comes to dealing with numbers. Heck, she's head bookkeeper at the Hotel Marengo, and has to deal with numbers in the hundreds of thousands (I'm talking about dollars here), but she doesn't have enough imagination to fill a thimble. She could never even come up with bed-time stories for Walter, Daphne, and me when we were kids. It was Pa who had the imagination in the family. Well, Pa and me. When it came to imagination, I was a chip off the old fatherly block, in fact. But Ma…well, she was a swell person.

Therefore, when Ma endorsed my idea, I looked at it again, worried that Rotondo was right and I was a moron.

Oddly enough, it was Billy who came to my rescue. Since he'd come back to me, broken and wasted, I'd taken over the job as rescuer in our marriage. "It makes more sense to head for the ocean than to drive to the border, now that you've brought the desert into it, Pa." He called my father "Pa" out of habit, since his own parents were gone.

"Exactly," said I, pleased that Billy was actually agreeing with me for once. "That's why I suggested that Detective Rotondo call on the Coast Guard to patrol."

On a sigh, Pa said, "It's a long border between Oregon and Mexico, and it's a mighty big ocean, Daisy. It might be more difficult to find a man on water than on land, where motorcars have to drive on roads."

I'd actually thought about that, too, and had an answer handy, more or less. "True, but they have new equipment. What do they call it? Radio? They can communicate from boat to boat using it. I read about it in the *Star News* a while back."

"That's right," Billy said, sounding enthusiastic for once. "I read about that, too. The article said that one of these days, and not far off, either, people just like us will have radio-signal-receiving sets in our houses. Wouldn't that be something?"

"It sure would." Pa sounded even more enthusiastic than Billy. He always did.

"I guess," I said. "But why would you want to listen to what the Coast Guard boats are saying to each other?"

"It wouldn't be just the Coast Guard, Daisy." Lord bless him, Billy didn't scoff at me for my question. Much. "I read in a magazine you got from the library that once you've got your radio-receiving machine hooked up, you can listen to music or even hear stage plays over the receiver."

"Really? Gee, I wonder what it would be like to hear a play and not see the actors acting in it." A couple of times we'd gone to see Gilmor Brown and his Savoy Stock Company at the Old Savoy Theater on Fair Oaks.

I liked going to the theater, but it was difficult for Billy, since he had to climb up stairs, which spoiled him from doing any other kind of exercise for hours afterwards. And then somebody had to heave his wheelchair up the same stairs, and he had to sit in an aisle in order to watch the play, because he was too winded to climb out of his chair and sit on a real seat.

He'd *never* allow Pa to lift and carry him. Plus, he hated being noticed except when I wheeled him down Colorado Boulevard during the annual Armistice Day Parade, because he was only one of several other men in wheelchairs, most in even worse shape than he was. At the theater, people couldn't help but notice him in his wheelchair because it blocked an aisle.

"I'm not sure I'd enjoy listening to a play without being able to see the actors," said Ma, giving an example of that defective imagination I mentioned earlier.

"I think it would be great," I said to her. Because she needed more explanation than most people due to the one flaw in her essential composition, I added, "It would be like reading a book, Ma. When you read a book, you see the words but supply the characters with their looks and so forth in your head."

Ma said, "Oh."

"Exactly," said Billy. "Boy, it would be great to be able to listen to the news on a radio-receiving set, too."

"But we get the news in the *Star News*," said Ma.

"True, but maybe we'd get it faster over the radio-receiver than the newspaper. Even when newspapers print specials, it takes time."

"And don't ever forget that people are always coming up with new ideas," said Pa, who actually *did* come up with new ideas occasionally, unlike Ma. "I'd bet my entire fortune"—this, needless to say, was a joke, since he didn't have one—"that if radio-signal-receiving sets become popular, folks will begin writing stories specifically for them."

"Oh, boy, I hadn't thought about that. What fun, to be able to sit down in your own house and listen to a real, live play on a machine!"

Okay, that made a dog and a radio-receiving set I was going to buy for Billy as soon as I could. For all I knew, radio-receiving sets cost a mint, but I was fairly sure I could get Mrs. Bissel to give me one of her dachshunds without much trouble. Mrs. Bissel was a sweetheart, but she was even dimmer than Mrs. Kincaid, and she absolutely loved people who loved her dogs. I expected her to call me to conduct a séance any day now, and I was going to see if she'd trade a séance for a dachshund.

Sometimes when I think about it, my life seems kind of strange. But it was mine, and I lived it as well as I could.

To my shock and intense pleasure, not to mention Billy's, Mrs. Kincaid didn't telephone the next day. Or the next. Or even the next. I went to choir practice on Thursday, praying I wouldn't return home to a message begging me to race to the Kincaids' house, and there wasn't one.

We went to church on Sunday morning, and there was no Sam Rotondo sitting in the congregation to sabotage the service for me. As luck would have it, I didn't have to sing any duets that day. He'd chosen the one day during which his presence would upset me to show up. I considered such behavior typical on his part.

He and Billy, however, were becoming closer and closer. Darned if the man didn't come over twice that week to play gin rummy with Billy and Pa. He wouldn't talk about the Kincaid case, claiming it was against police procedure. I just bet.

I chose to ignore them and make myself a new dress in a gorgeous cream-colored silk, having found the material on sale in Nash's Department Store's fabric department. I usually wear dark colors, but I'd rationalized the expenditure by deciding the creamy color would blend in with my skin tone and make me look mysterious. And if it didn't, I could always wear the dress to church.

Billy must have told Sam—I was beginning to think of the man as Sam now, too, drat it—about radio-receiving sets, and they talked about them during one entire gin rummy evening. Pa joined in the conversation with gusto, as usual. As Ma brought out the hemming stick and stuck pins around the bottom of my cream-colored dress—it had one of those modern, up-and-down, uneven hems so Ma had to adjust the metal measuring stick every few pins—we could hear them, yakking away like gossiping women.

"I don't care what anyone says, Ma. Men are as bad as women when it comes to talking about silly things."

She glanced up from her hemming stick, pins fanning out from her mouth and making her look like a gargoyle. "Do you think so, dear? I rather enjoy hearing Billy and your father enjoying themselves."

When she put it like that, I felt guilty. "I do too, Ma," I said, lying through my teeth.

What was the matter with me? I knew good and well that I was jealous of Sam Rotondo, and I couldn't figure out why. Perhaps because we'd gotten off to such a rocky start (Sam and me, not Billy and me. Our rockiness had come with the war), I didn't like the fact that Billy liked him, if that makes any sense.

Or maybe—and this scared me even more than the above—I was beginning to find Detective Sam Rotondo attractive. He wasn't handsome, like my Billy or Del Farrington, but he had a sort of rugged charm.

No. Not charm. Rotondo definitely possessed no charm. I don't know what it was, but it worried me, and I wished he didn't come to our house so often. Which was selfish of me. Billy needed friends almost more than he needed his morphine.

In other words, I was totally confused and didn't like my state of mind one little bit.

Mrs. Bissel called me on Monday, almost as if she'd heard my thoughts about trading séances for dachshunds, but there wasn't a peep from Mrs. Kincaid. Harold had called me once or twice during those few days, but he only claimed nothing new had happened and that there had been no word from or about his father. I didn't ask about Stacy, and he didn't volunteer any information, so I assumed she was being as bratty as ever.

When Tuesday rolled around, I was starting to wonder if Mrs. Kincaid had found herself another spiritualist. Now that would put a serious crimp in my business. Harold called again that night to chat. He was a great one for chatting, and was very entertaining, although I didn't suppose Billy would think so. I almost asked him if his mother didn't like me any longer, but couldn't quite make myself do it.

On Wednesday, I was just about to take a bold step and call Mrs. Kincaid for myself to see what was going on, when the telephone rang in the kitchen. My cream-colored silk slithered to the floor when I jumped up from the sewing machine. I didn't even stoop to pick it up, I was so eager to get to the phone.

After persuading Mrs. Barrow and Mrs. Mayweather to get off the wire—I presumed Mrs. Lynch and Mrs. Pollard were off shopping or visiting somewhere—I recognized Mrs. Kincaid's voice. Barely. Her voice was raspy, sounding amazingly like leaves scraping against a window on a dark and creepy night.

I wasn't even sure it was her at first. "Mrs. Kincaid? Is that you?"

"Y-yes," she whimpered.

Oh, golly, something bad must have happened. "What's the matter, Mrs. Kincaid? What happened? You sound desperate."

Now, if I were truly a person who could communicate with spirits, do you think I'd have had to ask her what was wrong? Neither do I, which either means that Mrs. Kincaid was as stupid as dandelion fluff or that she didn't think like the rest of us do. I hope she never begins to, either.

"Oh, Daisy!" She started to cry. Of course. I was so

accustomed to her crying at me by this time that I didn't even wince. "It's Eustace. Mr. Kincaid."

Her voice choked to a halt, and I thought she was going to tell me they'd found his body buried in a remote spot on the desert and that Quincy Applewood really *was* guilty of murder, but I couldn't ask. Not right out loud over the telephone wire. Besides, I couldn't believe it of Quincy.

Instead, I donned my virtual spiritualist hat and crooned in a soothing tone, "All will be well, Mrs. Kincaid. The cards never lie." I trusted her not to remember that the cards had predicted undefined but harrowing problems for her. "And neither does Rolly," I added, just in case she did remember about the cards.

"Oh, Daisy, you're of such solace to me. I wanted to have you over yesterday and the day before and the day before that, but Harold begged me to give you a rest. He said you mediums—or should I call you media?—Oh, dear, I just don't know. But Harold said you needed a chance to meditate and center yourself or your powers would be drained or diminished or something like that, and I *couldn't* do that to you, Daisy. You've been my mainstay and my support. With, of course, Freddy and Algie and Harold, but they're men, don't you know, and you know what men are."

"I certainly do." I wasn't altogether clear on the rest of her speech, however. Her voice had picked up strength as she said the above, although it still didn't sound like hers. But I think I caught the gist of her message, even though I still didn't know if her husband was alive or dead. If it hadn't been Quincy who'd offed the buzzard, I'd personally prefer the latter scenario, although I didn't say so to Mrs. Kincaid. "Um, what exactly has happened, Mrs. Kincaid?"

"The Coast Guard caught Mr. Kincaid. And he hadn't got very far. His steamer was just about four miles out to sea, heading to Portugal or Spain or Istanbul or one of those countries over there."

I hadn't even thought about Portugal or Istanbul, because I hadn't thought a Spanish phrase book would do Mr. Kincaid much good in either place, but I didn't quarrel with her about it. Rather, I said, "Hmmm," mysteriously.

"It happened just as you said it would, Daisy. I told that Detective Rotund that he should listen to your suggestion. He balked at first."

Naturally. He would.

"But in the end, since they were having no luck finding him anywhere else, he decided to call upon the Coast Guard to search for a vessel containing Mr. Kincaid. And you were right, Daisy. They found him. With the bearer bonds. You were right!"

By golly, I *had* been right. Good for me. And take *that*, Detective Sam Rotondo! I couldn't understand why Mrs. Kincaid insisted on calling him Rotund. He wasn't fat. He was just big.

"I'm so glad they found him alive," I said, thinking it was the right thing to say even if I didn't mean it.

"Hmph," said Mrs. Kincaid. "I wish they'd drowned him. Oh, Daisy! He's going to go to *jail*! However will I withstand the gossip and talk. Think of the humiliation of having a husband in *jail*?"

That beat me, so I remained silent, hoping she'd take my silence as something to do with seeing mystical auras and so forth.

"I *need* you, Daisy! I know you need to rest your powers, but haven't they been rested enough? Are you able to come over to the house? Please, dear? I need you *so* much!"

Interesting, thought I, that she should call on a stranger—and a fake, at that—rather than her own daughter, when she was in trouble. Harold had an excuse for not being at his mother's beck and call each and every day, since he actually worked for a living. But all

Stacy ever did for a living was get into trouble and annoy people.

Still in my spiritualist voice, I said, "Of course, Mrs. Kincaid. I shall come as soon as may be." Calculating frantically in my head everything I had to do before I jaunted off to the Kincaids' mansion, I added, "I should be there within the hour." I didn't want to leave my cream-colored silk lying in a heap on the floor, nor did I want to leave the sewing machine set up in the back parlor, because it was in the way should Billy want to wheel himself in there for some reason.

And, of course, I had to change clothes. Right then, I looked like any old housewife who'd decided to make herself a new dress with fabric bought on sale at Nash's, but I wasn't supposed to be any old housewife. I was supposed to be a spiritualist.

I also had to break the news to Billy. I caught him reading on the sun porch and, after sucking in a gallon or two of air to brace myself, told him I was going away again. He took it fairly well, probably because I'd been home for several days running, which didn't happen often. True, a couple of ladies had come, by appointment, to have me read the Tarot cards for them, but Billy didn't mind that, since I did it in the back parlor (yes, the same room in which Ma, Aunt Vi, and I did our sewing) and we didn't get in his way.

"Sorry the old man's alive, but I'm glad Quincy's cleared of murder charges," he said.

"Me, too, on both counts. I wonder if Mrs. Kincaid allowed Quincy to stay at her place, or if they locked him in a cell once he was able to get around. He was in bad shape the last time I saw him."

"Must have let him stay at the Kincaids'," Billy said knowledgeably—he'd been talking to his favorite detective a lot lately and knew more about police business than he used to. "They can't very well arrest a person for murder if nobody can find the corpse, unless they have a whole lot of circumstantial evidence. From what I've gathered, they don't have anything against Quincy except people overhearing an argument in the old man's library."

"Well, they have the old man himself now. And the bearer bonds."

"Aha!" Billy actually smiled at me, something that seldom happened when I was running away from home. "So they found the bonds on the old devil, did they?"

"According to Mrs. Kincaid." I was surveying my wardrobe, trying to decide on an ensemble that would be eloquent of tragedy but not overwhelmingly gloomy and one that would, moreover, create the impression of a person in communication with the Great Beyond. Sounds complicated, but my wardrobe was geared to such conflicting necessities.

I settled on a light-weight, dark blue, poplin summer suit with shiny blue bias tape sewn on the long pointy collar and around the jacket pockets. I wore the suit with a white lawn blouse and topped it off with a moderate-brimmed blue hat with one white flower adorning the brim, modest cotton stockings, and white bag, gloves, and shoes. If I say so myself, I looked pretty classy. But arcane. Always arcane. I never allowed myself to forget the way I made my living. I walked out to the sun porch.

"Do I look mystical enough?"

"You look super, Daisy. You always do."

"Thanks, Billy." I bent and kissed him. "I hope this isn't going to take all day."

"Me, too."

As I might have predicted, had I been possessed of real psychic powers, it took all day.

 CHAPTER 17

I drove the Model T since neither Pudge Wilson nor Pa
was available to harness Brownie to the pony cart. I'm
sure that made Brownie happy, or would have, had he
been capable of happiness. I think Brownie enjoyed his
sulks.

Cranking the blasted Model T wasn't any fun, either,
but I did it. The days were getting much warmer, and the
haze, which I understood had always existed in this area,
blurred the San Gabriel Mountains to the north.
According to Miss Carleton, a librarian at the Pasadena
Public Library on Raymond and Walnut, the Indians
who used to live in the San Gabriel Valley called this
area "The Valley of Smoke." Pasadena was still a
beautiful town to live in, though, even if you weren't rich
and the day was hazy.

Gardens were bursting their buttons with roses and
other flowers. I hate to say it, because she's such a
terrible gossip and I don't really like her, but Mrs.
Longnecker's garden was spectacular, especially her
dahlias and roses.

Mrs. Weber, who lived a couple of blocks from us, had

planted a hedge of gardenia bushes several years earlier. On hot days, the fragrance of the blossoms seemed to get trapped in invisible clumps in the air. When the Model T drove through one of those airy clumps, the fragrance all but knocked me out. We had one gardenia bush in the back yard. I decided then and there, while under the influence of hundreds of gardenia blossoms, to plant at least one more.

And then there was the jasmine. Mrs. Phipps had jasmine that bloomed during the day and jasmine that bloomed at night, so you were treated to glorious fragrances no matter what time of day you passed her house. Not to mention the honeysuckle vines crawling all over her front fence. And all this glory was in our own modest neighborhood.

When I made a left turn onto Orange Grove Boulevard and started tootling through that neighborhood, the beauty was enough to make a person cry, if she were that sort of individual. I'm not. But I sure did enjoy the drive. Roses, roses everywhere, not to mention stock, ranunculus, dahlias, anemones, impatiens, hibiscus, bougainvilleas, wisteria, geraniums, bird of paradise, and approximately three million and ten other flowers the names of which I didn't know. Our own native California poppies, bright orange in the sunshine, grew in places where people hadn't settled yet, making the entire trip as lovely as if I were on a magic carpet flying through a rainbow. It seemed a shame that I was in our clunky old Model T.

And the lawns. My word, those lawns were really something. Nowadays you can't find lawns like that. Some of them seemed to roll along forever, dotted here and there with trees. Coral trees, palm trees, jacaranda trees, pepper trees, avocado trees, weeping willows, the occasional sycamore or oak, and even a few eucalyptus trees and monkey-puzzle trees imported from Australia. I tell you, you could do a lot of swell gardening if you were rich.

I got to the Kincaids' within the hour I'd specified, in spite of the beauty surrounding my drive there—I tended to slow down and gawk when I passed the most spectacular of floral yard displays. Since I imagined that Quincy must still be feeling pretty puny, and since James was probably doing Quincy's work as well as his own and didn't need my machine to fuss with, I decided to park spang in front of the mansion, in the Kincaids' circular drive. If Featherstone didn't like it, too bad for him. Two other automobiles, one of them Harold's snappy red Bearcat, were already parked in the drive, so I wasn't setting a precedent or anything.

Featherstone gave no indication either of liking or disliking my choice of parking spaces, but opened the door with his nose in the air, as ever, and I walked in. "Cheers, Featherstone," said I because I couldn't help myself.

He made no response other than a chilly, "Mrs. Majesty." He never did respond to my jolly greetings. Rather, he turned and I followed him down the hall to the drawing room. I guess it was inevitable that the first person I saw as I walked through the door was Sam Rotondo. I suppressed my sigh and braced myself for Mrs. Kincaid's greeting. Her greetings, since Stacy's arrest and her husband's bolt to unknown ports, had been a trifle hard on my own personal body.

Sure enough, as soon as Featherstone announced me in a voice that sounded like that of a judge pronouncing the death sentence on a murderer, Mrs. Kincaid squealed like a stuck pig and fairly flew off the chair in which she sat. It wasn't until she'd stopped hugging me and, I'm sure I need not say, crying all over me, that I got to survey the room.

All the people I was beginning to think of as regulars were there: Sam, Harold, Father Frederick, Algie Pinkerton, and, to my distaste, Stacy, all occupied space in the drawing room. There was no sign of Mr. Kincaid. I hoped this meant he was already in jail. Stacy looked at me as if she'd like to shoot me dead. I ignored her, although I greeted all the others.

"Good day to you, Harold, Father Frederick, and Mr. Pinkerton."

They good-dayed back at me.

Before Algie could ask me to call him Algie instead of Mr. Pinkerton, I turned to Sam. I still didn't like him, but he was being very kind to my Billy—mainly by behaving as if he wasn't trying to be kind—so I smiled at him, too. "Detective Rotondo." I wanted to ask him, "Do you live here?" but didn't, although he'd asked me the same question in a snide voice once. I felt rather virtuous for my restraint.

He nodded. No smile. Even when I tried, I couldn't get on that man's good side. If he had one. Oh, very well, I knew he had one, or he wouldn't play gin rummy with Pa and Billy so often. But it was irksome to have wasted a smile on him.

"Come sit beside me, Daisy, dear. I need you today so much." Mrs. Kincaid had reseated herself on one of the sofas and patted the space beside her.

I heard Stacy mutter something under her breath, although I didn't hear the words.

Harold, who was apparently as fed up with his sister as I was, barked at her, "If you can only be ugly, Anastasia Kincaid, leave the room. You're a bigger pain in the neck than anyone else I know! Other than our father, that is."

Mrs. Kincaid said, "Oh, dear," and pressed a hand to her plump cheek.

Stacy said, "Don't be such an ass, Harry."

Mrs. Kincaid, her head whipping toward her daughter, and her eyes bulging like some kind of South-American frog I'd seen once in an issue of *National Geographic*, whispered, "Stacy!"

She sounded so shocked at her daughter's vocabulary

that I nearly shook my head in wonder. I mean, if you're a mother, and you have a daughter as rebellious and unpleasant as Stacy Kincaid, wouldn't you notice something was wrong before she said a word like *ass* in your presence? The word *ass* is even used in the Bible, so it's not nearly as bad as some words I've heard. Or even, I blush to confess, spoken from time to time.

Sam Rotondo turned toward Stacy, too. "If you please, Miss Kincaid, I believe you needn't be involved in this conversation. I'd appreciate it if you'd leave the room."

Stacy's mouth dropped open until her chin almost knocked against her breastbone.

Harold said, "Thank God."

Mrs. Kincaid said, "Perhaps that would be best, Stacy, darling."

Humph. She never called *me* darling, although she had called me dear a few times. Then again, I wasn't her daughter, even though I was nicer to her than was Stacy. There's that family connection that always gets you, I guess.

"Great idea," said Harold, frowning at his sister.

"I won't!" Stacy said. Looking pouty and rather like a mule digging her back legs into the mud and daring anyone to move her.

"Oh, please, darling, don't start a scene. Not today. Not now."

Poor Mrs. Kincaid. If Stacy'd been my kid, I'd have smacked her from here to next Sunday, and she'd never have defied me again. That, at least, was my fantasy of what true, disciplined motherhood entailed. I had no first-hand knowledge of the motherly state back then.

"I'll see you to the door," said the ever-watchful and prudent Father Frederick. Even though he seldom offered suggestions of a disciplinary nature to Stacy, he sure knew how to take advantage of one when he heard it.

When he took Stacy's arm tenderly with his hand, she

shook it off violently. "Why should *I* leave, when *she* gets to stay?" she shouted, pointing at me. I never did know why she disliked me so much, but she sure gave every indication of doing so.

Harold walked over and stood beside Father Frederick. He was decidedly *un*gentle when he took his sister's other arm and yanked her up from the sofa. "Get the hell out of this room now, and don't return unless or until someone tells you to come back in. And don't leave the premises."

Mrs. Kincaid said, "Oh, dear," again, but Harold and Father Frederick showed Stacy to the door and out of it. She looked as if she'd like to kill everyone in the room, starting either with Harold or me, depending on who was closer after she loaded her gun.

As she took off down the hall, Harold hollered after her, "And don't leave the house and grounds. The detective might have some questions for you."

"I don't care!" came shrilly back from the escaping monster-in-training. I wondered if she'd learned her disagreeable behavior from her father. I'd also have taken bets that she'd leave the house and grounds as soon as she got James to crank up whatever automobile she chose to use. I wouldn't have put it past her to snitch Harold's Stutz Bearcat and have an accident on purpose just for the heck of it.

"I don't think we'll need Miss Kincaid," said Rotondo. He sounded relieved because of it, and I couldn't find it in my heart to fault him.

"Good," said Harold, who belonged to the family and, therefore, felt no compunction about admitting his feelings aloud, unlike some of us present.

We were all quiet for several seconds, recovering from the Stacy incident. Then I saw Rotondo take a deep breath. He turned and spoke to me. I got the feeling he didn't want to, mainly because he looked more or less like a thunder cloud about to burst and rain all over me.

"I'm sure you were pleased to know that we ultimately took your suggestion about calling upon the Coast Guard for help, and that the Coast Guard found Mr. Kincaid and brought him back to the States."

"Very pleased," I agreed. I'm ashamed to say I smirked. It was a small smirk, but still...

His mouth thinned into a straight line, but he didn't speak sharply at me, probably because there were other people present. "Most of the bearer bonds were recovered with him."

"Most of them? What about the rest of them?" The fiend had probably cashed in the bonds to buy his boat. What a consummate rotten apple the man was.

Algie spoke up. "It will be my pleasure to replace the bonds that are unaccounted for." Then he blushed and tried to fade into the wallpaper. As I believe I've mentioned once or twice, Algie Pinkerton wasn't exactly aggressive about putting himself forward.

"Oh, Algie!" Mrs. Kincaid looked at him with love in her eyes.

Hmmm, wondered I. Did Episcopalians throw people out of their church if they were divorced, as Catholics did? Would Mrs. Kincaid divorce her worm of a husband even if her church recognized divorces as legitimate? I knew Mrs. Kincaid was terrified of scandal, but I still thought she and Algie Pinkerton would make a swell couple. They were both sort of dizzy, and they were both rich, which meant that neither one would be marrying the other for money, which was important. I mean, look at what had happened after she married Eustace Kincaid.

And where were Edie and Quincy? Since talk of the case had lagged while Rotondo got his temper under control and Mrs. Kincaid and Algie gazed adoringly at one another, I decided to ask. "Where are Edie Marsh and Quincy Applewood?"

Rotondo answered me. "Miss Marsh has been given a

leave of absence to tend Mr. Applewood, who's still in the room next to the breakfast room, recuperating." He didn't look as though he approved of these arrangements.

Mrs. Kincaid's gaze swiveled from Algie to me, and she clasped her hands to her bosom yet again. "It was the least I could do, after that poor Applewood boy went through so much to follow my wretched husband through the night. And then to be set upon and beaten over the head by a thug hired by Mr. Kincaid! And poor Edie. After what Mr. Kincaid tried to do to her! She was in such a state." Mrs. Kincaid gave us all a sappy smile. "They're planning to marry as soon as may be." She sighed happily. "Mr. Applewood, of course, always has a position here if he wants it. And dear Edie is welcome to remain, although I doubt that she will once she has a home of her own to care for."

I stifled the urge to ask her how the heck they were supposed to buy a home of their own on Quincy's salary as a stable boy. Rich people had no idea how the rest of the world lived. I'd discovered that much about life when I was ten years old.

"How nice," I said, meaning at least part of it.

Mrs. Kincaid leaned over and whispered in my ear. "I'm giving the Applewood boy a substantial raise in pay, because of the despair Mr. Kincaid caused Edie, and the terrible beating Mr. Applewood suffered in our service."

"That's very nice of you," I said, meaning every word this time.

Harold and Father Frederick had reseated themselves—Harold had taken the precaution of locking the drawing-room door in case Stacy decided to put on another one of her dramatic performances.

It was Harold who got the meeting back on the right path. "So, what's going to happen now, Detective Rotondo? Will Father be eligible for a bail bond? He's already skipped the country once."

"That will be up to the district attorney and the judge, Mr. Kincaid."

"Too bad Father's friends with so many judges," Harold muttered pensively. "If he does make bail, I suppose he'll come back here to stay until it's time for the trial." I could tell that Harold didn't like this scenario at all. "Unless, of course, he lams it again." That thought cheered him up some.

"Probably." Rotondo wanted Kincaid to stay locked up. It was obvious in his posture and tone of voice, and the fact that his teeth were clamped together so hard, his jaw bulged. I wondered if he was going to ruin his teeth doing that.

Mrs. Kincaid pushed herself up on the sofa until she sat as straight as a carpenter's level, only vertical. "He will *not* be coming back to *this* house! I shan't permit it."

Looking glum, Harold said, "California has joint-property laws, Mother. You may not be able to prevent him from coming home."

Turning to gaze at her son, Mrs. Kincaid gave him what I can only describe as a dazzling smile. "Ah, but you never knew, Harold, that my late father, your sainted grandfather, insisted that Mr. Kincaid sign a pre-nuptial agreement before he and I were wed. Papa was wiser than I, I must say, because I thought it was unnecessary and that Eustace would balk at the notion. He didn't, undoubtedly because he was so happy to be marrying so much money. That's also probably why he cleaned out the bank, because he knew if he left me without funds of his own, he'd be a pauper." She sniffed. "The vile beast. This house and property are *mine*, and Eustace shan't get a farthing from me if I can help it."

I'll be danged. I didn't even know there were such things as pre-nuptial agreements. For that matter, I didn't know what a farthing was.

For the first time in what seemed like ages, Sam Rotondo smiled. "That's good. Unless one of his judge friends wants to post bail for him, he won't be out of jail before the trial. If the case goes to trial." His smile faded on the last sentence.

"Why wouldn't it go to trial?" demanded Harold. "He stole half a million dollars worth of bearer bonds and tried to skip the country. If it weren't for Algie and Del, the bank would have folded and my dear father would have cheated three-quarters of the citizens of Pasadena out of their life savings!"

Rotondo sighed. "I hate to say it, Mr. Kincaid, but money talks."

"But my father doesn't *have* any money!" Harold paused, smiled, and added, "Not anymore, he doesn't."

"That's right," said Mrs. Kincaid, also smiling.

"We'll see," Sam said. He didn't look any too convinced to me. Probably because there were still all those judges. "He'll be arraigned today, and we'll find out if someone has posted bond for him."

"I believe it's time for me to use the telephone." Mrs. Kincaid sounded grim. I didn't know she had a grim bone in her body until then. And she still sat tall, as if someone had stuck a pole up her back. "I am friends with the wives of all the judges Mr. Kincaid knows. I believe I shall be able to exert some influence in this case."

There you go. What's that old saying about a woman scorned? I was proud of Mrs. Kincaid for her response to her husband's desertion. After all, she could have had a nervous breakdown and decided she was helpless and done nothing but cry and moan for the next six months. Instead, she did something useful.

She surprised me. She exercised a much greater degree of firmness about her husband than she did about Stacy. Still, I held some faint hope that she might gain strength through this ordeal and learn how to deal with her daughter effectively. Stranger things have happened. I think they have, anyhow.

Father Frederick stuck a boot into the conversation. Looking upon Mrs. Kincaid with fondness (I wondered if he was a single gentleman. If Algie didn't work out, Mrs. K. Could do worse than to marry Father Frederick). "I shall be happy to discuss your future plans with you, Madeline. Regarding your marriage, I mean, if you care to discuss such a delicate matter with me."

Lifting her chin, which made her look like an entirely different person than the soft, sort of squishy, giddy woman I'd known for ten years, she said, "I haven't yet decided what I shall do. I am contemplating securing a divorce."

"My goodness." Father Frederick appeared thunderstruck—and a tiny bit gratified. I guess he didn't like Mr. Kincaid any more than I did. "Please feel free to ask for my support and counsel whenever you like."

Borrowing from my own repertoire, Mrs. Kincaid gave Father Frederick a gracious smile. "You know I'd never do anything drastic without consulting with you, Freddy. You and Daisy and Algie have been my main guides and friends for years."

That meant I'd been one of her main guides and friends since I was ten years old. It made no sense to me, but I didn't argue. Far be it from me to question the judgment or logic of my main source of income.

"I *won't* have a jailbird for a husband," Mrs. Kincaid added uncompromisingly.

"If he gets convicted, I suppose he'll be a prison-bird," Harold said.

Mrs. Kincaid blinked at her son. "Is there a difference, darling?"

Another darling. I concluded that she reserved the *darlings* for her children.

Harold said, "Yes. I'll explain it to you later, Mother."

"Before I do anything, however, I need Daisy to read the cards and consult the board for me." She patted me on my dark-blue-poplin-covered knee.

I smiled at her, thinking *Oh, boy*. If my husband had run off with five hundred thousand dollars' worth of bearer bonds from the bank he was supposed to be head of, I'd be consulting a lawyer, not a spiritualist. Not that Billy would ever do anything of the sort. My Billy, while nowhere near as rich as any Kincaid extant in Pasadena, was an honorable man. It was strange, but I was actually luckier than Mrs. Kincaid, at least in this one element of life.

Rotondo stared at the two of us in clear disbelief for several seconds. His stare lasted fully long enough for me to register his distaste for such an agenda as cards and board, and to respond with an *I-dare-you-to-say-one-disparaging-word-about-my-business* look.

He finally said, "Yes. Well, if there are no more questions about Mr. Kincaid's capture and arrest, I'd better get down to the courthouse."

Harold exchanged a glance with his mother, then with me. I shrugged. Whether anyone in the room wanted to believe it or not, this Kincaid mess wasn't my problem.

Algie went to Mrs. Kincaid and stood before her as she sat on the sofa. "Is there anything I can do for you, Madeline? I had best go to the bank and help Mr. Farrington. We have to make sure exactly how many bonds are missing and how much they total in dollars."

"Of course, Algie dear."

So he was a *dear*, too. I felt much better.

"Maybe I should go to the courthouse with you, Detective Rotondo. Will you require a member of the family to be present?"

"It wouldn't hurt. Thank you, Mr. Kincaid. Er, would you care to drive in my police vehicle or take your own?"

I'm sure Harold could tell how little Sam wanted him to ride in his machine, because even I could detect Sam's reluctance to make the offer. I think it's a dirty shame that so-called "normal" men feared the Harolds of this world. Harold was about as dangerous as a powder puff.

"I'll take the Bearcat," said Harold. He didn't even sound snippy or cynical. He was probably accustomed to this reaction from men who weren't of his persuasion. "That is, I'll take it if Stacy hasn't stolen it and wrapped it around a tree somewhere."

"Harold!" cried Mrs. Kincaid, aghast.

I couldn't suppress a grin because Harold and I were on the same track. Harold Kincaid was a sweetheart; I don't care what anyone else said or thought about him. He was quickly becoming a good friend to me, as Sam was to Billy, and I appreciated having someone to talk to, as I could talk to Harold.

"Just kidding, Mother." Harold scurried over to the couch, kissed his mother's cheek, winked at me, and headed toward Rotondo, who stepped back a space, as if he expected Harold to attack him. Bigotry comes in lots of forms, I guess.

"Thank you, Mr. Kincaid." At least Rotondo *sounded* polite. Turning to Mrs. Kincaid, he said, "I'll return as soon as the arraignment is over, if that's all right with you, Mrs. Kincaid, and tell you how it went and what will happen next. We may have to execute search warrants on this house and the bank, but I promise you that we'll disturb you as little as possible."

"*Search* warrants? Good God!" Mrs. Kincaid's stiff posture slumped. I laid a hand on her shoulder and murmured in my best mediumistic voice, "This, too, will pass, Mrs. Kincaid. Recall the messages that came through for you in the cards and the board."

I could practically hear Sam Rotondo's eyes rolling even though I wasn't looking at him. Darn it, if he wasn't a friend of Billy's, I'd never let him in my house again.

"May I speak with you before you and Daisy get started, Madeline?" Father Frederick looked serious, and I instantly took the hint.

I stood up and smoothed my jacket. "While you speak

with Father Frederick, may I visit with Edie and Quincy? They're both good friends of mine." I smiled sweetly down upon Mrs. Kincaid.

She took my hand. "Of course, Daisy dear. I feel so bad about what happened to both of them."

Yeah. So did I.

Algie, Harold, Sam, and I left the room together. Harold gave me a peck on the cheek before taking off to the courthouse. Sam nodded curtly. Algie stuttered something I didn't catch. Father Frederick shook my hand, which was a departure, but I didn't mind. As for me, I hot-footed it through the kitchen, waving at Aunt Vi as I did so, and hurried to the room that was being used to accommodate Quincy as he recovered.

I made a big mistake when I got there. It still embarrasses me to think about it. But how could I have known that I should knock before entering a hospital room, and that room was being used as one, wasn't it? When I trotted through the breakfast room and got to the right door, I burst right in. My greeting stuck in my throat, and the sight that greeted me made me step back out into the hall and shut the door. Fast.

My goodness, but I didn't think people did things like that until after they were married. If I'd known what was going to happen to Billy in France, I might have availed myself of the opportunity beforehand, too, but, gee whiz. How embarrassing.

I heard some shuffling noises coming from inside the room, and stood there, wondering what to do. I really wanted to congratulate both Edie and Quincy for overcoming such terrible obstacles to their happiness, but I didn't think I could manage a chat with a couple of nearly-naked people. I wouldn't know where to look, if you know what I mean.

As I stood in the hallway for several moments, confused and flustered, the door opened and a red-faced Edie peeked out at me. "Daisy," she said.

I bowed my head. "I'm so sorry, Edie. I don't know why I didn't think to knock. I was so eager to find out how the two of you were doing, that I just walked right in." Guess I didn't have to ask now, but I did anyway. "Is Quincy better?"

"Much better." Her cheeks got even redder. "Thank you for asking." She stepped back and opened the door wider. "Please come on in, Daisy. We both need to thank you for suggesting the police get in touch with the Coast Guard."

"Right," came from the bed. I didn't want to go into the room, but after such a friendly greeting from Edie, I felt obliged to do so.

I waved from the doorway. "How are you feeling, Quincy?"

"Much better. And I want to thank you, too, because if the Coast Guard hadn't found that bastard—"

"Quincy!" Edie glowered at her beloved.

Quincy winced. "Sorry. Edie's making me watch my language."

I thought that was a splendid idea, although I didn't say so.

"Anyhow, if the police hadn't finally called on the Coast Guard for help, I'd probably have been charged with murder."

"Without a body?" I asked, thinking about what Billy had told me.

Edie said, "You know how it goes, Daisy. If you're not rich, they can do pretty much anything they want to do to you."

Pessimistic, but true. "Yes, I know. I'm sure glad they found him. They got most of the bonds back, too."

"Glad to hear it. I wish they'd toss a few our way. We could use them." Quincy grinned. I quailed to see the grin, but I guess his lip was healing fast, because nothing started bleeding.

"Quincy." Another glower from Edie. "Mrs. Kincaid

has been an angel. She's given me a paid leave of absence to nurse you, she's given you your job back, *plus* a raise in pay, and she said I could stay here and work—again with a raise in pay—until I don't want to any longer. What more do you want out of life?"

I wondered how these two were going to get along after they were married. Pretty well, I decided, as long as Edie held firm. You had to be strong to survive living with a man. I knew it for a fact.

"I know it, Angel Face, but I sure wouldn't mind being rich. Would you?"

Angel Face? I'm glad Billy only called me Daisy.

Upon a sigh, Edie confessed, "No. I wouldn't mind at all. But there's no use in longing for things that can't be."

Quincy shrugged, which didn't seem to cause him any pain, either. "You never know."

"True, true," I said, deciding I'd better get back to the drawing room with my Tarot cards. I suspected it would be Featherstone who brought Mrs. Kincaid's fancy Ouija board to the drawing room, and I wanted to see him do it. There was something about Featherstone together with an Ouija board that tickled my sense of the ridiculous.

I didn't get home that night until way past dark. I actually dined (the Kincaids dined; we Gumms and Majestys only ate) with Mrs. Kincaid, Harold, Father Frederick, and Algie (nobody knew where Stacy was, thank God) at the Kincaid's massive dining room table. What's more, I got to eat Aunt Vi's food, so I didn't miss out on anything.

The meal started out with a salad made with mixed greens and with a dressing that was so good I wanted to lick the bowl when the greens were gone. That course was followed by a poached fish of some sort served on a bed of spinach and with a sauce so savory, I decided that as long as I could eat Aunt Vi's cooking, I wouldn't miss not doing with Billy what Edie and Quincy had been up to. Not much, anyway.

I thought that was it—salad, fish, and spinach would be a full meal for us Gumms and Majestys. It wasn't it, however. Next to be brought in by Featherstone, who held the platter as if he neither knew nor cared what it contained, was a chicken pie. I was familiar with Aunt Vi's chicken pie, and wished I hadn't eaten so much fish. But what's a person to do in a situation like that? I ate my chicken pie with relish. That is to say, not with relish, but with pleasure. Oh, you know what I mean.

Dessert was a blackberry tart smothered in sweetened whipped cream. I understood now why Mrs. Kincaid and Harold were both on the plump side. If I ate like that every day of my life, I'd look like an elephant in no time at all.

# CHAPTER 18

It turned out that even judges have their principles (or maybe they were prejudices). Not a single one of the judges or lawyers or bankers who had been chummy with Mr. Kincaid before he stole the bearer bonds wanted anything to do with him after he was charged with several felonies.

He was not tried by a jury of his peers, either, since rich men always managed to get out of serving on jury duty. It was regular people like the Gumms and Majestys who served on his jury. Irate that a rich man like Kincaid had tried to swindle them out of their own paltry savings, they convicted him of everything. Plus, the judge (who, I later learned from Harold, belonged to one of Mr. Kincaid's clubs) sentenced him to ten years in prison.

So, there you go. Sometimes justice prevails. Sometimes it doesn't. Depends on how much money you have at the time you need a judge's influence. Fortunately for Mrs. Kincaid and the rest of us who loathed or had been oppressed by Mr. Kincaid, Mr. Kincaid had no money at the time of his trial.

Mrs. Kincaid filed for divorce, and proved Algie's prophecy by being the center of social attention in Pasadena for months after the news of Mr. Kincaid's theft and bolt to the ocean spread. She was the Queen of Pasadena until the next scandal broke and some other society woman took over the position. She enjoyed herself during her reign, too. I can't even remember the number of séances I held at her house during the ensuing six months, or the number of new clients I garnered from doing so.

I was glad for her and even a little bit proud. After all, I'd had a hand in helping her through her many travails, one of whom still lived in her house. Mrs. Kincaid never spoke to me about Stacy, but I heard lots of gossip when I conducted séances at other rich women's homes. It seemed to me that Stacy would never grow up, and I was glad I didn't have to run around in her circles.

As for Edie and Quincy, three months after Quincy resumed working as a stable hand at the Kincaid mansion, the two of them got married. What's more, Mrs. Kincaid insisted they do so in her garden, which still looked gorgeous even though September had crept in and fall was approaching fast. I don't think I've ever seen so many spectacular carnations and chrysanthemums.

Father Frederick performed the ceremony. Mrs. Kincaid cried. So did Algie Pinkerton, who sat next to her (I saw them holding hands at one point). So did I. How embarrassing. But my darling Billy understood. He even surreptitiously handed me his big white handkerchief at one point when my tiny lacy one was saturated.

I saw Stacy Kincaid sitting on a garden bench, a scowl on her face and her arms crossed over her chest, and I wondered who in the world had got her to attend the wedding. Had it been Harold? Or had Mrs. Kincaid finally acquired some backbone? I didn't like Stacy enough to find out for sure, but I was intrigued to see her there. She was even clad in a demure frock, and wasn't trying to shock the world by smoking cigarettes during the ceremony.

Billy got to meet Harold and Del Farrington at the wedding, and he was as polite to the two men as he would have been if he'd been introduced to a couple of "normal" men. I was proud of him.

Harold and I had become true chums by that time. We spent gobs of time together, and he gave me a tour of the Sam Goldwyn Studio, which was fascinating. I even got to see Douglas Fairbanks from a distance. I'd have fainted dead away on the spot had I been a woman with a weaker nature. I'd asked Billy to come with me, but he said he didn't want to, and that he considered men who acted in the pictures sissies. There you go. There's no reasoning with even the best of men about some things.

Sam Rotondo had already surprised and disappointed me by keeping in touch with Billy after the Kincaid case was concluded. Of course, his friendship was good for Billy. And Pa liked him, too. Aunt Vi and Ma thought I was prejudiced against him for no good reason. Ha! They'd never been regarded as a murder suspect as I'd been. Let me tell you, such an experience gives a person a poor impression of one's accuser.

The dratted detective gave me the shock of my life when he showed up at Quincy and Edie's wedding. Had they actually invited *him*? When I asked, Edie said, "Of course." I'll never understand some things as long as I live.

Edie had asked me to be her matron of honor, by the way, but I declined the offer with genuine thanks. I told her the truth: I didn't want to leave Billy alone in a herd of strangers. To tell the truth, I was also certain I'd cry, and I didn't want to be the only weepy member of the wedding party. Edie understood.

It was a beautiful wedding. Mrs. Kincaid had one of

her underlings build an arch, under which Father Frederick stood. The arch had been slathered with fall flowers. Edie wore an ivory satin gown (I would have been a little put out if she'd worn white, given what I'd glimpsed by accident that one time). It had a dropped waist and lots of beads and was perfectly gorgeous, especially since she'd had her hair bobbed, and she wore a short veil that went so well with the dress, I almost wished I could get married again and borrow Edie's ensemble.

The reception was held in Mrs. Kincaid's drawing room with Aunt Vi catering along with the help of several girls hired for the day. All of this, I'm sure I need not say, was paid for by Mrs. Kincaid. What a swell lady she was. The food was as delicious as ever.

After we'd all eaten as much as we could hold, a band started playing and people began dancing. Although I used to love to dance, I didn't dance at the reception because of Billy's problems. I'm sure he wouldn't have enjoyed seeing me having a gay old time dancing with other men.

Ma and Pa and I were chatting with Edie's mother (who'd also been crying throughout the ceremony) when I realized Billy wasn't with us. Somewhat alarmed (every now and then, when were at parties, Billy got spells during which he'd become depressed and wheel himself off somewhere to hide) I turned to survey the room.

"What is it, Daisy?"

"Billy's taken himself off somewhere."

Ma knew what that meant. She took my arm. "Try not to worry, Daisy. I'm sure he's only gone to talk to someone he knows."

That was the problem: he didn't know any of these people. Since the war, his mobility had been so limited that the friends he'd had in high school, and who were still alive after the war, were out of touch with him, except for an occasional letter or drop in. He hated it when old friends popped by, because he didn't like people feeling sorry for him.

Because I didn't want to upset Ma, I said, "That's probably it." I didn't believe it. I feared Billy had become discouraged by watching all the fully functioning people in the room and decided to wheel himself home. My heart thumped like a bass drum as I searched the crowd for him.

I was wrong. Ma was right.

There he was, across the room, and darned if he wasn't laughing it up with Detective Sam Rotondo. Billy had seldom looked happier. "Oh," I said to Ma. "There he is." I jerked my head in the general direction of Billy and Sam.

"Ah," said Ma. "I see." She smiled one of her warm, unimaginative smiles. "Isn't that nice?"

"Yeah," I said. "It's real nice."

"He's a good man, Sam is," opined my father as if he were Saint Peter at the Holy Gate passing judgment on a newly departed human.

"Right," I said, even as my insides were churning unpleasantly.

But I suppose I was glad Billy and Sam were friends. God knows, Billy needed friends.

After watching the two men chatter like a couple of male magpies for several minute, my brain in a whirl, I decided their friendship was fitting. They both drove me absolutely crazy. They might as well do it together. But suddenly I had an idea. If I could get Billy to persuade Sam Rotondo that I wasn't an evil person…well, it was worth a try.

And I'll try anything once.

Turn the page for an

excerpt from

FINE

SPIRITS

A Daisy Gumm Majesty Mystery

Book Two

Alice Duncan

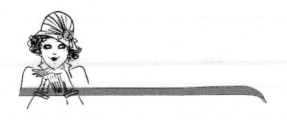

"Actually, it's not that *I'm* ill," Mrs. Bissel went on. "It's something else." Her voice dropped to a sepulchral whisper on the *something else* part of this speech.

This time I was successful in suppressing my sigh. In the time it would take her to tell me her problem, I'd probably have been able to sweep the kitchen and vacuum-clean the living room rug—or resume bickering with Billy. But instead of doing something useful, I had to stand in the kitchen with the telephone's ear piece jammed against my head, the black mouthpiece sticking out of the wall, and listen to a woman who wasn't accustomed to thinking think. Can you tell I was in a really bad mood?

"I'm glad you're not ill," I said pleasantly. I was always pleasant to the clients, even those whom I'd rather strangle. To be fair, Mrs. Bissel wasn't one of my imaginary stranglees. She, although daffy, silly, and a general waster of my time, was a very nice lady.

Besides, I had designs on one of her dogs. Her female dachshund, Lucille, had, with the help of her male companion Lancelot, just given birth to four of the most adorable puppies I'd ever seen in my life. They were black with little tan spots over their eyes, tan feet and muzzles, and were as shiny as the seals I'd seen in the

Griffith Park Zoo in Los Angeles. I wanted one. What's more, I suspected that Mrs. Bissel would be willing to trade one of the pups for a séance if I worked on her just right.

Mainly I wanted the dog for Billy. He often got lonely and angry when I left home to work as a spiritualist. Since he claimed it was *what* I did, rather than the fact that I had to work at all, that bothered him, I was supposed to understand that he wouldn't have cared if I'd left him every day to work at Nash's or as a typist for an attorney or done something else "normal."

I didn't buy it. I think he'd have hated my having to earn our living no matter how I did it. In a way I could understand his attitude. Until the war, Billy had never been one to sit idle and let others do for him. He'd done all sorts of things to earn money before he became a soldier, he was a whiz at automobile mechanics, and he'd had a job waiting for him at Hull Motor Company after the war...if he'd still been healthy and whole.

It was hard on his masculine pride to be unable to work. Heck, it was hard on me, too, although in my case pride had nothing to do with it. I hoped that a dog, especially one as sweet and funny-looking as one of those dachshund pups, would keep him company. At that point I was willing to try anything to make Billy happy. Well, except give up my work, because I couldn't afford to do that.

"It's something else," said Mrs. Bissel, still sounding as if she were buried in a tomb and attempting to communicate with a living entity, or *vice versa.*

"Ah," I said mysteriously. Sounding mysterious had become second nature to me years earlier.

"It's because my house is *haunted.*"

That took me aback, which was unusual, given my line of work. "Um, I beg your pardon?"

"Oh, Daisy!" Mrs. Bissel wailed. Being fair again, I must confess that Mrs. Bissel didn't wail at me very often. Mrs. Kincaid, my aunt Vi's employer and one of my very best customers, was a first-class wailer, but Mrs. Bissel generally remained calm when speaking to me. "My house is being haunted! By a spirit. Or a ghost. I don't know what it is, but it's belowstairs, and the servants are all terrified, and so am I, and I don't know what to do about it, so I called you. I need you to get rid of the spirit—or maybe it's a ghost—that's haunting my house!"

◆

FINE SPIRITS
available in
print and ebook

THE DAISY GUMM
SERIES

Strong Spirits
Fine Spirits
High Spirits
Hungry Spirits
Genteel Spirits
Ancient Spirits

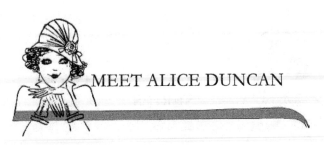

MEET ALICE DUNCAN

Alice Duncan expressed her creative side by dancing and singing in an effort to avoid what she knew she should be doing with her life (writing sounded so hard). She belonged to two professional international folk-dance groups and participated in a Balkan women's choir where she sang the tenor drone. In her next life, she'd like to come back as a soprano.

Alice finally gave into writing in October of 1992 and sold her first title in January of 1994. That book, *One Bright Morning*, was published by HarperCollins in January of 1995 and won the HOLT Medallion for best first book.

In September of 1996, Alice and her herd of wild dachshunds moved from Pasadena, CA, to Roswell, NM, where her mother's family settled fifty years before the aliens crashed.

Alice's favorite part about writing is that she can portray the world the way it should be instead of the way it is. She hopes she can continue to write forever!

You can visit Alice at www.aliceduncan.net

CPSIA information can be obtained
at www.ICGtesting.com
Printed in the USA
LVOW03s1330011117
554589LV00001B/10/P